Nobody's Children

Megan frowned. 'Do I know you?' she said slowly. 'I met you, I think, long ago . . .'

The girl stared back at her. She had very dark blue eyes, Megan saw, like her own. And then two slim hands came out and gripped Megan's and there was a shake in them, and a fierceness in her grip.

'You? Can it really be you? Oh, I've dreamed of meeting you again . . . you know me, don't you? I'm Marsha.'

'Marsha,' Megan said in a low, breathless whisper. 'Oh, Marsha . . . I'm Megan.'

The two girls smiled at one another, but Tony took a step back, looking as though he would have liked to cross himself.

'Dear God . . . you're identical! You could be twins!'

Megan glanced at him, then back at Marsha.

'Perhaps we are,' she said dreamily. 'Her hand stole out and the girls clasped fingers again. 'Perhaps we really are.'

Judith Saxton was born and brought up in Norfolk and now lives in North Wales with her husband and family. She has always been keenly interested in country pursuits – the family own cats, dogs and horses – and enjoys cooking and swimming. She has had over fifty books published under several names, one of which is Katie Flynn. For the past few years she has had to cope with M.E. but has continued to write, albeit more slowly

Also by Judith Saxton

Nobody's Children

JUDITH SAXTON

ARROW

Published by Arrow Books in 2000

1 3 5 7 9 10 8 6 4 2

First published in the United Kingdom in 1991 by GraftonBooks

Arrow Books Limited
The Random House Group Limited
20 Vauxhall Bridge Road, London, SW1V 2SA

Random House Australia (Pty) Limited
20 Alfred Street, Milsons Point, Sydney
New South Wales 2061, Australia

Random House New Zealand Limited
18 Poland Road, Glenfield,
Auckland 10, New Zealand

Random House (Pty) Limited
Endulini, 5a Jubilee Road, Parktown 2193, South Africa

The Random House Group Limited Reg. No. 954009

www.randomhouse.co.uk

A CIP catalogue record for this book
is available from the British Library

Papers used by Random House
are natural, recyclable products made from wood grown in sustainable
forests. The manufacturing processes conform to
the environmental regulations of the country of origin

ISBN 0 09 927817 0

Printed and bound in Great Britain by
CPI Bookmarque, Croydon, CR0 4TD

For Ann Saxton, and my favourite twins,
Lucy and Kirsty

Ford Focus. Moneyphone.

07546929604.

Acknowledgements

First, my sincere thanks go to Rhys Bebb Jones, the Holyhead Community Librarian, who found me ancient books which contained just the information I wanted, introduced me to people who knew all about Holyhead in the forties, and made the research so smooth and easy that I got it done in record time.

Still on Anglesey, Mrs Gabrielle Beardshaw of Holyhead Library told me what life was like in Holyhead during the war, helped by Captain Idwal Pritchard, who put us right on such details as blackout, convoy duties, etc.

On the subject of the cross-channel ships which ply between Holyhead and Dun Laoghaire, David Emrys Evans of Min-y-mor Road, Holyhead was the expert – and he also explained the dispositions of the armed forces, the shipping in the harbour and all about Salt Island.

Mrs Lyn Williams of Penrhyn, who remembers everything with the most astonishing clarity, took me through an average day in old Holyhead. I only used a fraction of her wonderful reminiscences, but there is always the next book!

My editor, Nancy Webber, with the help of her family, the Aucklands, was able to tell me about Bolton during and after the war, and Carol Morley of the *Bolton Chronicle* sent me some very helpful reference material and also pointed me in the right direction for finding out how Mancunians coped during the war years.

CHAPTER ONE
1927

It was a hot day, hot enough for August although it was only June. The sun glared down on the station platform, on the gleaming rails, on the painted metal seat on which Madeleine Ripley-Trewin sat.

There had been quite a lot of people on the platform at various times, but now for some reason Madeleine was almost alone. Other travellers had leapt on and off trains, young men with their Oxford bags flapping, young women with skirts so short that you could see silk-stockinged thighs, but still Madeleine waited, too shy to ask anyone to tell her when the London train arrived but terrified of missing it.

It had been a long day already. Up early, packing a bag with essentials, running down Markland Hill on to Chorley New Road, the leaves of the trees scarcely stirring in the breeze, the light mist over the flat meadowland glimpsed from the top deck of the omnibus a harbinger of the bright day to come.

She had caught a train within minutes of arriving at Trinity Street station and had travelled the short distance from Bolton to Manchester, and there she had caught another train as far as Crewe, the station at which she now waited. She just hoped no one would chase after her, though it seemed unlikely, since Mother and Father had gone gaily away for a few days on their own. The thought of such unfairness made the tears well up again, but this time Madeleine was determined that they should not fall. She dug her nails into her palms and tightened her lips and stared at the shimmering refreshment room on the opposite platform – shimmering because of the pool of unshed tears in her eyes – and longed for a train to come and take her farther away from the area where she might be recognized, to show everyone that her wishes were not to be denied just because they thought she was still a child!

But the rails next to her platform refused to vibrate and hum with the approach of a train, although one seemed to be arriving or departing elsewhere on the station every few minutes. And even if someone did recognize me, Madeleine reminded herself, they wouldn't have much luck if they tried to tell Mother and Father. Having announced that she might not go to France for another week, her parents had driven up to London to visit friends for three days whilst she was left in Markland Hill to twiddle her thumbs.

She had got special permission to leave school early, too, before term had officially ended, because she meant to go to France with Fanny and Bernice Hockton. Mother *knew*, what was more, that if Madeleine was to get a really interesting job when she left school then she needed languages . . . she had said she understood, had even argued with Father when he had insisted that a girl in her position did not need to work and might indeed be keeping someone in difficult circumstances out of a job.

'It's no use saying that Madeleine would be taking work from a girl who really needs it,' Mother had said mildly, but with the firmness Madeleine only admired when it was directed against someone other than herself. 'Young ladies these days do work, and the sort of girl who desperately needs a job is unlikely to have languages. If Madeleine has French and German there's absolutely no reason why she shouldn't aim for one of the embassies.'

Madeleine's father, who had been an ambassador himself some years earlier, thought there was no better life, so he agreed with this in principle. Yet they still refused point-blank to let her go to France *now*, only a week before they had planned it, accompanied not only by Bernice and Fanny but by an older sister, Althea, and her husband George as well.

'Althea will take the greatest care of us all,' Madeleine had assured her parents. 'She's most awfully responsible, truly, and she and George have been married nearly a year. They're just as good as Mr and Mrs Hockton would have been.'

But to Mother and Father, there had been no question. Lindbergh might fly the Atlantic, Gertrude Ederle, a girl not much older than Madeleine, might swim the Channel, but Mr and Mrs Ripley-Trewin would not hand their beloved only child into the custody of newly-weds.

So she had left, and it served them right. The servants wouldn't realize she had actually run away because she had told Mrs Owen, the housekeeper, that she was following her parents to London at their request. She had not enjoyed lying to Owen, but she had had to get away before cousin Ethel returned, with her faint moustache and her horrible habits. Cousin Ethel would have been on the telephone before you could say 'knife', checking with Mother, and the girl on the exchange would listen in, as they all did, and would spread the news that Madeleine had fled. Whereas Owen simply accepted that the arguments which she must have heard earlier, unless she was stone-deaf, had been resolved by an invitation to join the older Ripley-Trewins in London.

Madeleine heard a clatter and looked up. It was the signal, sending a message of some sort further up the line. She sighed and looked down at herself. Did she look like a runaway, a schoolchild? She had done her best to choose her most sophisticated garments, but her choice had been limited by her mother's insistence that sixteen was not adult, and a child should not make herself hideous by flattening her bosom or denying her waist and hips.

Still, the blue and white linen dress was rather pretty, with its dropped waistline and short pleated skirt, and she had unplaited her wheat-coloured hair so that it rippled loose around her shoulders. That would annoy both her parents, she knew, for although they refused to let her have it bobbed or shingled, they also made her wear it neatly braided into a long tail or disciplined in some other fashion.

Beneath the blue and white dress, though, real glamour started. She had stolen silk stockings from her mother's undies drawer, together with a pair of camiknickers in pale green crêpe de chine and the garters necessary to keep the stockings up, though they were horribly restricting and uncomfortable. She thought wistfully of the liberty-bodice she had worn as a child to keep her black woollen stockings up, then resolutely turned her mind from such mundanities. She had quite decided to defy her parents and go to France with Bernice and Fanny, because she was jolly sure that, when it came to the point, Mother and Father would not admit that they had not trusted George and Althea. They would have to accept that she had managed to get her own way – and they would have the satisfaction of knowing that she still had her long hair, for she would not punish them twice over by cutting it. Not yet. Not until she was considered old enough for all the other lovely things which went with bobbed hair – cloche hats, very high-heeled shoes and a cigarette-holder made of amber or ivory, with a packet of cigarettes to go with it!

She was still dreaming happily of the clothes she would buy one day when she heard, at last, the humming vibration of an approaching train. She half got to her feet, then sat down again, suddenly aware that the palms of her hands were damp and that her heart was pitter-pattering rather faster than was its wont.

It was all very well . . . she knew where the Hocktons lived, of course, but she had never travelled to their home by train before, and found herself dreading the explanations. The invitation to go to France with them had come from Fanny and Bernice, but now she came to think of it Mr and Mrs Hockton had not actually been consulted. What would they say when she turned up on their doorstep with one small suitcase of clothing to last her for the whole of the summer vacation? Would they suspect? She was jolly sure the girls would – but she would say her stuff was being sent straight to the Lascelles, who had hosted them last year. Was she really going through with it? She could see the train now, clacketing along the rails, steam coming steadily from its smoke-stack, the fireman hanging out to shout something to a man in uniform who had emerged on to the platform and was doing various official-looking things with heavy bags of mail.

Rather timidly, Madeleine approached him, but he was too busy to notice her and she turned away, fighting tears. How could she find out where this train was going if the man wouldn't even look at her?

But when the train stopped, porters appeared as if by magic and hurried along the length of it, peering into carriages and seizing heavy cases – making sure they weren't losing any tips, Madeleine thought with unaccustomed cynicism. She stood up again, preparing to go and ask where the train was heading . . . and it started to move.

Madeleine ran towards it but she was too late. The doors were all shut and it was gathering speed. Around her the people who had got off the train called to friends, shouted to porters, made for the exit. Madeleine turned blindly away from the edge of the platform. She had missed it. In her disappointment she walked straight into someone, who steadied her, hands on her shoulders.

'Hey-ey! Hold up, li'l maid!'

'What . . . where was that train going?' Madeleine gasped, pulling back and looking up at the man who still held her. 'It was my train, I'm sure it was . . . oh dear, whatever shall I do now?'

'There are more trains,' the man said soothingly. 'Sit down, maid, and get thy breath.'

Madeleine obediently sat on the seat again. She looked up at her companion, and her heart did a little double thump with sheer pleasure. He was tall and dark, his hair a little too long and very curly. But because he looked concerned the tears which she had been denying forced their way to the surface, coming too thick and fast, now, to press back. They brimmed, toppled, fell.

'Oh, I'm making such a mess of things!' she said shakily. 'I meant to do so well – I meant . . .' She broke off. 'Why did you stop? Everyone else just went on. Do I know you?'

He smiled. It transformed his face; now she could see he was very good-looking, his teeth white and even, his skin glowing with health.

'Good question. Do you know me?'

'No,' Madeleine admitted after another long look. 'If I'd met you, I wouldn't forget.'

He sat down beside her, leaned back, turned to face her.

'That's nice! Now, what ails thee, maid? Missed a train? Well, that's no great matter; there'll be another one by in a moment.'

He took her hands, his own warm and comforting. His eyes, she saw when she peered up at him through her lashes, were so dark that the pupils merged with the irises.

14

Covertly, she summed him up. Broad cheekbones, a chin tapering to a point, a deep amusement crease in one cheek. He was wearing a pale blue shirt open to the waist, and some darkish flannel trousers. He had sandals on his bare, brown feet, a very large knapsack was slung round his shoulders, and he carried a roll of material, stained and fawn-coloured, which Madeleine felt she should have recognized but did not, quite.

'Know me again? Now tell me what's gone wrong.' He let go of her hands for a moment so that he could wipe the tears away with the broad, hard palms of his hands.

'Was I staring? I'm s-sorry,' Madeleine stammered. 'I know there'll be another train, but . . . oh, nothing's gone right today. You see, I'd arranged to go to France with two friends . . .'

The story tumbled out breathlessly, interspersed with gulps. Madeleine, who was considered shy, found that she could have told this man anything. Yet when he said his name was Tarot she did not immediately volunteer her own. He was not a boy, he was a man, and who knew what was in the head of such a person? Certainly not she; he might leave her presently and go to the police for all she knew – after all, she was under age and alone.

The thought brought a fresh onset of tears. This time he put his arm round her.

'Come on, li'l maid, you're off to France despite them, so why the tears? What's your name, child?'

Madeleine stiffened indignantly, scowling; she was most certainly not a child!

'My name's Madeleine, and you're right: there's nothing to cry about, because I *am* going to France!' She looked up at him, trying to stop her lower lip from trembling, seizing it with her top teeth to hold it firm. 'I will go to France! I won't be treated like a baby all my life!'

He shook his head, smiling at her, with something in his expression which Madeleine did not understand but found she enjoyed.

'Nor me. Go where I want when I want, that's how I live. You sure you want to go to France?'

Madeleine hesitated. France no longer seemed quite so fascinating somehow. She remembered last year; kind though the Lascelles had been they were also very old-fashioned and strict, and their daughter Claudette had kept interrupting Madeleine's increasingly fluent French with petty quibbles about grammar. *Did* she want to go to France? She would spend the summer as fenced-in and kept-under there as she would in Bolton.

'We-ell . . . I won't go home, anyway,' she said defiantly. 'Where are you going, then?'

'Not home; haven't got one, right now. I'm going to wander down south, sketching as I go, selling my work to eat. I'll meet other painters . . .' He grinned at her, putting out a long finger to lightly touch her nose, then her enquiring mouth. 'It's a grand life – you'd enjoy it. I've got a little tent and a few quid, the sun by day and the moon by night. I'll get by.'

Madeleine stared, round-eyed and envious. He smiled again and reached out a big, gentle hand, curving it round her neck, drawing her close to him. He smelled lovely, of the earth, of hay and grass, with a certain salty something else which she decided to recognize as the sea.

'Why don't you come with me? A few of us are going to meet up on the Downs – mostly artists, but a few poets too, I expect – to see in the summer solstice and worship nature together.'

'Artists?' Madeleine had heard vague rumours of the way artists behaved; the very word had a romantic ring. She looked down at Tarot's tanned and dusty feet, the toes strong and straight, as though he had never worn shoes. 'Are you an artist, Tarot?'

'I paint,' he acknowledged. 'But this summer I'm not just going to draw; I'm learning about life. You could learn more about life with me than with your friends in France. There's room in my tent for a little one.'

A part of her was downright scared, wanted to draw back, to hastily deny any interest in things artistic. But his fingers on her bare arm were sending thrills up and down her spine, his dark eyes were making her stomach clench with excited anticipation. If she walked away from him now, caught her train and went to France, she would never know what might have happened, never find out just why he had stopped, sat down beside her, started to talk. And she was a woman, wasn't she? Other girls . . . women . . . no older than she had Relationships, she knew they did. Girls in her class at school talked of canoodling and kissing. She wanted to be one of the new generation which took these things for granted, not like her parents, hidebound, stifled by convention.

'In your tent? But I haven't much money with me.'

It was true. The Hocktons, she supposed, would have paid her fare to France. She had a few shillings, nothing more. Mother and Father did not leave money lying around and Madeleine had never had much need for cash, until now. But it seemed money did not matter to Tarot, for he shook his head reprovingly at her.

'I've enough for us both, but we shan't need much. We'll live on the country. I can sell my sketches, or we can work on the land, and rest up when we're in funds. If you come with me, you'll see.'

Oddly enough, that decided her. He did not want her for her money; he had scraped acquaintance with her because he liked the look of her. Well, she liked the look of him, from the dark curls to the strong bare feet. She

17

felt instinctively that he would not harm her, would treat her as an equal . . . but . . . alone in a tent, with a *man*?

'Yes, I'll come with you. Will you buy me a tent, then?'

He looked at her, shaking his head slowly, his eyes alight with laughter.

'No, only one tent, but you'll be as safe with me as though I was your brother, if that's what you want. Come on.'

He stood up and held out a hand. She got to her feet, hesitating still, just as a train roared in on the opposite platform. She had been so fascinated by Tarot that she had never even heard it until it was upon them. And now he acted so quickly that she had no time for regrets. Hand in hand they raced over to it, leaping aboard as soon as the carriages slid to a halt. Tarot sat down, tucked her into a seat beside him. They were off, committed. He slung his pack on the sagging hammock of a rack above their heads; covertly, she examined it. It was a very small tent, she thought rather apprehensively, and a very thin bedroll. Still, even as she wondered just what she had let herself in for, she found that she really did trust him, new acquaintance though he was. And they were going to some big party or other – she was a bit vague about the details – where there would be lots of other people, handy to help if she needed it. Not that she would.

They were not alone in the carriage. Four elderly women sat opposite them, knitting, gossiping, sharing sweets in a rustling brown paper bag. Madeleine edged nearer to Tarot; idly almost, he put his arm round her and pulled her close. The elderly women noticed but pretended they had not. She could see them signalling to each other how young she was, how depraved.

It gave Madeleine an enormous thrill – she was young, and she was without doubt very depraved indeed to be going off with a young man to whom she had not been

18

introduced, a young man with only one name, further-more, and a foreign-sounding name at that.

Tarot's fingers were teasing the long locks of her hair, twisting a shining strand round his fingers, releasing it and catching another, crushing a handful absently in his palm. Madeleine found that she was wildly excited by this small intimacy. When the backs of his fingers touched the flesh of her neck she thrilled all over, arrows of feeling darting from all the sensitive places in her body down to her stomach, almost painful in their intensity.

The women's eyes were all otherwise engaged, lowered to work or raised to the passing scene, but Madeleine knew they were envying her in their hearts. Her breathing quickened as she imagined what they would say if they knew that she was going with Tarot wherever he wanted to lead her, that she would sleep in his little tent tonight, eat breakfast with him tomorrow. That she, Madeleine Ripley-Trewin, spoilt sixteen-year-old daughter of one of the oldest and richest families in Bolton, was tossing her cap over the windmill and running away with an *artist*, which was only one step removed from a gypsy – and she did not know whether it was a step above or a step below, either!

The train clickety-clacked away and now and then clouds of steam were blown back, temporarily obscuring the view of sunny meadows, hills and woodlands. Madeleine felt her lids growing heavy, her breathing slow. She had had a more than usually exciting day and the train's music lulled her so that she leaned drowsily against Tarot's shoulder. She could feel the coarse cotton of his shirt cradling her, the lovely masculine smell of his sun-warmed skin reassuring her, the firmness of the hand which held her against him making escape not only impossible but totally undesirable.

Tickety-boosh, tickety-boosh, tickety-boosh. The train

19

rattled along soothingly, now and again crossing the points so that the rhythm changed to *tickety-tackety, tickety-tackety, tickety-tackety* before returning to its former note.

Madeleine's body relaxed bonelessly, shamelessly. She cuddled against Tarot, as fond and secure as a babe in its mother's arms. And, presently, slept.

CHAPTER TWO

The weather was still delightfully hot when they reached
the Downs a day later. They had changed trains twice
and then taken to the road twenty or so miles short of
their target, camped overnight in the small tent, and then
walked the dusty lanes, up and up, until the freshening
of the wind and a certain clarity in the air spoke of the
approach of the Downs.

It was mid-June, with one more day to go before the
solstice. Midsummer day, to Madeleine, was a vague date,
a festival remarked on but never celebrated. Until now.
Now, according to Tarot, the celebration would be something the like of which she had never experienced. He
was excited by its approach, as indeed was Madeleine.

She now knew that he had spoken no more than the
truth when he said she would be as safe with him as with
a brother. When night-time came and they entered the
tent he had rolled himself in one blanket, she had covered
herself timidly with the other, and they had slept.

At least, Tarot had slept. Madeleine, made uneasy by
this strange, detached intimacy, by the flimsiness of the
tent's walls and by the stuffiness, had scarcely closed her
eyes. Also, unromantically, Tarot had snored. Not a bubbling, grunting snore like her father's, nor a whiffly, nervous snore like cousin Ethel's, but a snore, nevertheless.
It had not helped, any more than her inadvertent sleep
in the train had done.

But she had not greatly resented her wakeful night. It
had given her the thinking time that the various activities
of the previous day had denied her, and she had been

glad of it, coming to the conclusion, eventually, that she stood a very good chance of having her cake and eating it too in this strange, adult adventure.

Mother and Father must never know that she wasn't in France – that stood to reason. But they would not suspect anything if she sent a number of postcards to Fanny and Bernice with instructions to post one off at weekly intervals as if they came from Madeleine herself. She saw no reason why the Lascelles should think it odd that she had not gone to stay with them, because she would prime Fanny and Bernice with the story that she had been sent, instead, to Germany. It was quite possible, too, because her German was nowhere near as good as her French.

But right now they were approaching the place where Tarot would meet his friends. High up on the windy Downs, it was marked by an immense circle of Stones standing on the short turf surrounded by a thin belt of trees. They were not the first to arrive – Madeleine could see two or three tents already set up in the shade – and as they got nearer she spotted several people strolling and talking under the noonday sun.

A long stare at the women showed them to be dressed in long, rather old-fashioned clothes with a great many heavy necklaces and bracelets adorning their persons. Most of them were young, all were quite pretty, but, clearly, fashion was despised amongst them. Madeleine was glad, then, that Tarot had made her discard her neat checked dress and smart shoes. He had acquired from somewhere a long dark garment in a soft, droopy material with a waist around knee-level – which was fashionable – and a skirt almost to her ankles, which was not. Her elegant high-heeled pumps had been changed for ugly flat sandals, but they were comfortable to walk in and if Madeleine had felt rather wistful when she put her things into her case, and even more wistful when Tarot had hidden the case in the middle of a haystack, at least she still had her pretty undies – or Mrs Ripley-Trewin's pretty undies – to bolster her confidence. And now, she was glad of her changed image. How odd she would have looked in her short pleated dress and high-heeled shoes . . . how lucky that she had not bobbed her hair, when all the young women here had flowing locks!

'Well? What do you think, maid? Have you ever seen the like?'

Tarot was standing in the great open space which seemed right on top of the windy world, pointing to the Stones. They stood, timeless and time-conquering, great dolmens and single columns, in the rough circle which her teachers at school had described. Through Madeleine's head ran jumbled thoughts of ancient Britons, vague half-memories of old legends that Stones such as these had once been young maidens . . . or giants . . . or warriors . . . turned to granite by some malignant power. Yet in the sunlight, with the lichen on their shaded side and the sunny side bare and bright and clean-looking, it was hard to think of witches and wizards, of days so distant that they were not even taught as history.

'No, I never have,' Madeleine said now. Her hair was being blown gratefully away from her hot neck; she smiled at Tarot, knowing whom she had to thank for the sudden delight which filled her. He was special, though she did not know what to make of him, knew less now that she had known him for twenty-four hours, which was odd but true. He changed his voice according to the way he felt, speaking sometimes with a warm Somerset burr, sometimes with the Lancashire accent she knew so well, and occasionally the clipped, correct English used by the upper classes. Were they all put on or all natural? She had no idea, simply trusted him completely, taking it for granted that his changing tones were neither sinister nor wrong but merely a pleasant eccentricity.

'Nor you ever will,' Tarot said. He held out a hand. 'Now let's put our tent up before anyone else takes our place.'

He had found a good spot, near the Stones, yet in the shade of a big tree. Madeleine went with him, though she would be little enough help, she knew. But she could hold a string, push blankets this way or that, do as her lord and master bade her. If there was one thing an English boarding school for girls taught its pupils, it was obedience and submission, she thought, laying out the groundsheet on Tarot's instructions. Though if Miss Hepplewhite and Miss Constance could see her now . . . her thoughts broke down into giggles pierced, as always, by the sudden arrowing of strangeness, the fiery excitement, which invaded her whole being with uncomprehended surges of innocent desire.

As she worked, Madeleine glanced about her. Tarot had described his friends as artists and nature worshippers, but so far as she could judge they were all quite ordinary. Everyone dressed carelessly by Ripley-Trewin standards, and most of the men had hair which her mother would have described, repressively, as 'too long for a gentleman', but other than that . . .

Then she began to look more closely. One of the beautiful, shiftless-looking girls, wearing nothing but a thin, smocklike garment, was posing, leaning against one of the Stones. Two or three men were sketching her, making ribald remarks, occasionally strolling over and moving an arm, feeling the muscle in her calf. There was a casualness in the way they touched her that sent prickles of excitement and embarrassment up and down Madeleine's spine. So this was the bohemian life, this was how real artists behaved to their models! No wonder the girls seemed so self-confident, so indifferent to what they wore. Probably they wore nothing most of the time!

But this particular meeting was not just about art. This was a special expedition when people gathered to worship the beauties of nature through the power of the Stones. Tarot had explained that it was the exact position of the rising moon, in conjunction with the ritual which would be performed, which made this occasion something special.

'When the moon is in line with the biggest dolmen, then she is at her most powerful,' he had said as they walked the dusty lanes, and he had told Madeleine that she must remove her footwear, as he would remove his, on the grass of the circle. He had explained that only barefoot could she gain direct access to the life-force which flowed from mother earth. She had looked at him a little suspiciously because already, after a mere twenty-four hours, she knew that Tarot did not always mean what he said, but he stared back at her gravely, so when they reached the Stones she tossed her sandals down with his and ran about on the grass, feeling with sensual pleasure the heat of the dust, the coolness of the vegetation, and above all the sudden freedom of being barefoot.

The people in the other tents were mostly couples, she saw, but occasionally there would be a group of young men or a group of girls. Next to them, another couple had set up their own small shelter. They had introduced themselves earlier – Tarot and Maddie, Fez and Junipa. Fez was a painter, like Tarot, with a lot of light brown, slippery hair and a beard so thin you could see through it. Junipa was a small girl with bobbed black hair and conventional clothing – a neat gingham dress with a grey cardigan over it. But Junipa was very young, like Madeleine herself. We're not really artists and we're certainly not models, Madeleine told herself now, holding a stake for Tarot as he skilfully hammered tent-pegs home with a chunk of fence-post. That's why Tarot put our tent near Fez's, so that Junipa and I would be company for one another.

They had not talked much, though. Just a few soft words, during the course of which each had undoubtedly noticed that the other had a low, unaccented voice. Some of the other women had soft country accents or London twangs; some swore when they tripped over their dress-hems or trod in cow-muck. They're almost like gypsies, Madeleine thought, as two young women wandered past, beads swinging. They were deep in earnest conversation and she caught a bit of it.

'My dear, he'd used ochre for her complexion . . . ochre! And of course she was annoyed – wouldn't you be? – but she didn't want him to know she'd slept with most of his friends . . . not that he'd expect anything else. It's these communes, you know, they lead to so much . . .'

Morals are different for artists, Madeleine told herself. They're free, unconventional. Living with nature, like me and Tarot.

'Let's eat,' Tarot said presently, when the tent had been erected. 'Big do later. We'll hit the hay for an hour.'

'Right,' Madeleine said. She wanted to be just like him, to use few words, to take it for granted that he understood her and she him. But there was so much to talk about, so many questions she longed to ask. Still, for now it should be enough to eat the bread and cheese he had bought, and then crawl into the tent to rest.

The food finished, Madeleine drank warm and brackish water from the bottle Tarot had filled earlier in the day, when he had seen her pulling a face over a mouthful of his bitter beer. Then, a little reluctantly, she followed Tarot into the tent.

It was her least favourite place, the hot air thick with the smell of bare feet and bodies, and she hated the flies, great buzzing black things which came in through the flap and then refused to leave again. What with them and the heat and the odd sort of feeling that Tarot might pounce at any moment, Madeleine did not expect to get much sleep now, any more than she had the previous night. She was longing to be deflowered, if that was the correct expression for what she was almost sure Tarot would do to her, but stupidly enough she found that all her sneaky reading of the human biology books used by the Upper Sixth, all the talk in the dorm, even her sly peeps when the dog was put to the bitch or the stallion to the mare up at the farm where she kept her pony, had not prepared her at all for the reality. She was afraid she would do the wrong thing, scream with pain, bleed to death, let Tarot down in some mysterious way.

But at least her man would be Tarot, not some dreadful boy with sweaty hands and more eagerness than knowledge. There had been rumours in the dorm, after Ailsa Collins had left so suddenly, that a young man had persuaded her to 'give him what he wanted' at a wild London party. Suzanne, Ailsa's dearest friend, had given them a blow by blow account of the affair, in which, she said, poor Ailsa had suffered more pain than pleasure since the young man had insisted on prodding away at the wrong place.

The wrong place? Madeleine thought now, puzzled. But what was the right place? Still, Tarot would know . . . and he had made it crystal clear, by his actions as well as his words, that he would not touch her until she was ready. Which, thought Madeleine darkly in the stuffy yellowish light under the canvas, might be a very long time indeed.

She was aware, of course, that a girls' boarding school,

despite the constant talk of boys, is not a very informative place. And Madeleine herself, an only child with no boy cousins or close neighbours, was really rather ignorant. She had never seen a naked man, and since Tarot appeared to live and sleep in his old flannels she doubted that she ever would . . . not until she decided to let him pounce – if she did.

Of course there was Geoff, Madeleine reminded herself, dutifully lying on her blanket with her eyes closed, trying to ignore the buzzing flies. In fact, though she had not mentioned it to either her parents or Tarot, one reason for her wanting to go to France had been Geoff.

She had adored him for most of her life, first as the brother she had never had, then as the lover she wanted. And how had he repaid her? First, by plainly finding her boring, and then by squiring her about once or twice as a duty, never a pleasure.

'Madeleine will be immensely rich one day,' Geoff's mother had once said, not knowing Madeleine was near and listening as hard as she could. 'Believe me, I'm not asking you to be nice to her for my sake, Geoffrey!' Even at twelve or so she had been hurt, but the pain had not lasted. She supposed that every mother felt like that about her child – certainly there was much talk of marriage in her own family, and how important it was to match estate to estate, land to land. Not much talk of love, but lots about duty and how doing the right thing brought its own reward.

So if it ever did come out that she had run away with Tarot, wouldn't it just serve that smug Geoff right? Not only would he never lay hands on her person, but he would never touch her lovely money, either!

Beside her, Tarot began to snore. Madeleine rolled over and looked at him. Oh, but he was gorgeous! Sometimes she thought he looked vaguely like someone she knew, but it was just wishful thinking, she supposed. Now, she saw that his face looked younger and smoother asleep and his mouth had fallen open, showing his strong white teeth. Mother would approve of his teeth, Madeleine found herself thinking, and had to stifle a giggle. Honestly, what a thing to think! Mother did notice nice teeth, but whether she would care about them when she found out what the rest of him intended to do with her only child was another matter.

Having sat up, however, Madeleine decided she simply couldn't bear the tent a moment longer. A huge bluebottle was buzzing over Tarot's quiescent face, hovering around his open mouth. Hastily, she inched over to the tent flap, lifted it, and was out in the blessed air once more. She felt mean deserting Tarot, but it didn't really matter, and she would have screamed if he'd swallowed that bluebottle, she really would. To be sure, he had decreed a rest, but if she moved over to the nearest patch of shade, then she would either sleep in the cool grass or amuse herself by watching the youths building the bonfire.

It was quiet out here in the heat of the afternoon. The young men were making the fire outside the Stones, because Tarot had explained that true believers would not desecrate the holy inner circle. Their worship was a silent, personal business, he said, but the food, music and dancing which would follow it was a wild pagan rite enjoyed by all.

Tomorrow night they would not light a fire, but would watch as the moon and the Stones conjoined to form a particular shadow-pattern, a particular path of moonlight, and then they would offer up their devotion to the dark arch of heaven, worshipping the white goddess in the sky above them.

But now, in the afternoon hush, Madeleine lay on the cool grass and watched the young men piling the great bonfire higher and higher. With a little stab of doubt she thought she recognized the chestnut paling fence they had passed earlier in the day when they had bought bread and beer in the nearest village. And was that a door? Surely they could not be about to burn a *door*? She sat up, eyes rounding. Yes, it was a door, and the next object to be flung on the bonfire's crown was a sturdy five-barred gate. Madeleine's soft brows drew into a worried frown. These were Tarot's friends, young and creative people who believed in the power of love and the forces of mother earth, who wanted to change society, make this land a better place to live in. If a gate had to be sacrificed for the Cause . . .

She lay back again, only half-satisfied with her own glib explanation. Her grandfather had been a big landowner and Madeleine knew that a farmer valued his gates and fencing. No matter how loudly these bohemians said that property was meant to be shared, a farmer would not agree that the fence he had laboured to build, the gate he had erected and paid for, could in any circumstances be put on a bonfire and burned just for the fun of it.

But it was none of her business. Madeleine was almost snoozing again when a young man passed her, treading heavily on the hem of her dress as he did so. He glanced down, began to apologize, then grinned. It was Fez.

'Sorry . . . oh, it's you, Maddie,' he said. He was a gaunt youth with a quick, nervous smile and a talent, Tarot said, for watercolours. Madeleine had seen two of his bright, clean-looking landscapes and liked them, though not so much as Tarot's extraordinarily arresting oils. Right now the artist was carrying a window-frame.

'Hello, Fez,' Madeleine said rather guardedly. 'Where did you get that window-frame?'

He stopped by her, looking uncomfortable. 'Oh . . . there's a derelict cottage back there,' he said vaguely, gesturing with the frame. 'That's where the door came from – see it, did you?'

'Yes. But it's wrong, Fez, to take things, even if the cottage is derelict,' Madeleine said, feeling heat flame in her own cheeks as she saw his skin reddening. 'Someone owns it.'

'Oh, sure. But do they have any right to it? I mean, our need . . .' His voice faded as he looked at the bonfire growing higher every minute. He bit his lip, turning away from her. 'Got to get on.' He moved away, then glanced back, face still pink. 'Where's the man? Too hot even for Tarot?'

'Asleep. As I will be, in a minute.'

Madeleine watched Fez stagger off towards the bonfire, his skinny figure sagging under the weight of the frame. She knew she had somehow spoilt his pleasure in the barbarous great bonfire, shown up his ability to find fuel for what it really was. Well, I was right, she told herself, settling back on the grass. He had done wrong and should know it. But she still felt uneasily that a free spirit, such as she, should perhaps not have taken such an old-fashioned stand.

She must have dozed a little, for the smell of roasting mutton woke her and when she sat up it was evening, the sun long gone though it had left a legacy of warmth in the still air. The fire had been lit and what looked horribly like a whole sheep was turning on a hastily rigged up spit, but there was no denying the smell was delicious after nothing but bread, cheese and beer. Madeleine got to her feet, stretched, yawned, then looked about her. People were emerging from tents and making for the fire, their faces bright with anticipation. Should she wake Tarot or would he be angry to have his sleep disturbed? She did not know, but had just decided to risk it when the tent flap opened and Tarot crawled out. He sat back on his

31

heels and knuckled his eyes, then rose to his feet and loped over to her. He had a powerful, springy sort of walk which always reminded her of the great cats – lions, tigers, leopards. When he put his arm round her he smelled of sleep, of sweat and of the linseed oil he used to clean his brushes. Madeleine shivered with delight and sniffed him as a puppy sniffs its dinner, which made him grin his lovely, lopsided grin and hug her to him.

'Little stray bitch,' he said, making the insult a caress. 'Grub up! I've got you a plate.'

He had two tin plates in his other hand and a couple of tin mugs swinging from his index finger.

'I wonder where they got the sheep?' Madeleine said tentatively, but Tarot just ran his hand round the curve of her hip and made a growling noise and it no longer seemed to matter whether or not the sheep was stolen. It tasted better than anything had ever tasted before, the flesh crisp outside, soft within. Fat ran down their chins as they ate and hot, strong tea was a lovely change from beer. Madeleine ate and drank and laughed when Tarot marked her forehead with mutton grease, and when the meal was over she curled up with her head on his shoulder and watched the play of the firelight on the intent young faces, watched a bearded man with a fiddle begin to tune up, watched as people called out suggestions for songs, as they began to sing.

Presently, cigarettes were produced. Madeleine had never smoked, but when Tarot caught her head in his arm and held the cigarette to her lips she drew on it, obedient as a child taking medicine.

'More,' Tarot said, turning her face to look into her eyes. 'You want more.'

She inhaled as he told her and then he kissed her, his mouth soft, caressing, the contact going on and on as her mind swooned with the suggestions his lips made, with the soft seduction of this, her very first kiss.

'Again,' Tarot said presently, and she smoked more and the firelight on the faces was so beautiful that she cried a little, and Tarot cradled her in his arms and crooned to her and blew smoke in her face, and when she wanted to stop, when the colours and the magic grew too much, somehow hurt too much, he would cuddle her for a little while and kiss her into compliance and hold the cigarette to her lips once more.

Suddenly, Madeleine pulled away from him and sat up. She was on the verge of an enormous discovery, the ultimate happiness. She tried to tell Tarot but her words got tangled somewhere between her mind and her lips so that all she could say was 'Want you, want you, want you' over and over, instead of giving tongue to the astounding truth she had uncovered.

Tarot grew very small, and he was laughing at her, teasing her, but she was far away, she had soared out of her body and high into the sky from which lofty perch she looked down on the colourful assembly around the Stones. She saw strange things. Young men, bare-chested, in white tunics, young women in flowing garments with hair to their knees, whilst others wore nothing but garlands of flowers round naked waists, necks and ankles. They were all gathered about the fire and the fire burned all around the Stones, and it was no longer one bonfire but a dozen or so and you could see, now, that the people were worshipping the Stones as they needed to be worshipped, as they had always been worshipped.

She gazed down as at another world, another life, and she the Goddess who ruled them all. When would the sacrifice take place? For it must happen soon, as the moon rose. And who? Who?

* * *

33

Madeleine woke to find herself alone. The ground on which she lay was damp, but so hot from her body's warmth that as she got up it steamed, the mist rising from it in the shape her body had left in the grass. She rose slowly, standing upright, and felt the cool wind blowing on her skin as if to remind her that the day's heat was done and the night was mistress, now.

She was naked. She could not remember taking off her clothes but was not worried by her state. Ahead of her the Stones stood against the moon, their shadows so black that they looked more like holes in the earth than mere shades.

For the first time since waking, Madeleine felt uncertain. What on earth was she doing out here, with no clothes on? And where was the tent? She tore her gaze away from the Stones, which was strangely difficult, and looked behind her. No tents. Not just Tarot's tent but all of them, gone, disappeared. She looked further. No people wrapped in shawls or blankets, no sign of human occupancy of any kind. She could see the ashes of the fire, some of them glowing still, but there was nothing else save for the fringe of great trees round the perimeter of the grassy space, and the Stones and the little wind.

Her first thought was that she must have slept for a week or more, because the grass showed no signs of recent stress; there were no bare patches save for that where the fire had burned, no crushed and broken grass blades, no scatter of food, paper, bottles, which had marked the site.

Yet Madeleine was not afraid. She walked forward carefully, gracefully, looking down at the whiteness of her own body and the dark smudges of her nipples. She entered the circle, going in under the big dolmen. There had been a young man . . . something to do with the fire . . .

34

She reached the centre of the circle; it was marked, on the grass. She stood for a moment gazing straight ahead, then turned until she was facing the full moon whose white eye was directly in line, now, with the big dolmen. Then, very slowly and deliberately, she knelt down. She knew what she must do without knowing how she knew it and stayed thus for a moment, then raised both arms and fixed her gaze on the moon. She knew she must stay here until . . . until she must leave, and naturally she must worship the moon. It was huge and white and wonderful, bringer of beauty, slayer of darkness, a goddess both powerful and benign to those who worshipped her.

She could not have said how long she knelt there, her arms and her eyes raised to the moon, but presently she felt a presence and a shadow came between her and the shining white orb. A man. Naked, as she was herself, with long black curls and a powerful torso which was as familiar to her as her own slight body.

The man knelt directly in front of her. She knew he was there though her gaze was still fixed on the moon overhead. Presently he reached out and took hold of her breasts. His hands looked black against the whiteness when she looked down, but they were warm, living. His touch brought her eyes and mind back from her contemplation of the goddess and she looked straight into the man's face, into those dark and passionate eyes.

'Tarot?'

She had forgotten his name until she spoke it, but he nodded and pulled her against him, his arms locking round her, keeping her close, breast to breast, thigh to thigh.

They stayed like this for a moment and Madeleine could feel her whole body beginning to respond to him, to tingle, to ache, to come alive. Cool, passionless marble became hot and living flesh. Her mind no longer lay captive of the moon and the smoke, but told her clearly that this was her man; that she was virgin now but would soon be virgin no longer.

She would be the sacrifice, here on this sacred spot where the power vested in the Stones had scorched the very grass away. He would lay her down and take her beneath the steady gaze of the Stones.

But first he made love to her so that when the moment came her body was eager, her hunger roused to fever-pitch. She forgot the staring standing Stones, the menhirs and dolmens, she forgot the dew-wet grass beneath her body and the great white eye of the moon overhead. She knew only the joys of the flesh, only the soaring of the spirit as their loving reached its climax.

When they had done they lay on the scorched grass like two broken dolls, languorous, sated. Then Tarot knelt and pulled her into his arms. He got to his feet and carried her small, warm weight across the circle and out, under the biggest dolmen, over to the familiar, stained tent. He crept inside in the grey dawn light and cuddled her down in the smelly, earthbound blankets. Then he chafed her cold hands and kissed her soft lips and violet-tinged eyelids until she slept.

Next day Madeleine was sick when she woke, but after bread toasted over a camp-fire, and a mug of weak tea, she felt better. She kept staring at Tarot, longing to ask him just what had happened last night yet oddly reluctant to do so. Had they really done . . . that . . . in the circle of Stones, where anyone might have seen them? Surely not! And why had she thought the place deserted? When they had eaten breakfast she went and stood outside the circle, regarding the Stones almost fearfully, but they were just Stones, bland-faced in the early sunlight, deny-ing their power, rejecting their significance. Had they been able to talk they would have told her she was over-wrought, Madeleine thought wryly. And they would be right; undoubtedly she had dreamt the whole strange episode, after smoking the cigarettes which Tarot had pressed upon her.

Presently, emboldened by the sunshine and the buzz of voices as the camp began to wake up, she went right into the circle and looked down as she reached the centre. The grass looked a bit crushed, as though someone had been rolling around on it, but it did not look scorched . . . she had definitely dreamt it.

But she knew she and Tarot had made love; her body told her every time she moved, and besides, you only had to look at him when his eyes fell on her. So alive with love, so warm and bright with it, that she felt ashamed of her own much more mixed feelings. Oh, it had been marvellous, that loving, she had enjoyed every minute, but it had been uncanny as well, and Madeleine liked her world to be clear cut, black and white, without that blurring of the line between reality and fantasy which had occurred the previous night.

'What are you looking at?'

It was Tarot. He had come up behind her and now he locked his arms round her and drew her hard against him, so her bottom was pressed against his thighs. His hands took liberties now, reminding her that he had made good his promise, that he had made her his woman when she wanted it and not before. Fingers touched, squeezed, bringing a fluttering gasp to Madeleine's throat, making her turn in his embrace, put her arms up round his neck, press against him as he had pressed against her.

'Oh, Tarot! Was . . . was it here, last night, that we . . . you know?'

He smiled, a lazy, sleepy smile. A smile of lust remembered. A conqueror's smile.

'Maybe. Maddie . . . shall we move on?'

'If you want,' she said drowsily. A bee hummed past, its honeysacks full. 'We'll do whatever you want.'

He held her easily with one arm and with the other hand pressed her head against his chest. She licked the bare skin beneath her mouth and heard his sharp intake of breath, felt his body surge into delighted life.

'Whatever I want? Then let's go back to the tent.'

She went with him eagerly. Even knowing it could never be quite the same, she wanted it – and Tarot.

CHAPTER THREE

The summer passed in a dream for Madeleine. She and Tarot tramped the length of the West Country, putting up their little tent if the weather stayed fine, sleeping in barns and old sheds when it did not. They had left the artistic community at the Stones and Tarot had filled a sketchbook and sold several landscapes. To keep themselves they worked spasmodically, but always in country ways and at country tasks. They helped with the harvest, picked fruit, dug potatoes, and throughout it all Tarot could not do enough for her. He told her constantly, with a light of wonder in his dark eyes, that he had never known a woman like her, never had such loving.

Madeleine, who had never known any loving other than his, could say with complete honesty that she, too, revelled in their love. But she knew that her own feelings were far more ambivalent than she dared let him believe. He was sharply intelligent when he needed to be, yet he did not seem to know or care that it had been neither his doing nor hers that they had come together. It had been the will of the standing Stones, those strange monuments to a violent and bloodstained past, which had lured her into being, for them, a virgin sacrifice.

Madeleine never voiced such thoughts aloud, however. Was she afraid Tarot would scoff? She did not know; she just thought the whole episode with the Stones was best forgotten. Tarot had told her he had given her a reefer to smoke that night, swore he had done it to relax her, make it pleasanter for her when they first made love, but she only half-believed him. Oh, she knew she had inhaled a drug all right, but she could not believe it had led to hallucinations so real, so weird. No, it was the Stones themselves. But she would never use the stuff again, not as long as she lived.

And she loved him; she had no doubts on that score. Her parents loved her calmly, coolly, almost as a duty. They had never been demonstrative, never cuddled her or made much of her. Tarot alone could comfort her by his physical presence, only he could speak to her with a touch.

When he said that they must return to civilization for a while, she agreed to go with him to London. He was an artist, after all; he needed a studio in order to translate his sketches into oil paintings which he could frame, exhibit and sell. But she did not like the thought of leaving the countryside; somehow she knew that the Tarot of meadow and moorland would disappear once they reached a town once more.

'There's a reasonable house in Soho where a few of us stay,' Tarot had explained when she had wondered aloud where they would live. 'Can't put up a tent in Hyde Park.'

He had used his drawling, announcer's voice for that remark, a voice which always made Madeleine a trifle uneasy. He produced it usually to impress or confound – why should he use it now?

But she was still too deep in his thrall to question his decisions, even though she knew he cared deeply about her, more deeply than anyone else had ever done. Father and Mother loved her, but not with warmth or passion. Her old nurse, Nanny Evans, felt more warmly about Madeleine than her parents . . . or so Madeleine told herself, as she and Tarot climbed stiffly out of the train at Paddington and prepared to make their way to the commune, where Tarot said the artists took turns with the housekeeping, shared the two big attic studios and where the women worked, modelled or painted too if they had any ability.

Autumn was whirling the leaves down even in city squares, Madeleine saw as they trudged through Hyde Park and along Piccadilly, dodging the muddle of building materials which surrounded the new underground station. A cold wind whipped her long skirts about her legs and she scarcely envied the flappers their brief skirts and smart stockinette suits. Her sandalled feet were cold, though, and she could have done with the expensive silk stockings she had abandoned in that haystack, to say nothing of the stout shoes she saw all about her.

Sometimes she thought about her friends at school, talking about their holidays, wondering whatever had happened to Madeleine Ripley-Trewin, who was so bright and such a good little scholar. Her parents must know by now that she was missing, but there had been no outcry so far as she knew.

She had tried to keep up the deception, or at least to keep them fairly happy, by continuing to send them cards. She would seal the card in an envelope and give it to anyone with a destination far from wherever she and Tarot happened to be. They must have received cards from John o'Groats to Land's End by now, and she just hoped they had more sense than to try to trace her. She had left them, they were a part of her past; all that mattered to her now was Tarot and their life together.

But in fact Madeleine was restless, uneasy about she knew not what. The small group of artists and their women had rented a tall old house in Wardour Street whilst the owners were abroad, and here they would live until the weather was sufficiently good for them to take to the road once more. Fez arrived soon after they did, and an older man with a long brown beard and a fat, cheerful lady-friend who liked cooking. Madeleine

41

decided they were lucky to be under a roof, for the autumn weather had turned wild and windy, with frequent rainstorms and gales which made her quite unable to regret the tent.

'Nice to be back,' Fez had said when he arrived. Madeleine asked him where Junipa was and he looked confused, his eyes darting everywhere and failing to meet her gaze. 'Junipa?' he said at last, looking down at his dusty shoes on the blue and gold peacocks of the hall carpet. 'Oh . . . she went back.'

'Back?'

But she was not asking, really, because she guessed. Junipa had gone back to her parents, to her nice safe ordinary life, to school or college or her governess . . . whatever she had escaped from, in short. Junipa had only stolen a summer. She had not been greedy, like Madeleine, wanting more, making it less and less possible with every day that passed to retreat to ordinariness.

As she and Tarot settled into their room, Madeleine considered, for the first time, going back, and found the thought both fascinating and repulsive. How would she stand being a dependent daughter again, doing as she was told, living by the clock? And she would have to forgo Tarot's lovemaking, a fate which she simply could not envisage. From a schoolgirl with a body all her own, albeit sleeping, she had become Tarot's woman, her body very much awake to every nuance of feeling, every subtlety of touch, smell, sensation.

The house unsettled her, too, with its echoes of her own home. Yet she had no desire to return to The Limes; far from it. She was still too deep in Tarot's thrall. Even living in a house again seemed bearable when one could hear the rain beating on trees and rooftops and know oneself safe from it, and it was good to have regular meals, to sleep in a proper bed between real sheets and bath in hot water. These were pleasures of the senses which reconciled her to community life and made her recent wanderings seem far less attractive.

The studios were the best-kept rooms in the house, though she and the other women did their best with the place. The owners had left all the carpets down and what you might call basic furniture, but locked all the decent stuff in the cellar. And with so many of them living here, the house tended to wear a scruffy look. In the studio, however, Tarot was almost obsessively tidy. He had a place for everything, all his paints were kept in sealed enamel tins, his brushes were always cleaned and put away. Fez, Johnny, Bobby and the others seemed almost proud to throw down their tools and let their women clean up after them, but not Tarot. The room in which he worked must be just right. Forgotten now was the smelly, untidy tent, the casual way he would sit sideways on a stile, sketching with quick, sure strokes. And his paintings were a good deal better than those of anyone else in the house – and a good deal more saleable. Tarot was working, now, towards a small exhibition and no one seemed to doubt that it would be both a financial and an artistic success.

Madeleine should have been in her element, and so she might have been except for her conscience, which seemed to have slept all summer and come awake with the autumn. This house was beautiful, and the communal lifestyle was ruining it. One cold evening they chopped up and burned a little half-moon table with a marquetry top which they had acquired by the simple expedient of breaking down the cellar door and selecting the table from amongst the other furniture. Madeleine was angry and showed it. She could have cried for the little table, which had stood humbly in someone's home for two or three hundred years, growing more beautiful every time

43

it was polished. And now it had perished in the flames so that a group of selfish, thoughtless gypsies could keep warm.

Artists, not gypsies, her thoughts tried to tell her, but Madeleine, still aching for the table's fate, was scornful. Artists did not take other people's furniture and destroy it, she told herself. They lived simply, loved beauty, and should have been growing their own food, cutting their own trees for their fires. It was gypsies who lied and stole, a hen for the pot, a fence for the fire, not artists, people with sensitive souls, and she wanted no part of it.

She struggled to express her feelings to Tarot, and he tried to explain how he felt – that every human being had a right to live, to be warm, to be sheltered from the elements. He agreed that it had been wrong to burn the table – he had been as angry as she over that – but not that it was particularly wrong to break down the door and use anything they fancied. He believed that people should share what they had, not hide it uselessly away.

'The table was bad, but it isn't just that,' Madeleine told him. 'They aren't taking care of the house, Tarot. They scuff the carpets, they don't clean their shoes properly before coming indoors so they trek in mud, they put hot cups down on shiny surfaces . . .'

'But they don't care about inanimate objects,' Tarot said. 'They feel one should share, and the people who own this house have so much, why shouldn't they share, too?'

He was older than she, but the sheer stupidity of the remark silenced her. For the first time, she questioned his supremacy over her. If he could rationalize like that, think he had won the case with superior logic, then how could they ever be happy? She had been tempted to go on arguing, to try to make him see that for all he knew the people who owned the house might not be idle rich but folk who had worked hard for their possessions. But there was no point. She was still bound to him, by his assumption of her faithfulness, his command over her physical needs.

He was working well, too, and she approved of his work. He painted in a way she had not seen before; there was a sort of spikiness, a vivid, uncomfortable strength, about some of his pictures which unsettled her, but nevertheless she liked to see him concentrate like this, recreating many of the times they had enjoyed together.

He painted obsessively when he was working, piling up the canvasses to take down for framing when he had time, his eyes smouldering with passion when he thought a picture was going well. He used all sorts of mediums, unlike Fez, who stuck to watercolours, but whether he was slashing charcoal on to thick, grey paper or using oils or pastels, his pictures shone with vitality and life.

What was more, they were only in London until after Christmas, when he seemed sure that his paintings would have sold sufficiently well for them to move on, back into the country. And Madeleine would be glad to go, because she thought the city diminished her lover. In the country he worked in the fields, trapped rabbits, strode out along dusty lanes with a hand on her waist to help her along, a thousand tricks, learned the hard way, making their wandering life easier. Here in the city he seemed smaller, less capable of coping with whatever befell them. His tent was thrown in the downstairs cloakroom, he worked like a madman and then lazed for days, content that money would come in after the exhibition.

He stole in the city, too. He had acquired from somewhere a great-coat and stout leather shoes, galoshes, even a suit complete with waistcoat. She tried to tell herself that he had bought the things, but how could he? He didn't have that sort of money, not until he had sold his paintings, yet . . . the clothing fitted him perfectly, the suit looked tailored, with none of the faults of an off-the-peg garment. She loved him but he worried her.

'I need a decent suit to go round the art galleries,' he had said abstractedly when she had asked him where the clothing came from. 'Don't worry, the coppers aren't feeling my collar.'

He was using his Oxford English voice and suddenly he grabbed her, holding her close. 'What's wrong with that? God, your eyes sparkle like champagne when you're cross!'

He disarmed her, of course, made her wish she had not been so sharp. But she felt different, in the city. She supposed vaguely, that it changed her as it changed him, made her more aware that she was behaving out of character. Out of class? It sounded awful, put like that, but sometimes in her secret soul she acknowledged that the class barrier, which she had denied when she ran away with Tarot, really did exist and that, in some ways, she felt more comfortable on her rightful side of it.

And then she was ill.

She woke very early on the first morning of her illness, to find the sky grey and heavy with rain, the trees weeping with it, their sodden yellow leaves spiralling down to float on the puddled paving, to swirl away down the suddenly running gutters. She and Tarot had commandeered a very good bedroom and had managed, so far, to keep it to themselves, though Fez had introduced another girl into their ménage and now clearly coveted the master-bedroom with its mirrored walls and white carpet so thick and soft that Tarot had several times carried her out of bed to make love on the floor.

But Tarot had simply said he and his woman were settled and would not move out, and now, lying between the sheets and gazing out through the opened curtains at the streaming panes, Madeleine was glad that he had stood up for their rights, even if it did go against his oft-repeated remarks that they should share everything. Come to that, she mused, he had been furiously angry when Bobby, the elderly man with the beard, had come into the kitchen once when she was making a jelly and first lied to her to persuade her up to his room and then tried . . . well, he'd tried to get hold of her. Truth to tell, she had been very upset, had run downstairs crying, and Tarot had stormed into Bobby's studio, hurling the door wide open, shouting . . .

Bobby had defended himself, Madeleine remembered, with the sharing theme. 'You're welcome to Freda,' was the phrase which had suddenly turned Tarot from an avenging fury into a stiff and outraged aristocrat – he had told Bobby to get out and stay out and Bobby and Freda had quite meekly packed up and left. Since then there had been anxious looks whenever a man emerged from the wrong bedroom, but Tarot, it appeared, genuinely did not mind if others shared their possessions. It was just his possession – Madeleine – who was different.

'You're too young for that sort of thing,' he said half-guiltily. And then he hugged her. 'And too precious,' he finished defiantly. She had loved him terribly then, without caring about the mysteriously appearing clothes, or his odd, uneasy morals.

Lying in bed thinking over these things, she became aware of a hotness in her stomach, a discomfort, to put it no stronger, in the area below her ribs. She sat up . . . and flew out of bed, a hand going to her mouth, her chest heaving.

Fortunately, the master-bedroom had an adjoining bathroom. Madeleine reached it and vomited all over the hand-basin, unable to get as far as the lavatory itself. She also made terrible retching and screeching noises, unable to stop as her stomach relentlessly emptied.

Tarot came in after a few moments, to find Madeleine, empty, sitting on the edge of the bath mopping her watering eyes.

'You all right?' he enquired anxiously. 'Baby, you're ill. Come back to bed.'

'I'm fine now,' Madeleine said. She felt fine, too, fitter than she had done for days. 'Gosh, whatever did I eat for supper last night?'

Tarot gave her a long, severe look.

'For supper? Why blame supper?'

'Well, why else should I have a bilious attack?' Madeleine asked reasonably. 'Unless I've caught a germ. I feel most awfully well now, anyway.' She turned her naked back to him and ran the taps, beginning to clean down the basin. 'I say, I'm absolutely starving . . . what's for breakfast?'

Tarot cleared his throat a couple of times and then said, 'Well, toast, I suppose. Coffee. Umm . . . Maddie . . .'

Madeleine finished cleaning the basin and turned back to him. He looked odd – she stared. Yes, he looked like a puppy caught chewing the shoes you bought for that special wedding. She looked harder. Worse, he looked like that same puppy who knows you've found the shoes and fears you will presently discover the hat. Whatever could be the matter with Tarot, famed for his lack of conscience?

'What do you mean? Oh, darling Tarot, don't say you feel ill, too?'

He grinned, came across and hugged her, then turned her in his arms and kissed her damp cheeks, her brow, the tip of her nose.

'I'm fine. You go back to bed, and I'll bring you a treat.'

48

He did, too. A tray with a late rosebud on it, complete with earwig, only Madeleine knocked it off the bud when he wasn't looking, so as not to spoil the surprise. And tea, which for some reason she just couldn't face, and toast, only a bit burned, with marmalade spread straight on to it because they'd run out of butter.

For the rest of the day she felt fine, working in the kitchen, singing to herself, exchanging jokes with the new girl, Mollie, and cooking one of Tarot's favourite dishes, baked plaice stuffed with shrimps and served with duchesse potatoes. Tarot had advised her to have a quiet day so she had done so, and gone off to bed feeling absolutely first-class.

And awoke, sick.

It fell into a pattern, though not every day. Some days she would wake fine and stay fine, other days would start off with violent retching. She might have worried, but no one else seemed to, and Tarot said it was one of those things which happen and would clear up in a week or two.

And it did. After three mornings in a row when she woke late, ate breakfast in bed and only went downstairs in time for lunch, it was clear she was cured. She was delighted and began to suggest to Tarot that, with so many of his paintings complete, they might think about putting the exhibition together and then returning to country living. They discussed finding work on a farm or renting a small cottage, even joining another commune, but though Tarot agreed with her that London was dull, he seemed reluctant to move on.

'Wait until you're a hundred per cent fit,' he said lazily, sitting cross-legged on the living room floor and sketching Madeleine's profile as she lounged in her chair. 'We'll go then, I promise.' He put his pad down and held out his arms. 'Cuddling time,' he announced. 'Maddie come to Tarot.'

Madeleine went, but she was getting close to rebellion. The house was growing dirty and shabby despite her efforts, which no one else made. Fuel for the fire in the living room had run out and she had made such a scene over burning furniture that Tarot had dissuaded the others from doing such a thing again. He told them that it had all the cleverness of a starving man eating his own leg, which had impressed Fez, though not Johnny Stripp, an out-of-work cartoonist, who pointed out that it wasn't their own leg they were eating (or burning, in this case) but someone else's.

'Winter will end,' Tarot pointed out, 'and someone will have to explain that missing table to the owners when our time here is up. No more, lads.'

'Where will we spend Christmas?' Madeleine asked him that night as they lay in bed, but he only rolled over, kissed her cheek and told her to go to sleep.

The mere mention of Christmas, however, had made Madeleine think. Last Christmas she had been fifteen and a half, most of the child's magic over but still young enough to be thrilled to find a fat yellow labrador puppy sitting on the end of her bed as her main present, and to be delighted with new jodhpurs, a hacking jacket and a brown, velvet-covered hard hat in place of her old black one.

If they were still here, what sort of Christmas would they have, she and Tarot? He might steal her a present but she would not reciprocate; she still could not bring herself to take what did not belong to her. He did not seem to realize that the first casualty of the way they lived was likely to be her love for him.

What would Mother and Father do for Christmas, without her? They would take Goldie for his walk and buy the servants little presents and give them money, as they always did. They would be sad because Madeleine was not with them, but she'd been away at Christmas before. And they knew she was alive and well, because she still continued to send them cards . . .

It was then, for the first time, that Madeleine began to imagine her own homecoming. She would come up the long drive by taxi, stop at the front door, get out, knock . . . the scene went on and on, with tears and love and cuddles and of course forgiveness and saying sorry – her parents saying sorry for driving her away – and Mother would say how sensible she had grown and Father would kiss her and say she must never be made unhappy again, and Geoff would come round and stare open-mouthed at this vision of sophistication which was Madeleine, eager now for a glance or a word from her, a kiss or a hug being beyond his wildest dreams.

But even whilst she dreamed of home, Tarot was woven into every fantasy. He was there, watching, godlike, from above, whilst she preened and kissed and showed off. He would adore her home, he would think Goldie the nicest labrador in the world, he would be impressed by Father, would simply love her fair-haired, blue-eyed mother.

Yet another part of her knew this could not possibly happen. If she went home it would be alone. And even though the homesickness grew harder to bear as Christmas approached, she sensed that the Tarot-sickness, if she left, would be worse. So she stayed. But there was an element of desperation, now, in the way she clung to him. The face she turned to each new day was a little sadder, a little paler. If only he had let them return to the country, to their wandering life! But he wanted them to stay in the city.

'Just for now,' he said when she asked, fretfully, how

long they must remain. 'Trust me, sweetheart. We'll go back again, after . . .'

'After what? After Christmas?'

He chuckled and squeezed her.

'Perhaps.'

Her sickness long over, Madeleine was cheerful, happy because, with the approach of Christmas, she had gone out and got herself a job and everyone else in the house had done the same without having to be nagged. Of course, Madeleine could not have nagged Johnny Stripp or Fez or Mollie, to say nothing of Luke or Mambo or Felice, but she could have nagged Tarot. She was quite nasty to him sometimes and felt ashamed when he humoured her and triumphantly superior when he mumbled and would not fight back.

Her job was a temporary sorter in the post office. She stood at a long table for eight hours at a time sorting letters into their different postal districts. Tarot was a postman, delivering. He did not have a uniform because he was temporary too, but he had a badge and turned up for work looking quite suitable, in a navy blue fisherman's jersey and matching trousers. It was getting very cold, but even so he had rebelled at first over wearing shoes. Good sense prevailed only after Fez, clad in flimsy sandals, cut his heel on a broken milk-bottle hidden under a mound of fallen leaves.

Madeleine liked her work. It was not taxing on the intelligence but it meant working with a lot of other young people, chattering was allowed and they served coffee for elevenses and tea around three-thirty. The money seemed marvellous, and with all of them in jobs of some sort Christmas presents became a reality and no longer an impossible dream. Madeleine bought Tarot a thick white jersey, warm and tough; she almost swooned when she thought how marvellous he would look in it. She got small things for the others and rather to her own surprise bought presents for her parents and for the staff. She bought George, the gardener, a jolly expensive pipe and some tobacco, and Mrs George, who was over seventy and had, as she was far too fond of remarking, dandled the small Madeleine many a time on her knee, a silk scarf with hand-painted wisteria all over it. She even bought little presents of perfume for 'the girls', that anonymous trio of constantly changing domestics who kept the house half-way clean, as Mother was wont to put it.

Why did you do that? she asked herself, hiding the presents in the bottom of the built-in wardrobe in the room she now thought of as hers and Tarot's. Are you planning a visit?

She told herself that she would post them . . . but how could you possibly post an antique rose-bowl, or a shooting stick? She had chosen Mother and Father the sorts of presents she knew they would like without ever considering how she would get the things to them. Father's shooting stick was awfully shabby and Mother did so love her roses . . .

She had made Tarot promise not to look in the wardrobe and knew he would keep his word. He might lie to others, probably did in fact, but he would never lie to her.

And then, snugly in bed one night with Tarot making the preliminary moves to loving, she almost screamed as his mouth closed round her nipple.

'Aah . . . don't, it hurts!'

She had not thought much about it, but her nipples had been swollen and sensitive to the touch for a couple of days. She found this often happened when she was about to start a period – what a nuisance, she thought crossly, that it should come back now, with Christmas so close.

She had always been irregular so had not worried over her long and happy holiday from the miserable business, but now she heaved savagely at Tarot's head, whimpering as her breast was freed from his weight. Now that it had been brought to her attention she realized that her tummy had been swollen and full-feeling for a couple of months. No doubt the curse would arrive shortly and ruin Christmas for her.

'Oh, honey-chile, I didn't mean to hurt you; I'm so sorry.' Tarot heaved himself up on to his elbows and leaned over her, kissing her mouth, then running his hand gently over her body in a way which made her breathing quicken. 'I'll be careful, really.'

He was careful and Madeleine, in the pleasure and excitement of it, forgot all about swollen stomachs and tender nipples. If it came it came, she decided. There was more to Christmas than making love.

Two nights before Christmas she couldn't sleep; she had heartburn, an ailment which had never troubled her before. Indeed, she had not known it was heartburn until Tarot told her that a sensation as of burning oil heaving up from one's belly was usually only that.

'But it happens whenever I lie down,' Madeleine whimpered presently, as they clung in the friendly dark. 'Oh, *damn*, I'll have to spend the whole night sitting up . . . the whole of the rest of my *life*, probably.'

Tarot chuckled and sat up himself, then heaved his legs over the side of the bed.

'Get you a cure,' he promised. 'Stay where you are, Maddie-baby.'

'Maddie-baby' stayed where she was, though she wondered rather apprehensively just what sort of cure Tarot had in mind. She had heard all about his belief in 'natural' medicines, as well as various outlandish things which he had picked up from foreigners and old crones in country districts. If he came back with boiled frogs' eyes or stewed snails . . .

But he returned, mundanely, with a glass of milk.

'Drink it slowly,' he advised. 'Milk's great for heartburn; I remember my Aunt Flippa saying so when she was . . .'

He stopped abruptly. Madeleine, sipping milk, looked up at him, big-eyed, over the rim of the glass.

'When she was what? Oh, Tarot, what was wrong with her?'

Tarot laughed.

'Nothing, stupid . . . except heartburn. Sometimes people get it from eating too quickly, or from eating unsuitable food, or just because two things you've eaten don't mix. Drink your milk.'

Madeleine drank the milk and then lay down, not flat but using Tarot's shoulder as a pillow. To her relief, the heartburn did not return but she stayed propped up just to give herself a chance. Outside the house the wind howled mournfully between the tall houses and they could hear what sounded like sleet occasionally gusting against the window panes.

'Tell me about the countryside,' Madeleine said presently, her voice drowsy, slowing with incipient sleep. 'Go on, you know how.'

Tarot was good at talking about the countryside so that Madeleine almost felt as if she were there, and it reassured her to hear in his voice how he loved it, because it made her feel certain that they would go back. Now, his arm curled comfortably round her, he began.

'Out there, way out there, far from London and the squares and the underground and trams and taxicabs, the trees are waking. It's night, and the great trees wake at night, and thrash their branches in the high wind and seek with their roots.'

'Why seek? What does it mean?'

'We've had a long, dry summer,' Tarot said, using his Somerset voice now. 'The trees be thirsty, maid. So they send their roots seeking, out into the surrounding earth. They seek beneath houses, hunting for the water they can smell as it seeps through drainage channels, they seek near streams, their great roots burrowing under the grass like snakes who thirst. They seek under great roads and the tarmac rises up, heaving and cracking, and the little animals think an earthquake's come, and run to their holes to hide.'

'Mmm, lovely,' Madeleine murmured, on the very brink of sleep now. 'What else is happening, Tarot?'

'The streams are drinking,' Tarot murmured. 'Picture the great trees, Maddie-baby, with their roots writhing after water, standing a-tiptoe on the edge of a stream. And now, far away in the mountains, the rain is pouring, running down rocks, pelting on the leafless trees, turning a thread of water into a gush, a gush into a torrent. And all the torrents are joining up there, high in the hills, so that presently they'll rush down to the lowlands, to swell brooks into streams and streams into rivers and the rivers into deep lakes.'

Maddie was half asleep . . . more, two-thirds asleep . . . and she could tell from the deepening of Tarot's story-telling voice that he, too, was drowsy.

'When can we go back to the streams and the trees, Tarot?' she asked, her voice as gentle as his. 'When can we go back to the real countryside?'

'After the baby's born,' Tarot said. 'Then we'll go back, Maddie-baby, back to the streams, and the trees with their seeking roots, and . . . what's the matter, love?'

Madeleine had jerked herself upright, away from Tarot,

and the cold air rushed between their bodies, waking her up fully, finally, as though she would never sleep again.

'Baby? What do you mean? What baby?'

'Oh-oh,' Tarot said. His voice was sharply awake too, with humour in it, and apprehension, too. 'Maddie, why do you think you were sick a few weeks back?'

He was using his wireless announcer voice, but Madeleine was too preoccupied to care. What on earth did he mean? What could he mean? Not, surely, what she thought he meant?

'Sick? But that was ages ago – I've been fine since. Tarot, you surely don't think *I'm* having a baby?'

'Well, I'm not certain, of course, but you haven't been able to get your blue cotton skirt done up round the waist for a couple of months, have you? And your little breasts are bigger breasts, sweetheart, darling, love.'

He touched one and Madeleine struck his hand away, her whole body trembling with rage and fear.

'Don't touch me! I'm *not* having a baby, I won't, I won't! I'm not old enough for babies . . . I don't want one, I won't have a baby!'

'Well, perhaps I'm wrong,' Tarot said peacefully. 'When did you last menstruate?'

'Don't call it that,' Madeleine snapped. 'If you mean the curse, I'm not very regular – I never have been. It might have been April . . . or May.'

'Then you've missed seven months,' Tarot said. 'That I do call irregular.'

She could hear he was smothering a laugh and it made her so angry that she jumped out of bed and stood in the dark which is never quite total, shivering in her white cotton nightie, hating him as thoroughly as, five minutes earlier, she had loved him.

'I . . . don't know why you think it's funny . . . I'm so

57

confused . . .' She choked on a warm rush of tears.'Oh, Tarot, make it go away!'

'I can't,' Tarot said ruefully. 'It's too late, Maddie-baby. I did wonder whether you knew, but then I thought perhaps it was better, by and large, if it just sort of happened. Was I wrong? I'm sorry, love.'

He rolled across the bed and tried to put his arms round her, but she snatched herself free of him, the urge to lay blame too strong to allow her to hear the remorse in his voice.

'Don't touch me!' she shouted, not bothering to keep her voice low. 'I hate you, Tarot . . . you did it to me! You put the baby there, and I thought you said . . . you said . . .'

'Yes, honey, but the sheath can't stop you being pregnant, it can only stop you getting pregnant. It must have been the first time, at the Stones . . .'

He had an arm round her waist and she beat on it, digging her nails into his flesh, wanting urgently to hurt him as his revelation had hurt her.

'I won't have your baby in me . . . your vile baby! I won't let it stay there, I won't, I won't! I'll kill it, that's what I'll do. When I have babies I want them to be decent people, not thieves and gypsies.'

'Maddie, you don't mean . . .'

'I do! I hate you, hate you! I want you to go away now, this minute, and I never want to see you again.'

He sighed, a deep, shuddering sigh, then laid his cheek gently against hers, still holding her prisoner in his arm.

'It's my fault, you're right. I'll do what I can to put it right in the morning,' he said. His voice was tender and presently he got out of bed, picked her up and slid her between the sheets. 'Sleep; just forget all about it and sleep. We'll tackle it in the morning.'

Madeleine was worn out and did sleep, for a little,

though she was conscious of him climbing into bed beside her and even in her sleep when he tried to put his arms round her she rolled away, out of his reach, muttering that he was to leave her alone.

She woke in the early hours and lay on her back staring up at the slowly lightening ceiling and thinking. She must get away. Whatever Tarot promised, he would never help her to get rid of a baby. It would be going against all those wonderful principles he talked about when he was feeling expansive. The sacredness of life, the trust which exists between living things. What was more, once she had a baby she would be tied to him, would accept his thieving, his taking of other people's property. She knew babies changed girls, she had seen it happen. And she would not even have a nice house of her own, or maids to do the work. Tarot believed she would grow to enjoy scrubbing floors and washing babies' napkins . . . he would see her grow old and plain and think it did not matter, because they had each other.

But I'm too young to be roped and tied and dragged off to look after a baby, she told herself, whilst the big tears formed in her eyes and ran out of the outer corners, because she was lying on her back. I won't let anyone make me into a woman with a baby when I haven't been a girl at all yet.

She put her hands flat on her belly; she had wind again, could feel it uneasily stirring. And then it occurred to her that what she was feeling was not wind but the tentative movements of the child and for a moment she felt softened and tender, marvelling at the life within her young, rounded stomach.

But then she remembered that it was Tarot's baby and he would expect her to bring it up in a tent or in a communal house and she hardened her heart against the child and its father. She would go. Right now, before he woke. She had some money, enough for a train ticket to Bolton. She regretted the Christmas presents but she dared not stop to take them. If he were to wake . . .

He did not wake. She dressed and, shoes in hand, stole down the stairs and out of the house. Halfway down the street she stopped and looked back and knew that more than half of her wanted to turn round, give him a chance.

But it was no use. He would want her to keep the baby, she was sure of it, and she did not intend to do so. She would go home and explain to Mother and Father and they would send her to a clinic somewhere, as Auntie Ellen had done with cousin Deirdre. She would go to sleep and wake up just as she had been before she met Tarot.

I'll go back to school, she told herself as she struggled along the wet and slippery pavement, her feet slopping in the only shoes she had been able to find in the dark – a pair of Tarot's old sandals. I'll tell Mother and Father a bit, because I'll have to explain about the baby, but I won't tell them much. And I'll never go near painters or artists or anything like that and Tarot will never find me because he only knows my Christian name and I never said where I'd come from . . . it didn't seem to matter. I'll forget all about Tarot, and the baby-that-never-was, and sometimes, when I'm old, I'll remember the badger that night in the wood, and the way the vixen looked when she came out of her earth to find food for her cubs. When I'm old I'll remember the good things and the bad won't hurt any more.

She reached the nearest tube station and caught a train to Euston, then had to hang around the platform for an hour until the first train left for the north. She felt conspicuous in her droopy clothing, with the old sandals on her feet. Everyone else was going home for Christmas and was in their best, whereas Madeleine had not even

60

managed to find her own coat but wore, instead, an ancient burberry belonging to Sprat, a new resident of the house.

Once on the train she felt a little better. She bought some sandwiches from a man who wandered up and down the platform selling them and sat eating ham and pickle and trying not to think how frantically Tarot would be combing the house for her – then the street, then the area.

She had arrived at Trinity Street station before the first faint tuggings of regret warned her what was to come. She felt . . . as though there was something missing, something which was essential to both her health and her happiness.

But it would pass, she told herself, climbing into a taxi and telling the man to take her to The Limes, Markland Hill, off Chorley New Road. The driver swung round and gave her a long, not unfriendly stare.

'Markland Hill. The Limes. Right you are.'

Madeleine began to feel excited as the taxi followed the familiar route, through the familiar streets. Chorley New Road seemed to go on for ever, but at last she saw the shape of Christ Church on the corner and the driver stuck his hand out, slowed, and swung right. Up the hill, the road narrowing, and then left, between the big stone gateposts, under the winter-bare trees. The driver slowed again as they approached the house and Madeleine saw once more the grey stone façade, the stable block peering round the side like a child examining guests. She felt a little thrill of . . . was it fear? The house looked empty and deserted, the windows unwelcoming, the circular lawn before it grey and furred with frost. There was not a soul about – suppose her parents had gone abroad for Christmas?

As the taxi drew to a halt the man turned and, through

the little window, named his fee. Madeleine scrabbled in the pocket of Sprat's horrid coat and found just enough money to pay him. She handed it over and then climbed down. She turned back to ask him to wait at least until someone had answered the door, but he was moving, the tyres kicking up the gravel, the driver clearly intent on finding himself a fare, next time, with a bit more class.

Madeleine set off for the front door. She had jumped out in such a hurry that she had left one sandal in the cab, but it was no use repining, with the vehicle halfway back to town already. She limped briskly over to the porch. Someone would be home, even if it was only the servants.

She rang and heard the bell sounding far off, a deep and mellow tone. It faded into silence. Madeleine found that she was listening, dry-mouthed.

Footsteps. The door grating open. Her mother's face in the opening, hair surely greyer than she remembered, face thinner, more lined.

'Mother? It's been a long time.'

Her mother's hand flew to her mouth and she swayed where she stood, yet even as Madeleine climbed the steps to catch her, she straightened, smiled.

'Oh, my dear child! How *very* strange that I should have been passing through the hall when you rang . . . but I had such a strong feeling! Come along in . . . what a sight you look . . . we've thought such dreadful things . . .'

Madeleine stepped forward and her mother's arms closed convulsively round her. Her mouth kissed air first, then Madeleine's cheek, nose, forehead. Random dabs of kisses with her whole undemonstrative soul in them.

Madeleine hugged too, and kissed as well, and the two women clung, almost relaxed, almost natural. Tears were running down Madeleine's face; am I to do nothing but cry, she asked herself crossly. Why should I cry, when I'm back and happy and it'll soon be over? This is my mother, and she loves me very much. I'll explain and she'll arrange everything and I'll put up with whatever I must and then I'll be myself again. So why on earth do I ache so, why on earth do I weep?

Why, indeed?

CHAPTER FOUR

Madeleine sat curled up in the big armchair in front of Nanny Evans's fire and dreamed into the flames. She was warm and comfortable today and the baby, an active little creature usually, had stopped kicking an hour or so ago and did not seem inclined to start again. Having been uncomfortable for several weeks, Madeleine felt she had earned an easy birth.

I look like a mountain, she thought resentfully. And though Nanny is sweet and Wales beautiful, it's a long way from home and civilization. Damn Tarot, it's all his fault, yet I can't help thinking about him, wondering what he'd do and say if he was here.

He had been right about one thing. It had been too late to have an abortion, which was what she had wanted, even if she had not actually put it into words. She had visited a doctor, not kindly old Dr Prosser who had seen the young Madeleine through chicken pox and similar childish ailments but a younger man, who had told her that it would be more than her life was worth to do anything other than give birth to the child within her.

'It would mean a considerable risk,' he had said gravely, speaking not to Madeleine but to her mother, who had accompanied her. 'There are worse things, Mrs Sidmouth, than bearing an illegitimate child. Losing a daughter, my dear ma'am . . .'

Madeleine had seen her mother wince and got just the faintest inkling of how her parents must be feeling. The Ripley-Trewins were an old and distinguished family; their girl-children were brought up carefully, guarded from the world, as Madeleine herself had been. Now, 'Mrs Sidmouth' was shocked and disgusted at the fate which had befallen her only daughter, whilst at the same time feeling that she herself, and her attitude, had been at least partly responsible. Yet even her guilt could not justify the part which Madeleine must have taken in her seduction by a wicked older man . . . she clearly could not bring herself to believe that the sex-act, outside marriage, could ever be enjoyable.

Madeleine, of course, had done her best to portray Tarot as a despoiler of innocence. Her father had swallowed this hook, line and sinker; he had trumpeted about horsewhips in a very satisfying way. But Madeleine's mother was both practical and a member of the female sex herself; she knew that Madeleine might have been seduced, could even have been raped, but her daughter had not stayed away for six months under a duress which had sent her home fitter and rosier than she had ever looked.

It had been taken for granted by all the Ripley-Trewins, parents and child, that Madeleine would go away somewhere quiet to give birth to the baby, would afterwards hand it over for adoption to some suitable couple, and only return to Bolton when she could appear as chaste as she had left it last June. Madeleine had to agree once the doctor had forbidden an abortion, but she was not looking forward to the birth and was delighted to stay with Nanny Evans.

'You will have a first-rate midwife in dear Nanny,' Mrs Ripley-Trewin had explained. 'And an excellent medical man will attend the birth. I'd prefer to be with you myself, of course, but that's impossible. It really would cause talk if I were to disappear for a number of weeks. However, as soon as . . . as it's over, I'll come up with Father in the Lagonda and fetch you home. We'll say you've been in France.'

France, that so-convenient country. Madeleine found that her parents had carried on the fiction that she was over there improving her knowledge of the language, even writing to the school to explain her absence. It did not shock her that they had not got in touch with the authorities when her cards started arriving with English stamps – as Mummy had explained they knew she was alive and well and wanted to save her having to suffer from her foolishness – but sometimes, when she lay in bed and the baby kicked and squirmed and kept her wakeful, she wondered what other parents would have done. Ordinary parents, of ordinary girls, the sort of parents who could not have got away with pretending their child was in France. But it did not worry her much. Tarot, she told herself, was just an episode which was over and now she must forget him and carry on with her life.

So now, curled up in the big chair, Madeleine remembered the journey to Wales, tucked up in the back of the Lagonda with lots of rugs and flasks and sandwiches so that they would not have to stop for a meal on the way. Father had driven – he often drove himself, so that would occasion no remark – and Mother had sat beside him making light conversation in her languid, gentle voice until the big car turned into the little winding lane at the end of which Nanny Evans's cottage crouched like a rabbit hiding from the hunt.

They had taken her in, given Nanny money and gone, relieved, Madeleine could see, to be rid of her and the guilty secret which they had been so anxious to avoid talking or thinking about. And suddenly Madeleine was almost happy again, almost able to enjoy her nice hot meals and her nice warm bed and Nanny's enveloping love.

Nanny told everyone she was a young cousin from London, come here to have her baby. Madeleine didn't know whether people believed this or not, but she knew it didn't matter anyway. They saw so little of Madeleine, bundled up in her coat and hat against the cold when she went for walks through the snow, or cuddled down in the big chair before the fire, hands folded on her bump, hair loose, eyes dreaming into the flames, that they would never know her even if they saw her again, some time in the future. No, she would have the baby because they said she must and then she would go home and start being Madeleine Ripley-Trewin once more.

But oddly, as the birth grew imminent, so Madeleine began to suffer from a constant, nagging ache, the ache of losing Tarot. She had been wrong to run away from him like that, wrong and cruel. He was not a bad man, for all she had painted him as the villain of the piece, and now she saw, over and over in her mind's eye, his loving look, his tenderness for her, the way he had tried to persuade her to come to terms with her pregnancy.

Once or twice she woke in the night, tears on her cheeks, convinced that he was outside the cottage, calling for her. She heaved her bulk out of bed and padded over to the window, but there was never a man outside. Only the cold moon shone on the snow, and the barn owl floated over the winter-bare trees, and the little wind moaned around the eaves and mocked her desperately searching eyes. Gone, gone, gone, the wind seemed to whisper. You didn't value what you had and now it's gone, gone, gone.

Climbing back into bed again, Madeleine told herself that she had done a dreadful thing to Tarot but would undo it as soon as the child was born. Then she would make some excuse to visit London, find Tarot, and tell him that the baby had died and persuade him to forgive her. Oh, they could not marry or be together, she understood that. Mother had already made it clear that she must marry a man of their choosing as reparation for her sins, and she supposed that it was fair enough, really. After all, she had gone her own way and look where that had led her! Now she would do as they wished. She lost herself, then, in dreams of a perfect marriage . . . it never occurred to her that the perfect husband persisted in looking a lot like Tarot.

It was fortunate, really, that she could feel no affection at all for the baby. She resented it, seeing it as the main cause for her parting from Tarot, her banishment to the country, even for the feeling that she must acquiesce over whatever husband her parents decided to choose for her. The baby was to blame for all these things, and yet she had hit out at Tarot, shouted at him . . . run away from him. So she must find him again as soon as she was free and beg his forgiveness.

Did she believe that she could see him again and not go to him? That her summer love had no substance, no resilience? She did not know herself, because she was able to rise above the very real pain of parting, the ache of what she had done to him. Time, for her, was suspended until her body had rid itself of its burden. Until the child was born she lived in a sort of placid dream into which reality seldom intruded. Helping Nanny with the cooking, tinkling out popular tunes on Nanny's small upright piano, reading the limited supply of books which Mother had been able to send down with her, was enough. Madeleine yawned and reached for her knitting. It was meant to be a matinée jacket but it bore a far stronger resemblance to a string vest, so many and various were the holes where the inexpert knitter had dropped stitches.

But Nanny had insisted that she employ her time some-how, and so far three pairs of bootees, one greyish pink, one greyish blue and the other merely grey, half a matinée jacket and some cobbled-together mittens were the results of her labours.

One day I might have a *real* baby, Madeleine told herself, looping the wool round twice, casting the stitch off, making another one. A real baby, with a proper father and lots of lovely little clothes and a nanny all of its own to take care of it whilst I go dancing. And inside her, the unreal baby kicked sadly and Madeleine's hands went to cradle it and then remembered that she hated it and curled back round her knitting needles instead.

Pain and confusion and the hurt of rejection, were they all there, in the dark inside her? As they might have been in her mind, had she not been a sensible person? But there was no one to tell her, only the fire on the hearth and the subdued hum of the wireless in the corner bring-ing dance music from far-away London and, presently, the soft sounds of the back door opening as Nanny came back from her afternoon's whist in the village and started to make them some tea.

Madeleine awoke in the dead of night. She was very hot and her back ached. She sat up on one elbow and looked at the bedside clock, and as she did so a sinister sort of pain, a mean, griping pain, slithered and slid from her shoulders down to her lower back.

Damn! Was this it, then?

Madeleine groped for the matches and lit her bedside candle. Having ascertained that it was only a quarter to two, and that it would be many hours before anyone was up, she blew the candle out and lay down once more. She had asked Nanny whether childbirth was painful and Nanny had been very bracing, talking of ladies she had nursed who had had a few pains, just five or six, and the baby had popped out like a pea from a pod. Clearly, the most sensible thing to do was to go back to sleep until the pains got a bit more pressing. After all, if the pain would go away . . .

An hour later Madeleine realized that it hurt like anything and no amount of lying in the dark was going to get her back to sleep, so she might as well wake Nanny and suggest a cup of tea. She sat up, found the matches, lit the candle, swung her legs out of bed, and was stopped in her tracks by a fierce and fiery pang which reverberated through her, leaving little room for doubt about the pains of giving birth.

Nanny lied to me, Madeleine thought, staggering to her feet and heading determinedly across the chilly linoleum. She said it didn't hurt and it jolly well does . . . I'll make her get me a cup of tea and then I've a good mind not to drink it!

By five o'clock the tea had been drunk and Madeleine had vomited it all up, taking a dreary pleasure in seeing the tea for the second time in ten minutes, this time puddling the blue linoleum beside the bed. Nanny anxiously mopped it up, wiped her charge's sweaty face and announced with rather less forcefulness than Madeleine would have liked to hear that babies always started in the early hours and then got themselves into the world much later, that first babies always took their time and that she would just pop down the road on her bicycle and get good Mair Davies to go along for the doctor, just in case.

'But Nanny, you said you could manage without the doctor,' Madeleine reminded her, doubling up as the pain struck her again. 'Oh, oh, make it go away!'

'I can't, my lovely,' Nanny said distractedly. 'Better get the doctor, eh, girl?'

'No. You mustn't leave me,' Madeleine said. The pain was changing, moving round so that the tiger-grip encompassed her abdomen as well as her back. 'Nanny, my stomach's gone tight. Oh, I think I want to be excused. Can you help me to the lavatory, do you think?'

'Ah, that's not such a good idea; use the chamber pot,' Nanny said. But no sooner was Madeleine on her feet than she gave an apologetic shriek and deluged the lino once more.

'Your waters have broke,' Nanny announced, not rushing for the mop this time but helping Madeleine back to bed. 'Baby won't be long now, love. Better stay with you now, I had.'

'I have to go to the lavatory,' Madeleine insisted, red-faced and eyeing the puddle on the floor with mixed feelings. It had something to do with the baby, she knew, because her stomach no longer felt quite so tight. In fact . . . 'Nanny, I have to do big jobbies!'

'No, no, love. It's the baby,' Nanny said reassuringly. 'Lie back now, and grip my hands, and then bear down for all you're worth and it'll be over in no time.'

'If I bear down . . .' Madeleine said warningly.

Too late. All of a sudden, she was heaving herself upright in bed, the better to bear down. Her body was taking control, giving the orders, and it seemed to think that bearing down – pushing – was the only activity now which it could recommend.

So began the most strenuous couple of hours Madeleine had ever spent. She crouched and heaved and clung to Nanny's hands with her own small, wet paws, and between them, like sailors heaving on a capstan to bring up an anchor from the deep, they got into the rhythm which would see the dawn, welcome the sunrise.

They did not actually break into a chorus of yo-oh heave-ho, but probably a good few of the uninhibited

71

shrieks and grunts Madeleine gave, combined with Nanny's encouraging shouts and little cries, were not unlike that well-loved sea-shanty.

There was no suggestion, now, that Nanny might leave her and go for the doctor. Both women were too absorbed in their task. Madeleine pushed, grunted, occasionally gave vent to a thin, exhausted scream, but for the most part she worked and Nanny encouraged and though, as the pain intensified, she occasionally broke off to demand of Nanny how much longer it would take, on the whole Madeleine behaved well. I am not a coward, she reminded herself, as she rested between pains and Nanny gave her a sip of water and mopped her face, neck and breasts. I am going to get this baby out and then . . . oh, then, how I'll sleep!

And then, quite suddenly, there was a purpose in all this pain and pushing, a light in the darkness. She crouched, gave the biggest push of all, and felt the soft slither, the unbelievable relief, of the moment of birth.

At first she could not believe it. It was over! It had been born! Nanny was fussing round, talking about 'a lovely little girl' as if that mattered to Madeleine, and then, grinding and wicked, low in her back, came the mutter of a further pain and something warm and nasty happened to her lower regions.

'Nanny . . . what is it?'

'It's the after-birth, my lovely,' Nanny said soothingly. 'Always comes after the babe, see? Don't push too hard, just let it happen.'

Madeleine tried to obey, but the urge to push was too strong for her. She did just glance sideways at the baby in the moses basket which Nanny had stood ready by the bed, and then, once more, came the urgent demand from her body to push.

'Nanny, I'm . . . it's . . .'

72

Nanny was there, holding her hand, then releasing it to bend and catch the thing which shot forth from Madeleine's quivering body.

'Madeleine . . . it's another one,' she breathed. 'You've got another one! Them's twins, Maddie dear – twin girls!'

'Like as two peas in a pod,' Nanny marvelled a couple of hours later, when Madeleine had been cleaned and tidied and popped back into bed in a freshly laundered nightgown. 'Two beautiful little girlies, just like their mummy. Shall I bring 'em over to you?'

But Madeleine, after one cursory glance and a noticeable wince, looked away.

'It's over, and I'm glad,' she said feebly. 'But I don't want to look at them, Nan; what's the point? Can I have a cup of tea, please?'

'Yes, of course you can,' Nanny Evans said. She had pulled the blanket down so that Madeleine might look at the two fair faces, but now she pulled it carefully up again, tucking it warmly round the two small, sleeping bodies. 'You don't want a hold of 'em? No? Well, plenty of time for a cuddle, later.'

'They're going away,' Madeleine reminded her. 'I needn't touch them.'

'Well, we'll leave it for now,' Nanny said diplomatically. 'I'll just give your mam a ring . . . will you be all right for twenty minutes or so?'

The telephone box was a short walk away, so having made Madeleine a pot of tea on a small tray, with milk, sugar and biscuits handy to the bed, Nanny Evans put on her thick wool coat, her fawn muffler, her galoshes and her best hat, and sallied forth. The snow was clearing nicely from the roadside, though if you looked up at the hills you could still see it lingering, reluctant, it seemed, to let spring take over the land. The little breeze was chilly though the sun shone, so Nanny walked briskly, rehearsing what she should say to Mrs Ripley-Trewin. With most grandparents, it would have been wonderfully good news, but in this case . . . dear me, it made you wonder what to say for the best.

Nanny got through to Mrs Ripley-Trewin's number easily enough, speaking first to Owen, the housekeeper, and then being connected to Madam herself, but at the last moment she said nothing about the second baby. Mrs Ripley-Trewin had impressed upon her that none of the servants at the Markland Hill house knew anything about Madeleine's condition – though Nanny, from her wide experience, rather doubted that. They had evolved a fictitious niece of Nanny's, Siân Rhys-Evans, who was expecting her first child. No sooner had Nanny said that Siân had given birth to a beautiful baby girl than Mrs Ripley-Trewin interrupted her, saying, 'Oh, thank God!' with sufficient fervour to cause any servant, overhearing, a good deal of surprise, Mrs Ripley-Trewin not being a lady given to great enthusiasms, as you might say.

And somehow, after that, Nanny said nothing about the second baby. After all, she reasoned, making her slow way back along the lanes to her cottage, if dear little Madeleine was really not going to keep either baby, and Mrs Ripley-Trewin had only arranged one adoptive home, then why should not the second twin go to Nanny Evans's daughter Menna, in Aberystwyth? Menna and her husband were childless and longed for a little girl; what better gift could a loving mother give? It wasn't as though she would be taking the baby from eager adoptive parents, and Menna had been fair as an infant so no one would wonder if she gave birth to a child with silver-fair hair. Besides, Nanny had long known that Mrs Ripley-Trewin

74

was a lady who panicked easily and was, at the best of times, a mass of nerves. What a state she would be in if she suddenly found herself with two children to find homes for instead of just one! Better, by far, that Menna should be given the unexpected and unwanted child.

Home at last, Nanny divested herself of her outer garments, kicked off her galoshes and put on her cosy house-shoes, made of lambswool and felt and embroidered by dear little Menna's own hands. She went into the kitchen, got out the muffins she had made the previous day, toasted and buttered them, and took them up to Madeleine together with a slice of rich fruit cake and some homemade biscuits.

With some trepidation, she told Madeleine what she had done, and explained about Menna as well. Madeleine, heavy-eyed now, sat up, sipping her tea and smiling. She ate two muffins and a slice of cake and three biscuits, then she drank another cup of tea and snuggled down again.

'Better say nothing to Mother, though,' she said, as Nanny finished her explanation. 'I don't see any harm in your Menna having one of them, Nan. The adoption people won't tell us who's having the baby – or they won't tell me; I dare say Mother knows. Mother says it's better that way, and they'll be nice people from London or somewhere who'll bring the baby up properly.'

'My Menna's the same,' Nanny Evans assured Madeleine. 'She's got a good man and she'll stop working right away when she hears the good news. A nurse she is, you know, in a big hospital, down Aberystwyth. Your little girl couldn't be with a better family, though I says it as shouldn't.'

'Fine,' Madeleine said, clearly indifferent. 'Then you give her one of them before the adoption people come for the other.'

'It'll be a few weeks yet,' Nanny said comfortably. 'What do you want to call them?'

'Do I have to give them names? It seems silly.'

'Might as well, though they're so alike it'll take a while to tell one from t'other,' Nanny said tactfully.'How about Elizabeth for one of them, like the Duchess of York's little girl?'

'No, not Elizabeth. Well then, the one on the left's Megan and the one on the right's Marsha.'

'Marsha? That's a funny sort of name,' Nanny Evans began, but was speedily silenced.

'Don't you like it? Then send Megan to your daughter and Marsha can go to London. Oh, dear, I am *so* tired.' Madeleine opened her big blue eyes very wide and gave Nanny a sweet smile. 'You don't mind if I close my eyes for a minute, do you?'

Before Nanny Evans could say she did not mind in the least, Madeleine was fast asleep. And since the babies were mumbling and grumbling, Nanny picked up the cradle and took it out of the bedroom and into her own room, with the fire burning on the hearth and all the necessities she could think of standing ready.

She wondered if Madeleine would feed the babies . . . well, of course she would, once she knew it was the best thing, at first, she told herself. But herself remained unconvinced. Madeleine's whole attitude to her babies remained a mystery to Nanny Evans, though she must, in her time, have attended a hundred births. Still, Madeleine was a good girl, a loving girl, if you treated her right. Nanny had said nothing about the babies' father, but she had heard Madeleine, some nights, walking the floor, leaning out of the window into the icy air. And weeping. Not that it was any of her business, of course, and Madeleine, she well knew, was too young to be a mother, particularly with all the stigma attached to giving birth to bastard twins. She was better off without them, better off without *him*, too, taking advantage of her, ruining her life.

It was not as if she wanted the babies, either. She clearly did not. In fact, Nanny was beginning to feel quite apprehensive about the next six weeks, until the adoption people came for the little girl. What would she do, in a small cottage, if Madeleine refused to be in the same room as the twins?

On this point at least she need not have worried. The following morning she got up early, checked that the babies were sleeping soundly and went through to suggest to Madeleine that she might like to have a go at breast-feeding them.

Madeleine's bed was empty. She had left a note assuring Nanny that she was fine and had set off early to walk to the station. She had to call on some friends in London and would make her way back to the cottage in a week or so – if her parents rang, would Nan kindly stall them for a few days by pretending Madeleine was still with her?

I ought to ring Madam and tell her that Madeleine's gone off again, Nanny thought anxiously. But if I do the Ripley-Trewins will be down here like a ton of bricks and they'll find out about Menna's baby and want to take her away. On the other hand, Madeleine's note clearly says she won't be gone long. It might be best to play along with her, for a while at any rate.

Resignedly, she went back to her bedroom and peeped at the twins. They lay drowned in sleep, small faces set, eyes screwed tight so that not even a line of lashes showed, hair in damp, flattened curls on their small, egg-shaped skulls.

They're real pretty, Nanny said to herself, touching a cheek as soft as silk. Better make up a few bottles, see which they like best. I don't want to bring no wet nurse in, gossiping, carrying tales . . .

And then, in a couple of weeks, I'll drop Menna a line, tell her to come over on the bus because I've a surprise for her. She can stay here for a month or so, and then take the baby – Megan – back home. Yes, that'll be best. Madeleine will come back quite soon, she said she would. She's a good girl. I won't say anything to Madam, it would only upset her.

Nanny bustled into the kitchen, tipped milk into a pan, sweetened it, added water, and put the pan on the stove to boil. Some liked honey, she reflected, fetching a jar from the larder. Or there was golden syrup . . .

CHAPTER FIVE

Madeleine sat down on the station bench, leaned back and closed her eyes.

She was so tired! And if she stood up she knew her head would feel light and odd, her legs would ache, and the awful giddiness which had haunted her over the past two or three days would return.

She had not eaten much lately, not since she had given birth to the babies and left Nanny Evans. She had no money, so she only ate what she could beg or steal, and the wearier she grew, the less eating – or stealing – seemed to matter.

She knew she was ill, of course. Occasional glimpses of herself in shop windows or mirrors had shown her gaunt, sickly pale, her hair tangled, her skin dirty. But it no longer seemed to matter, for she had not found Tarot despite the most ardent and furious search.

It had taken weeks to search London, trekking the city streets, in and out of art galleries, visiting every place they had been together, shamelessly questioning everyone she met as to whether they knew anything about Tarot.

It had led nowhere. First, she had visited the house in Wardour Street, only to find a neat maid answering the door. That had been the first shock because, in her heart, she had expected to find them still in residence, even though it was spring. But they had gone as completely as the winter snows, vanishing totally as though they, too, had been absorbed into the earth.

From the house she turned to the streets. Other women discussed the flapper vote, talkies, the floods which had devastated London. Madeleine's only subject for discussion, as she searched cheap lodgings, Salvation Army doss-houses, was Tarot's whereabouts. The Army people were good to her, though, feeding her in the soup kitchens they had set up in the East End, encouraging her to talk about Tarot, trying to persuade her to go home to her people.

But she never told them her name or any other detail which might lead to her being returned to Bolton. She dared not give up; she had to find Tarot!

After London, then, the countryside he and she had wandered over and worked in, last summer. The farms, the fields, the haystacks even, were visited, on foot when public transport could not help.

She stole, of course. It became the only way she could eat, stealing or begging. She very soon had no pride left, anyway. She stole a shawl dropped by a fat old woman in a market town somewhere, tossing it round her shoulders and pretending not to hear the outcry behind her. She stole fruit from barrows, loaves from bakers' shops, vegetables which she ate raw, still dirty from field or garden. She would have stolen medicine, once she acknowledged she was ill, but she did not know how. Instead, she begged like a gypsy round a fairground until she had enough for the train fare to the Downs, because she had faced up to facts.

She would have to visit the Stones.

She did not know why she had left the place until last, save that she feared them still, the menhirs and dolmens, the Watchers who had overlooked the coming together of herself and Tarot, when they had made the babies. Could the Stones tell her where Tarot was? Would they, if they could? She had given birth to the Stones' little maidens and then she had abandoned them. The Stones would undoubtedly be angry with her. But she must face them, because they were her last hope.

When the train came shouting and muttering in she got to her feet, crossed the platform and collapsed into a seat. She was alone in the carriage, which was a good thing, because she felt ill unto death. She hoped, vaguely, that she would be able to get to the Stones, but at least, if she died, she would have died trying.

The thought stirred her mind out of its frightening state of exhaustion into another state, even more frightening. Death. She was near death. She had never looked it in the face before, and now that she did so she found she did not want to die. She was too young . . . but what was the use of living, if she must live without Tarot?

The train chugged on, through the June countryside. People came into her carriage, stayed a while, left again. And at last she reached her destination.

A friendly woman told her she looked ill, half-starved. Then she gave Madeleine an apple and a bag of fudge. Madeleine had eaten the food slowly, carefully, but even so she had felt, once more, that terrible, cruel pressure, the rushing sensation, as milk roared like a river into her aching, empty breasts.

No one had ever tried to explain to her about childbirth; she had given birth herself with no inkling of the after-effects, the painful emptiness of her womb, the swollen fullness of breasts which throbbed with milk – milk which seemed to Madeleine to curdle within her for want of someone to suck.

It all added to her sense of guilt, her helpless longing for Tarot. Only he could make her whole again, only he could understand! She must find him, explain, beg his forgiveness, and then lie back and bask in the warmth he would give her, the gentle, tender love she had thrown back in his face when she ran away.

81

The station platform looked like all the others; she still had a long way to go and she was very weak. She needed more substantial food than the apple and the fudge, delightful though these had been.

June is not a good month for living off the land. Too many things are in blossom, not enough in fruit, and there is a limit to the amount of young lettuce and tiny radishes which can be eaten by a starving girl who is intent on preventing her body from making more milk to fill those aching breasts.

Madeleine got off the station somehow and looked around. She found a man cleaning ditches and asked for one of his sandwiches. He gave her one, smiling, then looked puzzled when she thanked him and downed it in two bites. He asked her when she had last eaten and she explained that she was trying to get home, that she lived quite near, would eat in an hour or two . . .

He gave her some money and advised her to try the vicarage. Madeleine asked directions, set off towards it, then abandoned the road and walked the fields for a bit. She had no intention of getting mixed up with a vicar and besides, strange things were happening to her. Her head kept swelling up, larger and larger, like a balloon, and once or twice she found she was floating, actually progressing along without having to put foot to ground, which was convenient but horrid, because it made her feel so wretchedly giddy, and when she closed her eyes she fell over, and lay for a long time in the sweet meadow grass, unable, or unwilling, to move.

Presently, she got up and continued on her way. She found a stream and drank. She was dry as a desert, terribly thirsty, but she dared not drink her fill. As soon as the first sweet mouthful trickled down her throat her breasts began to swell. The pain was terrible; it made her want to lie down and scream, and put her head under the surface, and breathe in water instead of air until . . . oh, until the pain went away and she was clean and white and the old Madeleine, the one who had never gone with a man, never borne a child.

She took another mouthful, then another . . . and then lay down in the water and felt its coolness envelop her, and heard the gurgle and chuckle of it as it flowed round the rocks and swished softly against the banks. She put her face close to the surface and saw, in that kindly mirror, that she was still young, still beautiful, and imagined herself floating downstream like some modern-day Lady of Shalott, to where someone would find her, fall in love with her . . . mourn her loss . . .

'My God! Come along out of it, gal! She's fainted . . . give us a hand, Frank!'

Madeleine felt herself lifted out of the water. She was heavy, her head drooped forward on the slim young stalk of her neck, the water wanted her, grudged her sudden leaving of it.

She began to cry, very feebly, and then they got her into a sitting position on the bank and the sudden change of posture, for her head had been hanging down, brought darkness at last, and oblivion.

She came round in a hospital bed. It was clean and white and someone had washed her beautifully. She saw two clean hands on the top sheet and they were her hands, she recognized them from before.

Before what? She frowned down at her hands, trying to remember, but nothing would come, nothingness flowed into her mind like a physical presence, frightening her into breathlessness, her heart hammering, her lungs sucking air, her whole being suddenly panic-stricken.

'Name, dear?'

What a gentle, soft voice! It reminded her of

someone . . . Nanny! Yes, it sounded just like Nanny, and all nannies, everywhere, have to be obeyed.

'Madeleine.'

'Madeleine what, love?'

'Madeleine Ripley-Trewin.'

'And your address?'

'The Limes, Markland Hill, Bolton.'

'Well done. And is that on the telephone?'

A child again, Madeleine basked in the praise. Well done! It was a *long* time since anyone had said *well done* in just that tone of voice. She yearned for more such comfortable words.

'Oh, yes. Bolton 202.'

'That's fine, lovey. Now we'll just get you up the bed a bit, so's you can have a little drink of this . . .'

She was all child; she tried to get herself further up the bed and was hot-faced with shame to realize she could not do it. Something had stolen her strength, reduced her to this impotent kitten whose small paws clawed in vain at the covers to help her upright. But the kindly one put a strong arm round her, raised her, held the little teapot thing with the spout up to her lips.

Madeleine the child drank; Madeleine the woman cried out, clutching her breasts with thin, frail hands, weeping because the pain was so sudden, so unexpected. And because it brought with it a faint recollection of what had happened to her, why she was here, threw into the emptiness of her newly conscious mind echoing nightmares. Childbirth, loss, deep and terrible unhappiness. Loss. And not just the loss of her babies. The ache in her breasts was mirrored by the ache in her mind as she remembered that she was only half a person without Tarot.

The hospital in which she lay was only a cottage hospital

in a small town, but she soon realized she could not have been in better hands. Gentle, practical women nursed her, brought her food and helped her to eat, understood without words why she ached and wept and ached again. They must have contacted her parents but her parents did not come, not because they did not want to do so but because the authorities thought it best that she should be allowed to recover a little first.

'I lost a baby, once,' Sister Trett said to her, practical hands busy brushing and plaiting Madeleine's hair, practical mind giving a comfort only she could offer. 'My first, it were, as well. No one explains that your body goes on believing the babe's there and needing sustenance, that your belly's emptiness is a cruel thing, that even your arms are your enemy, when they ache and ache for a little light burden to cuddle and hold. Oh ah, a woman has to learn such things the hard way.'

'Yes,' Madeleine said timidly. 'It goes on and on, and your mind won't believe either, will it, Sister? And you know how angry They are . . . how They'll make you suffer, one day, for what you did.'

'That's no way to think,' Sister Trett said bracingly. 'You're just a little bit of a thing, far too young to take on a baby . . . reckon they said it 'ud ruin your life, eh?' She tutted and shook her head, stroking Madeleine's hair back from her brow, comforting as a nanny to her charge. 'Well, who knows but what they're right? Now your little'un's gone, lovey, and you must put it right out of your mind, make a new start. You've done no wrong and you've given great pleasure and happiness to another woman, a woman who can't have babies of her own, very likely. Cling to that thought, my maid, cling to that thought.'

Madeleine tried. It was not too bad in daylight, but with darkness her thoughts turned dark, too. The Stones

85

sometimes seemed to stand round her bed, accusing, like great, pointing fingers. She shivered in the middle of the circle, longing to run, fearing Them, knowing she was the sacrifice, that presently . . .

When she had been in hospital five days, she slept, and dreamed. It was a good dream because Tarot was in it, and she knew he was no longer angry with her; he understood her dilemma, and sympathized with her. They were in the circle, with the Stones standing round them, and he took her in his arms, but gently, and tipped up her chin and kissed her mouth, light as a feather.

'What ails thee, maid? Thou wert Their sacrifice – not willing, forced. No harm shall come to thee through this.'

She woke on the words, to find her mother bending over the bed. Her face was pale, tearstreaked.

'Madeleine! Oh, my dear . . . we wanted to come before but your father had a stroke . . . he's getting better . . . he would have come with me, to bring you home, but he can't . . . can't . . .'

Her mother's voice broke; more tears stood in her eyes.

'A stroke? Oh, Mother, was it me? Was it because I worried him so? If I've hurt Father . . .'

Even though she had been so ill she had intended to go to the Stones, to continue her search for Tarot. Now, that plan faded, suddenly meaningless, simply a further selfishness, a further means of causing pain. What use to weep for Tarot, when she had cast him off? What point in mourning her babies, when she had run away from them, denied them?

But there was one thing she could and should do: she could make up to her parents for the way she had behaved, what she had done to them. Lying there in bed, still weak and empty, still aching, she vowed she would do just that.

I'm young, she reminded herself, and I've got all my

life ahead of me. Father's fifty-nine, Mother only a couple of years less. It's time I thought of them, for a change.

Her father would recover; the doctor said so, and very soon Madeleine herself began to believe it. But the stroke had aged him; aged her mother, too. They were wary now, cautious in a way she had never known them before. She was taken home by train and taxi, because her parents did not trust the chauffeur they had been obliged to engage not to let slip that he had fetched Miss from a hospital in the West Country. Then she saw for herself how she had shaken their faith in themselves, their place in society.

'If I should die . . .' was a normal part of her father's conversation, now. 'After I'm gone . . .' figured quite heavily, too, and both remarks distressed Madeleine only marginally less than they distressed Mrs Ripley-Trewin. Madeleine knew that her behaviour had brought their own mortality near and there was nothing she would not do, she told herself, to put things right, to give them peace of mind.

But when she realized what they wanted, ah, then that was different. Marriage, and not to someone like Geoff, a young man of her own age with whom she had a good deal in common.

'Young men are wild, uncertain, and want to know too much,' Madeleine's father had said, according to Mother. 'My poor girl's been in hot water, and now I want security for her more than anything else. She needs a husband who'll take care of her, keep all worries from her . . . and never enquire too closely into the past year. And I know just the man.'

He did. Dickie Steadman, forty-two years old, managing director of a famous animal feedstuffs firm, fellow board-member of Golden Grape Fine Wines, a small but thriving wine importing business which Madeleine's father had helped to start ten years ago. What was better, he wanted to move into a very imposing house in Victoria Road, not a stone's throw from The Limes. And best of all, he had lived for the past ten years or so on the other side of Manchester. It went without saying, therefore, that so far as gossip went, he was out on a limb. He would not be sniffing round to try to discover just what Madeleine had been doing in France for a year, and he had already accepted that Albert Ripley-Trewin's stroke had been caused by overwork.

'He'll give you the moon, if you ask for it,' Mrs Ripley-Trewin assured her daughter. 'Generous to a fault . . . a handsome, friendly man, marvellous with children . . . he's most awfully keen to have kiddies of his own. His first wife couldn't have any. Poor Cynthia.'

But forty-two years old. A heavily built man with a big laugh, a long chin with a cleft which he rarely managed to shave properly, and an air of self-satisfaction. Coarsely handsome perhaps, but she hated the way his light blue eyes flickered hotly over her when they met. Assessing, anticipating.

'I don't like him much.'

One comment, diffidently given, hotly denied.

'Darling, you don't *know* him! Father's known him for years; he's often said he'd trust Dickie with his life . . . you'll be in safe hands, I promise you.'

Safe hands. Hot, sweaty, eager hands. Clutching, greedy hands.

'Yes, but marriage . . . it's a bit different, Mother.'

They knew what was best for her. Far be it from Mother to hurt her, but did she know what 'damaged goods' meant when applied to a young woman? Fortunately, Dickie had been married before, and was unlikely to expect . . . but a younger man might . . . not that we're old-fashioned, but you know that despite what you modern young things say, men *do* like their wives to be . . . well, untouched, I suppose I should say. I wouldn't reproach you, dear, but it's difficult for Father to answer the sort of questions which a younger man might feel justified in asking, whereas Dickie – well, he absolutely adores you, has done for years, said ages ago that he'd never seen a prettier girl . . . wished you were nearer his age . . .

'What about Geoff?'

Baldly said, blushingly, because if she could not have Tarot, if she was to be sold off to the first man willing to support her without too many questions asked (damaged goods, damaged goods!) then why should it not be Geoff?

Geoff, it seemed, was now out of the question. If Madeleine remembered, Geoff had been in France when Madeleine was supposed to have been there. He would expect Madeleine to discuss France with him, would ask questions . . . it would all come out, Mother would die of shame . . . she had told *lies*, you see, after a lifetime of meticulous truthfulness . . . and of course, it would kill your father.

It was the threat she most feared, that she should do them further harm. She had seen her father's brusque, kindly self-confidence fade into uncertainty, and though Dr Prosser very kindly took Madeleine to one side and assured her that he had been warning Albert Ripley-Trewin for years that he would have trouble if he did not regularize his life-style and eating habits, nothing could convince her that the stroke had not been ninety-nine per cent her fault.

She gave in, as they must have known she would. She rationalized her decision, telling herself that she was doing the right thing for a number of reasons. One, that all the troubles of the previous year had come when she did as she wanted, not as her parents thought right. Two, that the ache of missing Tarot, the guilt-feelings over the twins, would disappear once she had a husband of her own, and the children he wanted so badly. And she would have her own home, too; a house to run, a staff. She would learn how to give dinner parties, to socialize. She would enter society at last . . . she could bob her hair, shorten her skirts, learn to drive a car.

But she would not smoke – she would never smoke. Or walk barefoot through the meadows, in a long, swishy skirt with a hem discoloured from dust. Or visit Stone circles. Or love a man again.

The wedding was the social event of the season and Madeleine looked beautiful; she heard it on every side. The bridegroom was described as distinguished which, Madeleine thought fairly, he was, but no one stinted their praise of Madeleine's golden looks.

They honeymooned in the south of France, in a borrowed villa, and on the second day Madeleine got sunstroke. Dickie was wonderful, holding her head when she was sick, bringing her long, cool drinks, and leaving her alone in bed.

She had really looked forward to bed. To find that making love was not something everyone did naturally was a shock, but she did her best to put up with Dickie's ineptitudes. He had been married before, yet he used no gentleness during the act of love, attacking rather than persuading, putting all his considerable physical strength into subduing Madeleine, as though she were a victim rather than a partner. They slept under a sheet, nothing more, yet Dickie was always as hot as though he had a private little boiler burning away inside him. And the hair on his chest was like wire-wool scratching Madeleine's still-sensitive breasts.

But honeymoons are not easy, and Mother had murmured that she might find things difficult, so Madeleine endured, and enjoyed the good things: the lovely food, the marvellous weather, the milky warmth of the sea.

At home she found more problems, but told herself that she would enjoy overcoming them. Dickie bought her a horse, but it was at livery on a farm up on the moors so that she had to learn to drive or the chauffeur would spend all his time, Dickie said, ferrying her about.

In the end Johnson, the chauffeur, taught her because Dickie was always too busy. He was young and handsome and once, because she was unhappy and bewildered, she let him kiss her, and cuddled in his hard young arms she wondered what would happen if he carried her out of the car and laid her in the sweet grass and made passionate love to her.

But he did not know what she was thinking, so he drew back, apologized, and behaved very correctly for the rest of the day. And that night, in bed, Madeleine let herself imagine that it was Johnson who was digging his elbows into her breasts and kneeling on the soft part of her thighs and for the first time she responded to Dickie, who was touched and softened and wept a little, and held her gently for once, when their shared passion was over.

Gradually, Madeleine began to grow into her new role. She respected Dickie for the things he did well and tried not to resent the things he did badly. When she had her hair bobbed he sulked and was more violent than usual in his lovemaking, and Madeleine apologized and said she'd grow her hair again and he wept and said he was a fool and she the best little wife in the world.

But she did not become pregnant despite Dickie's grunting and sweating.

And then, one afternoon, when she was cutting roses in the garden and wondering what treat Dickie had in store to celebrate their first wedding anniversary in a few weeks, the maid came on to the terrace and called her.

'Madam, there's someone at the door . . . a policeman. He's asking for you.'

A slow saunter with the sweetly perfumed roses held in a shallow basket on one arm. Her straw hat shading her fair complexion from too much sun, her body in its pale cotton easy, comfortable.

'Yes, officer? Have I done something awful? Look, do step inside.'

He stood on the step, sweat glistening on his brow, his helmet in one hand, a fatherly-looking man with a ruddy, countrified face and hair cut cruelly short, and recently, too, so that his forehead was fringed with white where the sun had not yet had a chance to redden.

'There's been an accident, miss . . . ma'am. A car accident.'

Dickie? But he had telephoned only an hour before, to say he would be late for dinner. Nevertheless, things did go wrong . . .

'Not my husband? Mr Steadman?'

'No, ma'am. Mr and Mrs Ripley-Trewin. On the Wigan Road. The car seemed to go out of control . . . Mr Ripley-Trewin was driving, and the doctor seemed to think he might have been taken ill at the wheel . . .'

'I must go to them,' Madeleine said. She felt as if someone had cunningly erected a glass screen around her through which she could see perfectly well, but which deadened sound, cut her off.

'Of course, ma'am. Is there someone who could go with you?'

'My husband's away . . . I'll ask Johnson, my husband's chauffeur.'

Johnson drove her round to the hospital, though they were already dead. Killed instantaneously when the

Lagonda had veered directly into the path of a lorry carrying building bricks. There had been nothing the lorry driver could do about it; the Lagonda had driven straight at him and there was little room for manoeuvre on the winding road.

She went to The Limes, then, to do what she could to sort out her parents' affairs. Dickie came over too and helped her because he had known the Ripley-Trewins all his life. He arranged the funeral, put the house on the market and paid off the servants, whilst Madeleine received condolence visits and worked with her father's lawyer to see that the terms of both wills were properly carried out.

After the funeral they went back to The Limes and friends and relatives came and there was a very subdued funeral tea, with everyone talking in hushed voices because it had been so sudden, because Madeleine was only nineteen and an orphan now.

Home once more, in the big house on Victoria Road, Madeleine tried harder than ever to fit into Dickie's life. She tried to enjoy the things her mother had liked. She shopped at Whitakers with her friend, Fay Justian, and had coffee at the Kardomah Café; drove her little red sports car into Manchester and went to the cinema or the theatre. She tried to imagine her parents smiling approval from heaven but could not quite believe it. She had sacrificed her chance of happiness for them, and they had left her. The sacrifice seemed pointless now.

But she was a well-brought-up child. She had made her bed and now she must lie on it, and with a good grace.

Madeleine settled down to do her duty by Dickie, to be faithful and affectionate, and to give him the children they both longed for.

She reminded herself constantly that she was luckier than most, and she worked harder than ever to fit into the place Dickie had made for her. She tried never to look for Tarot at horse-fairs or race meetings, when she and Dickie went to one or the other in their 'county' clothes, with shooting sticks and binoculars. She tried not to gaze wistfully at fair-haired two, three, four-year-olds, nor to wonder whether, by some chance, the child was actually hers.

She saw in the mirror that she was changing. Her face wore the rather bored, slightly guarded look she had seen in other wives of older men. Yet she made friends, built up a social circle, became a good dancer, a useful rider to hounds, a noted hostess.

But inside, deep inside where no one else could see, she was still the old Madeleine Ripley-Trewin, with long, sun-bleached hair and quick, fluid movements, who loved Tarot and wanted him still, could never love another.

CHAPTER SIX

1939

'Megan Prydderch, will you get yourself out of that bed and down them stairs, before I come up to you meself?'

Megan had been playing a game she often played on sunny mornings, seeing pictures in the sunlight which danced on her bedroom wall, made more interesting because of the spindly birch which cast its constantly moving shadow on to the whitewashed surface.

At the sound of Mam's voice, however, she rolled over from her back on to her stomach and knelt up in bed.

'Righto, Mam, shan't be a tick,' she shrieked, because the attic was a long way from the kitchen in the tall house in Newry Street and past experience had told her a shriek carried better than a mere call. 'Just gettin' out of bed.'

This was not strictly true, but Megan made it so by leaping gigantically out on to the chilly linoleum and then pattering across it, through the door and out on to the little square landing at the head of the attic stairs. As she passed her washstand she grabbed her enamel jug, because cleanliness was not just next to Godliness so far as Mam was concerned; they were neck and neck. No matter that it was Sunday, or that Megan was on her school holidays – Mam would expect that jug to be filled in the kitchen before her foster-daughter put a thread of clothing upon her small person.

There were three attic bedrooms. One held the boys, Dewi, Henry and Peris, and the other was Mam and Da's. Because money was tight in this house, two lodgers slept in the bedrooms on the first floor: Mr Elias Jones, a clerk at the railway station, and Uncle Reggie Brittain, who had sailed out of the port of Holyhead all his life and couldn't think of living anywhere else, so that when he retired he had moved in with the Prydderchs and looked like dying here, too. He was white-haired and bearded, was Uncle Reggie, and everyone loved him, though when he remarked, as he was fond of doing, that he had to live within spitting distance of sea water Mam frowned a bit.

Mr Jones was all right, as well. Tall, thin, stooping, with odd little spectacles called *pince-nez* on the end of a long, bony nose. He had a surprisingly beautiful tenor voice and could be persuaded, almost at the drop of a hat, to give the family his renderings of old favourites. 'The Ash Grove', 'Danny Boy' and 'Speak to me of Love' were popular with Mam and Da, though Henry, who had developed a taste for jazz, pleaded for 'Bye-bye Blackbird', 'Chinese Moon', and 'Yes sir, that's my Baby'.

With her jug in her hand, Megan cantered down the attic stairs, tiptoed across the first floor hall, and went fast but quietly down the staircase. She loved Sundays because the whole family went to chapel together and then had a proper dinner if they were in funds, and afterwards she and Peris could spend the afternoon as they liked, provided they were in for five o'clock tea.

Down in the kitchen, Mam was making two breakfasts with her usual speed and despatch. Bacon and egg for the boarders, porridge and bread and scrape for family. Not even the lodgers had bacon and egg every day – times were too hard for that – and the family did not usually have bread as well as porridge either. It was a Sunday special, a treat.

'Getting up, Meg, then? There's good you are! Rouse that lazy Peris, will you, so's he can give a hand. Da and the boys need a rest, Sundays.'

Megan held out her can and smiled up at Mam as it

was filled by vigorous heaves of the pump handle. Water gurgled, coughed, then gushed into the jug, icy cold from its long stay underground but sweet and clean, as clean as Megan herself would be once she had got to work with it and her trusty flannel.

'I'll give him a shout,' Megan promised. 'He do love porridge!'

Mam smiled back, the smile making her look so beautiful that tears came to Megan's eyes and had to be sternly ordered back. Mam was small and strong, with hair black as jet except where some white had crept in, and lovely dark eyes. When she was young her skin had been white as milk, she told Megan, but working in the sun and the wind had coarsened it so that now it was gently tanned, with golden freckles across her nose which darkened to tea-colour in the summer sun. Megan knew her foster-mother was beautiful even with freckles, and envied her the black, naturally curly hair, the dark eyes, the sturdiness, even. What use is hair so light it can scarcely be said to have a colour, or eyes of blue, when the sea and the sky are bluer, or thin little legs and arms like sticks of celery?

Still, Mam would be the first to remind Megan that beauty was only skin deep and character counted for more, and besides, Mam thought Megan was lovely. 'So fair you are,' she teased gently, brushing the long, light locks. 'Oh, you make me look coarse and brown and hefty you do, Megan my little one.'

That made Megan laugh, and Mam had hugged her and the talk had turned to other things, but nothing could stop Megan secretly hoping that, one day, she might look just like Mam, black curls and all.

She had worshipped her foster-mother for five years now, ever since the day they had first met. Mam had come to the mainland from the Isle of Anglesey because she and Da had decided to take on another lad. They had

97

been taking children from the social for some years, ever since they had realized they would not be able to have babies of their own, but now Samuel and Arthur, the first two, had left home, and Dewi and Henry, the second two, were out of school and earning.

There was very little money in Holyhead, Megan knew, but Mam and Da did better than most. They had the big old house in Newry Street which had been Mam's family home until her parents died, and they had the fishing boat which Da took out every day of the year save Sundays, Christmas Day and days when the weather was so foul that he could not leave the port. The house enabled them to have boarders and to take the boys in, and the social paid for the children's keep until they were old enough to earn. And lads, even quite young ones, could help in the house, dig the back yard and the allotment down by Salt Island, and make themselves useful in a variety of ways. And when they were old enough they could go to sea with Da and haul the nets and bring home the catch. Samuel, though in business for himself now, still helped, because he bought the fish off Da and took it over to the mainland and sold it to the fancy hotels in the seaside towns, who could then boast that their fish came from Ynys Mon and was the freshest available.

So Mam went to the Deiniol Evans Children's Home, as she had always done, and talked to the superintendent, Mr Glasse, and as a result of that conversation was led to the room where the little ones were doing what they called handwork.

Usually, Mam had boys of ten or twelve, but this time, for some reason, she and Da had decided to have a younger one, a child of no more than six or seven. Perhaps they wanted someone to stay a bit longer. Megan did not know – all she knew was that her life had changed, that day, and that she had never looked back.

When Mam came into the room Megan had been sitting in a chair, cuddling a kitten, sucking her thumb and dreaming of nothing in particular. Peris, who was her special friend, had been taking a box to pieces. He should have been mending it, but found it more pleasurable to rip out nails and unscrew screws and reduce the box to pieces of wood. He was a very naughty boy.

The superintendent had been furious and had begun to berate the pair of them, Peris for the wickedness of ripping the box apart, Megan for even blacker sins. The trouble was, Megan thought now, looking back indulgently down the years, I never did see what was naughty the way the Deiniol Evans Home did. She knew that the kitten was meant to stay in the kitchen, that thumbs were not built to be sucked, and that she should have been industriously knitting woollen squares to make a blanket, but even so . . . dirty habits, idle hands, the words flapped round her head like ill-omened bats whilst the kitten was snatched from her grasp, the thumb was popped out of her mouth, and the knitting was thrust into her lap.

'A child who dreams is an idle child, open to mischief,' Mr Glasse said crossly, turning to Mam. 'Mrs Prydderch, if you knew the trouble that's caused by simply doing nothing . . . the wicked thoughts, the evil ideas . . .'

'Even at six?' Mam said blankly, and the superintendent said *especially* at six, because a child of that age was more impressionable than an older one.

Mam nodded impatiently and tapped her fingers on the table whilst the superintendent droned on about children and responsibility and the importance of cleanliness and regular churchgoing, and all the time her eyes spoke to Megan, and seemed to promise things only Megan could understand, only she could interpret.

At last Mam stood up and Megan, as though someone had pulled unseen strings, stood up too.

'Right, Mr Glasse, that's settled then. And I'm takin' that little one, too,' Mam said, pointing at Megan. She had already brought Peris to her side, despite the fact that Mr Glasse had spitefully tried to persuade her to change her mind and take someone a bit more responsible.

'*That* one? The fair one? Oh, but Mrs Prydderch, you always have boys. You never take a girl, and that one . . . she's been out more times . . . no one ever succeeds with her. She's a bad girl, she wets the bed, she's sly, she's spiteful . . .'

Mam had cut across the tirade with marvellous brevity.

'Yes, that one. Come along.'

She had held out a small, capable hand. Megan had grasped it, and heeded nothing after that save for the strong feeling that Mam's hand had rescued her from stormy water, hauled her ashore, and would keep her there, safe. Loved, even.

Because she had been in and out of the Deiniol Evans Home so often, though, Megan found she was afraid as they neared her new home. They walked into the kitchen and there was Da, and tall Dewi, and hefty Henry, and they were sitting round the table with tea spread out before them and they looked like great gods to small little Megan.

'Hey-up, what's all this?' said Da, who had expected a boy, and Megan had been so terrified that she had wet herself, the warm, guilty wee running down her skinny legs and puddling the kitchen floor.

'Now look what you made her do,' Mam had said reprovingly. 'There's scared of you she is, and you such a big softie, really. Fetch us a mop, Dewi my little one.'

And huge Dewi had fetched the mop and winked at Megan. Winked! And Da was looking sorry and smiling at her and saying he hadn't meant to worry her, and she was a godsend, that she was, another woman for the household of men, and wasn't he proud to have her?

Megan looked around her. No one, absolutely no one, had that look on their face which she had grown to know and dread. The look which said, *Oh God, we've made a dreadful mistake, and how in heaven's name can we get out of it?*

Even the boarders were indulgent with the small, yellow-haired girl who wanted so much to please. She endeared herself to Uncle from the start by admiring his parrot, Screech, which lived in a big wicker cage on the half-landing and could actually talk. She liked Uncle's monkey, too, a chilly creature with a sad little blue face who wore woolly coats and breeches in winter and loved small pieces of raw swede or potato. Mam did not care for the monkey, who was called Bertie, though it was a while before Megan realized this since Uncle always referred to the little creature as 'Face-ache', which seemed far more appropriate for an animal cursed with such a lugubrious expression. But Mam disapproved of creatures in clothing, even after Uncle had explained that the monkey would die of cold in the Anglesey climate without his winter woollies. Mam told Uncle he ought to ship the poor thing back to foreign parts and explained, in a whisper, that Bertie smelt and wet in corners instead of using the tray full of sawdust which Uncle provided. But, being Mam, she tolerated the monkey and pretended not to hear when Screech came out with what she called, rather obscurely, 'sailors' talk'.

And so we came to Newry Street, me and Peris, Megan told herself now as she climbed the stairs with her jug held carefully so as not to spill a drop. And we've been here nearly five years and no one has tried to send me back, not even when I've been really naughty, which I am from time to time.

101

Peris, of course, was a child of the devil, always in trouble and quite often dragging her in after him. He was a year older than she and a great deal wickeder, with a mind full of inventive naughtiness which often started out innocently enough. He had taken her climbing for gulls' eggs at South Stack because Mam liked them, and had somehow stranded the pair of them on a very small ledge with an enormous drop down to the rocks below. The lighthouse keeper had sent for the lifeboat, and it had taken the crew the best part of three hours to rescue them.

Then there had been the apple-stealing from the convent, which had seemed a good idea at the time when Peris had explained that nuns were holy women who would not grudge the apples to a couple of poor waifs and strays.

Sadly, the nuns had not been as holy as Peris had assumed, and had grudged the apples to the extent of chasing the delinquents half a mile across town and finally cornering them down by the harbour, where Peris had confidently expected to escape by scrambling over a high wall. But Megan had gone and got herself caught, falling over and squealing like a stuck pig, and he had been forced to return to rescue her and had been caught himself.

Megan loved all her foster-brothers, but Peris was her especial friend. He was thin and agile, with a wedge-shaped face and a wide brow across which fell fine toffee-brown hair, and he had eyes the colour of strong, milkless tea set on the slant which had won him the nickname 'Chinky' at school. He had eyebrows which rose at the corners like those of fauns and satyrs in Greek mythology, and a three-cornered smile which tended to make him look mischievous even when he was merely happy.

Megan reached the top landing without incident and gave a soft tap on the boys' door. All three boys slept there and it was only a small room, so when she heard nothing she stood her jug down, opened the door and slid inside.

The curtains were still drawn across the window and the window was shut, which meant that the room smelt strongly of boys' feet and sweat. In fact the air was so thick with it that Megan held her breath, scampered across to the mound in the single cot which she knew was Peris, and put a cold hand under the covers. She found a face, slid her fingers across it and grabbed an ear.

From below the bedclothes came a subterranean rumbling including some language which, Megan knew, would qualify as sailors' talk should Mam ever get to hear it.

'Get off, you poxy brat! Sod off, Meg! Oh, damn you, girl, swing for you I will one of these days.'

'Mam says to get up,' Megan said, keeping her voice low. The big boys would not be pleased if she woke them betimes on a Sunday morning, when a bit of a lie-in was much prized. 'Get out of that bed, boy, or I'll pull the ear off your head.'

'Damn you, Megan, I tell you I'll . . .'

A ruffled head appeared above the blankets, towed up by one reddened ear. It was wrathful at first, then it grinned ruefully.

'All right, all right, you've made your point. I'll get up. Out of here with you . . . hey, spare some water, eh?'

'No fear, Mam would scalp me,' Megan said righteously, backing towards the door. 'Get your own, Peri, or she'll throw you in the harbour. Hurry, now.'

She returned to her own room. Since it was a partitioned-off bit of the boys' room, she could hear Peris blundering around, then crossing their shared lino and thundering down the stairs, no doubt carrying his water jug. She sloshed water into her own basin and dropped in her facecloth, then squeezed it out and applied soap. The flannel was then rubbed vigorously over her face, neck and upper body, Megan having cast off the hand-me-down nightdress which kept her respectable in a house full of males. Presently, washed, she donned a cotton dress, knickers and her old sandals, got out her hairbrush and sat on the edge of her bed to brush.

This was her favourite task of the morning. Mam was proud of Megan's hair and the rule was one hundred strokes night and morning. During that time, who could blame Megan for dreaming, for going over her past and anticipating her future? It was practically the only time in the whole of her busy life when she sat and did nothing – apart from in school, she reminded herself ruefully, and then one was all too apt to suddenly find oneself the centre of attention, blushingly aware that one had not heard a word the teacher had been saying.

But now . . . the brush smoothed away, her hair crackled, and she remembered.

Megan had one of those incredible memories which people smile and shake their heads over, the sort of memory which could look back to a time before speech, to a particular ceiling crack shaped like an old man with a huge nose, to a face hanging over her, smiling, always smiling, whilst grey eyes twinkled behind round, wire-rimmed spectacles, a voice cooed lovingly, and comfortable hands lifted her into comfortable arms. And she knew when she was lifted out of her warm nest that she had left someone behind, that there was someone else who was always with her, a presence so akin to her own that the two were almost one, almost physically as well as mentally joined.

Then, one day, the round, bespectacled face had disappeared, taking with it that other. Instead there was a pretty, anxious face with a soft, uncertain voice. Another voice, a man's, harsh and often angry, entered her life.

Megan had known even then that the anger was directed against her, and because she had not liked the change, because she was suddenly alone for the first time in her short life, she began to grizzle and cry a lot, to weep and wail, to search with small, helpless hands and mouth for that other; but her companion had gone like the crack on the ceiling, the smiling face.

Other things changed, too. Food was never quite right, either too sweet or not sweet enough, and hands trembled, threatened to drop, to let slip her small and tender body, her frail, newly-hatched head. She was perpetually tensed against being allowed to crash on to the floor, which she sensed was hard and unfriendly. And through it all echoed the loneliness, the hollow ache of her loss.

Things got worse, not better. She sensed sadness, as the anxious one went about her business, and a growing depth of bitterness. The prettiness faded as the sadness grew, the voice which had quavered grew shrill, food was not always given, now, to calm hunger, and there was discomfort too as soiled clothing was ignored, sores multiplied and stiff, ammonia-reeking nappies chafed spindly legs, tiny buttocks.

But worse than all this was the coldness against her side where there had been warmth, the emptiness where there had been that other person, that kindred spirit. She ached with her loss and tried to show someone, say something . . . and so she had cried and whimpered and threshed around and her small stomach perpetually rumbled with wind and tightened into cramps from the stresses and strains of her own loss and the sadness around her.

Then, confusion. Many faces, all strange. Many other babies, but never the voice she longed to hear, the presence she longed to feel. Toddling for the first time, Megan had tried in vain to find her other half. She had staggered about, clutching the furniture, falling, crawling, always searching, always crying because the Other had gone and left her lonely, with an ache which it seemed no amount of time would cure.

Time passed. There were more strangers, more unfamiliar beds. And dreams which taunted her, haunted her. Always she was sure the Other must be near, wanting Megan as Megan wanted her, needing Megan as desperately as Megan needed her. But never near enough, never quite coming close.

Despair, then, for a while. Spreading wet in the bedclothes, wet of tears on her pillow and of wee beneath her body. And the cries, presently, of adults who declared they had tried everything . . . she's such a miserable kid . . . a real whiner . . . she doesn't want us, doesn't love us . . . we're sorry, Miss Scott, Jenkins, Adlington, we'll have to send her back, we just can't cope.

Later, when she was big enough to talk, to understand what was happening, there had been foster-homes by the score, for lots of people want a little blonde girl for their very own. She had never fitted in; every attempt had ended in failure. She meant to be good, but somehow it never worked out. She had let caged birds free, had nearly drowned in a forbidden pond, eaten prize-winning fruit and been sick on a treasured rug. She had fed poisonous berries to a younger child and been instrumental in the breaking of a foster-father's leg. But worst of all, she had wept . . . and searched, endlessly, for the Other.

The searching had led, inevitably, to the running away. Not just from foster-homes but from institutions, too, until she had lost count of the times she had set off, doggedly, taking any money she could lay her hands on, determined to go . . . where? Just away. Because the only conviction she had held in those early years was that she was in the wrong place. Not wanted, not happy, not fitting

106

in. So it had been natural to run away from the adoption attempts and the foster-homes and the institutions which smelt of boiled cabbage and urine, trying always to find the Other, to find that elusive bluebird, happiness.

Then she had come to Holyhead and found all the things she wanted, save for the Other. In the sideways-leaning row of terraced houses with their whitewashed walls and wavy, lichen-patched roof-slates, there was a warmth and a love which the small, six-year-old Megan had immediately recognized and wanted for herself.

She had earned it, what was more. For goodness, which doesn't come naturally to any child, fell on her like a benison when Mam was near, and the hungry searching for that Other slowed and ceased. She became careful of the feelings of others, grew less anxious, and almost as a reward, it seemed, discovered that there was a way to find the Other once more.

Sitting on the bed in the dappled sunshine, carefully wielding the brush from hair root to tip, Megan closed her eyes and willed the pictures to come. First, she just saw the pinky-gold of sunlight through closed lids, but then she emptied her mind deliberately, thinking of nothing, letting her thoughts dance, suspended, like a cloud of midges above a still, reflecting pool.

And the pictures came. A girl, very like herself, riding a pretty pony across a stretch of grass, ducking her head under trees, now and again rising in the stirrups to reach up for something above her head.

Megan was near her, willing her to turn round, to come and play, and presently the girl dismounted, looped her pony's reins up over the top of the saddle, and sat down in the grass. In imagination, Megan sat beside her. The girl closed her eyes and then smiled. Now they could see each other, Megan was sure, as they sat on the grass, basking in the sunshine, and she put out a tentative hand to touch the other girl's arm in its smart velvet riding jacket.

The Other smiled, and then their fingers met, clung . . . and they were holding hands, and though Megan knew that this was a sort of dream, that she was really in her bedroom brushing her hair before breakfast, she also knew that it was happening, that the hand in hers was a real, flesh and blood hand, that the Other existed. Now that they were both happy they relished their coming together but had no urgent need of it, as Megan once had.

'Megan, my little one, come you and stir the porridge; I've got to get the bacon and eggs on to the trays, see.'

Megan opened her eyes; she was sitting on the bed, the brush cast down beside her, and her hands were lightly clasped in her lap. Was that all it was, then? Had she taken the hand, not of the Other, but of herself? But she thought not; her two hands were warm, but the hand she had held in the meadow under the oak tree had been cool from the wind, the nails longer than her own, whitened in some mysterious way, the skin soft, smooth.

We are eleven, she and I, she told herself, as she called to Mam that she would be right down. No one in the world was ever born a waif and stray, Mam says so. And she's real, I know she is, which means that I had a sister once.

She didn't die, either, because the Other is no ghost. Ghosts don't ride ponies and have picnics on sunny beaches and wear beautiful clothes and have a whole shelf of picture books all their own. But I'm not a ghost either . . . so how do I go to her? How do I know what she's like? Sometimes I get the feeling that I shall always be the one to go to her, never the other way around. I need her, but she's never needed me.

* * *

108

Presently, sitting at the kitchen table with a mug of weak tea and her dish before her, Megan reached for the golden syrup and drew a woggly M on the surface of her porridge. M for Megan and M for Mam . . . if the Other has a name, I wonder if that begins with M, too? Peris passed her the skimmed milk and she poured it on, creating an outer rim of bluey-white around the grey and gold of porridge and syrup.

'What'll we do after chapel, Peris?'

Megan kept her voice low; whatever he wanted to do she would follow him, of course, but it would be rather nice if he suggested something good for a change.

'Get the lines and go to Soldier's Point,' Peris said briefly, through a mouthful. 'There's crabs in the rocks.'

'You'll both get me some runners first,' Mam announced. 'Take the big basket, because I'll salt some down for winter.'

'Sure, Mam,' Peris said easily. Like Megan, he adored their foster-mother and gave short shrift to anyone unwise enough to suggest that the Prydderchs had children for the money and not for love. 'If we get dabs, you and the boys can have 'em for supper.'

'Dirty little dabs taste of face-flannel,' Henry remarked. 'Do you go for something tastier, Peri, my little one. There's plaice off Penrhos, they're good to eat.'

'We'll get whatever takes our bait,' Peris admitted, grinning across the table at Henry. 'Anyway, boyo, you shouldn't grumble. At least you get supper!'

It was a sore point with Peris and Megan that they were sent to bed before supper was served, Mam thinking that young stomachs should not eat just before bed. And it was true, thought Megan ruefully, that for someone who suffered from nightmares, as she still occasionally did, a late meal could prove a mistake. All the same, it was galling to go up to bed whilst downstairs Mam, Da, Dewi and Henry tucked into Mam's famous vegetable pie or a lovely fish cobbler.

Presently, when everyone's belly was lined with hot porridge, the family left the table and went to change into their best. Mam was chapel and Da was church, so they went alternately. But although Mam was staunch Methodist she was by no means devout enough for their minister, who preached that Sunday was a day of rest and tried to persuade his congregation never to cook, garden or enjoy themselves on the Sabbath. However, everyone knew that Rhiannon Prydderch was a good woman, the best of neighbours, who would do anything for anyone, so the minister never thundered against her from the pulpit nor held up her foster-children to scorn when their behaviour left something to be desired. Besides, with so much poverty on Holy Island, each minister needed natural organizers in his flock, and Mam was one of those all right! She was always busy, yet she found time to take the bus to the mainland twice a week to visit jumble sales and bring home quantities of clothing for the very poor, and she helped the Sally Army with vegetables to enrich the broth they handed out daily in their soup kitchens. The minister told her now and then that she should not let the children go for fish nor Dai Prydderch take his boat out on a Sunday, and Rhiannon said she wished things could be different so that she didn't have to work on the Sabbath to feed her little flock, and didn't the minister think that someone should have a word with the good God, now, who asked people to choose between filling their children's bellies and pleasing those who preached the gospel? And when she said that the minister put his hand across his mouth, and smiled at her, and probably went on his way feeling better for her plain speaking.

Da's church was St Cybi's, overlooking Landsend and the docks. Megan liked it best, with its magnificent views

110

and the quiet, white-haired old vicar who never thundered at them but preached a good sermon nevertheless. And she liked the churchyard, with the old slate gravestones and the low wall, ideal to sit on whilst you waited for a service to finish.

It was a fair walk to St Cybi's, but further to the chapel Mam favoured, and today was chapel; Megan dreamed along beside Peris whilst above her head the adults' conversation rolled and soared. They were talking about Germany, and Poland, and what someone would say on the wireless at dinner-time, and Dewi said he would join the Navy and Henry said the Navy wouldn't have a fish-head like Dewi and Da told them both to pipe down and he and Mam discussed going over to see Great-aunt Blodwen and Great-uncle Eifion, who lived very frugally indeed in a tiny harbourside cottage in the fishing village of Moelfre. Mam wanted to take them some food and bits and pieces, but Da said they were very proud and it would have to be done tactful, like.

'I could go over with you,' Megan suggested hopefully at one point. She loved Great-aunt Blod's tiny quayside cottage. Last time they had gone Mam had taken homemade bread and butter from the farm and Great-aunt Blod had provided lovely fat brown shrimps . . . Megan had eaten until she was sated, and Great-aunt Blod had cackled at her appetite while all the time she was swallowing down Mam's good bread and butter as though she had not eaten for a month. Which, when Megan remarked on it later, Mam had said was likely true.

'All these means tests and public assistance – you can't expect old 'uns to take to it,' Da remarked. 'Independent, they are, and proud, too. The old boy keeps his pig and grows spuds and still catches any fish foolhardy enough to approach the shoreline, and they manage. But manage it is, just. Small appetites he says the old have – small appetites they need, the way things are.'

But the visit wouldn't be today, because it was a long way to Moelfre; you had to catch the blue bus which sauntered across the island, taking the easy route, so that it might be a couple of hours before you reached your destination. Not that anyone minded, when the women could sit comfortably on the inward-facing seats, like a sewing circle, all gossiping away like mad, whilst the children and the livestock took up the middle of the bus and the driver stopped when little Eirlys wanted to pee, and stopped again to chase a calf back into a field or a pig into its sty.

'Mam, can Meg and me go down to the Point, after chapel? We can have our dinner later.'

An old trick, but one which always made Mam smile. As if she would dream of allowing a child to miss its hot Sunday dinner . . . as if a child would dream of missing it! Good Welsh lamb today, with potatoes and greens grown on the allotment, followed by plum pie, the crust dusted with sugar, and a thick custard poured over it. The only meat meal of the week, and them to miss it?

'Not today, Peris. But one of these days I'll say yes and you'll find Dewi and Henry won't leave you so much as a lamb's whisker.'

Everyone laughed, but they were almost in the chapel porch now, so the laughter was hushed, respectful.

'Only joking, I was,' Peris said hastily. 'Are you going to sing, Megan?'

A family joke, that her skimped pink dress would one day split asunder as she reached a top note, had them all grinning again.

'She do need a new one,' Mam muttered, as they collected the hymn books from the deacon at the door. 'That pink is indecent, just. The Girls' Friendly will be having

112

a rummage sale out at Valley . . . they've hired the Mill-room . . . but I'd thought for a Sunday best dress it would be nice to go down to the Emporium; lovely stuff Miss Williams makes. But no time, yet, to do anything about it. Next week, perhaps, eh, Megan, my little one?'

'I'll sing soft,' Megan promised, as she always did. 'I'll not take big breaths . . . I'll save the pink for this week.'

The family filed into the chapel and took their places about halfway up the aisle. Already in, Samuel and his young wife turned to smile at them. Samuel's Angharad was going to have a baby soon; her stomach was one big, soft curve.

'Da and me will be grandparents at last. You'll all have to call us Nain and Taid,' Mam had teased. Her a grandmother, and looking young as Angharad herself!

'We are gathered together . . .'

The service slid into its accustomed routine and Megan allowed her thoughts to wander comfortably. Another Sunday well into its stride, dinner getting closer, Soldier's Point beckoning, with all the joys of cliffs rich with gorse and smelling of chestnuts in the hot sunshine.

This is the best life in the world, Megan told herself. I don't ever want it to be any different. The Other has a pony and beautiful clothes, but she hasn't got Mam and Da, or Peris, or the boys, and she hasn't got Soldier's Point, and Penrhos beach, and Great-aunt Blod and Great-uncle Eifion at Moelfre. Oh, I hope it never changes!

The minister announced a hymn and Megan prepared to sing carefully.

And the future, which seemed so sunny and safe, spread itself out before her, unchanged and unchange-able.

Except that the date was the third of September nine-teen thirty-nine.

CHAPTER SEVEN

Marsha had been riding all morning, taking Robin from his stable right down to the meadows near Ladybridge, and then she had thought about luncheon and decided to go home for it. Sometimes she popped in on her cousins, Sarah and Simon, and Auntie Phyl fed her, but that meant ringing Mummy and Daddy to explain where she was, and she rather thought she'd be obliging today and go home.

Robin was in full agreement with this decision. Lazy little beast, she chided him, digging her heels into his barrel-sides and trying to get him to trot rather than saunter. Mummy and Daddy had bought Robin for her when they first moved into Gablehurst, a big house with its own stable on Chorley New Road, but since then Marsha had grown a lot. She really could do with a bigger, faster mount, but Mummy and Daddy were such fusspots, always terrified she'd fall off and break her neck, that for the time being she had to make do with Robin.

That was the trouble with being an only child. It was spiffing in some ways, because mostly you got what you wanted, but in other ways it was a dreadful nuisance. You had to take all the fussing and all the worries on your own shoulders, whereas for Simon and Sarah there was always someone else to blame.

Simon was thirteen, two years older than Marsha, but Sarah was the same age, and they got on most awfully well. Indeed, Marsha had insisted that Mummy and Daddy send her to Sarah's school, on Chorley New Road, because she just knew she would like it there. And she did. Marsha was no genius but she had a natural gift for languages. Provided she could gabble French and German well enough to come top of the class it was sufficient to make up for her failings in other subjects.

When she led Robin into his stable, though, Mummy was actually at the kitchen door, shading her eyes with her hand and looking worried.

'Oh – Marsha, darling, come in at once, will you,' she called. 'Daddy wants a word.'

Oh, does he, Marsha thought, taking Robin's saddle off and humping it towards the tackroom over one arm. Well, he can jolly well want, because John Holloway, who was groom, chauffeur and general handyman, always made her rub Robin down and generally take care of him herself. 'I've got enough to do with your father's hunters and the cars,' he was wont to tell her. 'I believe kids who are lucky enough to own horses should know how to look after them, so you get on with it, young Marsha.'

He was nice, was Holloway, but you did as he told you or there was trouble, so Marsha hurried back to the stall, took Robin's bridle off, slung it on the hook and then seized a handful of hay from the net which hung above his manger and began to rub him down. Robin, who was a thirsty horse, had his nose in a bucket of water and made no objection to her ministrations – in fact, the objection came from a totally unexpected source.

'What are you doing, may I ask? I thought I heard your mother calling?'

It was John Holloway and he was scowling.

'You did, but I've got to rub Robin down,' Marsha pointed out virtuously. Had he not told her, over and over, that it was wrong to leave a pony to grow cold in its own sweat? But adults, as everyone knows, are a mass of contradictions. Now, instead of praising her, the groom jerked his thumb decisively towards the yard.

'Out! When Mrs Loxley calls, my girl, you run! And don't say I've ever encouraged you to disobey your parents, because that I never have. Off with you. I'll finish Robin myself.'

Marsha was halfway across the stall when she stopped abruptly, swinging round to face the groom.

'Mr Holloway, why does Daddy want to see me? And why are you letting me off from grooming Robin?'

Holloway laughed.

'You're no fool, young Marsha! Go and see.'

Marsha continued on her way; she knew Holloway far too well to think he might relent. She would have to go indoors and find out for herself.

Inside, it struck her at once that the kitchen staff were very quiet. Serious faces stared back at her as she popped her head round the door. She asked Mrs Roberts, the cook, what was up, but Mrs Roberts just said, rather woodenly, that Mr Loxley and madam were in the drawing room, and she had better hurry.

Eager to know just what was happening, but not at all worried, Marsha actually broke into a trot and hurried down the long, dim passageway, through the baize door at the end of it, across the wide, echoing hall and into the drawing room. Mummy and Daddy were both there and she saw that neither had made a move, yet, towards the dining room. Usually, at this hour, they would have gone through, for though they had a cold meal for Sunday luncheon, to save the staff, they liked to have it fairly early. But today they were waiting for her.

'I untacked Robin and then gave him a bit of a rub down before Holloway came and finished him off,' Marsha announced. Daddy was looking red and perturbed, Mummy pale. What on earth had happened? She voiced her thoughts. 'I say, what's up, Mummy?'

'We've just been listening to a wireless announcement

by the Prime Minister,' Mummy said. 'Darling, something rather dreadful has happened. The Germans were given an ultimatum to get out of Poland by a certain time, and since they've not moved nor answered the ultimatum we are now at war with Germany.'

'Gosh,' Marsha said inadequately. 'What will it mean, Daddy?'

'It'll mean every able-bodied man who can fight to defend his country must do just that. We'll probably have to get out of this house, for a start. It'll be wanted by the forces, I dare say. And they'll take the horses, too. They did in the last war.'

'What, *our* horses? Fly and Jostle? And my dear little Robin? I won't let them – Daddy, you mustn't let them. Robin's mine!'

Gone the annoyance over his fatness and his small size; he was hers and therefore sacrosanct.

'War's a funny business, pet,' Daddy explained patiently. His high colour was higher than ever, his eyes pale and fierce in contrast. 'When a country's at war the government of the day can do all sorts of things. They can take over big houses, requisition horses and cars, make women work in factories or on the land . . . and we just have to make the best of it, I'm afraid.'

'I don't see what they can want with Robin, or with our house,' Marsha mumbled. She was fond of her big airy bedroom with its lovely built-in wardrobes and cupboards and the window-seat with its squashy, chintz-covered cushions. 'Where are we supposed to live if the Army moves in here?'

'Well, sweetheart, that is rather the point. I want you and Mummy to go to Auntie Eff and Uncle Teddy, in the States.'

That night, in bed, Marsha cried until her eyes ached.

Everything was happening too fast for her, that was the trouble. In the end, almost without consulting her, they had decided that Mummy would stay and she, Marsha, would go to America.

It was bombing they were afraid of, it seemed. They thought the Germans would bomb England, and despite Gablehurst's being on the outskirts of Bolton – practically in the country, really – Daddy feared it might be in danger. In terms of air war, it was too near Manchester and Liverpool for safety.

So now Marsha cried into her pillow, totally unable to forget her troubles in dreams, as she usually did. And then she thought of the Other. The girl she had invented as a some-time companion, the one who looked a lot like herself. What would the Other recommend her to do? What would she think if Marsha was sent far away, to America?

Of course she'll come with me, Marsha reminded herself as she lay on her damp pillow and tried to think of a plot which would foil Daddy's evil plan. The Other's just in my imagination, so she has to go where I go. It cheered her up a bit, but not enough. She did not want to be sent away from all the action and excitement of a war – it was her parents' over-protectiveness coming to the fore again. Marsha can't have fun in case she hurts herself; she can't have a bigger pony, or a proper, speedy bicycle or a glass of wine at dinner, just in case.

In the early hours she fell into an uneasy doze and woke at her usual time, tired but more cheerful. All she had to do was go round and see Sarah and Simon; Daddy had a lot of regard for Auntie Phyl and if Auntie Phyl was keeping Sarah and Simon in England, then it would not be that difficult to persuade Daddy to follow suit.

Feeling sure she had found a solution to her problem, Marsha got up, washed and dressed, ate a hearty breakfast and then went down to the stables to saddle up her pony. School loomed, but not for another couple of weeks, so she was fairly certain to find Sarah and Simon at home.

She did. But one glance at Sarah's face took her mind off her own troubles. Sarah looked positively agonized.

'Sarah? What's up?'

'Oh, Marsha, we must do something to stop them! Daddy spoke to your daddy on the telephone last night and they're sending us off to America until the war's over. And that might not be for months and months!'

After that, things happened fast. Too fast for Marsha, who had planned a number of scenes in which Daddy's heart was to be melted so that he allowed her to stay. Instead, she found herself bundled around the shops, introduced to a woman called Mrs Tavistock who would be accompanying her grandchildren to the States and had agreed to 'keep an eye' on Simon, Sarah and Marsha, and then bidden to help with the packing.

Daddy was in the Army already, looking very smart in his uniform, but he got time off to drive her over to Liverpool to catch the ship. And despite her first misery, Marsha found that she was rather excited by it all. Mummy had put some lovely clothes into her big cases, and treats for the voyage, even a Brownie camera and some films so that she might take pictures of her new surroundings to send home. And luscious chocs, too. Usually Mummy was too concerned about Marsha's skin and teeth to allow her many sweets, but it seemed when one was going on a long journey to a foreign land chocolates might make one feel a bit more cheerful.

Furthermore, Auntie Eff and Uncle Teddy, Daddy's cousin and his wife with whom the children would stay, lived in New York but had at the other end of Long

119

Island what was really a farm – and they kept horses, not just ponies, so Marsha would be able to ride.

In fact by the time she found herself climbing into the back seat of the Armstrong-Siddeley, she was almost resigned, though, as she told her parents, why they had had to put her in the Tavistocks' charge she had no idea. Still, it would make arriving in America a positive relief.

Her father, who had never liked the Tavistocks himself, sympathized with her, but when she tried, rather half-heartedly at this late stage, to turn his sympathy into a tool to keep her in England, he only sighed and shook his head.

'Darling, how do you think I'd feel if I came through the war all right, only to lose my little girl? It's bad enough Mummy insisting on staying where there's so much danger, but on the other hand she is, as she says, old enough to do a good deal towards the war effort. You, my lamb, are just another mouth to feed, another reason for Mummy to have to stay at home instead of working. No, you and your cousins will love Auntie Eff and Uncle Teddy, and you'll adore the life they lead. Just go on loving us too, won't you, sweetie? Because we couldn't bear it if you decided you wanted to stay in the States when the war's over.'

It melted her, as he might have known it would had he been a more devious man. Marsha clung to him and cried a little, and said she would always love him, always always, just as she would always love Mummy, and he wasn't to think for a moment that an aunt and uncle, no matter how nice, could ever mean what her parents meant to her.

And the house was being closed up. Robin, Fly and Jostle were going into the country, where they would be used as farm horses by a friend of the family.

Mummy was moving into Manchester, to work in a

munitions factory, which seemed very strange to Marsha. But of course Mummy's family had come from there, so perhaps it was only natural that she should want to go back to her childhood friends. Daddy would visit her on his leaves and Marsha would write to both parents at the new address.

'I suppose it'll be after Christmas before we leave, won't it?' Marsha had said hopefully, helping Mummy to pack china in a series of large tea-chests. 'I mean, it must take a lot of arranging, mustn't it?'

'It's all done,' Mummy said cheerfully, wrapping the Sèvres vase in soft white tissue paper and then enfolding it lovingly in newsprint. 'You sail the day after tomorrow. Daddy and I have arranged to take you to Liverpool to see you off.'

So in the end it was time that defeated her. No time to work on Daddy's susceptibilities or Mummy's conscience; only just time to tell everyone at school that she really pitied them, left behind to be bombed; time enough to ring Sarah up three times in one morning to remind her to pack essentials such as bathing things and tennis racquets. And then leaving day arrived, and Marsha was woken up early, bundled into warm clothing, pushed into the Armstrong-Siddeley without being fed first, and driven off, with Daddy at the wheel and Mummy in the passenger seat while poor, sleepy, hungry Marsha huddled in the back.

They arrived in Liverpool in time for lunch, which they shared with Simon and Sarah and their parents, and then the fathers went to the shipping office whilst the rest explored Liverpool. After that they had a convivial evening together in their hotel lounge, playing a variety of childish games. Marsha, who usually noticed things that people hoped she would miss, saw Mummy and Auntie Phyl start to cry at least four times in the course of the evening, but since they had both sided with their husbands in insisting that the children be sent out of danger, she did not feel a great deal of sympathy for them. After all, they only had to say the word, and Simon, Sarah and Marsha would jump back into the cars and be driven home again, happy as happy!

But of course they did not say the word. Instead, they took the children up to bed, where Marsha was tucked in, kissed goodnight and left to sleep.

'Mummy and I are just going to have a nightcap with Unks and Auntie in the bar,' Daddy whispered as he cuddled her. He had grown a blond and bristly moustache and it tickled when he kissed her, so Marsha giggled, and touched his face with her fingertips, and let him go without further ado. Besides, she was very tired.

She woke later, though, when her parents came to bed. She did not let them know she was awake, but instead lay there, listening, still hoping against hope for a last-minute reprieve.

Instead, she heard something very odd – very odd indeed.

Mummy and Daddy were not quarrelling – she knew they very rarely quarrelled – but they were having a sort of disagreement, and though she listened to every word, Marsha realized afterwards, when silence reigned once more, that she really had not understood what they were talking about. And, since she was eavesdropping, she could scarcely ask them.

Mummy started it.

'James, my darling . . . she's going such a long way away – don't you think we ought to tell her?'

'Certainly not, old girl. As I've said before, the time to tell her is when she's old enough not to be hurt by it, and that's not yet. She's only a little kid.'

'Oh, darling, I agree. But she's going so far away from

us . . . suppose something happened to you or me? Or suppose she found out by accident? Whatever would she think of us?'

'How can she find out? No one knows. I must say, when the adoption people suggested it and we agreed, I never thought we'd manage to keep it dark. But we have, so why spoil it?'

In the dark, Mummy sighed deeply. The bedclothes shushed as she turned.

'I don't know. It just seems unfair to let her go on believing an untruth.'

More little noises. Marsha knew that Daddy was now hugging Mummy, and Mummy's cheek was nestled into that soft, safe spot just below Daddy's chin.

'Nell, my love, it isn't an untruth. She's all ours and no one else's. Right? Legally, bindingly. Her real mother didn't want her – she was only a child herself – but we did, and now she's ours. Give us a kiss, just a little one.'

More soft sounds, and then the happy, breathless giggle which Mummy gave when she was pleased.

'I don't think we should, James. Suppose Marsha wakes?'

'Oh, come on, sweetheart, she's had an exhausting day, our little lass. She'll sleep like a log until morning.'

And oddly enough, very soon after that, Marsha did fall asleep. She rather thought it was when she started counting the rhythmic squeaks of the bedsprings, as one counts sheep. The squeaks went on and on, and she was just about to reach a triumphant fifty when sleep overtook her and she knew nothing more until a maid knocked on the door with tea and biscuits at seven o'clock.

When the ship left the harbour, Marsha stood next to Sarah, waving energetically towards the shore. Sarah was the sort of girl who gets made a prefect without ever opening her mouth. She had a sensible, practical face and stout, hockey-player's legs. Her straight, honey-coloured hair was bobbed, she had a dusting of freckles and wore glasses to correct a lazy eye, and she was a great organizer. She liked young children, thought boys were a nuisance and had quite unconsciously developed a motherly attitude towards Marsha, probably because Marsha was small for her age and so at least six inches shorter than Sarah herself.

Once they had left the docks behind, Marsha looked about her. An exceedingly cold wind blew in their faces and sailors were working around them.

'We're really off now,' Simon remarked. 'Let's go up to the bows and watch out for shipping.'

Both girls agreed and left the rail to walk along to what Marsha would have called the pointed end. There was no sign of the Tavistock party, presumably either down in their cabins or on some other deck, for the SS *Hardcastle* was a big ship, used for cruises during peacetime.

The three of them settled themselves comfortably by the rail where they could look ahead as the ship steamed out of the port of Liverpool. A member of the ship's crew, seeing them there, came over to talk to them.

'Hello, kids. Everything all right?' he asked breezily. 'Going to take a mile walk before your dinner? That's three times round the promenade deck, you know.'

Sarah started to answer him, with Simon chiming in now and again, but Marsha was no longer listening. There was a little boat with a rusty brown sail down there, far below, bouncing on the waves, for it was a rough and windy day. And as the ship lost touch with the port, as the estuary of the Mersey widened into the ocean, there was more land on her left, with mountains rearing up into the sky.

'Where's that?' Marsha demanded, pointing.

124

'Welsh coast,' the crew member said. 'See that? That's the Isle of Anglesey, the most westerly part of the peninsula. I used to go there for my holidays when I was a kid. Marvellous place.'

Marsha stared at the island, which was falling behind fast as the ship put on speed. It seemed . . . how very odd, it seemed like a place she knew, or would like to know. She stared at its misty outline. She did know it! She must have been there, once . . . oh, it was a wonderful land, the best place in the world to be!

The crew member was talking, Simon and Sarah were moving off, following him, but Marsha still stood, glued to the rail, staring out to where the Isle of Anglesey was getting fainter and fainter as the SS *Hardcastle* sheered away from land and headed towards the Atlantic.

That island! It meant something to her, she knew it. Something really important, what was more. She stared and stared, and then she closed her eyes, not because she was tired but because she had such a strong feeling that it was the right thing to do.

Immediately, a picture began to form behind her lids. A girl and a boy, down on a rocky shore. The boy was small and dark, the girl fair. Marsha knew without seeing the girl's face that it was her imaginary playmate. She watched as the boy reached a grimy hand into an equally grimy pocket and drew out a length of what looked like string. He then produced a tobacco tin and opened it. *Things* wriggled obscenely inside, fat brown wormy things fringed on either side by millions of legs. The boy seized one of them and impaled it on the string, which must be a fishing line since Marsha could now see a hook on the end of it. Then he cast the line into the sea which sucked and rushed at the rocks on which the two children stood.

The imaginary playmate watched, and then took the line which was handed to her. She didn't want to put one of those worms-with-legs on to her own hook, and I don't blame her, Marsha thought. She saw the girl squat down, staring intently at the sea into which the line fell, and then the boy got out his tin again and began to bait another string.

'Marsha, I never knew what a dream you were until now! Did you hear what the sailor was saying? His name is Alan, by the way. He said we'll see Ireland presently, quite clear! And we're travelling in a convoy, with gun-ships and things, to protect us from the German navy!'

Marsha opened her eyes. Sarah was staring at her, her surprised-looking, slightly prawnish blue eyes fixed on Marsha's.

'Er . . . gosh!' Marsha said obligingly. 'Where are the other ships, then?'

'Waiting for us, out there.' Sarah gestured towards the empty horizon. 'I think this voyage is going to be fun!'

The children were supposed to do lessons on board ship, but they usually got out of all but a few classes. There were teachers on board, some of them with their own children in tow, but once they got well out into the Atlantic, where the big rollers never stopped, several of the staff and a good many of the pupils became very ill indeed.

Sarah was sick for a whole week, and then recovered slowly. Simon and Marsha were fine, and they became good friends whilst Sarah was laid low and unable to organize them with her hearty, hockey-playing attitudes.

Simon was tall for his age, with the same honey-coloured hair as his sister but with acne and a stork-like, stooping figure. Marsha had seldom taken any notice of him. He had always tried to keep a distance between himself and his sister's little friends, but now, suddenly, Simon discovered that Marsha could be fun and Marsha discovered that Simon was interesting. A member of a whole gender which until recently she had scarcely considered human, he taught her that there were boys who could do things other than fight, brag and bully. Simon was funny and clever, and enjoyed playing all sorts of games. He found his sister rather boring, but soon realized that Marsha was another kettle of fish altogether.

'You're pretty,' he said to her one day as they walked the three times round the promenade deck that tradition, it seemed, required. 'You'll be even prettier when you grow up.'

Marsha, whilst secretly agreeing with him, was surprised, flattered and even a little shocked by his declaration. She was beginning to think about boys, but had never considered Simon as anything but Sarah's brother.

'Will I?' she asked innocently, however. 'I'm only eleven. Isn't that too young to tell?'

Simon went red, then grinned.

'Probably. Race you to the dining room!'

They saw their first action in the middle of their second week out. Sarah was up, though tottery still, and she was with Simon and Marsha on deck when they heard a ringing of bells and shouting from a nearby frigate. In two minutes, so it seemed, everything was happening at once. Guns were fired, a great many people screamed, and although they did not at first realize it, one of the slower ships in the convoy was mortally wounded.

'There's an awful lot of black smoke,' Simon said presently, peering through a porthole. They had been told to keep below decks and well clear of the portholes when enemy action was in progress, but no boy worth his salt could fail to try to see what was going on. 'I think something hit something else.'

'Oh, I hope not,' Sarah said. Her voice still lacked its

former strength and resonance, and she was lethargic and easily tired. She had not yet regained her appetite, either, though at least she appeared at mealtimes now and usually ate a little of whatever was put before them. Simon and Marsha, who were positively enjoying a life on the ocean wave, always finished up Sarah's portion, so no one noticed.

'Let me have a look,' Marsha said. She pushed Simon to one side and knelt by the porthole herself. They had been sent down to one of the lounges and children were everywhere, playing cards, chattering, shouting to one another. Mrs Tavistock came over to them, waving a box.

'Come along, you three,' she said in her bossy, brisk old voice. 'Let's see you joining in with the smaller ones for once. Come and play tiddlywinks!'

'Mrs Tavistock, there's a war going on out there,' Simon said severely. 'I can't play tiddlywinks when sailors are risking their lives to keep us safe.'

'Don't be so pretentious, Simon,' Mrs Tavistock said. 'It isn't as if you could do anything, and a game will keep the little ones occupied. Your parents left you in my charge and I'm no longer asking you, I'm telling you. Come along with me, please.'

Sarah went at once. She enjoyed playing with the little ones. But Simon and Marsha stayed where they were, watching through the porthole.

Which was why, when the enemy submarine managed to sneak through the outer ships of the convoy, they actually saw with their own eyes the torpedo which was destined to strike the SS *Hardcastle*.

'Look at that white streak of foam coming towards us,' Marsha said excitedly. 'Is it a shark?'

Simon stared for a second, then turned towards the mass of children and accompanying adults.

'We're being torpedoed,' he shrieked, in such a high

and urgent voice that the children stopped squabbling to listen. 'It will hit in a few seconds . . . *get out of here, everyone, or you're dead!*'

Megan was woken by a bang so tremendous that it brought her out of sleep in one moment. She found herself sitting up, heart crashing against her ribs, staring into the dark with fear-widened eyes.

But why was she afraid? What had happened to wake her up? The house was quiet around her; through the partition which separated her from the boys she could hear Dewi snoring, Peris breathing heavily – he had a nasty cold – and Henry moving restlessly, coughing, settling.

She lay down again, closing her eyes, feeling her heart-beat return to normal – and suddenly, as though she had been seized by the hand, she was somewhere else. Also in darkness, still very afraid, but somewhere else. No longer in her own bed in her own room, but called out of her warm sleep by the Other.

For a moment she knew great gladness, a comfortable sense of warmth and closeness. For once it was not her need. As clearly as if she had shouted 'Megan', the Other had haled her out of her bed, her room – indeed, out of her whole life – to bring her to this particular spot.

Cautiously, she looked around her . . . and found herself falling, falling through space. She felt the uprush of wind lifting her clothing clear of her body, and then she was hit violently, as though a great hand had slapped her with all its strength, and she was under the waves.

She knew a moment of complete panic, of choking fear, and then the darkness cleared a little, and she could see about her. She was no longer under the sea but sitting on a bundle of some description, with ripples breaking over her bare toes, and beside her, huddling, was the Other.

Megan gazed at her. She looked so different! Straggly hair, a blue tinge to her complexion, her clothes all covered in thick, black sludge which smelt foul. What had happened to that pretty, self-confident child who had everything? But now she was holding out a hand towards Megan.

'You've come! I knew you would – well, you have to, don't you, because my mind made you? Hold me!'

It was a command, even coming through the blue and shivering lips. Megan obediently caught hold of the Other's chilled and soaking hand. Her own, she noted with almost clinical interest, was warm and dry despite her recent encounter with the water. This dream – it had to be a dream – was really very rum indeed!

'What is it?' Megan whispered at last, when the two of them had sat on the bundle of floating stuff for a while without exchanging another word. 'Where are we?'

'We're in the sea. A German ship torpedoed the SS *Hardcastle*,' the Other said tiredly. 'You should know that!'

'Well, I didn't. What's that black stuff on your dress?'

'Dunno. Oil, perhaps. Smells like it. Will it be dawn soon?'

Megan looked up, into the dark sky overhead. But it was no longer dark; the stars were paling, and dawn could not be far distant.

She told her companion so and the Other almost smiled.

'Good. It'll be easier when it's light,' she remarked. 'Will someone find me?'

'Of course they will,' Megan said.

She had no idea whether she spoke the truth or not, but felt she must give whatever reassurance she could. That the Other, who had never really seemed to notice her, should suddenly be talking was miracle enough for

130

now. But she could see that the girl was in a poor state . . . what could she do to help?

She voiced the thought aloud. The Other looked thoughtful.

'Can you take me somewhere safe? No, of course you can't. How silly I am – I made you, so you can only do what I can make you do.'

This got Megan so angry that she was tempted to turn round and leave the other girl alone on the heaving ocean, except that she knew very well such a thing was impossible. You couldn't just get in and out of dreams as you wished. She would have to hope that this particular dream – no, this nightmare – would soon be over.

'Why won't you answer me?' the Other said plaintively, presently. 'You should, you know.'

'If you made me, how can I answer? I can only say what you make me say, you said.'

'Ye-es,' the Other agreed uncertainly. 'But tonight it feels different. You feel . . . realer.'

'So do you,' Megan admitted. 'I say, what's your name?'

'Marsha. What's yours?'

'Megan. Look, there's someone else!'

Marsha followed Megan's pointing finger and suddenly knelt up, waving vigorously.

'It's Alan . . . Alan, row your boat over here! Alan, it's Marsha! Are Simon and Sarah with you?'

Megan watched as the boat came nearer, doggedly rowed by a smallish, stoutish man in nothing but pants and vest. All around her the sky was growing lighter and she could see, now, that there were other boats, other bundles. She could see a couple of ships, as well . . . but Marsha was taking no notice of her, being too busy shouting to the fat little man in the rowing boat.

And then Megan realized that she was looking down

on the scene from quite high up, that she was leaving, leaving, leaving . . .

She woke.

Dawn light streamed grey into the room and she could hear gulls coming in with a fishing boat, squabbling and cursing each other as they fought over the guts which the fisherman was throwing out as he neared the quay.

In the next room, Dewi snored, Peris breathed heavily and Henry coughed, settled.

What a weird dream! It seemed to have taken no time at all, except that it had been full dark, earlier, when she woke. She hoped the Other . . . no, Marsha . . . would reach safety, but she was pretty sure she would. There had been no lingering sadness in her mind as she plunged up through sleep to wakefulness. And anyway, Megan reminded herself with a secret smirk, if she invented me, then I invented her, and I want her to go on living. I wouldn't like it at all if she drowned. So I shall imagine her getting safely into Alan's boat and being taken on board one of those other ships. And the others . . . Sarah, and was it Simon? They'll be all right too, safe on a ship somewhere.

She settled comfortably on her side, hand under the pillow, thumb hovering to be popped soothingly into her mouth as soon as she slept. But, unbidden, other thoughts came and would not go away. They were torpedoed; a lot of people will have died. Children, too, probably. *Can a person like me dream a dream so horrid yet so real?* But I did, of course. Unless it wasn't a dream. Unless, somewhere, there really is a girl called Marsha.

She knew she believed completely in Marsha, that girl so like her that they could have been twins, but suddenly the whole thing was too much for her. She did not want to have to accept a reality which included the torpedoed

132

ship or the people struggling in the water. She would *not* believe in them; they were just a dream, only a dream.

And, presently, Megan slept.

CHAPTER EIGHT

On 12 December 1939, after ten years of marriage, Madeleine Steadman discovered that her husband was unfaithful to her and had been unfaithful many times over the past half-dozen years.

The words rang in Madeleine's head like a litany of truth. Dear old Dickie, Daddy's friend, married to a girl more than twenty years his junior, had simply not been satisfied with just one woman.

But first he had poured reproaches on her head because they were childless, refusing to accept even a hint of blame himself because 'Everyone knows that in nine cases out of ten it's the woman's fault'.

Then he had begun to take his business much more seriously, staying away at first for one week in every four, then every third week, then every other. He telephoned her quite often, urged her to enjoy herself, apologized for his absence, explaining that because the wine importing business had expanded so fast he was needed in France more than ever before.

Now that she knew, Madeleine wondered why she had ever believed him. But the answer was that she believed him partly because she wanted to do so and partly because she didn't really care what he did so long as he was temporarily absent from her bed.

For, with his increasing absences, his sexual attacks on her had become fiercer, more frightening, somehow. He pretended to believe she would quicken with child if taken violently, but now she realized he behaved like that to salve his conscience. He was telling his new woman that he no longer loved Madeleine, and only stayed with her for some obscure reason to do with loyalty and duty. He probably said his wife was cold, didn't enjoy sex, and therefore it behoved him to make sure that neither of them enjoyed it.

He had certainly succeeded so far as Madeleine was concerned. She realized with dismay that she now hated the thought of sleeping with a man as much as she had once relished it. Tarot's lovemaking had been so marvellous! But she hardly ever thought of Tarot now.

With the coming of the war, of course, Dickie had had to stop pretending to be in France, but he had an excellent alibi in the War Office, where he now claimed to be spending most of his time. He had a little flat in London which, he said, was far too dangerous a place for his young wife. So he left her in Lancashire and courageously spent weekdays in Baker Street, 'managing for myself', as he put it. And Madeleine struggled to keep the big house clean alone, because the staff had either gone off to help the war effort or had been called up.

Until now. Until the letter.

She would not have opened the letter except that it was addressed, unexceptionally, to Mr and Mrs Steadman. It was a Monday and Dickie had departed on Sunday night for London, so having turned the letter round and round in her hands for several moments, and decided that it could scarcely be personal or business since it was addressed to the pair of them, Madeleine had opened it.

It was from a business acquaintance of Dickie's in London, and it was just a pleasant, ordinary thank-you letter, what Madeleine's mother would have called a bread-and-butter letter. It thanked Dickie and his charming wife for entertaining some people called Ned and Stella to a dinner-dance at the Savoy the previous week, and added that Ned and Stella had seldom enjoyed an evening more.

Our fond love to you both, the letter ended; next time we'll treat you, and let's make sure that next time isn't too far distant.

There was a postscript.

I enclose a couple of photographs taken during the course of the evening, the letter continued. *Aren't you a couple of lovebirds???*

The first photograph showed Dickie and a plump and smiling young woman in each other's arms on a dance floor. A purist might have said they looked as if they were not so much dancing as fornicating, Madeleine told herself judiciously. The second picture showed Dickie, very red in the face and very smiling, sitting, legs spread, with the same young woman sprawled across his lap whilst one of Dickie's hands fatly fondled her thick upper arm.

It would not have been so bad, Madeleine thought, if Dickie had not clearly told everyone that the plump young woman was his wife. But he had, so how should she behave if she and his London friends ever met? She hated to think, for Dickie could not bear to be made to look a fool.

Perhaps he's going to divorce me, Madeleine thought next. Hopefully. But she didn't think he'd want to do that, because although her money and his were by now indistinguishable, the Ripley-Trewin name had given Dickie the entrée into places closed to a mere Steadman.

So it seemed as though he intended to continue to live a double life. Unless, of course, he were to become a widower through some accident, Madeleine thought, and felt a cold shiver run through her. If she were to die, then Dickie could remarry and still have the kudos of having been married to a Ripley-Trewin. Could it be that which kept Dickie more or less by her side?

She had read the letter in the living room of their house in Victoria Road. Outside, the weather had been mild for December, the trees which massed between them and the curious eyes of passing Boltonians still clinging to a few brittle, golden leaves. Thinking about it afterwards, it struck Madeleine as almost funny that the letter should have revealed such a petty, lower-class type of deception to one in such circumstances. Houses here were amongst the most exclusive in the area and the inhabitants, surely, should have been above tawdry little affairs, not of the heart but of the lower regions of the body! But that was three days ago, when she had first opened the letter. Since then she had read it and looked at the photographs a dozen or more times, still without coming to any firm conclusion. And then this morning, when the lawn was furred with frost and the first real nip of winter was in the air, she found that her mind was made up, and with that realization came a wonderful lightness of heart.

She would leave him. She would prop the letter and the pictures up on the mantelpiece and add a note apologizing for opening what was obviously a personal letter – she would leave the envelope up there too – and then she would go. She could not go back to her parents' home because that had been sold, but she could go somewhere else, though she was not yet certain where. Dickie would scarcely follow her once he had read her note, and she intended to make very sure that he was not the only one who read it, either. She would not cancel Mrs Figgins, who did the heavy cleaning and was the most dedicated gossip, nor would she discourage her neighbour, Elsie Tuddnam, from popping in later in the day for a chat. She would leave Elsie alone in the room for ten minutes – that should be long enough for a notorious snooper to memorize the note.

It was a strange thing, though, to be leaving after ten

years. I came here a trusting girl and I'm leaving a dis-
illusioned woman, Madeleine told herself as she packed
her case. She would not need much, and anyway she
found that most of her more expensive clothes reminded
her of Dickie, so she just packed necessities, plus her
jewellery, some of her favourite books and small things
which she felt were peculiarly her own – the carriage clock
which her mother had given her, a Regency writing case,
some silver which had once graced her parents' mantelpiece.

She was ready to go when the doorbell rang. She knew
it would be Elsie and hurried down to let her in. Elsie
was all smiles. Did Madeleine know that they had found
a German spy dressed as a nun down on the South coast?
And they were starting up a crèche for young children in
the town so that their mothers would be able to help with
the war effort. Did Madeleine intend to take some sort
of a job? Though of course the house alone kept her busy.

Elsie had once been beautiful, Madeleine imagined,
and was still attractive, but Madeleine thought her shallow
and occasionally spiteful and did not see much of her.
Now, however, she explained that she was going away
for a few days, apologized for leaving her guest alone,
and hurried back to her room.

She completed her packing and heaved her cumbersome hide suitcase as far as the head of the stairs. Then
she descended them, humping the case crashingly down
behind her. Despite the noise, though, Elsie was still
riveted in front of the mantelpiece when she got back to
the living room, and Madeleine had to actually start talking before the other woman could tear herself away from
the revealing letter and yet more revealing photographs.

Clearly, she longed to mention them; her eyes kept
flickering back to the note no matter what the subject of

conversation, but she lacked the courage to come right out and ask Madeleine what she intended to do about it.

Finally, it became clear even to Mrs Tuddnam that she could linger no longer. Regretfully, and with many a backward glance at the mantelpiece and its extraordinary burden, she left at last, Madeleine seeing her right off the premises and promising to return the visit immediately on her return.

I'm a mean bitch, Madeleine thought cheerfully, as she put on her dark brown coat with the mink collar and cuffs and pulled the matching fur hat down over her curls. Why couldn't I have put Elsie out of her misery, and told her I was leaving Dickie? She would really have loved a nice chat about it all. But never mind. It'll be all round the neighbourhood in a day or so. She'll probably dine out on it for years, and who am I to grudge her that?

Outside in the garage was Madeleine's beloved little red two-seater. She had had the MG Midget for almost two years and could scarcely imagine life without it. Should she take it, then, or would it be better, more independent, to go by taxi?

But the car, though it had been bought by Dickie, was very much hers; why should she not enjoy it whilst she could? Madeleine remembered, without regret, all the money she had poured into Dickie's various business ventures – she would not see a penny of that again – and walked purposefully round to the garage. She backed the car carefully out of its place and drove it round to the front door, where she loaded the case into the boot – not without difficulty, for it was exceedingly heavy – and climbed back into the driving seat.

It was a cold day, clear and sparkling. The sun had come out as though it, too, applauded Madeleine's behaviour, and Madeleine, who had wondered whether to crank up the hood, decided to leave it folded down. It would be good to feel the rush of the cold, free air on her cheeks as she drove.

She reached the end of the drive, conscientiously slowing and looking right and left, then turned on to the road. As she did so, she felt a tremendous sense of elation and adventure, so strong that she could have cheered. Indeed, she did cheer, loudly, three times, and then she burst into song, feeling, for the first time for more than ten years, that she was Madeleine again, her own self, unadulterated and whole.

She had driven a good few miles through the December countryside, not at all depressed by the bare trees, the faded grass or the cold, when two things occurred to her. One was that she had run away in December before, and how very different that had been! Running away from Tarot, not towards him, regret dogging every step, every inch of the way. The second was that she was starting afresh. She owed no one loyalty, save perhaps herself. If she wanted to, she could begin a new search for Tarot where the old one had left off.

And all of a sudden, she knew that was what she wanted to do more than anything else. To find Tarot. Oh, they would be different people now, no doubt about it. She was twenty-eight years old, settled, sensible. Well, she was settled and sensible to outward appearances, anyway. And he would have changed, of course. She was sure he must have married, probably had a parcel of kids. She knew that if she and Dickie had had children she would never have left him, but despite having given birth to twins she had still allowed Dickie's attitude to affect her a little. It must have been at least partly her fault; she must have held back in some essential way, the sort of holding back she had certainly not indulged in with Tarot.

The car was heading south, eating up the miles. Where had she been going when she had collapsed? Back to the

Stones, of course. But was there any point in going back after a dozen years?

The afternoon was advancing now, and it seemed like a good idea to put up the hood. Madeleine got out, cranked it up, got back and started the engine. She still had not made up her mind what to do, but with her gloved hands on the wheel once more it seemed as though her fingers made it up for her. When the turning came which would lead her back to the West Country she took it, as she had done once before. Only this time she would follow the road all the way, until she found the Stones.

It was weird to drive, mundanely, the way she had twice before covered, once as a shy child with the man who was to become her lover, once as a half-crazed woman from whom childbirth had temporarily stolen her senses.

She drove slowly, taking a whole day over it, having put up the previous night at a comfortable roadside inn where they had fed her well, given her a soft bed, and probably discussed her coming, in hushed voices, until the small hours.

Next day she set off as the sun rose, with a good breakfast inside her and hope warming her even more than the food or her fur-trimmed coat. She had walked a good few of these lanes, and found they were still clear in her memory. She stopped at little wayside stations and gazed nostalgically over winter-cropped hedges at deserted platforms, bare flowerbeds, miles of shiny, empty railway lines, remembering how young she had been then – how heedlessly happy!

She reached the last village, the one where they had bought bread, cheese and beer. She was getting near, now. She could have guessed her whereabouts, she thought, by the freshness in the air, the sense of tingling excitement as the little car toiled up a steep hill and down a hollow, up another . . . and she knew she had arrived, though there were no signs to say so, no litter of vehicles or people to warn her that this was her destination.

She parked the car in a gateway grassy with age, mossy with disuse. She did not bother to lock it up, but put the key in her pocket, just in case. The place was deserted as she had never seen it, save in that strange, awe-inspiring, drug-induced dream.

Madeleine climbed over the gate, crossed a meadow, pushed her way through a hedge and then began the climb, and presently, she saw them.

The Stones. Standing, gaunt, against the December sky, rimed with frost, mighty with power.

Suddenly, Madeleine felt sixteen again. Soft and vulnerable, aching to undo the harm she had done as an innocent girl. She wanted to confront the Stones, to make Them understand the pain They had caused, to make Them show her Tarot, wherever he was.

But before she did anything she must look round, take it all in. And of course it had not changed at all, not in a mere twelve years. It had stood here since the world was young and innocent, when Man had been a grunting child himself, without sophistry or deceit yet with the urge to worship strong enough to move these great obelisks from the place of their creation to this high and sacred spot.

Madeleine stood outside the circle and just looked for a long time. She was remembering, and the hair on the back of her neck kept tingling, until her body ached with memories and her soul sang with them. Oh, that first time, which had caused so many people so much heartbreak! Oh, the strength of Tarot's arms, the tender warmth of his love! If only, if only . . .

At last she bent and took off her shoes and stockings and walked, with slow deliberation, under the biggest dolmen of them all and right into the very centre of the circle. She looked down, half-hoping that the grass would be scorched, but it was not, only perhaps a little more crushed and flattened here than on the surrounding ground. She had meant to speak to the Stones, only half-believing herself that to do so might help, but it was as though, with the touch of the grass on her bare feet, a Power mightier than her will took over.

She knelt, not voluntarily but as though a huge hand had pushed her down, and her arms jerked up. She raised her face to the sun's red disc as it rose and shone down on her over the top of the tallest menhir in the ring, and foolishly, like a puppet, she stayed where she felt she had been put until the sun was right up, shining into her eyes and turning yellower and more powerful by the minute. And then it was as though the Stones no longer cared to be worshipped, for she was at liberty to regain her feet, to look around her, puzzled and even a little indignant, feeling a trick had been played on her.

She left the circle slowly, dragging her feet on the wet grass. She passed under the big dolmen and began to push her cold, sodden feet into her shoes, bundling her stockings into her coat pocket. Then she stood up and turned, saluting the Stones half ironically, half respect-fully, before making her way down the hill once more. Back to the car. Back to the twentieth century.

Returning the way she had come, Madeleine pondered on what had happened to her, what she had learned from her experience. She had acted strangely – but then the Stones had always had that effect on her – had allowed herself to believe in Them, put herself in Their power.

And she was glad she had done so, for if the Stones had not been able to bring Tarot to her – or perhaps had not wished to do so – They had given her a message so powerful that she felt it might as well have been burned in letters of fire on her forehead.

Good will come to you from this, the Stones had seemed to say to her as she knelt, subservient and crushed, awaiting Their will. Not at once, and perhaps not in the way you expect, but happiness will be yours one day, little Stone maiden, willing sacrifice.

CHAPTER NINE

Madeleine was coming home from work with a precious cabbage in the string bag swinging from the handlebars of her bike. She caught a glimpse of herself in a shop window as she pedalled by and smiled at the change which had come over her in twelve short months. She was a driver and fire-fighter in the Manchester Auxiliary Fire Service and the navy blue coat, the trousers and the tin hat were a far cry from Mrs Richard Steadman with her gleaming blonde curls and fashionable clothes.

Dickie probably wouldn't even recognize her should they meet, she mused, cycling along. Not that they would. Dickie had moved a young woman into the Victoria Road house, ostensibly as housekeeper. He was welcome to her.

Times were hard, though. Rationing was really biting if you lived in a flat and didn't have a garden, and although as yet Manchester had not been bombed Madeleine and her crew had been over to Liverpool twice the previous week to help with the fires raging there. It meant a long drive in both directions, hard work in between, and a struggle against unwarily falling asleep on the way home through the pretty Lancashire villages.

But Madeleine did not care. For the first time since her marriage, she was genuinely happy. Oh, she missed the luxuries which had been hers, she supposed, but not very much. Certainly she would not have changed her present way of living for that other way, abandoned along with the big house, the beautiful clothes, and the uncaring husband.

It was not easy, though, to become an independent working woman after years of reliance on others. She had sold the car and rented a tiny flat above a cycle shop on Cheetham Hill Road, and because she knew the car money wouldn't last for ever, she had gone out and got herself a job.

At first she worked in Woolworth's, which was where she met Lizzie. Lizzie was skinny and active with a thin face, black, sparkling eyes and lank brown hair. She was twenty-seven and engaged to the first officer of a destroyer, and she had left home when her parents discovered she had slept with her fiancé before he sailed.

'Boring buggers, me mum and dad,' Lizzie said laconically. 'Think they own me – small chance!'

No one, Madeleine quickly discovered, owned Lizzie. She was very much her own woman, with a caustic tongue if you annoyed her and a lot of native shrewdness. Indeed, it was her idea that the two of them should share a flat and that they should change their jobs and work for the AFS.

'What will your Alex say when he hears you've moved in with me?' Madeleine asked curiously when she saw Lizzie penning a letter to him. Lizzie looked up, shrugged, grinned.

'He'll be delighted,' she observed in her flat Lancashire accent. 'Never did get on wi' me parents, him. Besides, he'll get his end away more when he has leaves, now I'm in a place half me own.'

'Scarcely, with me in the same room,' Madeleine had said, and Lizzie smiled more broadly than ever.

'Fool! Why d'you think I suggested t'Fire Service? Happen we'll be on different shifts most nights.'

Madeleine reached the part of Cheetham Hill Road where the word 'Hill' became a reality and dismounted. She would push her bike the rest of the way, she decided, and besides, it was getting dark. She had a bicycle lamp, discreetly dimmed and fixed to point downwards, but she could turn it off and save her batteries if she walked.

It was bitterly cold. Christmas is coming, Madeleine reminded herself. Indulgently, she let her mind dwell on what she would most like for Christmas. Top of the list came finding Tarot, but she was beginning to realize that without his real name she was unlikely to trace him. Instead, she told herself that she must be content with a lesser miracle.

The right man, she dreamed, as the bicycle wheels crunched across the loose shingle of a builder's yard. Someone who will love me for myself, someone who will be content with a little home and an ordinary wife . . . someone who will give me babies.

Because she wanted a baby terribly badly. She had given up hope of ever finding the twins, who would be young people now, with no interest, she was sure, in the woman who had given them birth. No, she wanted a child of her own . . . though it did not help that in her secret heart she believed she would only become pregnant by Tarot. Surely there must be another man, somewhere, who would be right for her?

Would I take on a man who could give me kids, though, if he was a dead bore? Madeleine asked herself just as a blacked-out bus swooshed past her, its papered windows showing the dim, unearthly blue light to which she had become accustomed over the past fifteen months. No, not even a beautiful baby of her own would make up for having to live with a boor or a bore; she would rather remain childless than get landed again with a man like Dickie, for instance.

The bus drew up just ahead of her and Madeleine saw Lizzie amongst the people getting down.

'Hey, Liz, wait for me,' she called as the bus drew off

again and Lizzie began to trot up the hill ahead of her. 'Did you see your mother-in-law?'

Lizzie, who had been to visit Alex's parents, turned back, peered, then grinned. It was not full dark; there was a romantic slice of silver moon overhead and by its light Madeleine could see the other girl's face quite clearly.

'Maddie! Yes, I saw all of them, even his Auntie Maud and his little brother. Sammy, the kid's called. And Alex's brother Jim was there, too. He's a messenger boy with another of the AFS crews, so we may see him, sometimes. How did you get on?'

'Not bad. I slept all morning, then went into the city and actually found a greengrocer with some cabbages. Then I went to the Piccadilly and saw Ronald Colman's new film. It was most awfully good . . . though I admit I fell asleep at one point.'

'It must have been awfully good,' Lizzie said sarcastically. Madeleine laughed and continued to hurry up the street, her breath clouding before her face. Frost glittered on the pavement and the other people who had got off the bus had dispersed, eager to reach their homes. A car passed, gliding along quietly, its hooded lights showing twin slits of brightness where they struck the icy road surface.

'Isn't it quiet?' Lizzie's voice rang out, unconcernedly shattering the silence she was commenting on. 'Look at the size of those stars, Maddie! That's one good thing about the blackout, you can't half see the stars.'

'Wonderful. Only a few more days and it'll be Christmas. I'm on duty from tomorrow on, but we're only on standby on Christmas Day itself, aren't we?'

'That's right. Look, Maddie, would you like to come with me on Christmas Day, to Alex's mum's place? You'll be welcome, you know that.'

Maddie could feel her cheeks warming with surprise and pleasure, but even so, she shook her head.

'I couldn't do that, Liz, but thanks for asking.'

They had reached the small parade of shops now and Madeleine pushed her bicycle across the wide stretch of paving and down the passageway which led to the side entrance. Lizzie unlocked whilst Madeleine turned off her rear light, unhitched her string bag and took the rest of her shopping out of the saddlebag. Then the two of them manoeuvred the machine into the short entrance hall, locked the front door and made for the stairs.

Talking about Christmas made Madeleine wonder just what she would do over the holiday, with Lizzie out of the flat. But it would be restful, if not particularly jolly, to spend a quiet day alone with her wireless set.

But presently, when she and Lizzie were settling down in their beds, she decided that she must begin to come out of her shell. Next time a young man asked her out she would jolly well accept and give the bloke a chance, instead of letting her memories of Tarot ruin everything before it had even begun.

Live your life, Madeleine commanded herself. Stop just existing and live while you can!

The next day Madeleine and Lizzie went down to the station and found themselves more or less alone.

'Call from Liverpool,' a senior fire officer told them. 'Two hundred men and thirty pumps were sent there last night; you two were lucky to be on your day off. They've not got back yet. It was murder in the 'pool last night, I believe.'

The day was quiet but the girls were working a double shift because of the men still missing, so they got out their sleeping bags and were actually sitting in the bunkroom,

149

eating sandwiches which had been brought in for them, when the sirens sounded.

'Someone's off-loading early, on his way to the 'pool. He'll turn round and swear he pasted 'em,' Lizzie said thickly, through cheese and pickle. 'Any more tea int' pot?'

It was the last lighthearted remark either girl would make for forty-eight hours.

'Hey, Liz, is that you?'

Two tattered and exhausted figures, soaked to the skin, blackened by fire and soot, stopped momentarily in their task of handling the heavy hoses.

'Hello, Maddie. Gawd, have you ever known anything like it? Where've you been until now?'

Madeleine raised a filthy hand to a filthy forehead.

'Everywhere at once. Have you seen Deansgate?'

'Have you seen Market Street?'

Someone shouted. Madeleine acknowledged the shout and turned in one direction, Lizzie turned in the other.

Seconds later, more hoses hurled their fountains of water at the burning buildings and Madeleine and Lizzie forgot each other and everything except fire-fighting as the conflagration raged around them and farther off the high explosives and incendiaries seemed to rain down on the city, thick as locusts but more destructive.

'Will there be anyone left alive after this?' Madeleine said exhaustedly to an ARP warden as they took a brief break for a cup of tea, standing back from the scene as others took their places.

'There'll be a good few gone,' the warden agreed, sipping his tea. 'Those fires . . .' He shuddered. 'Once they get out of control the city's done for.'

'They've called in the Royal Engineers to blast fire-breaks,' another man informed them. He was elderly and

150

grizzled, with a rosy face and a little goatee beard. 'No help for it. The wind's strong, and it's carrying the flames towards parts of the city that escaped the bombing. But the engineers will do the trick.'

'I hope to God they do,' Madeleine said, with a strong shudder. 'Nothing could live in that . . .' She gestured to the fire, raging behind them. 'I'm completely disorientated – I've no idea now where I am, or where the fire's reached. It's not got as far as Cheetham Hill Road, has it? I live there.'

'No, but there's been a good few bombs up that way,' the elderly man said. 'I've been getting folk out . . . them as can be taken to rest centres.'

'It's Christmas Eve tomorrow – or is tomorrow today already?' Madeleine said, her voice thick with exhaustion. 'This little lot will ruin a good few Christmases, I reckon.'

From behind her a small, husky voice said soberly, 'Aye, lass, you're right there.'

Madeleine turned round. She and the wardens were grouped round the van which had brought the tea and some sandwiches to the workers. The person who had spoken was a messenger, still holding on to his bicycle. He grinned uncertainly at them, but addressed himself to Madeleine.

'I'm trying to find my brother's girl, Lizzie Allington. Someone said her lot were here, fighting the fires.'

Madeleine stood her mug of tea down on the portable table the local women had erected. She looked hard at the pale and filthy face staring into her own.

'Jim?' she said uncertainly. 'Are you Jim Cox, Alex's brother? I'm Maddie, Lizzie's flatmate. What's up? Can I help? Lizzie's here somewhere.'

'Oh, hello, Maddie.' Abruptly, Jim knuckled his eyes, whether from tiredness or grief Madeleine could not be certain. 'Lizzie were having her Christmas dinner with us, weren't she? Well, the house was flattened, so no dinner for any of us.'

'Oh, Jim!' Maddie could have cried for him. He was only sixteen, Lizzie had told her, awfully young to face up to tragedy and loss. 'Are your family all right?'

'Me mum's all right, and most of the others . . . we don't know about our Ned or me dad, because they weren't home. But our Sammy . . .'

He stopped, biting a lip, staring at her helplessly, his eyes large with tears.

'What? But Sammy's only a baby!'

'Aye, but he got hysterical-like, when the big bombs fell near. He had a sort of fit, went all blue and foamed at the mouth. Me mum was real scared, so she carried him up the shelter steps, thinking he needed air. And he came to himself out there and squiggled out of her arms and just ran . . . the blast got him. Me mum said he was . . . he was . . .'

'Oh, Jim,' Maddie mourned, feeling tears rise to her own eyes. 'Oh Jim, poor little Sammy. I'm so sorry.'

'You'd best get back to your mum,' one of the wardens said gently. 'It's no time to leave her, not even for your job.'

'She told me to fetch Lizzie; she reckoned Lizzie 'ud know what to do,' Jim said. 'She needs another female, does me mum.'

'I'll find her for you,' Madeleine told him. 'You stay here, and I'll bring her to you.'

She could see the crews at work and visited each one until she found Lizzie, grimly hanging on to a hose which fought and weaved like a python intent on escaping from its captor.

'Liz, Jim's over at the van; he wants you,' Madeleine said briefly. 'I'll take over here.'

'Jim?' It was impossible to tell whether Lizzie's colour faded beneath the layers of grime, but Madeleine heard her friend's voice sharpen with fear. 'Oh, Mad, is it his mum?'

'No. Do go to him, Liz.'

Lizzie stared at her for a moment, then thrust the hose into Madeleine's hands and turned away.

'Not me mother-in-law? Oh, God, not Sammy . . . don't let it be Sammy.'

The man holding the hose with her turned a dark face towards Madeleine.

'Not the kid? The little'un? What happened?'

Madeleine told him, her voice breaking. None of them would be spared completely, she was sure; tragedy would touch each of them. But a child of less than two . . . it seemed wickedly hard.

When she could do so, she glanced towards the small group round the tea urn. Jim and Lizzie spoke and then Lizzie put her arm round Jim's shoulders and the two of them made their way around the corner and out of sight.

Madeleine's partner on the hose shouted to her to keep the end high and she wrenched her attention back to the job on hand. And when, at last, she was able to return to the station, Lizzie and Jim were long gone.

But Madeleine relived the stark little scene over and over, in her dreams.

'Well, honey, you sure do play a hot game of tennis!'

A brilliant afternoon, the beach glimmering under the sun to her left, the tennis lawn vivid green from the constant spraying, the constant sunshine. Marsha, elegantly tanned to a pale fawny-gold, her hair bleached by a proprietary brand of lightener to the colour of Devonshire cream, smiled at her partner.

'Well, thank you, Gary! I won't say the new racquet does wonders, but it certainly helps!'

The two of them sauntered off the lawn, heading for the house, Marsha tapping the fearsomely expensive racquet thoughtfully against her knees as she walked. Her other one had been good, but this was a real winner. And now they would change into swimsuits and plunge into the pool and later there would be a barbecue on the beach . . . Marsha had a brilliant new outfit, casual yet elegant, in her favourite powder-blue with a matching scarf to tie round her hair. As she stripped off the white blouse and skirt in her room, she thought what a picture she and Gary would make tonight, both so fair, blue-eyed and golden-skinned. Auntie Eff was as proud of her niece as if she had given birth to her. She was always buying Marsha pretty things and drove her miles to attend the horsy meetings which Marsha adored.

She was proud of Marsha's command of languages, too . . . Spanish had just been added to her French and German . . . and boasted that the gift of tongues, as she called it, sure did run in the Loxley family!

The swimsuit was deep blue, the wrap, Marsha's own choice, a brilliant light tangerine. Marsha surveyed her reflection in the mirror in her room and found it good. She had thought the two colours would clash satisfactorily when she had insisted on the tangerine, instead of the matching blue which Macy's had recommended.

Sandals seemed silly, so she left the room barefoot, the wrap around her shoulders. Sometimes she thought about Sarah and Simon and how lucky she had been, but not often, not any more. Her life with Auntie Eff and Uncle Teddy had spread a thick, soothing patina of forgetfulness over that dreadful voyage. Sometimes she was vaguely aware of the Other, Megan, but she had not needed her

154

for ages so didn't bother to conjure her up. She had plenty of friends, she was popular, sought after . . .

Marsha tripped lightly down the stairs, humming the latest tune to take her little crowd by storm. *Don't go under the apple tree with anyone else but me . . .*

'Oh Meg, don't just stand there laughing! Run or we'll be in dead trouble!'

Megan and Peris were playing street tennis outside the house in the evening hush, and Megan's terrible old racquet, with its saggy strings, many of the gut ones replaced by fishing twine, had suddenly caught the ball just right and lifted it over the houses and down the hill. And even as she broke into a trot, Megan heard the crash, closely followed by an ominous tinkle.

'Hell, that was *glass*, girl, and glass is bloody pricey,' Peris panted in her ear as the two of them on suddenly winged feet abandoned Newry Street and tore down Newry Fawr. 'That'll be my earnings and yours gone for a year if they catch us!'

'Oh, come on, we don't know it did much damage,' Megan said breathlessly. 'Why don't we go quietly home and hope for the best?'

'Because where's the first place they'll go when they find something bust? Our house,' Peris said bitterly, slowing down as they reached the Green. They turned left, their run changing to a saunter. 'Oh God, girl, couldn't you have chucked away the evidence?'

'Evidence?' Megan looked around her, then wagged the dilapidated racquet. 'Oh, you mean this!'

'*Oh, you mean this,*' Peris mimicked savagely. 'Mam will tear our heads from our bodies if she finds out it's us and we've denied it. Chuck the bloody thing in the harbour, and we can say we were rabbiting in Penrhos woods.'

'No need; we'll go down the shore and get the crab-pot up and hope there's a crab inside. Mam will think we've been fishing; we shan't need to lie at all, hardly. And anyway, who'd believe this old racquet could hit a ball a yard, let alone about a mile?'

Megan smiled fondly at the racquet. To think that only a week ago she would have given a year of her life for a new racquet, a really good one with which she could dazzle the girls at school and get into the tennis team. But now – well, this one wasn't a bad old thing really. She was used to it, and it certainly could whack if you got the ball in the right place.

'Hmm. Well, all right.' Peris began to trot down the sloping green. 'Good thing we found that old pot, eh? And Mam's always glad of a crab or two.'

Megan nodded. Following in his wake, swinging the racquet in graceful forehands and wicked backhands, she began to hum under her breath.

Don't go under the apple tree with anyone else but me . . .

CHAPTER TEN

It was always lovely weather when Dai's ship came home, Rhi Prydderch reflected, and today had been no exception. She had welcomed him with homegrown peas, beef stew and dumplings, and of course with news and kisses. But she had shared him, too, because Peris and Megan were all over him, like the neighbours and the boarders, all anxious for news of the war beyond the confines of Holy Island.

The children had spent the afternoon fishing off Soldier's Point. They had come home with a string of mackerel, Peris triumphant, Megan with a sunburned nose which made her wail and fly for the butter in the vain hope of calming its raging red. With Dai Prydderch now working as a stoker on HMS *Blackbird*, Dewi on the cross-channel ship *Hibernia*, and Henry aboard a minesweeper, it was up to Megan and Peris to get what fish they could catch, though it was no longer as important to the family as it had been.

Because, Mam reminded herself, the war had changed a number of things, the miserable poverty of Holyhead amongst them. Now there was full employment, and rationing, though a nuisance to some, at least meant that everyone was fed. Indeed, with ships going to and from southern Ireland daily, no one with a few shillings in his pocket need go hungry. The Irish were rationed for tea and sugar, but whatever else you desired you could just walk into a shop and buy.

Another source of comparative riches were the forces personnel who now thronged the island. Penrhos House had been requisitioned by the Army and a huge number of men were working at Valley Airfield, all friendly, cheerful and hungry for whatever the islanders could provide in the way of entertainment and unrationed goods. There was the Dutch navy, too, and the British, and the Cheshires in Treaddur Bay, the lads in the training station on Turkey Shore, and, last but not least, the evacuees.

Rhiannon had taken two more boarders last year and regretted it when the evacuees came. Bright-faced boys, mostly, who would have been glad of her easy-going ways and good meals. But they were in and out of the house all day anyway, coming round to fetch Peris and staying for a meal and a chat, and everyone cracking their jaws to speak English when they would normally have spoken Welsh. Not that it mattered. Megan's English was lovely now, a joy to hear, where before it had been a bit stilted, a bit dot and go one.

Eh, but Megan was growing into a lovely lass. Dai couldn't get over it. Whenever he came into port, straight to the house on Newry Street it was, and a big hug for Megan first go off . . . after the big hug for his Rhiannon, that was.

'There's lovely is our Megan,' he would murmur, when he and Rhi were alone at last. 'But not a patch on you, girl . . . only different she is, see?'

Mam did see, and grudged not a tithe of his affection for their girl, who was not only pretty as a picture but a good child, too. Oh, she'd follow Peris through fire and water into any mischief, but that didn't make her bad, because she had the kindest heart in the world and would do anything for anyone.

She said as much to Dai as they lay in bed together that night, which brought to mind another of her husband's worries.

'Have you told her about men an' that?' he asked

anxiously, putting his arm round Rhi's plump shoulders. 'Meant to tell you I saw her up at the Laugh and Scratch I did, last time I come from sea. Talking to some feller in uniform, she was. It made me think, because she's not too young to be taken advantage of, and to my way of thinking she looks more than her age, besides having so much sweetness to her.'

The Cybi Cinema, known locally as the Laugh and Scratch, was a famous rendezvous for young lovers, but the kids piled in, too, especially for the early shows. Rhiannon knew that if Megan had been at the Cybi, there could be no harm in it.

'Good sense has our Megan,' Rhi averred stoutly. 'Won't do nothing I wouldn't like, you know that, Dai.'

'I know. But have you told her what it is you don't like, girl?'

In the big, soft bed where they had lain as newly-weds twenty-five years earlier, Rhi sighed and shook her head, and, dark though it was, knew that Dai would feel the movement of her hair under his chin.

'Not in so many words, no. Awkward, it do feel, to say such things to our Meg.'

'Well, it isn't my place to speak of it, but if you can't, Rhi, then I've no choice, for I won't have our girl taken advantage of by some young sailor or a lad from Valley.'

'But she's a *good* girl . . .' Rhi began, only to have her words stopped by her husband rolling over and bringing his mouth gently but firmly down on hers. When the kiss finished he leaned up on his elbow, looking down at her in the dimness.

'Rhi, girl, *that's* what it's all about! Warmth, and love, and giving! Between married people no sin but great pleasure, and great comfort, too. Our girl could give, unthinking, to any man far from home who asked the comfort of her body, don't you see that? These days, a man doesn't know whether he'll ever see land again; a pilot flying off the coast of Ireland risks storms, engine failure, constant harassment by enemy aircraft. If he loves a girl, he'll ask, and our Meg won't know enough to refuse.'

'And if I tell her to say no that makes me the spoilsport, the grudging one, and she probably won't listen, anyway,' Rhi said sadly. 'But I'll talk to her, Dai, love. I'll tell her there's other ways of giving love than lying with a lad.'

'Good. Because a great fool I'd feel tellin' her not to do what I spent three years of courtship tellin' you *to* do – to give in to my wicked wiles,' Dai said, and she could hear his grin in the darkness, though she could see nothing, now, with her head resting, comfortable-like, in the hollow of his shoulder.

'Don't worry any more, love,' Rhi murmured, cuddling close. 'There's enough worry coming from me, with you and the lads at sea day in, day out.'

'Aye. It's no picnic,' Dai said drowsily, his mouth against her hair. 'Do I ever tell you how much I love you, Rhi, my little one?'

'Often. But never often enough.'

He chuckled, a calloused hand stroking down the creamy flesh of her upper arm. She lay still until the caress slowed and stopped and she heard Dai's breathing change and deepen, and then she turned in his embrace to court sleep herself.

It should have been easier to rest, with him here. For twenty-five years they had lain together, night after night, with love, with humour, with passion too. A poor fisherman, her own mam had called him – but the old lady had grown to appreciate Dai Prydderch before the end, to acknowledge his worth.

And now the war had torn Dai from Rhiannon's bed, her foster-sons from the shelter of her roof. But she could not entirely regret something which had brought life back to the dying town. How long would it have been, but for the advent of war, before children had starved in the streets, old people in their beds? The authorities had done what they could; the local people, God bless them, had given until they had nothing left to give; the Sally Army had set up their soup kitchens. But there were always some who got left out, some who were too proud. How long would it have been before the first deaths, had not war been declared?

It was a puzzle to Rhi why war should have brought good in its train, but she was sensible enough to know that it had – and to realize that it would bring sorrow, too. A good many islanders would mourn their dead before this lot was finished, for it had been going on for nearly two years now, and showed no signs of slackening.

Some had died already. There had been fearful carnage at Valley Airfield in the early days because the runways had been built on sand and had been surrounded by the sandhills piled up behind Rhosneigr beach. No grass would grow there to bind the sand into a firm surface, and an Air Force sergeant who came into town and drank at the Five Sisters, the public house along Holbourn Road frequented by seamen using the port, had once told Dai that sand got in everything, not only into the food and the men's ears and nostrils but also into the engines. Planes took off and climbed into the sky to accompany convoys or to harass an enemy submarine and were never seen again. The insidious, clogging sand had claimed more victims as engines coughed, failed, died.

The problem had been cured, in the end, when the authorities brought bed-soil from nearby lakes and spread it thickly over the sand and rocks, so that grass could actually grow and thrive. But still accidents were rife. The three-man crew of a Botha bomber were drowned when their aircraft came down in a storm off Rhosneigr, and no fewer than thirteen anti-aircraft gunners, who had tried to go to the rescue of the wrecked plane, died too. Rhiannon had not been there, but there were plenty who had watched, appalled and helpless, as the ancient rowing boat which the lads had commandeered for their rescue attempt simply turned over in the mountainous seas, drowning the gallant young men just as it seemed they really might win through.

And then there were the ships. Rhi hated hearing about the ships that were attacked, the convoys sunk, the young men drowned. Especially she hated to hear about those who had died in the engine room. *They didn't have a chance* was a favourite expression and the pictures these words conjured up were too terrible to contemplate. Three of her men were in engine rooms, Dai, Dewi, and Arthur. Arthur had been her first foster-child . . . God, dear God, keep Arthur safe. He's a man grown now with a wife and two little ones, but he had a bad start, see, and he needs more care than some . . . ah, dear God, keep him safe!

But to think that made it seem as though she would not grieve so much if it were Samuel, Dewi or Henry, or her heart's darling, Dai, who died. Superstitiously, she crossed the fingers of the hand cuddled beneath the pillow, then equally hastily uncrossed them. She was a good chapel-goer and had no desire to be punished by Fate for believing in the Old Ones, the Ones for whom crossed fingers held off disaster.

Beside her, Dai slept. Not soundly, as in the old days, before the war, but restlessly. Sometimes, Rhiannon knew, he would talk in his sleep, shout, cry out. It disturbed her, and not only because he had a whole life, now, in which she could bear no part, ease no strain with her love and understanding. It disturbed her because Dai was a simple man, a good father, a loving and generous husband, yet now there were pictures in his head he dared not let her see, could not contemplate himself without a shudder. Dai's ship was on convoy duty; he had seen vessels torpedoed, had watched as survivors were torn to pieces by an explosion. He had fished the near-dead out of the water, burned, mutilated, smothered in the thick, killing oil.

She did not know of this because Dai had ever consciously breathed a word to her. He never would. She knew because he talked in his sleep and because his dreams were accompanied, sometimes, by verbal wanderings of such a horrific nature that Rhiannon herself could not rest for nights afterwards. And now, instead of going to sleep which she most urgently wanted to do, she was lying awake fearing that at any moment one of Dai's dreams might start.

To take her mind off it she turned her thoughts to the thin partition above her head which separated her from the boys' room, where Peris slumbered. For now, just, Rhi reminded herself grimly. Peris was fourteen and was out of school almost as much, now, as he was in it. He was a hardworking lad, and would harvest a crop, row second oar in a fishing boat, put down the crab-pots, drive a team of horses . . . anything which would help the war effort and earn a bit of money.

Not that they were short, not now. They had three new boarders who paid more than dear old Uncle Reggie and Mr Jones – and, because they all worked, were less trouble, too.

Beside her in the bed, Dai moaned. He said, 'Crabs!' in a horrified mumble and then, louder, 'Never no more, never no more.'

Hastily, Rhiannon rolled over and put her arms round him, tight, tight. She rubbed her face against his, and kissed his rough cheek, for he did not shave aboard ship and had not bothered to do so when he arrived home earlier in the evening. She kissed him with quick little kisses, plonk, plonk, plonk, and he relaxed and then woke, suddenly laughing low in his throat and catching hold of her, squeezing her harshly, convulsively, to his breast.

'Dai Rhys Prydderch!'

He began to stroke her back, his hand travelling from the nape of her neck to the curve of her buttocks, whilst the other hand held her captive still, against him.

Rhiannon made a small, purring sound. It was going to be all right! They would make love and then they would sleep, and the war would be over.

Until tomorrow.

This week, it was local kids in the morning at the County School and evacuees in the afternoon. Megan was glad because, much though she loved summer mornings, summer afternoons could go right on until eleven or so at night, thanks to double summer time. So if you were off in the afternoon you could spend up to ten hours in the open, working or playing under the sun.

Up in her room, Megan, having cast her homework aside as something she could scrape through in the morning before classes, examined herself in the mirror propped up beside her wash-bowl and decided that, though far too pale as to hair and face and far too flat as to figure, she was coming along nicely.

At thirteen, Megan was beginning to feel grown up, although Mam had assured her she had a long way to go yet, and must make the most of her childhood. But then Mam didn't know about Danny.

Danny was beautiful. He was also seventeen and would be going into the Navy quite soon, but at the moment he lived over at Penrhyn with his nain in a low white cottage with a cement-rendered roof and roses round the door. It looked pretty from the outside but inside it could best be described as basic, Megan knew. Earth floors in all the rooms, very little daylight coming in through the tiny windows, no electricity or gas or running water, and the bedrooms under that whitened roof so low you had to bend almost double to get to your bed.

Danny's da was a Swedish seaman who had been killed when Danny was not a year old, and his mam lived with the baker on London Road in a little flat above the shop. No one said much, but Megan knew they weren't married because the baker had a wife somewhere. Whilst he was at school Danny had lived with his mam weekdays and with his nain weekends and holidays, working on her smallholding and fishing the bay in his taid's boat. He kept ferrets for rabbiting and he had half a dozen crab-pots and he knew everything there was to know about the wild life of the island: all about the birds and beasts, the name of every wild flower, the habits of each insect which visited them.

Danny and Dewi had been friends in school so the Prydderchs knew him pretty well. Mam said he'd had a miserable time as a child because kids know when they aren't wanted and Danny's mam had made it pretty plain how she felt. His nain had not been overfond either, but he was useful so she paid for his keep whilst he was with her. He had stayed at school longer than most, but had left a year ago to work full time on the farm, still living with his nain and keeping her place going too. Megan heard Mam saying that Danny wasn't appreciated, but it meant nothing to her. She knew he was clever, miles ahead of Dewi in class, but so far as she was concerned Danny was an exotic and exciting figure, someone to be envied, not pitied. What was more, although she would have loved him even if he had been plain as a boot, Danny had deep yellow hair that he didn't bother to cut often enough, and a fascinating downy yellow beard. He had blue eyes and a strong, cleft chin which was still just visible through the beard. Dewi had once been heard to refer to it as 'Danny's bum-fluff', which made Megan blush because it was rude, though she could not, for the life of her, understand why it should be referred to thus. She had seen the bums of brothers on and off for years and they were as pale and beardless as her own, but that was boys for you: never said a word without a rudeness in it somewhere.

Actually, Megan was deeply interested, just now, in body hair, due to a certain lack of her own. Constant watching, peering into her pearly armpits, had done no good at all, so at present she was treating the absent hair as one is supposed to treat a kettle – she never looked to see if it was boiling – and she had great hopes that in three weeks, when the month she had allowed herself was up, she would discover a positive forest of pale hair flourishing beneath each arm.

And then I'll raze it all off with Da's razor, Megan thought happily. She saw no inconsistency in this; underarm hair was a sign of adulthood, but according to her mam's magazines it was something which Nice Girls disposed of briskly as soon as it reared its head. And since she had every intention of being a Nice Girl, because Mam and Da would be so disappointed if she became Fast, or even Fresh, then no sooner would an underarm hair appear than Megan would strike it down.

She had noticed that Peris was growing hair in all the right places, though, and he was only a year older than she. With unaccustomed delicacy she had not mentioned his new attribute to Peris, and last time they had gone fishing and Peris had cast off his shirt she had been pleased

166

to see that his chest was still bald as an egg. Danny, on the other hand, had a delicate tracery of blond hair all over his bronzed and manly bosom.

'Meggie, are you coming or aren't you?'

The shriek, echoing up the stairs, told Megan that she had better get a move on. Peris was not by nature a patient lad, and today she realized she would have tried the patience of a saint.

The trouble was, she was so terribly excited. At last Danny had asked her for a date! Oh, she had been out with him a hundred times – rabbiting, fishing, simply trailing behind him and Dewi whilst they walked miles, deep in talk – but this was different. This was a real date! *Meet me on the Green; got a surprise for you*, he had said. *Go off for a ride, shall we?* And if that wasn't a date Megan didn't know what was! She had not said a word about it to Mam, who would worry or possibly say she was too young and forbid her to go, and since telling Peris would almost certainly have resulted in her foster-brother's insisting on accompanying her, she had not told him either. But she was definitely going with Danny, and she did not intend to reappear until quite late at night. After all, once Mam found out there would probably be trouble, so she might as well have some fun before the storm broke.

Now, however, she had better get rid of Peris. She crossed her floor, padding barefoot on the lino, and tugged her door open.

'Go on ahead, I'll follow,' she bellowed, secure in the knowledge that all the boarders save for Uncle were at work and he, dear old chap, would be sitting on the wooden bench down by Quiet Corner, having a pipe and watching the comings and goings at the Toc H club there.

'Don't be a fool, girl,' came an exasperated roar in

answer. 'Mam won't let you bicycle off alone, so lovely you are, such a beauty!'

'Shut your gob, you!' shrieked Megan. 'Sarcasm's the lowest form of wit, Miss says.'

'It's good enough for you, girl,' Peris retorted. 'Are you coming or do I have to come up and drag you down by that stringy stuff you call your hair?'

Megan sighed deeply. Getting rid of Peris would be no sinecure, evidently. She pushed her feet into her old sandals, checked her appearance in the mirror – blue cotton dress, blue ribbon, soft, freshly washed hair – and then set off down the stairs at a heedless gallop, skidding on the landing, swinging round on the newel post with a cruel disregard for Screech's feelings, so that he told her, in outraged tones, that she was a stupid sodding sailor and a buggering bum-boy.

'I'll tell Mam on you and she'll wring your skinny old neck,' Megan informed him, whereupon Screech put his head on one side and announced that he was a pretty boy and would like some peanuts.

'Oh, yes, I suppose you're going to tell me you didn't mean a word of it,' Megan retorted, crashing down the remainder of the stairs into the hall. 'One of these days, Screech, you're going to become dish of the day at the NAAFI – parrot pie and chips!'

Screech, who adored attention of whatever kind, promptly burped, blew a raspberry, and then said, 'Pardon me, I'm sure,' in the very tones of Hermione Gingold, a lady much admired by Uncle.

Megan giggled and opened the kitchen door. Mam was standing by the sink shelling peas very fast into a blue and white enamel saucepan and Peris was sitting on the kitchen table swinging his legs and beating something in the big yellow mixing bowl. He had succeeded in splattering his mixture all over the table and his grey shirt was speckled with batter. He looked up as Megan entered.

'Good lord, Mam, she's actually here! Does Her Majesty have any small jobs to perform or can we leave now?'

'I told you to go on ahead, if you're in such a hurry,' Megan said. She dipped a finger into the batter and tasted it. 'What's this? Yorkshire pud?'

'Cow shit,' Peris said amiably. 'Have some more.'

Megan choked on a laugh but Mam, turning from the sink, said, 'Yes, it's a Yorkshire, and that's enough of that dirty talk,' and continued to rattle peas into the pan as fast as artillery fire.

'Mam? Is there anything you want me to do?' Megan asked, walking over to the sink. She picked up a peapod, stripped it neatly of its contents, and popped the peas into her mouth.

'Yes, leave them peas alone,' Mam said crossly. 'Oh, and if you're going by Parry's, on Market Street, you might pick me up a new scrub-brush. My old one's worn right down to the wood.'

'Right, we'll do that,' Megan said.

She recognized the request for the command it was, and also realized that Mam was feeling low. It always happened after Da sailed, especially when he'd been at home for a while. His ship had been struck by a shell and though no one had been killed they had been forced to put the old *Blackbird* into dry dock whilst the damage was repaired. This had given Da an unprecedented three weeks at home, but now they would all pay the penalty, first with Mam's understandable unhappiness and second in missing him even worse than usual.

'Thanks, love. Biking, are you?'

Mam sounded almost like her old self and Megan put her arm round the older woman's waist and squeezed.

'Oh, Mam! Why don't you come out with us, for once?

169

We needn't take the bikes – we could walk or bus some-where, and we'd love it, Peri and me.'

At once she could have bitten her tongue out, but as she might have guessed Mam laughed, put up a caressing hand and stroked Megan's cheek, but shook her head.

'Nice of you to suggest it, my little one, but there's a meal to prepare and when that's eaten and cleared I'm going down to the Institute. We're making raspberry jam for our boys this evening, and Mrs Evans-Hardware is going to find me up some wool so I can knit a few pairs of gloves and a balaclava or two. It's as good a way of relaxing as wearing yourself out biking miles over the island.'

'Whatever made you say that to Mam?' Peris said incredulously as they got their bikes out of the shed which had once contained half a dozen scrawny hens and smelt as though they were in residence still. 'What would we have done if she'd said yes? Answer me that, girl.'

'Scrapped our plans, of course,' Megan said promptly. 'Needs a break, she do. Still, since she said no, we might as well get a move on.'

'Good. Then we'll buy the old scrub-brush first and then forget about it. Right?'

Agreeing, Megan wheeled her bicycle down the short path and out of the green painted wooden door which led to the back lane. The back lane was just about wide enough for Megan and her bicycle to go side by side, between the old stone walls which lined the back gardens of the houses on Newry Street and the houses on Queen's Park.

At the end of the lane they were on Stanley Street, with the sun beaming down on the shops and people hurrying about their business. Despite her urge to get to the Green and find Danny, Megan left Peris in charge of her bicycle whilst she went along to Parry's. She passed

Boots, glancing in the window, but apart from the two big flasks full of coloured water everything looked dull today. She crossed the road, waved to Beth behind the counter in the Maypole using the bacon slicer, then turned into Parry's. Inside it was cool and dim, the smell of polish, candles and the paraffin oil they sold mingling with the smell of new bread from the baker's opposite. Megan selected the best scrub-brush, paid for it and took the parcel out to her saddlebag.

'Why don't you run it home?' she asked without any real hope. 'I could just cycle down to the Green and see who's around.'

'No fear,' Peris said promptly. 'Come on, I'll come back with you, if you really think Mam needs it now.'

'Oh, later will do,' Megan said. It began to look as though she would have to quarrel with Peris to get away from him, and she hesitated to do something which was really foreign to her nature. On the other hand, though, for a date with Danny she would do a lot!

The two of them got on their bikes and freewheeled blissfully down Market Street, hands on brakes, for morning shoppers wandered across the roadway as though the last thing they expected to encounter was traffic. At the bottom, they turned sharp left on to Landsend.

'We'll see what's come into the outer harbour,' Peris said, standing up on the pedals the better to push. 'Then we'll go by the Gors and feed the ponies. Then we'll go on to the wireless station.'

'Sure,' Megan agreed, hurrying along beside him. She was quite happy to visit the outer harbour, where the British vessels were snugged down behind the long arm of the great breakwater, partly because it was always interesting to see what vessels had arrived since their previous visit and partly because Danny and she were to

171

meet at the Green, which was the stretch of grass above the harbour.

'Did you get some carrots?' Peris asked presently.

Dismayed, Megan was forced to admit she had forgotten. She had hoped, of course, to escape from Peris before they began the long ride over Holyhead Mountain to the Gors so had not bothered to beg carrots from Mam, nor to dig any up from the clamp in the back yard. But Peris was too resourceful to be beaten by mere forgetfulness.

'You fool, Meg! Well, we'll just have to visit the allotments, that's all.'

'But the ponies aren't so keen on cabbage, and that's about all that's up,' Megan demurred. 'There's no root on the swedes or parsnips yet, and ponies don't care for peas and beans.'

Peris made a derisive noise in his throat.

'Megan Prydderch, don't you ever *think*? Old Daddy Williams-Bread has his carrot-clamp down on his allotment. What harm to take a few of his carrots for the ponies?'

'It's stealing?' Megan hazarded. 'Old Williams-Bread would kill us if he knew? Mam would kill us twice over? No harm other than that, of course.'

'We'll give him some of our broad beans and tell him it's a swop,' Peris suggested. They waited till the road was clear and then retraced their steps and headed for the allotments.

As luck would have it, Williams-Bread was there, along with several old men digging and weeding and young boys either helping or barrowing manure begged from the farms on the mountain. He waved to Peris and Megan and gave them a handful of elderly carrots cheerfully, refusing their broad beans until Megan had assured him that Mam wouldn't mind at all as she had done well out of their allotment this year, and anyway had enough ration

172

books, what with boarders and her lads, to mean that they never went short.

'Oh ah, and your Dewi's on the *Hibernia*, of course,' Williams-Bread said, letting Megan pile broad beans into his basket. 'Next time he's home, I wouldn't mind some baccy.'

'I'll tell him,' Megan promised, meaning it. Dewi would get anything for anyone, good lad that he was, and in Ireland most days. 'We're off to feed the ponies, Mr Williams.'

'Have a good time,' Williams-Bread said drowsily. He was sitting on an upturned wheelbarrow, watching whilst his grandsons dug a big strip of ground.

While they had been talking to Williams-Bread Megan had been scanning the area for Danny, hoping to pick out his figure amongst the dozens of young people sprawled on the grass above the promenade, but there was no sign of him. It was beginning to look as though she would have to be content with Peris and the ponies after all. And then, just as she and Peris mounted their bicycles once more, a voice hailed them.

'Afternoon, Prydderchs! See what I got!'

It was Danny, and he was sitting astride a very large motor bike. Peris promptly ran his bicycle up the short allotment path, across the road and over to Danny.

'I say! Is it yours? Isn't it smashing! Can I have a go, boy? G'won, Danny, say I can have a ride of it.'

'No fear; doubt you can ride a bike,' Danny growled. 'Give you a ride behind me later, though, if you behave.'

It was odd, Megan thought, how Danny treated Peris like a very young boy, definitely an inferior, whilst he treated her like . . . well, like a young lady, she thought triumphantly, which just went to show Peris, only he never noticed things like that.

173

'I'll behave,' Peris said earnestly. 'Where d'you get it? Is it yours?'

Danny smiled secretly. His teeth looked very white against his tan and his blue eyes sparkled with hidden amusement. He looked marvellous astride the motor bike, Megan thought blissfully; his denim trousers showed the swell of his muscles as he gripped his steed and his blue cotton shirt had the sleeves rolled up to show his tanned and competent arms, lightly covered with blond hair which glinted in the sunlight.

It seemed almost unfair that one man should be so beautiful. Peris, small, square and dark, stood beside him chattering away, and Danny stroked the glinting gold of his beard and nodded and looked as though he was giving Peris all his attention, except that Megan knew better. He was seeing her all the time, not staring but still seeing.

Presently Peris turned to her.

'Megan, my little one, you don't mind? Danny says he'll just take me for a spin . . . it won't take more than ten minutes . . . fifteen, perhaps.'

'I'll take you next, Megan,' Danny promised. 'Going to the sandhills by the quarry, me and Peris.'

Megan smiled. Smugly.

'That's okay, Danny. I'll talk to Siân until you come back.'

Mam didn't think much of Siân, who the boys said was 'hot stuff', but Megan got on well enough with the older girl. Siân was small and trim, with black, almond-shaped eyes and fawn-coloured hair. She had a secretive smile and prim ways with her, but despite appearances was known to be free with her favours. She was also fifteen, and going with, amongst others, an Australian pilot from Valley Airfield.

'Let's walk along the beach,' Megan said to her now. 'Been ditched, I have, by that old Peris.'

'Oh, they'll come back,' Siân said. 'Like 'im, do you, girl?'

'Who, Peris? He's not bad, for a boy.'

Siân made an impatient noise in her throat.

'Peris? He's your brother, or good as. No, tatty-head, Danny!'

'Oh, Danny. Don't know him that well, do I? A friend of Dewi's he is, see. But I suppose I like him all right.'

Siân smiled; the long, liquid eyes slanted expressively sideways for a moment, knowing, triumphant.

'Oh, yeah? Expect me to believe that, do you? When Danny's easily the best-looking feller for miles around! So you suppose you like him; how does he feel about you, girl?'

'Don't know and don't care,' shrugged Megan, but inwardly she was delighted with the turn the conversation was taking. Siân was nearly two years older than herself, yet she was talking to her right now, woman to woman, as though she and Megan had the same problems, the same feelings.

Siân slid her arm through Megan's. She was four or five inches the shorter but she was wearing high-heeled shoes which brought them nearly level pegging for height.

'Wish I could believe you, but there's hard I find it to credit that anyone wouldn't fall for Danny,' she murmured. 'There's older men and better lovers I dare say, but there's none of 'em I wouldn't throw over for Danny, given half a chance.'

'Why don't you go for him, then?' Megan demanded. 'He'd not say no to *you*, Siân!'

Siân drew herself up and tried to look haughty, but her small mouth was struggling not to laugh and the long eyes sparkled with suppressed mirth.

'Me? I don't lower myself to chasing the fellers, girl, I let them do the running! Just warning you I was, see, that if Danny ever did make advances, don't know as I'd find the strength to say no to him.'

'No? Well, if anyone makes advances to me, Siân, which they won't, I'd have to say no. My mam would murder me, else.'

Siân nodded. The two girls had been walking along the promenade, pretending not to hear the whistles and catcalls from the various craft moored nearby, but now Siân pulled Megan to a halt.

'There's proper, at your age,' she said approvingly. 'The same I was, when I was young. So no hard feelings if Danny and I should get together, eh? You wouldn't mind?'

'You're after a feller with a motor bike, that's what it is,' Megan exclaimed. 'You're welcome to Danny, Siân, if you . . . if you want him.'

She had been about to say 'if you can get him', but thought better of it. She was sure of Danny – fairly sure – but did not intend to tempt fate.

And presently, when Danny came back with a glowing Peris on the pillion, he took no notice whatever of Siân, but drew up alongside the two girls and addressed himself directly to Megan.

'Right, your turn now, Meg. Can you get on or shall Peris give you a leg up?'

Megan snorted and climbed nimbly on to the pillion.

'Are you ready? We won't go fast, not at first. Siân, you keep Peris amused for a while, will you? Hold on to me, Megan!'

Megan clutched his shirt; she found she was far too shy to clutch anything more intimate, but this was not good enough for Danny.

'Let go my clothes, girl. Put your arms round me and hang on tight,' he ordered. 'Later, when you've done a bit, you'll find you keep your balance best if you hold on to the back of the pillion, but for now just hang on to me.'

Timidly, Megan put her arms round Danny. He had a surprisingly narrow waist, sinewy and strong, but his shoulders were broad. The bike started up with a roar and Megan found she had to grip, had no option once the wind snatched at her hair and tried to get inside her blue cotton frock and whip it up above her head to show her navy knickers off to the world. She laid her face against Danny's back, therefore, and clung like a limpet whilst emotions roared through her almost as violently as the wind roared past.

They were well clear of the town before Danny slowed and spoke over his shoulder, and she had to shout at him to repeat it before she caught the words.

'All right are you, Meggie? Then we'll take a little trip along the coast a ways. Ever been to Porth Trecastell? In English it's called Cable Bay, because the first transatlantic cable was started there.'

'No, I never have,' Megan shouted above the noise of the wind. 'Why, Danny? What's there?'

'Nothing much. Quiet it is, and private. But there's something odd . . . oh, tell you when we get there.'

And with that Megan had to be content, since it was becoming increasingly obvious that conversations carried on between driver and pillion passenger on a motor bike were not an ideal means of communication. She found herself rather guiltily hoping that Porth Trecastell would prove to be neither too far nor too lonely. She liked and admired Danny more than any other boy she knew, except her foster-brothers, but beneath her clutching fingers she could feel the iron strength of his muscles. It occurred to her that if he did not understand that she was not allowed, by Mam, to be a bad girl, then she might have very real difficulty in persuading him to let her alone.

So when at last the motor bike drew to a halt in a scatter of sand, hard by a tiny bay, she dismounted with more alacrity than common sense, trying to tidy her hair with trembling fingers whilst eyeing Danny with all the wide-eyed suspicion of a very small kitten suddenly finding itself nose to nose with a very large tiger.

But if Danny noticed this, he was far too old a hand with girls to remark on it. Instead, he pushed his fingers through his own thick yellow locks, then looped an arm casually around Megan's shoulders.

'How d'you like her?' he demanded, plainly referring to the motor bike. 'Nice, eh, girl?'

'Very nice. It's noisy, though. And fast. And a bit cold,' Megan said. She reminded herself that Danny often put his arm round his friends' shoulders. 'Is it really yours, Danny?'

'Well, not exactly. I borrowed it off Eggy Carruthers, one of the fellers on the old *Hibernia*. Told him if I liked it, I'd have it off him. In instalments, mind, not all at once. I do like it, so I'll probably start paying next month. Done well with the fishing, see, and earning good money at the farm, too.'

'That'll be nice,' Megan said vaguely. She now realized that a push-bike had hitherto unappreciated virtues, like quietness and smoothness, which Danny's motor bike clearly lacked. 'I should think it's pretty horrid when it rains, though.'

Danny looked slightly affronted and Megan wished she had kept her thoughts to herself. Men, it seemed, loved motor bikes as women love clothes – you denigrate a bike or a best dress at your peril.

'Umm . . . not likely to have much rain now, though, seeing as it's summer.' He pulled at her shoulders. 'Take a look at the beach, shall we?'

'Sure,' Megan said obediently. There were American

Air Force units at Valley now, and it was almost obligatory to lard one's remarks with Americanisms, except that she, sheltered flower that she was, had to pick up her slang secondhand.

'Right, let's hit the road,' Danny said. The cinema was quite a good substitute, Megan realized, for meeting American Air Force personnel; she should have thought of that herself. 'The bike's safe enough; I've got the key.'

It was still a lovely evening with the faintest of breezes. The wind which had tried so hard to pluck Megan off the motor bike had been, it seemed, nothing but the wind of their going. The two of them walked down on to the sand of the sheltered bay, Megan a little stiffly because of Danny's arm around her shoulders, but as they scrambled down the bank which led to the beach itself Danny had to release her, and when they stood on a firm surface once more he took her hand, an easier and pleasanter way to walk.

'See that headland to the right? We'll go up there and I'll show you what I found a couple of years back.'

'Okay,' Megan said. She loved the beach and the sea and was incapable of remaining shy with Danny for long. 'Race you down to the water!'

It was the right thing to say. Racing across the hard sand below the high tide mark, Danny stopped being a slightly menacing male and became a friend again. They laughed, scrabbled in the shallows for shells, talked easily about their respective lives. Megan told Danny about school, and helping Mam when she did cricket teas for the evacuees from Liverpool, and Danny told Megan how he had decided to join the Navy because he could not bear the thought of working under a roof.

It was innocent talk but enjoyable, and when Danny said he thought they'd best start the climb up the headland or it would grow dusk before they knew it, she was

179

surprised, even a little alarmed. If Peris told Mam she had gone off for so long with Danny her life would scarcely be worth living.

She said as much to Danny, who reminded her that Peris had been happy enough to remain behind with Siân, and Megan decided that she might as well be hung for a sheep as a lamb and allowed Danny to take her hand once more to lead her up the cliffs on to the headland.

It was a stiff climb, with the sun now lower in the western sky and a sharp breeze lifting the hair from Megan's hot forehead. But they made the summit at last and stood looking out over the incredibly beautiful water-scape, the sea blue and silver, touched with the sun's gold, the tide creeping in over the hard sand and frilling the rocks with foam, and the gulls swooping and crying overhead.

Inland, the island lay peaceful under the sun, a green and gold patchwork, a giant toy farm with tiny cows and miniature sheep, and here and there a cottage huddled in its collar of trees or squeezed against a hill's gentle slope.

'It's hard to remember there's a war on when you look at that,' Megan said presently, gently squeezing Danny's hand. 'Now that the worst of the Liverpool bombing seems to be over, it would be easy to forget it altogether.'

'Here it's easy,' Danny agreed. 'But not out there.'

He gestured to the sea and just for a moment Megan saw it through his eyes, as a thing not beautiful but treacherous, one moment calm and the next stirred into fury, waves towering above the mariners, crashing down like bombs on a town, breaking up ships, drowning sailors, infinitely powerful, infinitely capricious.

And for Danny, fishing from his small boat, the swell hid another threat. He was not yet in the Navy, but even a fishing boat could be mistaken for an enemy vessel and torpedoed. She would never forget the night when she and the girl Marsha had clung to the wreckage, waiting and praying for the dawn. She had not understood what was happening, did not understand it still, but she knew that the other girl's ship had been torpedoed and sunk, and there had been dreadful danger stalking abroad that night.

Remembering, Megan drew closer to Danny, and when he slid an arm round her waist it seemed the sort of natural, comfortable thing anyone might do.

'Come and see what I found,' Danny said now. 'You'll be amazed, girl!'

Megan smiled but went with him – she had little choice, with his strong arm girdling her waist, his legs keeping careful time with her shorter steps. Presently, they came to a largish mound, rising abruptly from the flatter ground around it, and Danny stopped. Megan, perforce, stopped too, and looked enquiringly up at him.

'This is it,' Danny said. 'It's man-made, too – see how round it is on top? Like a pudding basin, almost? That was never done by nature – the whole landscape's wrong for it. That was built, and I can prove it.'

'I don't see why anyone would want to build a thing like a pudding basin,' Megan said doubtfully. 'Besides, it's miles and miles from anywhere. Why should anyone come out here? Unless it's an American shelter, of course,' she added jokingly.

'Not likely, is it, that I'd bring you out here to admire an air-raid shelter? No, this was put up a long time ago, before history. Stone-age man and all that.'

'Oh? I knew they erected stones but I didn't know they made pudding basins,' Megan said rather irritatingly. 'Go on then, prove it!'

'I'm going to, don't you worry. Come with me.'

They walked round the mound, reaching at last a place where gorse bushes grew so thick that it would, Megan

181

considered, be more than their skin was worth to attempt to penetrate them. She was about to say so when Danny simply plunged into the bushes, pulling her with him.

'Hey! You've got trousers. I don't want to get my skirt torn,' Megan objected, but Danny only turned and grinned at her before continuing to draw her after him.

'Here we are,' he said rather breathlessly, presently. 'Better bend down, Meggie.' He was crouching, heaving at a gorse bush which, Megan now saw, had a great mass of its branches roped up so that they could be tied back. 'See?'

Megan looked past him, and saw a gap in the smooth green grass of the mound ahead of them, and darkness.

'What is it? A cave?'

'Not exactly. Better than that. I'll show you. I've brought a torch.'

He produced a torch from his pocket and shone it into the gap. In its faint light Megan could see a passage, stretching into the bowels of the earth. She could just make out, on either side, great stones, some like pillars set into the earth walls, others slabbed across them to form square archways.

'Oh, Danny,' Megan breathed. She found that the hair was standing up on the back of her neck, prickling erect with a horrid fear that he was going to expect her to adventure into that darkness. 'Danny, I'm scared!'

'It's all right. I won't let you go,' Danny assured her. Holding her hand, he led the way into the passage, bending to get under the stones which held up the roof. 'Keep by me. You're safe as houses, honestly – I've been in here many a time when I wanted to shelter from the rain.'

Shelter from the rain! At that moment Megan would have welcomed a good old downpour, and herself, soaked to the skin, in the middle of a nice ploughed field with mud up to her ankles and a scolding ahead. She pulled back against Danny's impelling hand, for once inside he had pushed her ahead of him the better to guide her.

'Danny, don't. I'm really scared. I want to go out. It's too dark – I don't like it.'

'We're there now,' Danny's voice said close to her ear. 'Take a good look, girl. There's not many have seen a sight like that.'

Despite herself, her eyes followed the beam of the torch as it swung slowly round. The place was a big chamber, with more of the carved stones measuring out its width, breadth and height. And in the cold, dark space in the centre of the circle were the remains of a fire, the ashes long dead – she dared not think how long – with objects placed around it. Megan began to tremble, clutching Danny hard, aware that there was a great mystery here, one which she had no right to penetrate.

'Danny, it's – it's a secret place. We shouldn't be here. The Old Ones wouldn't want us . . . oh, please, Danny, take me back out!'

She turned to face him, eager only to prevent herself from looking at the pathetic bundles on the floor. She dared not run from the place alone, yet she could feel the dark mysteries of the Old Ones reaching out for her, drawing her in. Suddenly it seemed that Danny was her only hope, that without him she would never escape from here, for she had seen and understood too much. Desperately, she threw her arms round his neck, pressing her body against his, sobbing as she clung.

Danny's arms went round her almost unbelievingly, his grip as strong as hers, but it was not fear which moved him, but triumph. He had guessed that the weird atmosphere might work in his favour, and he had been right. He had liked Megan Prydderch for years, thinking she was only a child. It was not until he had noticed the budding of her tiny breasts, the burgeoning of hips, the awareness of her where once there had been simple friendliness, that he had realized how he wanted her. And as soon as he acknowledged his desire, he had planned to bring her to Porth Castell and this strange underground chamber.

He had been lying when he told her he had been here often. He had been here only twice before, once when he had first discovered the passageway, once when he had come back, with a torch and a spade, to dig his way through to the inner chamber which he could see but not reach.

He had not touched the things in the centre of the circle, but he had taken a good look at them. There were crude ornaments made of bone, objects which looked a bit like clumsy hair-slides similar to the little bakelite ones the girls wore in the playground, and pottery bowls holding grain and something he thought might be solidified honey.

There was the fire, too, dead these thousand years, he guessed, the sticks charcoaled long since in some distant ritual. And crude weapons – a dagger; what he imagined had once been a bow. He had found, as well, a long, pale strand of hair and had run it through his fingers, marvelling that after the weight of such aeons it should still feel soft and silky to the touch.

But what had moved and surprised him most was the bunch of flowers. He had never considered handling them, but as he had turned from them the delicate petals had crumbled into dust, just with the wind of movement he had stirred up in this still and ancient place.

Were they burial flowers, or was this a place of rejoicing? Did that long-ago tribe bring their women here to wed and bed them? It was impossible to know, irresistible to conjecture. Danny had found himself fascinated by the place, longing to return, wanting to conduct the experiment of taking a girl there, seeing what her reaction would be to this relic of a race long dead.

So here he was, and in his arms the delicate, golden beauty of the girl-child Megan Prydderch, just at the delicious threshold where a woman's desires and a child's fears fight for supremacy, whilst her slim, strong young body with its silken hair and petal-soft skin trembled alternately with fear and with the strength of her half-acknowledged, uncomprehended desires.

She is my captive, Danny thought exultantly, but I wouldn't hurt her for the whole world. What we shall do together will be for our mutual pleasure and delight. He ran his hands down from her shoulders to her waist, over the smooth curve of her buttocks and under the brief blue skirt of her cotton dress.

She cried out, then, and he released her for a moment to gentle her with caresses, to kiss across her face and neck, into the soft hollow of the shoulder bared by his impatient hands, careless of ripped material, of her sudden, soft sob.

He laid her down gently, away from the long-dead fire, with the torch, shining still, pointing at the big altar stone, its patterns looking one moment like men dancing and the next like the great rolling waves of the Irish Sea. He put his hands on her reverently, tenderly, touching for the first time those small, apple-shaped breasts, the soft, smooth swoop of her firm young stomach, the deeper softness . . .

'Danny! Get off!'

Her voice, sharp and shrill, surprised him so much that he rolled away from her, dismayed by himself, by what he had so nearly done. And in a moment she was on her feet and running like a deer away from him. He saw her outlined against the light as she stumbled down the passage, heard her sobs, knew that she thought of him now as a beast and herself as his terrified prey, and jumped to his feet, kicking the torch, breaking it, plunging the chamber into darkness even as he ran after her, calling her name, pleading with her not to do anything silly, that it was all right, he was sorry, he didn't know what had come over him . . .

He caught her up halfway down the cliff. Even in his panic he admired the way she climbed, with a swift neatness which came, he supposed, from years of robbing gulls' nests in company with young Peris.

'Meggie? Do stop, do let me explain . . .'

He would not have been surprised had she continued down the cliff, ignoring him, but instead she stopped short, waiting for him to come up with her. When he did so she smiled at him, a trifle tentatively to be sure, but with undeserved sweetness.

'Sorry, Danny. It was . . . I was . . .'

'It's me who's sorry.' His voice surprised him by actually sounding as humble as he felt. 'I had no right to behave like that – I didn't mean to, I swear, Meggie. I thought . . . just a few kisses, some cuddling . . . I know you're too young . . . I'm really sorry, girl.'

'It wasn't you, Danny. It was that place,' Megan said. 'I think it may have been because I was so scared, too. Perhaps it made you want to . . . oh, make me more scared. I don't know. Anyway, if you're sorry and I'm sorry, then we'd better forget it.'

'Yes. Are you all right? I didn't hurt you, did I?'

Megan looked down at herself as if searching for gaping wounds, then looked up at Danny again and grinned.

'You tore the neck of my dress,' she said. 'But I'm always ruining my clothes so Mam won't worry over it. And I think we'd better go straight home, because it must be late.'

'It is,' Danny said, casting a knowing eye at the reddening sun. 'You're a good kid, Megan.'

He knew, now, that she really was a kid still. A woman would have made far more fuss over almost being raped – or had she not realized, perhaps? What on earth came over me, Danny mused, as they reached the beach and raced across it, back to the grassy verge on which his motor bike still stood. Oh, sure, he had intended to take her into the mound and get her a little bit scared and kiss and cuddle her back to comfortable ordinariness again. But he had never intended to go as far as he had almost gone. Never.

He started the motor bike and jumped on, revving the engine. He felt Megan climb on the back and put her arms confidingly round his waist. He turned his head so that he was looking down on the neat white parting in her pale gold hair.

'Megan?'

'What?'

'It was the place, wasn't it? It made me . . . different. Won't go there again, I reckon, for a few years. Neither of us, eh?'

Megan looked up at him and grinned wickedly. His heart went out to her – she was too good for him, if the truth were known, far too good!

'No, I don't think I want to go back.' She hesitated, the mischief much in evidence. 'Well,' she amended, 'it's only fair to tell you that . . . that some of it might have been rather fun!'

He grinned back at her, then turned and kicked the engine into noisy, smelly life.

'It would have been enormous fun,' he shouted. 'But not there, not like that. Only . . . one day, eh, Meg?'

'One day.'

CHAPTER ELEVEN

It was late when Madeleine woke. For a moment she wondered where she was, for when she opened her eyes in Cheetham Hill Road she saw, first of all, the fluttering of the faded blue curtains at the window, then the houses opposite, and finally a very small patch of sky.

Here, the sky filled the window and the curtains – though they, too, fluttered as the breeze caught them – were pink with darker pink leaves on them. And the small room was brighter than the flat in Cheetham Hill Road, the air fresher.

The country! After spending so long in the city, it seemed a marvellous thing, now, to have some leave from her job and to come out here, into the quiet countryside, for a few days' complete rest.

Madeleine turned on to her back and contemplated the ceiling above her with a lazy, almost fond, eye. It had felt quite wicked even to think of a few days off, though goodness knew she deserved a break. She had stayed with the AFS until things in Manchester quietened down and then she had gone into munitions, making tanks in a huge factory, with cheerful young girls working alongside her and plenty of laughs to make up for the incredibly hard and dirty work.

She might not have taken her leave even so, for their work was much valued, had she not gone and caught chicken pox. For two miserable weeks she had been quarantined in the flat whilst Lizzie stayed with Alex's family and she scratched and roasted in the warm summer weather. And then, when the doctor had finally pronounced her fit, he had insisted she take a break before returning to work.

'You're absolutely exhausted. You're still working part-time with the AFS, you fire-watch, you help with your local shelter committee . . . it's too much. Take my advice, Miss Ripley-Trewin, and go away for a week or so.'

Lizzie had agreed completely with the doctor's verdict. 'There's a farm out by Knutsford that some of the girls talk about,' she had said. 'They take visitors sometimes, especially if you'll give a hand. They'll be haymaking about now.'

They were. Madeleine had helped, but they would not let her put her back into the work. Mrs Elton was a motherly woman with grey hair and rosy cheeks, and she insisted that they needed someone to lead the horses and help get meals for the haymakers. Telling Madeleine firmly that they had landgirls aplenty to do the turning and carting, she had roped the younger woman in for the job of housewife's assistant and carthorse-hand.

Not that Madeleine had objected, not after the first day. It had been so marvellous to walk with the huge horses to and from the fields, to smell again the strong, evocative smell of horseflesh and to feel, on her hair, the soft touch of Boxer's long, inquisitive lip. She watched him jingle his bit, sending it from one side of his mouth to the other with his long, sticky tongue. Markland Hill was not far from the real country, and as a child she had often ridden her pony out to the farms, helping with the animals, loving every minute. And of course, country life reminded her of Tarot.

She had thought of Tarot a lot since arriving at the farm. From Tarot she had first learned that deep, abiding affection for the countryside which was now so much a part of her. Living in the heart of a big city had not reduced that love; rather it had deepened it so that she found herself yearning for the old house on Markland Hill, with the great trees and hedges which had cut the Ripley-Trewins off from the ordinary life of other people. There at least she had been able to have her pony, her dogs and cats, without fearing for their lives, as she would have done had she tried to introduce an animal into the Cheetham Hill establishment. And there, although the town had been only a short walk away, she had felt as though she were in the country, the green of grass always nearer than the grey of pavements.

She had been tempted, sometimes, to go back. To stand outside The Limes and see what they were like, the family who had bought the old place. But those days had ended with her parents' death, and her separation from Dickie meant that she felt an intruder in Bolton now, a spy in the camp which had once been so very much her own.

And what of her marriage, her husband? She never thought of either, not any more. They were a part of her past she preferred to forget. Only occasionally did her thoughts return to the quiet of the large house with its open views, the meadows opposite the front gates, the air of being somehow superior to the rest of the world.

Lying in bed now, listening to the quiet sounds floating in through the open window, it occurred to Madeleine that despite the hardships of her present life, this short break excepted, she was a happier and more comfortable person than she had been in Victoria Road. She had recently bumped into an old friend from Bolton, Fay Justian, and Fay had almost passed her by.

'I never would have recognized you,' she kept saying. 'I couldn't believe my eyes! Is that little Madeleine Stead-man, I asked myself, as you walked towards me. No, it's just someone rather like, I thought, someone with fairer hair, rosier cheeks . . . more *life*, somehow, Madeleine.

Well, my dear, separation obviously suits you. What's his name?'

Madeleine had not understood. She had frowned, pulling a strand of hair across her mouth, uneasily chewing it. What on earth could Fay mean? Whose name? She repeated the words, gazing up at Fay, who was tall and dark and Jewish and great fun, too. It crossed her mind that she had been every sort of fool to have ignored her friends for so long, but it was because of the war, and a kind of dread of bringing Dickie down on herself.

'What's his name, Fay? I don't know what you mean.'

'Well, my dear, when I see a woman whose beauty has doubled, with animation in her expression instead of lethargy and boredom, then I usually assume there's a man in her life. Am I wrong? Don't say that little Fay's lost her touch.'

Madeleine had laughed then, relaxing, remembering all over again how nice Fay had been to her, wishing she had kept in touch after she left Victoria Road.

'I haven't got a man, if that's what you mean,' she said gaily. 'I don't need one, Fay. I'm happier on my own.'

'Ye-es, I can see that,' Fay had said, nodding slowly. 'But my gypsy blood tells me that you won't be alone for ever, Madeleine. No man can resist happiness, didn't you know that?'

Madeleine had laughed again and they had talked of other things, of Fay's successful husband, who had abandoned his business two years ago to fight for his country and was 'somewhere in the Western desert', as Fay put it, and of their two sons, David and Joe, who were away at school in Scotland, out of the way of the war, and who came home not to Fay's elegant house in Bolton but to what Fay described as a country cottage in the tiny Lancashire village of Slaidburn. Madeleine, who knew it well, thought of the cobbled pavements, the grey stone houses bowered in flowers, the smooth sweep of the moors above, the little river chuckling under the grey stone bridge, and wondered what on earth lively, intelligent Fay did with herself in such a quiet spot.

She asked Fay, who shrugged, smiling her knowing, somehow old-fashioned smile.

'I'm only there in the school holidays, remember. The rest of the time I'm in Bolton, and you'd be surprised at how useful I am. ARP warden, fire-watcher, leading light of the WVS – that's me. And when I'm with the boys, I relax. I help with country things like haymaking, have a drink down at the *Hark to Bounty*, splash my money around at the local fête, dig for victory . . . well, look at my hands!'

She held them out. Madeleine remembered Fay's hands, long, slim, white, with the nails always polished, always long and perfect. Now the hands were stained, the whiteness gone, and the nails bitten down to the quick.

'I see them,' Madeleine said quietly. 'And I see more than that – my gypsy blood says that though you put a brave face on it you're desperately worried about Phil.'

Fay snatched her hands back as though she had been stung, and then smiled slowly, shaking her head.

'Oh, Madeleine, you noticed my nails! Yes, it's a hard thing to have the man you love in danger. In a way, I envy you. The only person you worry about is you, I dare say.'

Madeleine shook her head.

'I wish it were true. But there is someone whose safety keeps me awake at nights. Someone I loved, once. Only I lost touch with him.'

'Anyone I know?' Fay said lightly, and sighed when Madeleine shook her head. 'Well, I hope you find him, I'll pray for your chap when I pray for my Phil.'

The whole conversation had taken place outside the

surface shelters in Piccadilly. Buses rumbled past, and a few cars, but both women had other things on their minds and when the sirens began their familiar wail neither turned towards the shelters behind them.

'Got to get to the station,' Madeleine called, and Fay, making off in the opposite direction, had merely replied that she really must change her library books.

Now, lying in her comfortable bed, in the country herself and relishing every minute, it was fun to think of sophisticated, town-dwelling Fay in these circumstances. What a difference it's all going to make to us afterwards, Madeleine told herself. And how strange if it turns a generation of townies into country-lovers.

But it was time she was getting up. The sounds floating through the window were the sounds of people going off to work in the fields and she had no desire to lie here and be forgotten. She got out of bed, tipped water from her jug into her basin, washed, dressed and then set off down the creaking wooden stair.

At the foot of it was the kitchen. Stone-flagged floor, beamed ceiling, vast, blackened cooking range. In front of the latter, frying bacon, stood Mrs Elton. She turned as she heard Madeleine's sandals pattering down the treads, a smile already on her lips.

'Mornin', luv! How about bacon and egg, eh? Bit of a treat.'

'It certainly is, Mrs Elton,' Madeleine agreed, with watering mouth. She was always hungry now; even with the lighter work she was doing here her appetite seemed to have doubled. 'I'm honoured, aren't I?'

Mrs Elton chuckled comfortably.

'Aye, well. Did I tell you, last eve, that my lad was home? John Frederick Elton, the spit of his dad, back for a fourteen-day furlough? He'll be down in a tick, and he'll give a hand down the fields, knowing our John. He's

193

brought a friend home, an' all. Scottish chap. Neil, his name is.'

'Oh, I *see*! The bacon and eggs have come out for Neil and John, but I'm benefiting as a sort of side-effect. Right?'

Mrs Elton chuckled again, trapping a generous slice of bacon against the side of the pan so that she could break one of the large, brown eggs into the spitting fat.

'We-ell, I'd have give thee bacon and egg anyroad. How about fried bread?'

'I adore it. But I don't want to see John and Neil go short, honestly. I'd be delighted just with an egg.'

'You work just as hard as them, I reckon,' Mrs Elton said placidly, breaking another egg into the pan. 'Lay the table, there's a good girl.'

'To think I've only known you a week!'

'Mmm,' Madeleine droned. She was nearly asleep, the warmth of the sunshine and total contentment doing for her what phenobarb had lately failed to accomplish.

'But you're the sort of person I feel I've always known. I can't imagine a life without Maddie. Can you remember what life was like pre-me?'

'Quieter,' Madeleine muttered.

Her eyes were closed against the sun and she knew she was probably freckling and her nose would be a cherry but she simply could not summon up the energy to care. Sleep was hovering, warm and pink and scented, and if Neil would just stop chattering for a moment she could let go, drift away; cease, for an hour or two, to be.

'Maddie? How can you sleep when we're alone, after five whole days when Johnny never left my side? Och, it's such a waste, sweetheart!'

'Mm hmm,' Madeleine hummed with desperate politeness. Damn the lad, why couldn't he sleep as well? They had had a hectic day so far, and it wasn't over yet by a long chalk. They had helped with the haymaking all morning, had a cold meal in the harvest field, carted and built the stack all afternoon, and then begged a picnic tea from Mrs Elton to bring up here, to Fettle Hill, whilst John and one of the landgirls went into Knutsford to the flicks.

John would not have approved at all, had he not fallen heavily for the snub-nosed charms of the Eltons' newest employee, Suzie d'Abeau. She was French and had escaped from her country as a girl of sixteen, driven by the Nazi invasion down to the coast and, eventually, over to Britain in a sardine boat. She had done various jobs before deciding on the land and Mrs Elton said she was a natural, a real daughter of the soil. John admired her greatly and had gone off happily in her company.

'Oh, Maddie, don't go to sleep! Look, will you not lean on me for a wee while? Honest to God, sweetheart, if you must sleep, then do it against me.'

Madeleine shuffled nearer to Neil, half-opening her eyes in order not to miss him altogether and find herself leaning fondly on the nearest sheep. But there he was, tall, young, extremely handsome, with reddy-brown hair, reddy-brown eyes and a straight Calvinist nose. With a little sigh she snuggled against him, trying to tell herself that now they could both take a nap.

'There, my darling, is that not comfortable?' Neil's hard young arm dragged the sleep-doped Madeleine into a most uncomfortable embrace, in which her head was forced to take up the angle of one recently hanged. 'Just you go to sleep, then, if you've a mind.'

It was strange, Madeleine reflected, how being virtually commanded to do what she most desired had somehow put her off the whole idea. Without conscious volition her eyelids popped apart and her brain dredged itself reluctantly back into capability. She was just about to damn Neil heartily for thoroughly waking her up when his hand, which had been lying innocently on her shoulder, dropped. With a resolute firmness far removed from his usual rather tentative approach, Neil cupped her breast in his hand and squeezed.

Immediately all thoughts of sleep vanished; strange, violent surges of feeling travelled from Madeleine's captured breast all over her body, culminating in a rush of what she recognized, shamefully, as red-hot desire arrowing into her most intimate parts. She gasped, feeling heat darken her cheeks, and turned her head, which was lodged just under Neil's chin, into the sun-warmed V of flesh nearest her. She put her mouth, open, on that flesh and ran her tongue over it, then bit. Quite hard. At the same time her right hand grabbed wildly somewhere in the region of Neil's thigh – or that was what she meant to grab. Merely to steady herself, she thought afterwards, with no malice aforethought. Or anything.

Unfortunately, her hand grabbed a part of Neil which her mind had resolutely refused to consider until now. It was what you might call a rampant part, what was more, a part which clearly thought being grabbed was a grand idea, and one which did not come its way nearly often enough.

'Och, Maddie, Maddie!'

Neil had somehow managed to swing her round so that suddenly they were lying nose to nose on the picnic rug. Except that Madeleine's nose only reached Neil's chin, of course. But they were breast to chest, Neil having abandoned his grip of Madeleine's bosom in order to strain her hard against him.

Oh no, Madeleine's cool, calm mind remarked. Oh, dear, after all this time you surely aren't going to give in to a Scot ten years your junior who is most assuredly a virgin? Have you no pride, woman? No shame, either?

196

Unfortunately, her body did not have the necessary detachment to act upon her mind's strictures. Her body, in fact, was all but yelping with excitement. So *this* is what I've been missing all these years, it remarked, moving, lifting, swaying, so that quantities of totally unnecessary clothing could be removed. Well, why don't we get on with it, then?

And indeed, Neil, virgin or not, seemed to have picked up quite a lot of theory. He had himself and Madeleine down to sweet, sun-warmed skin in no time, and although there was a certain amount of bungling and bumbling, in less time than it takes to tell he was gathering her naked body against him, murmuring sweet love-words . . . and preparing to consummate their affair as speedily as possible.

'Oh, Maddie, haven't you the loveliest tits I ever thought to see? Oh, how soft your skin is . . . how sweet you taste! Oh, oh, I must, I must . . .'

Madeleine knew no lady should encourage a man in such a position and at such a moment, but she was beginning to realize that she was no lady.

'Go on, go on,' she urged him in a mutter against his neck. 'Don't stop!'

He obeyed, of course.

There, on the picnic rug, in the hot sunshine of early evening, Madeleine and Neil kissed and cried out and enjoyed one another.

It was a joy to make love without pain or fear, with a young and beautiful man whose hands were gentle on her and whose mouth uttered not profanities but words of love and a desperate, fond desire.

They lay still at last, looking up at the tracery of boughs above their heads, and the blue sky beyond. Neil put on his trousers, for the sake of decency he said, and Madeleine left her bra and pants where they lay and pulled on her pink and white gingham dress. Their loving done, it was cool in the tree's shade, but although they lay close, side touching side, they did not cuddle or cling.

That was delicious, Madeleine told herself. But it wasn't anything more, really, than two people satisfying a hunger in each other and themselves. It would leave no lingering hurt when they parted, no desperate urge to be together once more. It was, quite simply, a physical thing.

'Och, Maddie, you're the best girl in the world.'

'You're not so bad yourself.'

His hand came out, smoothing her cheek, a gentle, affectionate gesture.

'Will you marry me, Maddie?'

'Well, no, Neil. I'm older than you, and besides we scarcely know each other.'

'Oh. I see.' He was trying to sound disappointed but Madeleine could hear the relief in his deep young voice. 'Och well, if that's the way of it . . . but I love you, Maddie.'

'Yes, but only for now, for the war. In peacetime, Neil, you'll find yourself someone who'll suit you a good deal better than I can. And besides, I told you, so far as I know my husband's still alive.'

'Aye, I remember now. I say, can . . . I mean, if I come to your room . . . I'm only here for three more days.'

'That would be lovely,' Madeleine said frankly. 'I can't think of anything I'd like more.'

'Thanks,' Neil said, his voice awed. 'Was I no so bad then, Maddie? Did I do okay by you?'

'It was grand,' Madeleine said honestly. 'You're . . . you're awfully good.'

She felt a fool saying it, as though pronouncing on an essay a pupil had written, but it was all right. She stole a sideways glance at him, to see him smiling, his eyes shining.

'You were awfu' good yourself, wee Maddie. I must say, it's fine to know what the fellers go on and on about – even to know *why* they go on and on,' Neil admitted. 'Will we sleep now, then? I'm really very tired.'

He sounded surprised. Madeleine, who was having difficulty keeping her eyes open, thankfully closed them and cuddled up to him, putting her head down on the broad young chest, smooth beneath her cheek as a baby's bottom.

He was a nice young man, Madeleine thought, a lovely, innocent young man, and he was lucky to have fallen into the hands of a woman who wouldn't take advantage of all that innocence.

'Yes, let's go to sleep, Neil,' she whispered. 'Morning comes soon enough.'

This time, she recognized the symptoms. She was sick before breakfast, her breasts ached, her stomach felt as full before a meal as after.

But this time she was older, and she had known the risk and hoped, in her heart, that she might bear a child.

She was sad when she heard that Neil had been posted missing when his fighter had plunged out of the sky, but only sad for him, not herself. She would have this baby and be a proper mother to it, but she had no intention of marrying anyone. She had put divorce proceedings into the hands of a solicitor, but despite the fact that Dickie was openly living with another woman the war held things up, and she was not particularly sorry.

Once bitten, twice shy, she told herself, stoically walking the empty streets one night, for she was fire-watching when she wasn't doing her ARP work.

But she had had to change her job; her lathe at the

factory had involved too much heavy work for her present condition so she had reluctantly given in her notice and gone to work in a large factory making small and fiddly wireless parts for the Air Force.

Lizzie worked at the bench by her side. The funny thing was that they were both pregnant, now. Lizzie's Alex had come home on leave and Lizzie's baby was due four weeks after Madeleine's.

The two girls managed their lives efficiently. They rushed off to work leaving most of the housework 'till later', came home and started on their ARP duties, or fire-watching, or, if they had an evening at home, knitting for their babies, and never exchanged so much as a cross word.

I wonder what it will be like when the babies are born, Madeleine thought now, her booted footsteps ringing out into the frosty dark as she walked along Heywood Street, glancing automatically up at the windows to check the blackout as she went. How will we manage in our little flat, with four instead of two? Well, in only another six weeks or so for me and ten for Liz, we'll find out!

It was a very cold night, and still; you could hear a pin drop, Madeleine reflected. She glanced at the luminous face of her watch in the faint starlight and realized that she would make it back to headquarters in nice time for a cup of tea before going home to bed. Sometimes she wondered how much longer she should work, but the consensus seemed to be that she should go on for as long as she could, and although she had periods when she was so tired she felt scarcely capable of putting one foot in front of the other, most of the time she was fit and energetic.

However, she was getting cumbersome. Lizzie, tossing her hair back and screwing up her eyes to calculate, had announced that she did not intend to work after seven months, and since Madeleine knew that her seven months had come and gone she supposed that she really should give in her notice. Still, she would leave it a day or so; perhaps at the end of the week . . .

Somewhere, far distant, a car cruised the streets, the first sound Madeleine had heard for what seemed like hours. Ahead of her, as she turned the corner into Bellot Street, she saw a lightening of the sky, a sign that dawn was on its way.

Suddenly, she was aware of a great lassitude waiting to pounce. Tiredness was something you took for granted now: pale faces, gaunt grey men leaving the nightshifts, people doing jobs all day and voluntary work half the night. Everyone looked worn out . . . how much longer could they all go on?

But the tide was turning; everyone said so. Soon, the RAF boys said, the boot would be on the other foot. When she heard the queer, echoing drone of bombers overhead, they promised, it would be our chaps coming home or going out and not Jerry attacking.

It may not come soon, then, the finish, the peace we all long for, but it's getting closer. What was it Churchill had said a few months earlier? *This is not the end. It is not even the beginning of the end. But it is, perhaps, the end of the beginning.*

Madeleine heard another car as she turned into Cheetham Hill Road, turned and saw it hugging the pavement, a lone man at the wheel. He slowed when he spotted her, leaning across to open the passenger window. She slowed too, recognizing the man as a doctor at the Northern Hospital. He could not have known her in her tin hat and uniform overcoat, but he smiled anyway.

'Hello! I wonder if you could help me? I'm a doctor, on a call . . . I'm looking for Wordsworth Avenue.'

'Go back and take the . . . oh, I think it's the third or

201

fourth right turn, on to Huxley Avenue. Then take the third left, into Galsworthy. The one you want is the second on your right.' His name came to her as he was thanking her. 'It's a pleasure, Dr Emmett – someone ill, or is it a baby?'

He peered at her, then grinned.

'You young women all look alike under those ghastly hats! Mrs Trewin, isn't it? Yes, it's a baby on its way. How are you?'

'Fine. You'd best get a move on, then.'

The doctor did a big U-turn in the empty road, then wound down his own window to call softly across the space between them.

'Should you still be working at nights, Mrs Trewin? Pop in and see me, and we'll have a chat.'

Nice man! Horribly overworked, probably horribly underpaid, and well past normal retirement age. Yet he still had time for her, would probably advise her to stop work and put her feet up for a few weeks whilst he, older, more tired, infinitely more valuable, worked on.

I'll go and see him, though, Madeleine told herself, beginning the long walk back to headquarters and that longed-for cup of tea.

'Fun, to retire together.'

Madeleine, who had been crying, snuffled into her handkerchief and tried to agree as the two girls walked away from the factory for the last time. It was the sort of day when sadness seems more apt than high spirits, with a leaden grey sky and a cold wind, bringing on its breath fine snowflakes which whirled briefly before settling in a very come-to-stay way on pavement, hedge and tarmac.

'Oh, come on, Maddie, just think! We'll still be doing our stint with the ARP, we help in the WVS centres, we

202

serve troops in the canteen . . . and you've only got five weeks to go! Do cheer up – what on earth's the matter?'

'I'll miss the girls,' Madeleine said. But she shoved her damp hanky into her overcoat pocket, sniffed defiantly, and then mounted her bicycle, smiling at Lizzie as she did so. 'You're right. I'm being a complete idiot . . . it was just that they were so kind!'

Both bicycle baskets bulged with presents, for it had transpired that every girl in their department had made something for her colleagues' babies. Beautiful little dresses and romper suits, tiny cardigans and cobwebby shawls, clothing sufficient for the next twelve months, had been shyly handed over and Madeleine, who had grown used to independence and even a sort of loneliness, had been overcome by such generosity.

Lizzie, equally delighted, had taken it in her stride, however. Now she spoke bracingly as the two of them wobbled up the long slope of hill which leads from the city centre towards the northern suburbs.

'Yes, I know. But think what we can do with all this stuff! Oh, I know we'll need lots of it, but you know that kid Beattie we felt so sorry for . . . I bet she'd be delighted with some of these things.'

Madeleine, agreeing, thought again of the pale-faced schoolgirl sitting alone on a long bench at the hospital, waiting her turn to see the doctor. It was impossible to believe that such a babe could be pregnant – until she stood up and you saw her thin little girl's frame distorted by her distended stomach.

The other girls had not bothered with her, but Lizzie had gone over at once.

'Hello . . . when's your baby due? Are you going to have it here, or at home? My friend Maddie and I are having ours in hospital because we've only got a tiny flat . . . what's your name?'

'Beattie,' the girl had muttered, hanging her head. She had long, pale hair which swung forward, hiding most of her face, but the rest bloomed poppy-red. 'I don't have a home here. I'm from . . . away.'

Cast out. Not yet fourteen, tricked by pity into giving, immediately abandoned by the young man, sent away by her parents to give birth in secret. Poor Beattie. Another of war's unlikely little victims.

She came from Wales, a good chapel family, mother distraught, father disgusted. The baby would be adopted, she had agreed to that . . . oh, but she was afraid!

They did their best to dispel that fear, Madeleine and Lizzie, but not by ridicule or false tales.

'We're scared as well,' Lizzie said. 'But I reckon we'll get through it, and once it's over we can all go back to normal again.'

'Yes,' Beattie had whispered. 'But . . . people die, having babies.'

'Not these days,' Madeleine had asserted stoutly. 'Now they take great care of mums, just you see.'

Beattie had looked at them through her hair, her light grey eyes reminding Madeleine of a puppy found abandoned, long ago, wanting to believe it was now secure but not quite daring to do so.

'Is that true? I think I can bear pain . . . if only someone I knew could be there!'

'We'll ask if one of us can stay with you,' Madeleine said, though without much hope. Hospitals were short of beds, short of staff, short of essential medical supplies. She doubted whether they would countenance a stranger's being present at a birth, but they could at least try and it was good to see Beattie's eyes warm with hope, her lips smile.

So now, cycling up the hill, saving her breath, Madeleine thought about the pleasure in store for Beattie, and was doubly glad of the beautiful, carefully made clothing. At least she and Lizzie had earned good money, had some put by, and would work again. Their children would not go short. But poor little Beattie, what had she to hope for? An easy birth, a pretty baby who would be quickly adopted, and then a return to the tiny Welsh village and a life of lies for the sake of the parents she had never loved and now feared.

'I'm going to walk,' Lizzie panted from the rear. She had never taken to cycling though she had little choice but to use her bike most days.

'Oh, all right,' Madeleine said good-humouredly, dismounting. She could have gone on for another forty or fifty yards, but what was the point, really? So she began to push her bicycle, heading homewards.

It was early evening and the roadway was full of cyclists, with the odd car and a good few buses. When Madeleine saw that Lizzie had fallen well behind she stopped, one hand to the small of her back, and waited for her friend, her eyes roaming incuriously over the traffic. A bus, bound for Bolton, drew slowly past her. It was crowded with people, mostly reading papers or staring rather vacantly before them, but a few did glance out, their eyes falling on the two pregnant girls pushing their bicycles. Madeleine glanced in, wondering if she might see someone from the old days – Fay, or Mrs Tuddnam, or old Mr Lofting, who had been her father's gardener and had once argued fiercely with the young Madeleine over the rights and wrongs of autumn pruning of roses.

Tarot. Sitting against the window. Unmistakable. Unchanged, almost. Hair cut, obviously, because he was in RAF uniform, the hair now curling crisply across his scalp, his dark eyes focused on something he held in one hand, a book, or a letter.

Madeleine screamed. She threw her bike down in the

205

roadway and jumped over it, reached out to heave herself aboard . . . and the bus moved. It had never stopped but it had slowed almost to walking pace. Now, however, it gathered speed with Madeleine grimly gripping the pole, one foot scrabbling for a hold, not finding one, then running . . . how she ran, because she could not give up, dared not give up . . . she must get on the bus and find Tarot. She heard someone call out . . . her fingers lost their grip but she ran anyway, unable to accept defeat.

And then the bus was too far away to hope to catch it, and the road was uphill all the way. She slowed. Sweat was running down the sides of her face, trickling from beneath her armpits, soaking into her undies. She felt a fierce and terrible stabbing pain in her breast, her side, and then saw the road rushing up at her, was suddenly aware of swirling snowflakes which were no longer white but black and red, bigger, more frightening, than anything she had ever seen before.

The road smacked into her face, breast and knee. It hurt badly and all the breath was knocked out of her and the red and black snowflakes whirled faster and faster, until they filled her vision.

Far away, someone was calling her . . . Maddie, Maddie! It was not Tarot, so it did not particularly matter. Someone heaved at her and the pain was terrible, worse than anything she had ever imagined, worse than child-birth. She opened her mouth and wailed, her voice faint and cold as the snowflakes which she felt, now, on her face. She was having the twins, only Nanny Evans was out and she must have followed her into the snow. She would take better care of the babies this time . . . don't punish me, God, for what I did last time; I was only a child myself. Let me have another chance, let me be good to my little ones, show me I'm right to believe you to be a merciful God.

Someone was crying, weeping, imploring the pain to go away, but it came in great waves, crashing down on her, invading her body and snatching her soul away, taunting her with her helplessness. Once, she became aware of a room, lights bright overhead, and a woman holding both her hands, telling her to push.

Push? Push what? Why? But she could not question, could only cringe and weep as the black and red snowflakes whirled once more and the pain enveloped her.

Where was the bus? Where was Tarot? Why had he not seen her, sensed her presence?

'Tarot, Tarot,' she called, and someone asked if he was a Pole and that should have made her laugh but she cried, instead. Because Tarot didn't come, though she had almost found him, almost touched him.

'. . . have to give her something,' someone said at one point, out of the whirling flakes. '. . . gone on too long. . . no reserves left.'

'. . . about the baby?'

'Too late . . . more important now . . . pass me that . . .'

A moment's pause, then incredible pain. And the whirling flakes all turned black and carried Madeleine down into oblivion.

'Maddie? You're all right, love. It's all over – you're all right.'

Madeleine heard the voice. She had heard it for what seemed like hours, now strong, now faint, but always there. It had almost tempted her back to full consciousness, but somehow she had been unable to answer its siren-summons until now.

And now, she opened her eyes.

Hospital. A certain smell which told of her whereabouts louder than any words. A feeling in her body as though she had been run over . . . aching bones, a hollow where her head should have been.

A face. Lizzie.

'Hello, Liz. What's happened?'

Lizzie had a bright face, laughing eyes. But now her eyes were sad, her smile tugged uncertainly at her lips.

'It's all right, Maddie. It's all over and you're fine.'

The baby! She was having a baby . . . of course! They had left work today, the girls had given them lots and lots of little clothes, and then something had happened . . .

'The baby!'

Madeleine's hands fell on the counterpane. It was flat over her ribs, flatter over her flat stomach. So she had had the baby . . . was it a boy or a girl? Where was it? Why had they not brought it to her?

'What did I have? I don't remember . . . only pain. Liz, what was it?'

'They didn't tell me. But it's over now, Maddie. No more pain, no more waiting. In a day or two you'll come home and then . . .'

Her voice faltered, stopped. Madeleine looked at Lizzie's face and then into her eyes.

'No more baby? Is that what you're trying to say, Liz? Did I lose my baby?'

Lizzie couldn't speak, couldn't even nod. She just held very tightly on to Madeleine's hands and tears squeezed themselves out of the corners of her eyes and trickled down her cheeks. A passing nurse paused by the bed. Her fat, red-cheeked face looked practical and unemotional, but her eyes were soft and sorry.

'Poor old girl . . . never mind, there'll be other times. You shouldn't have run for the bus. In future, let it go and wait for the next.'

She walked on.

Wait for the next. What next? How many chances does

a person have, for God's sake? How many babies do I have to bear, in pain and ignorance, before I have one of my own?

Madeleine turned her head sideways on the pillow. Away from Lizzie, and from the bustling life of the ward. She remembered now that she had lost Tarot, lost his babies, lost Neil's little one. It was as if the pregnancy had never been, as if she had imagined the whole episode. Desperately, she felt across her flat stomach, as though she could will it back to roundness, to fecundity.

'Maddie? Don't do that, love, don't carry on so! We'll share mine, when it comes. And I promise you'll have a baby of your own one day.'

Madeleine smiled, nodded. Her head felt very light and odd, her body small and empty, a husk, a hollow shell. The life of the ward hummed around her, other women had babies brought to the bedside, meals were eaten, husbands visited, mothers cooed.

In the midst of them, Madeleine existed. She was no longer inhabiting all of her body but only a tiny part of it. Deep down inside she was curled up, agonizing over her loss. She was polite when she realized someone was addressing her, ate at least a mouthful of each meal delivered to her bed, even admired someone's baby when it was put into her reluctant arms.

But within she was raw with suffering and unanswered questions. My baby. What did they do with my baby? When I'm strong enough to get out of bed I'll go and find it. I dare not believe it's dead because if it is I want to die too. My baby. What did they do with my baby?

CHAPTER TWELVE

'Cup of tea, please, miss, and a sticky bun. It says fried eggs on the menu-board – are they real ones?'

Megan, in her white apron with her hair tied severely back, smiled at the young Air Force officer. Men who had been abroad, or flying from other airfields, often went a bit goggle-eyed over the variety and quantity of food available to them at the canteen down in Quiet Corner. Especially eggs. Megan, who had tasted and discarded dried eggs some three years previously, had still not quite worked out why it was not simpler to use real eggs and cut out the middleman, but as people were so fond of saying, there was a war on.

'Yes, they're real eggs. And the sausages are pretty good. Where were you stationed before Valley, then?'

The officer couldn't have been more than twenty-two or three, but he had tired and knowing eyes in his tanned face. He grinned at her.

'In furrin parts, as they say. Not many places I haven't been, if I'm honest. I'm here now, though, to see to any repairs necessary on the Yanks' bombers. Still coming in, they are – well, it's no secret. You must have seen them.'

'True. And heard them,' Megan agreed. Everyone on the island had heard the constant roar of the huge Flying Fortresses and Liberators. Everyone had known that the planes were coming in for the second front, but now that it was almost over, with Paris liberated, American troops actually crossing the Rhine and the ARP told to stand down at the end of the month, it seemed as though a great lassitude had gripped the country. They had done so much, and now it seemed as though they had won – but to what end? So many men had died, so many homes had been razed to the ground, and this was only the war in Europe. In the Pacific soldiers were still fighting, ships were still at risk, death still rained from the skies. And here on Anglesey the airman smiling at Megan still waited to be served. 'What's it to be, then? Eggs and sausages, with some beans on the side and a nice slice of fried bread?'

The young man pretended to consider, then said cheerily, 'A full house, that's me.'

Once, Megan told herself, as she filled the plate, that expression would have been as foreign to me as Japanese. But now, despite having never shone at school unless you counted her drawing, she knew all sorts of things! She did evenings in this Toc H canteen, worked at Penrhyn, on the farm Danny had been at until he went into the Navy, and if she had any spare time she manned Arthur's fish and chip van with its blackened chimney and fryer full of pungent, smoking fat. Arthur had lost a leg during the evacuation of Dunkirk, and the van, specially adapted with hand controls, had been a godsend.

Now, the men ordered their food and took it to the small tables. The buzz of talk and laughter was especially loud this evening, perhaps because of all the rumours. The end of the war! They had been promised VE Day – Victory in Europe Day – when there would be no work, no school, only rejoicing.

'What'll you do when the war's over, Meggie Prydderch?'

That was Siân, helping out behind the counter. With her buff-coloured hair tied back and her black eyes cast meekly downwards, no one would ever have guessed what a demon she was for the boys. Except the boys, of course, who seemed to know by some instinct.

211

'Go on working on the farm,' Megan said flatly. 'Go on helping Arthur with the chip van. Or I might have a try for a job in the Glyn Café. Always fancied working there, I have.'

'There's a waste,' Siân said reproachfully. 'With your looks, Megan, you could do no end of jobs on the mainland. Go to London you could, girl! Live it up, see, instead of stewing round here. Besides, they won't want you on the farm when the fellers get back. When they send the troops home and the island goes back to normal, what'll you do then, eh?'

'I told you. As for the fellers going home, what's wrong with that? Our fellers will be coming back, Siân . . . not just the fellers either, but my da and Danny.'

It had been a long time since they had seen Da, who had been torpedoed on convoy duty and brought back home in someone else's clothes with a look in his bright blue eyes which had given Megan nightmares for weeks, though he had never said a word of what had happened to him. But the Navy, it seemed, did not much care what its ratings had been through so long as they were still alive. Da had been sent down to Southampton to join his next ship and had been off to the Pacific within days. The war there was still raging and Da was still away . . . all very well to talk of homecomings, but when would Da come back? Soon, she comforted herself, picking a fat golden chip out of the basket and dipping it in salt. It must be soon!

Danny had been torpedoed, too, and had gone off with Da on the new ship as well. The two men who mattered most to her in the world were far away . . . but they did write sometimes and Megan and Mam wrote often, glad that their men were together, could speak Welsh to each other, could share their letters.

And then there was Peris. She had missed him horribly

212

when he had first joined up, and feared for him, too. She was used to the Prydderch men joining the Navy because at least they understood the sea so far as any man could, but to join the Air Force . . . well, that seemed madness!

But Peris had always been different from the others. And he had always been intrigued by aircraft, cycling over to Rhosneigr, watching the planes go out and come back, counting them, knowing when one was missing, approaching the airmen when he saw them in the streets, full of questions, intrigued by their ability to fly whether in the great lumbering bombers or the slim, fast-moving fighters.

He was a bright boy, too. Clever with figures, quick to grasp a point, with all his wits about him. Naturally, he was Megan's favourite, because she had known him in the bad old days of the children's home, but his letters were cheerful and self-confident and since he was still learning to fly and not taking part in active combat she worried about him less than she worried about the others. Peris, she always felt, was the sort of fellow who would arise from a manure heap smelling of roses.

Behind the counter, Siân was serving an airman who had asked for toasted cheese with a poached egg on top. She handed the plate over, eyes down still, then glanced up at Megan.

'Our fellers won't come back right away, though. Soon the Americans will be gone, and the Dutch down at the outer harbour . . . the Belgians, the Aussies . . . we'll have nothing to do and no one to do it with, our Megan.'

Megan thought of the times she lay awake in her bed worrying about Da, and the boys, and Danny. She looked curiously at Siân, wondering how it was that two girls, so alike in some ways, could be so different in others.

'Ye-es. But that doesn't matter to me. I'd give up a lot just to know the lads were safe. Don't you worry about them, wonder what's happening to them? Those Japs . . . they aren't human, from what I've read.'

Siân flicked toast over on to its golden side and slid the wire grid back under the grill. Then she lined up cups before the big urn, splashed milk and began to turn the tap for tea.

'Too much imagination you do have, Megan,' she said crossly. 'No sense thinking what might happen. Think it'll go well and they'll all come home, that's what I do.'

A dark-haired young man in Army uniform leaned over the counter and touched Megan's bare arm, for it was a warm evening and the canteen, filled with humanity, was hot despite the open door and windows. She turned towards him and he leaned closer, speaking almost into her ear above the noise of the customers talking and the cook's clatter.

'Turn up the wireless, there's a good lass. It should be the news any minute now.'

The wireless was already playing quite loudly enough for Megan's liking, but she appreciated the importance of actually hearing the expected announcement when it came. After all, VE Day was to be a public holiday . . . and that would mean the shops would be closed, and the canteen too, she supposed. A whole day off! It would be marvellous to get on a bus and take Mam to some quiet spot somewhere for a real break.

'*Here is the nine o'clock news, and this is Stuart Hibberd reading it.*'

It was astonishing, Megan thought, how the quiet, unemotional voice made itself heard above the din. Men fell silent, the women in the kitchen stopped clattering pans. Outside, Quiet Corner and Market Street were gay with bunting. The ships in the harbour flew every flag they could lay their hands on . . . the whole world knew,

Megan thought, that the war in Europe was over . . . when, oh when, was it to be made official?

' . . . *that tomorrow will be Victory in Europe Day and Mr Churchill will address the nation at three o'clock in the afternoon.*'

There was a concerted sigh, a queer, almost wistful little sound . . . and then of course all hell broke loose. Someone vaulted the counter, grabbed Megan and Siân and kissed them both, then careered into the kitchen where sounds of giggling, shrieks and outraged smacks told their own story.

On the customers' side of the counter men kissed WAAFs and WAAFs kissed men, to say nothing of people bursting out to shout the news to anyone outside and people bursting in to demand if it were true. When the door opened for a moment Megan could hear the ships' sirens all lowing like demented cattle, and motorists hooting their horns.

'They left it pretty bloody late, mun,' someone grumbled that evening as, the canteen closed, the staff began to clear up preparatory to going home. 'We'll not be in tomorrow, then?'

'Shouldn't think so,' Megan replied, struggling out of her overall. Presently, making her way home through the still light streets, she wondered just what she would do. The chances were Mam would refuse to let the lodgers fend for themselves, even in the interests of celebration, and nice though it would have been Megan knew that Peris would be unlikely to get leave seeing as how he had barely joined up.

What an anticlimax, after all! A cockerel crowed as she approached the house, and the last pale breeze of evening brought seabirds' cries washing across the sky.

I am lucky, Megan told herself, pushing her key into the lock and turning it, walking quietly into the darkened hall. To live in such a place, to have such a good mam and da, such grand brothers.

She listened, but the house was quiet. She always popped her head round Mam's door, though, before going to her own room. Mam wouldn't have slept sound in her bed, she often said, if she knew Megan was still out on the streets.

'Make it sound far worse than it is, you do, Mam,' Megan grumbled, but there was a laugh behind the words, and love, too. It was so good to have someone worry about you, so good to be watched and waited for.

Now, stealing quietly up the first flight, pausing on the landing by Screech's cage to make sure that no one on the first floor was wakeful still, Megan remembered the girl Marsha, the one she sort of knew, in her heart.

The only thing she'd never had and always wanted had been a sister. So she had made one up, invented her. Once, she and her sister had been close, seeing each other often, concerned with each other, but of late years they had grown more independent. The Other is very involved in her life, Megan told herself excusingly. It's only me who still needs contact now and then.

Mam's door was ajar; Megan pushed it wider, put her head round the edge. Mam was sitting up, reading by the light of a flickering candle. She put her book down and smiled at her daughter.

'There's late it's getting,' she whispered. 'Glad I am that you're safe in, love. Sweet dreams, now, and I'll let you lie in tomorrow.'

'Don't you dare get out of that bed, Mam, until I bring you a cup of tea,' Megan whispered back fiercely. 'About time it is that you had a decent rest. Now don't forget . . . I'll bring you tea, tomorrow.'

Mam leaned over and pinched out her candle's wick

with a wetted thumb and forefinger, then snuggled down under the sheet.

'You spoil me, my little one,' she whispered. 'Very well, I'll wait for the tea tomorrow . . . get our day off to a good start, eh?'

'That's right. What'll we do, Mam?'

'What would you like to do?'

'Take a picnic . . . go out all day,' Megan suggested, still whispering. 'Like to go to Moelfre, I would . . . but there won't be buses, I dare say?'

'No buses. But we'll go down to Rocky Shore and you can show me those birds you're always on about. Suppose I borrow Peris's bike? We could get right down to South Stack – it's years since I've been there.'

'Oh, Mam, we'll do something *great*,' Megan hissed. 'Sweet dreams, now. See you in the morning.'

She made her way into her own room, threw off her clothes and fell into bed. The war was over! Well, the war in Europe, at any rate.

I'll sleep well tonight, she told herself, pulling the sheet up round her ears and plugging her thumb comfortably into her mouth. Yes, I'll sleep like a child!

An hour later, she was still lying in bed staring at the moonlight on the ceiling and feeling increasingly cross with herself.

What on earth was the matter with her? She had had an exhausting day, working a full morning in the shop, then doing an afternoon's work down at the WVS centre, and finally taking on the last and hardest shift at the Toc H canteen. Usually she fell into bed and slept like a top, but tonight all she could do was lie there and wonder. Wonder about the boys, wonder about Da and Danny, even wonder about Mam and what they would do tomorrow.

Counting sheep was no remedy, because she had tried it. She had tried counting puffins too, but nothing worked. Every time she tried to let herself drift off into dreams, something hauled her back. It was as though . . . as though a telephone was ringing somewhere, and she could not quite hear it but was still aware of its ceaseless belling.

Outside, now, it was quiet. The cheers and shouting, the sirens and honking, had all died away hours earlier.

Then it came to her. Of course, it was the Other trying to get through, she who had only once in their long acquaintance connected voluntarily with Megan! Fool that I was not to recognize it, Megan told herself, and began to empty her mind.

It was not as easy as it had once been because her head was still crammed with the events of the day, with anticipation of the holiday to come and with the sort of puzzled pleasure that was all she could summon up for the official ending of the war in Europe.

Anticlimax. That was how she had felt after the announcement. She had put it down to the fact that Da and Danny would not be coming home, not yet. But now, she must listen for the Other.

Once she knew what was happening, the link-up or whatever you called it came quickly. One minute the quiet darkness, the stars outside her window, a little wind blowing softly. The next, someone weeping. Someone hunched up in a heap in a huge bed, with soft blankets and sheets made of silk.

In the dark she held out her hand, to find it immediately and firmly grasped.

'What's the matter? Why are you crying? The war's over, you know.'

'Yes, I know. A-and I've g-got to go h-h-hoooome!' The last word was a wail. 'How can I bear it? They say Manchester's been bombed so probably Bolton has too and it'll all be grim and ugly and there's hardly any food and people are miserable and worried . . . why *should* I go back to that, when I'm so happy here, and doing so well?'

'You don't want to come back, then?'

Megan heard her own voice sounding sad, almost hurt. She knew the war had been harder on the mainland than it had been here, on the island, but even so . . . why should the Other, who had been so unhappy over being sent away, suddenly want to stay, to forget her home?

'There's no more bombing, you know,' she heard herself say carefully. 'Even those beastly V1s and V2s have stopped, now that Jerry's surrendered. You'll be quite safe.'

'Safe? Who cares about being safe? I'll be a million miles away from Gary!'

'You'll be a million miles nearer me, though,' Megan said. 'And a million miles nearer your people, too.'

The hump in the bed stopped snuffling for a moment to consider this.

'Nearer you? But you're where I am, aren't you?'

Megan felt quite impatient with Marsha, whom she still thought of as the Other, mostly. How could she so totally fail to understand their relationship?

'No, I'm not where you are. I think I come when you need me, and vice versa.'

'I haven't seen much of you lately,' the girl said. Her voice was unfriendly, yet the hand which clung tightly to Megan's spoke of wanting – affection, even.

'No. You haven't needed me and I haven't needed you,' Megan said, half-sorrowful, half-glad. 'I'm growing up and I'm very happy, you see.'

'Yes. Me too. Only . . . I'm kinda scared of crossing the ocean and leaving all my pals behind. I can remember

Mummy and Daddy, but five years is a long time. I was a kid when I left, and now I'm a woman.'

'You aren't a woman any more than I am,' Megan said indignantly. 'Sixteen's not a woman; Mam says so.'

'I am a woman! But if I come home and don't get torpedoed or anything we'll be nearer, you say.'

'That's right.' Megan had no idea how she knew, but she was absolutely sure. 'You won't get torpedoed, either. The war's over.'

'Yeah, but . . . all the submarines may not know. You hear stories . . .'

'They're stupid lies,' Megan said at once. 'Come home, Marsha. Come home.'

It was strange how the summer dragged, how change never seemed to be for the better, almost as though Siân had been right and Megan wrong. The airfield was almost deserted, save for the constant roar of Liberators and Flying Fortresses leaving for their own country once more. Their job was done, Europe was in the melting pot, and peace had begun to limp, slow and weary, across the land.

Several of the girls Megan had known at the County School had moved away to the mainland, or had joined the forces. Megan got itchy feet as they did, but resolutely ignored such feelings; she owed it to Mam to stay, and Arthur's fish and chip van suddenly had competition as it puttered round the streets of Holyhead. Besides, she was waiting for Danny.

And whilst she waited, she drew, and she was beginning to see that there might be some point in her one gift. A neighbour had bought a little watercolour and she had sold similar paintings to the troops going home. One day perhaps she might be able to earn enough from her drawings to leave the chip van – the thought was a heady one. Fish smells cling.

But now, with the war ending, the farmers needed all the help they could get until the men came home. Megan worked on the farm at Penrhyn and loved it. When the war started the Army had requisitioned sixty acres of the coastal farmland; that would be coming back soon, in what sort of state they hardly dared think, but in the meantime sheep still had to be dipped and sheared, fields sown and harvested. Rationing was as bad as ever – worse – yet on the island it was the least of their worries. Food in Ireland was still plentiful, Dewi and his friends now made the voyage more frequently, and they could bring back most things without any fuss.

Mam missed Da horribly, as indeed Megan did. She had his photo by her bed but his image in her mind was clearer; the tightly curling hair, the craggy, sun-tanned face with the white lines across his forehead and round his eyes which showed when he relaxed. Oh, Da was always in her mind, always close to her heart.

Danny, of course, was there too. He was beautiful, was Danny. But the years had gone so fast and he must have changed, as she had. Suppose he didn't like her when he got back, didn't want her? She tried never to think that he and Da might not come back, because it left such a black and aching void in her mind, but she knew from Mam's occasionally tight lips and too-bright eyes that she was not the only one fighting that thought. Oh God, keep them safe, she prayed on her knees by her bed each night. Oh God, let them come home to us!

It kept her a good girl, that fear. Not that she had any desire to behave like Siân; oh dear me no! Not a man she had met attracted her as Danny did, but even if one had she would not have dared. God would punish her the way that hurt most, through Da and Danny.

So Megan waited, and prayed, and stayed close to Mam.

CHAPTER THIRTEEN

It was a bad winter, but even a bad winter should have been bearable, because Da and Danny and the others were home.

Danny had changed. Not just in looks, though he had grown taller, his shoulders very broad, his waist very narrow. Quieter, too. He seemed much older than the teasing, good-humoured Danny who had gone away. He was moody and distant and sometimes there was a wariness about him which frightened Megan, made her unsure. She knew that he and Da had had it bad, that they probably had more than their share of remembered horrors, yet most of the time Da managed to throw it off, or so it seemed to her.

Danny was different. She was sure he still loved the island but he behaved as if he were bored with it. He was really strange, meeting her for a walk and then not addressing a single word to her save for commonplaces, ignoring half her remarks and finding fault with the rest.

Megan was frightened and bewildered by the change she saw in him and ran to Mam after the first week, desperate for reassurance.

'He's not the Danny who went away, Mam,' she sobbed, her head on Mam's shoulder. 'Finds fault all the time, he does, or else says nothing. But when I look into his eyes, there's so much unhappiness and uncertainty there . . . what does he *want* from me, Mam?'

'Patience and understanding, my little one,' Mam crooned, smoothing the long, dark gold hair back from

Megan's forehead. 'Lots and lots of understanding. You see, he've been strung up and uncertain, longing for home, scared that he'd never make it. And now he is home it's not the heaven he'd remembered, it's just a place and we're all just people.'

'Are you trying to say he misses the excitement of never knowing when the ship might sink?' Megan said incredulously. 'Because if so, he'll never settle!'

'He doesn't miss it in a nice sense; he's just too used to being afraid to settle at once,' Mam said reassuringly. 'It's hard on you both, but it's hard on a lot of young people. What's more, he's got no job right now, no sense of purpose. He isn't used to doing nothing, yet he feels that the world owes him quietness. Be kind and careful, my little one, and you'll find your old friend Danny's been there all the time, underneath the crabby, difficult young feller who seems bent on making your life – and his own – uncomfortable.'

'Well, I don't know,' Megan sighed, knuckling her eyes with the backs of both hands and sitting up straight. She had gone running to Mam in the parlour and now she looked round the familiar room. The grandfather clock with the moon chasing the sun round its face and the tides ebbing and flowing. The little tables, blackened with age and gleaming with polish, the china cabinet with the tea-services brought back to Mam's mam by her father from all over the world – he had been a seaman – and the pictures, crowding the walls, some oil paintings, some prints, some beautiful, some dreadful, but all a part of the house in Newry Street and so all a part of Mam. None of it had changed in three, probably four generations; so why had Danny changed? Da seemed no different.

She voiced the thought aloud and Mam put a hand

under her chin and turned her face so that they could look into each other's eyes.

'Megan, love, I won't treat you like a child. We are two women and we have women's troubles. I won't lie to you either, and pretend that your Da is the same man that went away two years ago. He isn't, any more than Danny is. Terrible dreams he has, and impatient with me he do get when I can't understand, or answer lightly something I was meant to grieve over. He wants to come close to me again, but something stops him. He's older than Danny, so it isn't excitement he's missing. I'm not even sure what it is myself. I suppose . . . I suppose it's the better world that wars are fought for . . . they don't exist, Meggie, love, they can't exist. But there's a terrible emptiness when first you realize it.'

'But Mam, we had it hard in a way . . . blackout, and worry, and never knowing if we'd see Da and Danny again. Doesn't that count? You and me, we aren't crying for the moon.'

Mam stood up. She held out her hands to Megan, still sitting on the hard little sofa with the wooden rail and the horsehair pricking into the backs of your legs through the velvety stuff covering it. She was smiling.

'We didn't leave the island, so our expectations weren't the same. Oh, we wanted peace and prosperity, but we didn't come to believe that just by winning the war we'd find perfection. They're disappointed, can't you see? Da has to accept that I've grown older. There are lines on my face which weren't there five years ago and I've put weight on. Then there's all the old arguments, which seem pretty trivial after you've fought for your life for years . . . you know: who owns the middle allotment, who's supposed to keep the paths clear of weeds, why Williams-Bread took down the beans flanking the hedge when Evans-Post swears he planted 'em . . .'

224

'Ye-es. Now we've talked about it, I know what you mean. Da isn't his old self yet. But Danny's sulky, sort of. Drums his fingers on the table whilst I'm talking, interrupts me in the middle of a sentence, makes me feel that I'm . . . oh, trivial, of no account. It's true, I dare say, but no one wants to feel like that.'

'It's not even vaguely true, love,' Mam said comfortably. 'What it is, the men don't listen properly, like, because their minds are too full of what they'd expected to find back home. Angels twanging harps, likely, and not ordinary women who get backache and who run out of vinegar when the shops are closed and we've got fish and chips for supper.'

Megan giggled. The incident over the missing vinegar had happened the previous evening; Da's incredulous face, his cheated expression, rose in her mind's eye to surprise her all over again. How could he be so silly, her dear Da, the best man in the world? How could he have made such a fuss, made Mam cry, over something as trivial as an empty vinegar bottle?

'Oh, Mam, his face when he picked up the bottle and it was empty! Like a child, finding nothing but a hole in his Christmas stocking! Oh, I wanted to laugh . . . good thing I choked it back, eh?'

'Well, I don't know. I got down my good tomato chutney, kept since last August because he do love it, and what does he do? Says he never could abide tomato chutney with fish, which was the *biggest* lie, as you know, my little one! Oh, I had to choke back the words, no doubt of that! The times I've seen him empty half a jar of the stuff on to his plate, and gobble it up and ask for more! But no point in saying so, only hurt he would have been, believing I'd made it up to shame him or some such nonsense.'

'Then Danny will get better? If I give him time and understanding?'

Mam stood up and went over to the big palm in the window. She felt the soil, digging her fingers well in; Mam loved her plants and would not think twice about getting her hands dirty, as long as she knew the soil was damp enough. She answered without turning round, her eyes fixed on the palm leaves.

'It may be that Danny expects more than you're ready to give him, my little one. He's been a far cry from home these past two or three years, and a man can grow used to women who – who think nothing of – of making free with their favours. But of course a decent girl, a good girl, like you, love, has to behave as she's been brought up to behave and sometimes a young feller wants . . . that is to say, he may expect . . .'

Megan had stolen up behind Mam; now she put both arms tightly round Mam's ample waist and squeezed, taking pity on the older woman's obvious embarrassment, her brave desire to speak of something about which her generation had always felt ill at ease.

'Mam, it's all right. I know well what you mean, and it really isn't that. Danny . . . if he wanted what you're trying to say he might want . . . he'd say. He'd make me feel guilty – or try to, anyway. But he doesn't. I'm as sure it's not that as I'm sure Da loves us all.'

'Oh. Well, good then, good for Danny. Because I won't lie to you, little one. It's what most men want, wrap it up how they will.'

'Oh yes, I know. But there's marriage, Mam. If Danny wanted me like that we could always get married. And he just hasn't said anything, apart from finding fault, getting his old motor bike out of the shed, taking it to pieces, polishing everything and oiling everything, and then saying he'll never ride it again . . . the fun's gone,

226

he said. And Mam, he and I went out together on that old bike, and happy I was, even though I was scared. And Danny too – many a time we laughed all the way home!'

'Give him time,' Mam soothed again. 'He'll come round to accepting that the only paradise he'll ever find is the one we make for ourselves, and that's a pretty ordinary paradise, in the end. No free rides, no fairy wand, no coach and horses from two white mice and a pumpkin. Just a little home, a lot of work, and the person you love to give you a kiss and a cuddle when the day's toil is done.'

'There's poetic!' Megan said, giving her mother another hug. 'Do you think Danny will settle for that, though, Mam?'

Rhiannon looked down lovingly at her girl, so beautiful, with the curtain of dark gold hair falling forward over one shoulder, the big, pansy-blue eyes staring straight into hers and the trembling of her soft, bee-stung lips. Was there a prettier girl in the world, she wondered, or a better? She would not lie to her, not for anything.

'I don't know, my little one,' Rhiannon said slowly, now. 'But if not, he isn't the feller for you, and he's not the feller I think him. It could be that the sort of life he's been living has spoiled him for the simple things; only time can tell us that. Now give over cuddling me and let's be getting the tea, eh?'

'Look at the bluebells, Marsha! I bet there was nothing like that in the States! Aren't they a picture?'

Marsha saw the misty blue beneath the trees, the misty green above, and reminded herself that it was scarcely Mummy's fault if she knew nothing about the breathless beauty of some parts of Long Island. Here, she realized, they thought of New York as a vast conurbation spreading out indefinitely, crushing the countryside. They had no idea that spring had as much significance to an American citizen as it did to his British counterpart, and that God's Own Country was not just a parroted phrase but a reality. Marsha thought of her home on Long Island, the old, grey stone farmhouse with its lichened shingles nestling amongst the trees, the long white beach before it, empty, washed by wind and sea.

'Well, darling? Aren't they the most beautiful things you've ever seen?'

Mustn't tell her about fall in the States, Marsha reminded herself, when the breathtaking colours stun the eye, when the scents in the woodland, so rich and varied, had made autumn her favourite time of year.

'Uhuh, they're very pretty. Is it much further, Mummy? I could just about eat a horse, saddle and all.'

Eleanor Loxley laughed, but uneasily. She and Marsha were driving back from the port of Liverpool, where the great liner had just docked, returning large numbers of evacuated children to their home country. Unhappy children, many of them, who had been in America so long that they could scarcely remember their own place nor their own parents.

When Marsha had left, Mummy had always been driven by Daddy or by a chauffeur. But throughout the war years she had driven other people – first a captain, then a general, then lots of other high-ranking officers. Now she leaned back in her seat, one beautifully manicured hand lightly grasping the wheel, and drove – you could tell – without thinking about it at all, effortlessly.

It wasn't only the driving which made her a stranger, of course. She was so self-confident now, so brisk! Gone the languid worrier, the sweet, anxious woman who had always asked her husband's advice before the most trivial act. She wore clothes, now, which she would not have

228

dreamed of wearing before the war – trousers sometimes, she told Marsha, and laughed when Marsha stared.

'Don't be so po-faced, darling,' she said, swinging the car expertly round a sharp bend. 'Trousers are such practical garments; why should men have them all to themselves? Besides, though Daddy really doesn't approve, he's come to realize that since I'm the one wearing them, I'm the one who has the last word.'

Marsha might have said something hurtful then, out of shock, not intent, but they were still in Liverpool and she had glanced at the street which she remembered from her last day in England more than five years earlier.

The street wasn't there, or not enough of it to recognize. She frowned; where were the tall buildings, the tree-lined square? Where the handsome Victorian office blocks with their intricate stonework, their sooty façades?

'Gone,' Mummy said briefly, when Marsha asked. 'You heard about the blitz, didn't you? Liverpool was almost flattened, you know. And you'll see changes in Manchester, too, though Bolton was luckier.'

It had silenced Marsha for several miles. She had heard about the blitz – but this! This wicked wasteland where once beautiful buildings had raised proud heads? This . . . this emptiness? She had imagined nothing so total, nothing like the piles of half-cleared rubble where kids played and already willowherb pushed its pink blossoms towards the sky.

'Bomb sites, they call them,' Mummy was saying instructively. 'It must seem terrible to you, darling . . . well, it was terrible . . . but I just tell myself that we're being given a wonderful opportunity to make things better. No need for slum clearance in some cities – the Jerries did it for us. But we've got to work together to see that the developers don't just build new slums – to make architects and planners and government take notice of us this time and get it right for a change.'

This was Mummy speaking . . . Marsha almost gaped.

'Yes, I see,' she murmured, however. 'What does Daddy think of it all?'

Immediately the friendly, informal atmosphere in the car seemed to chill. Eleanor, who had been driving with her eyes on the road and a little smile on her lips, glanced quickly at Marsha and then back again, but the smile had gone and there was a crease between her fair brows.

'Ah, Daddy. Well, I think you'll find Daddy rather changed, darling. Oh, he's still his old lovable self underneath, but . . . he's been away for a long time, you see, in charge of a very mixed group of men. Fighting in the jungles of Burma was the worst sort, and Daddy lost lots of men he was attached to. He had to write a lot of letters . . . he visited families when he came home, explaining how their men had died . . . it's made him seem rather grim, rather quiet. But he'll get over it, they all will, and we women have to help, darling, by being very understanding, very sensible.'

'I'll do my best,' Marsha said, but inside she felt like screaming. Why had they insisted that she come home, to this? To a changed mummy, a changed daddy, and a country that was flattened, beaten, rationed and crushed, even though it appeared they had won the war? She had been so very happy in the States, she had been doing so very well! And then, of course, there were her friends over there, all of whom would miss her horribly, and whom she, in her turn, would miss.

And there were the boys, coming back. She was deeply interested in young men right now, wanted to know lots and lots, enjoy herself whilst she was young. Not spend her time being tactful and understanding to Daddy and a little helper to Mummy, living frugally, doing without so that someone, somewhere, could replace the shattered buildings, repair the shattered lives.

'I'm sure you'll be very good for Daddy,' Mummy said now. Her voice sounded rather doubtful, Marsha thought. 'The thing is, darling, that what he went through has made him . . . well, rather odd. Church bells, for instance.'

'What about church bells?'

'He doesn't like them. The first week he was home he . . . well, he cried every time he heard the bells ring. And sometimes he wakes in the night and thinks he's somewhere else . . . somewhere in the jungle, I suppose. It could be a bit frightening if you weren't used to it. I mean, if you met him on the landing or anything . . .'

'I'll stay in my room,' Marsha said promptly. She had no desire to meet a sleep-walking Daddy lashing out at imaginary Japs with a bayonet! 'Mummy, are you trying to say that Daddy's gone a bit doolally?'

'Bless you, love, no!' Mummy said brightly. 'Or no more than most of the troops who came home after bad combat experiences. I didn't mean to worry you, but you're a young woman now, and you'll understand more than you did when you went away.'

'Yes, I'm nearly eighteen,' Marsha agreed. 'I've always got on well with Daddy. I'm sure it'll be all right.'

But she wasn't sure. Not by a long chalk.

The house was the next shock. It had not been bombed, but soldiers had been billeted there and it was . . . oh, battle-weary, Marsha supposed. Floors which had gleamed were scratched and scruffy from the tread of Army boots, paintwork was dirty, wallpaper peeling. The lawn had been dug up and potatoes planted, the asparagus beds were knee-deep in weeds, the flowers were all gone.

Never a gardener herself, Marsha noticed chiefly because she had remembered the garden's perfection so clearly, the smoothly shaven lawns furred with dew on bright summer mornings, the trees drooping new leaves as May burgeoned.

All changed now, neglected, allowed to die. In the walled vegetable garden there was order still, because old Mr Besdale had continued to plant and reap, but the vegetables were mundane – cabbage, potatoes, rows of broad beans. No delicious asparagus, no raspberry canes taller than a child's head, no Indian corn for Daddy to eat with his fingers, butter running down his chin.

Even the peach trees, the pears, apples, plums, had not been pruned or shaped, so though the trees would still bear Mr Besdale said it would be a year or two before they produced at the pre-war level.

Pre-war! It sounded very odd to Marsha. And then she had been taken into Manchester because Mummy wanted just one decent dress, and had been appalled by the bomb damage there. Market Street flattened, Deansgate in ruins . . . and perhaps worst of all, Mummy taking it so for granted, as though everyone knew and accepted this enormous change in their lives.

And the people. Returning soldiers with nightmares behind their eyes, skin darkened by tropic suns, or pale and emaciated survivors from prison camps. And those who had remained at home had fared little better. Strained eyes, pallid faces, drooping shoulders, all told their own story. When Marsha thought about the people back Stateside, the contentment, the good health, the lovely, smiling confidence of young and old, all of Britain made her cross. They had won, hadn't they? Then why on earth didn't they show it in their expressions, instead of looking so worried all the time?

Then, of course, she had found out about clothing coupons. You could not have the dress you wanted and could afford, the dress which made you look a million dollars

– all right, the dress which made you look mahvellous, dahling – unless you had the correct number of coupons, and the wretched allowance had just been cut, even with the war won, by a thumping twenty-five per cent!

And Daddy *was* strange, for all Mummy tried to pretend it was what happened to all the men returning from jungle warfare. When Daddy had an after-lunch nap he would whimper and thrash about, shouting aloud sometimes and bringing himself awake in a sweat of terror and embarrassment. Or she would notice tears running down his cheeks in the middle of a perfectly ordinary conversation, so that she did not know where to look, was forced to turn away, make some excuse to leave the room.

And the food was awful – diah, dahling – and there wasn't enough of it and when she suggested they might try the black market, which everyone knew about and most people with money used, Daddy had the most awful shouting fit and said his men hadn't died to let a spoilt little madam cheat on their wives and kiddies.

Marsha had been the one to cry then, and Mummy shouted too, and then Daddy cried . . . and how bitterly Marsha regretted ever getting on the ship and coming home and how she longed for that pre-war life which she had sometimes missed even amidst the fleshpots of New York.

Once or twice she thought about the Other, and wondered how she was getting on – except that she wasn't a real person, she was just a figment.

But at nights, when she was lonely and frightened and missed Uncle and Aunt so badly that she wept, she emptied her mind to let the Other in, figment or not. And the Other came to her, and they held hands, and they both grieved and worried without a word said. And felt better, afterwards, for the sharing of these bad moments, though it was only in their minds and in the desperate tightness of their grasping hands that the worries manifested themselves, because now that they were so old – eighteen very shortly – and both on the same side of the ocean, it seemed to have become impossible to exchange even the most mundane words.

Mummy said it was a bad time for everyone, and that they would all get through it if they believed in God and made allowances and loved each other. She said that Marsha must remember the country had spent every waking moment working to keep itself fed, to keep its troops supplied and to manufacture the weapons of war which would ultimately defeat the Third Reich. She said that in a year or perhaps less they would not need rationing and people would be less stressed. Life would be good once more, perhaps better because of the suffering which had gone before.

It sounded good when Mummy put it like that, and it was definitely possible – it had to be possible, or why had they bothered to fight at all? One day they really would find the Promised Land that the soldiers had died for. Mummy was convinced it was coming.

But Marsha doubted it.

CHAPTER FOURTEEN

'Well? Do you want to come or not?'

Danny heard the brusque note in his own voice and for a moment he felt as angry with himself as he was with Megan. But then she glanced up at him with that familiar puzzled look and his incipient pity for her was lost in impatience. Why could she never make a decision, for God's sake? Why did she always hesitate? He knew his own attitude had something to do with it, but wasn't he entitled to behave a bit badly after years of war? Why should Megan, who had stayed at home and got even lovelier, think she was entitled to understanding or even sympathy from a man who had suffered as he had?

He had been aboard two torpedoed vessels and had been one of the lucky ones both times. For the last nine months of the war he had been haunted by the chances of a third hit, a third tempting of fate. Could he possibly expect to get away that easily from the gods of wind and water who had twice almost had him in their grasp? No, of course he couldn't. It was just a matter of when the next blow would fall.

But the war had ended and he was still alive. He was back on Holy Island, the place he loved most in the world, and he was still Danny, with his mind, heart and body intact. Stronger, even, after the long struggle.

Yet he still waited for the dreaded moment when he would overstep some small god's private mark and bring retribution down on his head. When would the blow fall? When would all his hopes and dreams be scattered by a falling bomb or a stray bullet, or the strangling arms of the deep salt sea? He had expected to pay for his life by losing Megan, yet Megan was waiting for him, her eyes shining with love, her beautiful body still his if he chose to take it.

So why could he not accept this gift the gods had offered him? Peace, his own place, his woman? Something deep within him, some old, unhappy superstition, came between him and contentment, assuring him with every breath drawn that one day he'd pay. He might have escaped so far, but one day . . .

He tested Megan constantly, expecting to find her wanting. She would confess to having gone with a Yank, or she would tell him she was in love with someone else, or she would simply move away from Holyhead and the tall house in Newry Street, fed up with him and his unhappiness which must seem to her to have no real cause.

Yet here she still was and he had been home months now. Summer was coming and he hadn't settled to a job and yet she remained patient with him, and gentle. Loving, even, when he would allow her to be so.

'I'll come then, Danny.'

He had been so sunk in his own thoughts that he stared at her, speechless, for a moment. What in hell had they been talking about? What did she mean, she'd come? She smiled up at him, the mischievous look suddenly very much in evidence. He remembered it lovingly from long ago, when he had never doubted her, never doubted himself. Dear God above, why must he doubt now?

'I do believe you've forgotten what you asked me, Danny! You said you were going to take a look around Rocky Coast and did I want to come. And I do. Despite the fact that you managed to sound as though you'd only invited me because teacher said you must.'

'Oh,' Danny said rather blankly. So she did notice that

he was . . . the way he was. 'Well, let's get a move on, then.'

He loved taking her on the motor bike. He loved the feel of her soft cheek resting on his back, her arms tightening round his waist. And the bike gave him once more, for the duration of the time he was astride it, the masculine surge and urge which he wanted but seemed to lack.

But he could not tell her so. He dared not be nice to her because fate would not allow him to have what he wanted; he knew it in some dark part of his mind. If he had Megan then fate would cry 'Too much!' and would snatch from him . . . what? His sturdiness of body, his strength of mind? He did not know; he only knew that his luck had been overstretched, overstrained. Now it must be nurtured, cosseted, in case it turned on him, used its sharp blade to cut him off from all he held dear.

Carefully, Danny straddled the bike, waiting for Megan to climb on behind him. They were on the green above the outer harbour and it was a glorious May day. In normal circumstances he would have been working on the land – not a proper job, just helping out – but he had taken a day off. A real job, now – would that give him back his self-respect, if it was self-respect he lacked? But he did not think he could work in an office, and though he had been offered a job on the cross-channel ships he knew he would never work in an engine room again. He had had a bellyful of that during the war, and now he must be free, in the open air.

He coasted the bike down the green slope on to the road, then started her, the roar of the engine vibrating through him, bringing confidence with its burst of power. He shouted to Megan to hold tight and then they were off, the wind tearing at them, Megan clinging like a limpet, the petrol tank sending up its glorious smell of fuel, metal and hot rubber to tease and delight him.

237

It was not far to Rocky Coast. When they reached the wilderness of the clifftops, the rough grass sewn with spotted orchids, the gorse in golden blossom, he drew the bike to a halt and leaned it on a rocky outcrop. He came here often, now, because of the wild life and because here he felt no demands on him. He could lie on the grass and watch the birds, who had flown away at his approach, gradually forget him, return. Then they would display, court, battle even. And make love.

Girls expected you to make love to them in a quiet spot like this. Even Megan? No, not Megan, he decided, holding out a hand and getting immense pleasure from the feel of her cool fingers in his. She was wearing a faded cotton dress and old school sandals. The heavy weight of her dark gold hair tumbled between her face and his, but he knew her so well that he could guess just how she was looking. Eyes downcast to check on the uneven ground, skin dusted adorably with golden freckles, even the soft lips parting slightly to show the tip of her tongue as she picked her way amongst the rocks and gorse.

'Stop!' He hissed the word dramatically, pulling back on her hand. 'See?'

Two stonechats, a cock and a hen. The cock perched on the very tip of a bramble, its impudent eye cocked, its stone-drilling call loud in the still air. The little hen was lower down the same bramble, gazing up at her lord and master as though she had never heard anything lovelier than his odd little song and could not wait for the moment when she might applaud.

'Oh, how pretty! Are they rare?'

Danny laughed and squeezed her hand. Rare! Wasn't she a little sweetheart sometimes?

'Stonechats. No, not rare, but favourites of mine.'

They stood until the birds flew off and then Danny pulled her over to a convenient outcrop and sat her down.

238

'Stay here quiet and we'll see what comes.'

It was good to sit in silence on the grey nose of rock amidst the scented heather and gorse. Danny had his old binoculars round his neck and through them he found the birds and showed them to Megan. Her response was the best kind for she had a quick eye and an immediate appreciation of what she saw.

'See that? Long-tailed tit. Wonder if he's nesting? Don't often see them round here. Pretty, isn't he?

'And that. Goldcrest. Tiniest bird in Britain. Now I'll bet they're nesting. We'll have a quick look whilst they're searching for food, but we can't risk disturbing them by going too near.'

Together Danny and Megan made a nest of their own in the long, pale grasses and lay side by side, peering out at the life around them. A snake passed, its hard, bright eyes sending a shiver down Megan's spine. A tiny mouse scuttled between the bracken stems. And always there were birds, now landing on a bough so heavy with May blossom that even a robin's small weight sent the petals scattering, now rising in a cloud to dazzle and scold at a kestrel which had dared to hover over their gorse-scented hillside.

Drowsy at last, Danny laid down the binoculars and put an arm round Megan's shoulders. She snuggled closer and Danny rolled on to his back, carrying her with him, pillowing her head on his breast, knowing a moment of total, untroubled happiness.

A quiet girl was his Megan. A peaceful sort of girl, not the sort to bother a fellow with expectations which, for some reason he could not understand, he could not fulfil. He could cuddle her and kiss her smooth skin without either of them getting all hot and bothered, without feeling that he was letting her down by not wanting to go further.

The sun slanted golden through the grass; he had meant to take her down to the shore which was so beautiful that he had dreamed about it in his stuffy, smelly bunk somewhere on the Pacific Ocean. He closed his eyes, feeling the sun warm on his face, and saw behind his lids the freshwater fall as it cascaded down the cliffs, bringing fresh green to the salty rocks, ending its swoop in a flurry of white where it splashed into the natural basin at the cliff's foot.

There were big pools down there when the tide was out. Sea anemones, urchins, all sorts could be found there. He had planned to scramble down the cliff face, to show her the oddities, watch her wide-eyed wonder, her fresh and innocent enjoyment of things she had not seen before.

And the seabirds! Another day he would take her to Cemlyn, to the ternery. She would love that, love seeing the small, delicate birds so aptly named sea-swallows, as they forked the air, darting, swooping. They could go now, come to that.

He turned to her to suggest it, and saw she was asleep.

Danny looked down at her and felt tears come, unbidden, to his eyes. That she should trust him so, he who was disturbed, unhappy, no longer a safe harbour for her or any other girl! He wanted her but dared not take her, loved her but dared not confess it. What will become of us, he agonized, holding her gently, prizing her relaxed and confident slumber. What in God's name will become of us if I can't make love to her for fear the price she, or I, may pay for our happiness?

Megan woke. She was in Danny's arms and she could feel tremors running through his body. She knew he was crying and could have screamed aloud and shaken her fists for what they had done to Danny. The old Danny had never cried, his self-confidence had been total, but this Danny lacked even the assurance to examine the reason for his tears.

But it would never do to let him know she knew. Megan felt she was growing old and wise as a serpent so far as Danny was concerned. She seemed to know by some instinct what would upset him, how to handle this man of iron with his frail, spun-glass conscience.

She loved him. Who would not love Danny with his gorgeous looks and caring nature? He was as gentle with a tiny fieldmouse as he was with her, but she did not want his gentleness because a man should not be so afraid of a woman's reactions that he dared not even touch her.

But she was learning, and lately had done the right thing more often than not. She thought before she spoke, though occasionally she scolded him for harshness, knowing that the old Danny would never have spoken so to her. But this was a Danny who was hurt somewhere in his mind, and until his mind had healed he could not be entirely natural, even with her.

She had something to ask him, too, something which might cause the barrier he had erected between them to rear skywards once more. Even so. Megan rolled away from his side, sat up on her elbow and looked down at him. He looked straight back at her, making no move to wipe away the tear-trails which still shone on his lean cheeks. His eyes were as blue as the sky above them, his beard was thicker now and hid the jut of a chin she knew to be most determined. Tears on such a strong face hurt worse, she thought, than her own tears could have done. She must ask him now, before her courage failed.

'Danny, Da was talking to me this morning. He's got plans, and he wanted to ask what you think, only . . .'

'Oh? What sort of plans?'

Danny's hand came up and caught a strand of hair. He ran it through his fingers, doing it over and over until the hair crackled like a miniature bonfire, static electricity almost visible from the teased and gleaming lock.

'Work plans.'

Danny frowned, but she thought it was only because the sun was in his eyes. He put up a hand to shield himself and in the shadow his eyes seemed to burn at her. Was he angry? She did not want to make him angry, but she could not let Da down.

'What have Dai's work plans to do with me, Megan my little one? Is he going to stoke on the mailboats? I'm not. Not twice in a lifetime will I be nailed down below in that heat, and the water boiling past the plates not six inches from me.'

'Nor my da. Danny, he's buying a trawler – borrowing some money from the bank and using his savings. They'll fish Dublin Bay and anywhere else they can reach.'

She saw at once that he was excited by the idea. He sat up, leaning on his elbow, his eyes blazing into hers, their faces only inches apart.

'A trawler! It'll cost a mint, Meggie! But your Arthur will benefit . . . and it's a two-way thing, mind, for Dai will get more money selling direct than through a middleman. My, it's a good idea, no question! Who's in with him, then?'

'One or two. And you, if you'll go in as a working partner. Dewi's on, and a feller from the railways and another bloke who's been trawling for years. But it rests with you, Danny. Da says only he and you know the fishing and the weather round this coast. What do you think?'

'Dai doesn't need me. He could do it alone, with the lads. I don't have much money . . . well, I don't have any money. Dai knows that as well as anyone.'

'He knows. It's not your money he needs, Danny, it's your experience. Are you interested or do you want time

242

to think about it? Da said you could have a week or two, but he's seen a trawler he likes, it's quite cheap, and if you really aren't interested . . .'

'I'm interested,' Danny said at once. 'I'd be mad not to be, girl! It's what I need and what I want. Hard work and outdoors. Oh, Meg!'

He was grinning, his expression a mixture of amazement and pure delight.

'I'll tell Da you're on, then.'

'Wait! Why ask you to talk to me? Why not tell me himself?'

Megan thumped Danny's stomach, laughing at him as the air whooshed out of him.

'Because he thought you'd probably had enough of the sea, mun . . . those were his very words! Only I was so sure that it wasn't the sea itself . . . You haven't known what you wanted to do really, have you? With the war finished, lots of us have felt like that. I was going to join the WRNS, but then the war ended and I've felt let down and bored with the jobs I do ever since. Imagine, I'd have had that lovely uniform, and interesting work . . . it's not much fun to find yourself working in a chemist's shop and doing a bit of fish-gutting on the side, I can tell you.'

'I suppose,' Danny said vaguely. 'Tell Dai . . . no, I'll tell him myself.' He rolled over and stood up all in one movement. 'Come on, Meg, we've got to get back home before Dai thinks I'm not on, and asks someone else to go a-fishing!'

'Danny's a different person,' Megan assured Mam a week later, as the two of them prepared Sunday dinner. Megan was peeling potatoes – what looked like half a ton of them – whilst her mother made a Yorkshire pudding. 'Never have I seen a man change so quick and that's God's truth, Mam. It was as if the chance to work a trawler was so big that it shrank all the little worries to nothing . . . he's been almost his old self.'

'My Dai too,' Mam admitted, energetically whisking. 'It's *out of my way, woman, I've work to do*, instead of finding fault and trying to do jobs I can do myself in half the time. And no more sharp eyes at the boarders, nor nasty remarks that your da would have been ashamed to think, let alone say, before this old war. Too busy, see, for pettiness.'

'But will it last?' Megan worried, cutting the potatoes into pan-sized pieces and arranging them in soldierly lines along the draining board. 'What about when the planning is over and the trawler's in the harbour, waiting to go to sea? What then?'

'A challenge that will be,' Mam said robustly. 'And when they bring their first catch home how we shall sing their praises, even if it's three plaice and a couple of shrimps! Tell them we can't do without them, say they're indispensable. It's what they're missing, even if they wouldn't put it into words.'

'Mam, I think you're *brilliant*,' Megan said earnestly. 'Why didn't I see what was wrong? This peace has seemed a bit dim even to me, and I didn't ever go to war. But I was doing a bloody good job, until the men came back and us girls were told we weren't needed on the farms any more. Good Lord, Mam, I've been blind!'

'Don't let me hear you swear,' Mam said automatically. 'Nor there's no need to take the Lord's name in vain. But you aren't the only one that's been blind, girl. I didn't see what was under my nose until the trawler turned your da back into his busy self. Only then did I see.'

'And they won't go distant water trawling, Danny says, because the boat's too old to stand the strain,' Megan said gleefully. She opened a drawer of the Welsh dresser and fished out a handful of cutlery. 'Set the table, shall

I? So they won't be more than three or four days out of port, which isn't bad, eh, Mam?'

'Not bad at all. I just hope the boat isn't too old to stand our wicked old storms,' Mam said absently. Megan could see it was the least of her worries. 'Fret about borrowing money I do, but what with the boarders and you kids all working, I reckon we'll pay it off in a twelve-month, even if they barely cover their costs.'

'It's worth a bit of worry about money to have Da his old cheerful self, isn't it?' Megan remarked, raising her voice as she went from the kitchen to the lodgers' dining room. 'To say nothing of Danny!'

'True,' Mam called back. 'And Peris is home in less than a month.'

Peris had refused the offer to join the crew of the *Claudia*, as the trawler was called. He had been accepted for pilot-officer training and thought he would make the Air Force his career, he wrote.

'So he is. You don't mind him flying then, Mam?'

'Better a career he loves than one he just tolerates. He was never like the rest any more than you were, love. I thought . . . but I'm glad you've stayed with us, glad it'll be Danny.'

'What'll be Danny?' Megan began dipping the potato pieces in dripping and putting them round the joint. 'I'm very fond of Danny and he's fond of me, but . . .'

'But you don't love him? But he's not the one you want? Oh, Meg, and I've brought you up not to tell lies!'

Megan laughed, then bent and put the heavy pan into the oven, keeping her face turned away.

'Ye-es, but it can only be Danny if he asks.'

'He'll ask,' Mam said confidently. 'One way or another, he'll ask.'

Megan straightened up and closed the oven door. Sometimes, she reflected, she was sure that she and

Danny were destined for each other, but then she would be seized by painful and crippling doubts. He had thought her pretty once, but she had changed; she saw a different face in her mirror now from the pre-war one. Her hair was a darker gold and hung heavy on either side of her pale, ordinary face. Why could she not have rosy cheeks, curls, a bigger bust?

But even if he cared nothing about her looks, why should Danny love her? She was just a shop girl who had gone nowhere, done nothing. And Danny could have anyone, anyone at all.

She couldn't even dress the way she wanted. Mam disapproved of perms, too, and anyway every penny was going towards the *Claudia* now – which meant that Mam sold their clothing coupons and used the money to buy equipment.

They had got the *Claudia* cheap, though. She had been a minesweeper during the war but now she would go back to trawling, with Da as her master. Da raved about her, calling her his little darling, his sweetheart. Megan might have felt quite jealous had she not known how important the boat was to the men.

When they first got her, Megan had looked at her lines and her paintwork and suggested that Da should rename her the *Rhiannon*. To her secret amusement, Da had blushed beetroot red, the colour even visible through the whitening curls on his scalp.

'Oh, *no*, my little one,' he had said. 'I'd not want your mam's named bandied about with all them fellers . . . and unlucky it is, as well, to change a boat's name. She'll stay *Claudia* whilst I'm master.'

When Megan told Mam about it as they hung washing on the line Mam giggled and nudged her daughter so hard that a sheet almost bit the dust.

'Glad I am Dai sees it like that . . . I can just imagine

the jokes: "See old *Rhiannon* ploughing through them waves, mun? Many a good time I've had in her!", and all nudging and winking over the double meaning!'

'Oh, Mam, they wouldn't,' Megan said, shocked, but Mam explained that Holyhead had not had a fishing fleet before, and new things always came in for some stick. She had no doubt that the *Claudia* would set a fashion, though, which others would be quick to follow. And Megan should bear in mind that men would always find something to talk dirty about.

'Even Da?' Megan said, highly daring, and got her ear cuffed for her pains, Mam chasing her back indoors waving the peg bag and threatening worse.

But now, finishing off at the sink, Megan wondered whether Danny would take her out on the bike this afternoon. It was a golden day and Da would not let anyone work on the trawler on the Sabbath. They could go to Cemlyn, where long ago the two of them had found a white-coated seal pup curled up amongst the rocks. He had stared wonderingly at them with his huge, dark blue eyes, and when Danny held out a hand he leaned up to sniff it, white whiskers vibrating, and gave a little mew like a kitten.

But there would be work needing doing in the house; work on the allotment, come to that.

'You and Danny off anywhere when dinner's over, love?'

'He's coming round; but maybe he'll want to talk to Da, or put in some work on the boat.'

Mam laughed at her, shaking her head.

'If he comes round it will be to take you out. You go with him when he asks!'

'If he asks,' Megan said gloomily.

Mam reached up and kissed her, plonk, on the cheek.

'Oh ye of little faith! When!'

CHAPTER FIFTEEN

'Maddie? Could you spare me a minute, love? I need some info p.d.q. on the footballer George Harris – his son's got a trial for United some time next week and I'm doing an article on him.'

Madeleine looked up to see the sports editor, who was also features editor and Uncle Billy of the children's page, looming over her, looking distraught. With an inward sigh, she took her fingers from the typewriter keys and leaned back in her chair. After all, she could finish the wedding reports easily before they went to press.

'Certainly, Bill, if you don't mind these things . . .' she flicked a finger at her notebook '. . . being done tomorrow. Only I've never even *heard* of George Harris, so I don't suppose I'll be much help.'

Bill snorted. He was a tall man in his fifties, balding, pot-bellied, with glasses which he always wore well down on his nose so that he could look at people over the rims. He did this now, shaking his head in mock despair over Madeleine's admission.

'Not heard of our Georgie, and you a local lass born and bred – you should be ashamed to admit it,' he said reproachfully. 'Georgie was one of the finest right-backs this proud city ever produced, and his son may well follow in his dad's footsteps. We don't have much on our files, seeing as we've only been existence for a couple of years, but if you could just nip over to the *Chronicle* . . .'

'I know,' Madeleine said, pushing her chair even further back and reaching for her jacket. 'Go to their library and beg on bended knees . . .'

'That's right, lass. We'll mek a reporter of you yet.'

'I am a reporter,' Madeleine said with dignity, pulling a comb through her crisp blonde bob. Her flowing tresses had bitten the dust a couple of years ago, no longer considered by their owner to be suitable for a woman of thirty-three. 'I'm also the typist, the tea-maker, the general dogsbody . . .'

'Aye, well.' Bill stroked his big, fleshy nose reflectively. 'One of these days you'll graduate to Fleet Street . . . or mebbe the *Evening News* . . . and you'll be able to have them all gasping wi' tales of your humble beginnings on the *Advertiser*.'

'Very funny; and one day, I'll be Queen of England,' Madeleine said equably. 'Look, if I'm going to the *Chronicle* it'll hardly be worth coming back here afterwards. I could get in early tomorrow.'

Bill pretended to consider, then nodded.

'Why not? Tek the wedding reports home, and you needn't come in till your usual time.'

The *Advertiser* was a small paper, but it was doing well, and actually beginning to expand. With only four members of staff the wages bill was not large, and recently they had employed a rep, hoping to increase their circulation even more.

'Thanks, Bill,' Madeleine said. 'Got any notes . . . date of birth and so on?'

'Nay, lass. But he was at his peak, was George, between thirty-four and thirty-eight. Try them winters, then try the Royal Engineers from thirty-nine to forty-five.' He scowled, rubbing his enormous nose reflectively. 'The lad's just coming up to eighteen, so you could try his birth year, I suppose. Might turn something up.'

'Right.'

Madeleine put on her jacket, raised a hand to Bill and ran down the stairs. They were brass-edged and she never went down or up without wondering why anyone should have bothered with the brass. Was it to lengthen the life of the shabby brown lino, or to shorten the life of anyone slipping?

She was still wondering when she opened the door in the lower hallway and looked out into the street. It was a lovely afternoon, the sunshine giving the quiet pavement an air of holiday, schoolchildren scuffling along, blazers off, shirts unbuttoned, ties at half mast. A van, dispensing ice cream, was parked two doors along. Madeleine longed for a cone, but the staff of the *Chronicle* picture library department had enough on their hands without having to ignore a rapidly melting cornet. She began to stride out, then allowed her speed to slacken. It was silly to hurry; she could spend hours in the library now she didn't have to go back to work. And as soon as her pace slowed she began to be glad of the errand, to enjoy this quiet walk through the pleasant warmth of the afternoon.

A bus trundled past and someone waved to her from its depths. She waved back, then glanced at the number; a forty. It would be passing her old flat presently. She wondered how Lizzie was. They had not met for several months, though they were still good friends.

Lizzie had married her Alex when the war ended and Madeleine had moved out of the flat. It was hard for young couples to find accommodation they could afford, and besides, Madeleine's divorce had come through. To her astonishment, she suddenly found herself a woman of means.

The judge had ordered Dickie to give back a large sum he had taken from her parents' estate, and he was also paying alimony each month. She had enjoyed managing on whatever she earned, struggling and laughing with Lizzie, but with no Lizzie and no home the money had been a godsend.

She had bought a small house in a quiet, tree-lined road with Wilbraham Junior School at one end and Wilbraham Road itself at the other. The house had two bedrooms, a long, thin garden and a garage in which she kept her secondhand sports car. A thick holly hedge separated it from the road, a small, half-collapsed shed housed her garden tools and at the far end of the lawn, propped like a drunk against a rosy brick wall, an elderly greenhouse sheltered a vigorous black grapevine and some rather tentative tomato plants.

An old lady had owned the house before her and had, as the saying went, 'let it go'. Madeleine found she enjoyed the challenge of replanning the garden and trying to make the house a pleasant place to live. And in time, she told herself now, sauntering along the dusty pavement, in time it would be a little gem.

She had tried for the job on the *Advertiser* and been delighted when she got it. She learned to type, mastered the art of interviewing people, and knuckled down to becoming an independent woman.

And I'm not too bad at it, Madeleine thought, reaching the foyer of the *Chronicle* and avoiding the girl on reception, who was chatting to a young man with gingery hair which screamed abuse at his red tie. I actually like people, and I'm resigned to being an old maid now.

But she was not, of course. She was merely resigned to not finding Tarot.

God knew she had searched! Knowing he was in the RAF had not been the help she had hoped – like everyone else, they needed a surname – but she had spent every spare moment trying to track him down.

Unsuccessfully. She did not understand how two people who had loved one another as she and Tarot had could possibly fail to meet. Some sort of private and wonderful magnetism should have drawn them inexorably together.

251

But it had not happened. So now she just enjoyed her home and her garden, her job and a few carefully selected friends. And waited. He would be searching too, she told herself. One day . . . across a crowded room . . .

'Yes?'

That was the librarian, already up to his eyes in work, with *Chronicle* reporters staggering about clutching files of newspapers, notebooks lying around . . . Madeleine thought it would be just her luck if the *Chronicle* was also planning a feature on George Harris, but put in her request anyway.

Presently she picked up a vast brown folder full of newspapers and carried it over to a table, pulled up a chair and sat down. She fished her notebook and pencil out of her pocket and began to leaf through the pages.

George was easy to trace pre-war; he bounced across page after page, his long shorts almost meeting his long socks, his hair in a cowlick across his forehead, mouth perpetually open in a toothy, gormless grin. She got all the details down, feeling a virtuous glow. However, it seemed he had not been a particularly bright star in the firmament of war. She found that he had played football for his platoon . . . come home a couple of times on leave . . . attended the wedding of his elder sister's daughter . . .

I've got enough now, Madeleine told herself. But she continued to leaf idly through the papers. She saw faces she knew . . . once herself on an assembly line, her hair wrapped in a scarf, her lips smiling obediently in the direction of the camera. Once Dickie and his fat girl-friend, dancing cheek to cheek. She smirked at them and went on turning the pages.

Two sheets further on she found Tarot. After all the years, all the journeying, there he was. In Air Force uniform, with two other men. He was wearing what she thought of as 'high-up' insignia and she could see, even in the newspaper photograph, a trace of grey at his temples, but it was unmistakably he.

Below the picture there were a couple of lines of newsprint. John Foulds and Nicholas Byers with Wing Commander David Carding . . . Wing Commander Carding, in civilian life the well-known painter, had flown more successful missions . . .

She stopped reading, sat staring at the photograph, her eyes suddenly full. She had found him! Carding . . . no wonder they called him Tarot!

It was strictly forbidden to remove cuttings from the files. Madeleine tore the page out without a qualm, stuck it down the front of her cotton frock and left the building. She went along the street to the post office and found a telephone directory. He had been in the area all the time! He probably had a studio in London, a cottage in the country, but he had originated from Lancashire. She would surely get information about him from relatives?

Standing in a phone booth presently, with a list of Cardings and their telephone numbers written in her notebook, she dialled the first one, apprehension knotting her stomach as the tone sounded. Suppose he was married with lots of kids? Suppose he couldn't remember her? Suppose . . . ?

A woman's voice answered the phone after the fifth ring. She sounded young, breathless.

'Hello . . . Anne Carding speaking.'

'Oh, good afternoon. My name's Madeleine Ripley-Trewin. I'm trying to trace a friend of mine, David Carding, and I wondered if you . . .'

'Awfully sorry, my chap is Don Carding. But you could try Uncle Ronnie . . . his number's the next to last in the book. He knows all the relatives. He'll be your best bet, if your Carding is one of ours.'

Madeleine thanked her and rang off. She was

undeterred by the false start. After nearly twenty years of longing, what price a few phone calls? She dialled again.

Madeleine drove the car up the short, gravelled drive, parked it outside the front door and then just sat for a moment, gathering her courage. When old Mr Carding had told her he lived in Bolton, on Chorley New Road, her heart had almost stopped. She had known the Carding family vaguely all her life – not on a personal basis, perhaps, but by repute. And of course the one place she had never searched was Bolton, because . . . well, because she had always assumed that Tarot had come from somewhere far more . . . more exotic. Besides, she knew she had never seen him in her home town.

And now here she was. It was a very large and imposing property, the garden huge and heavily wooded though it was neglected now, the trees untrimmed, the lawns overgrown and weedy. Madeleine got out of the car and approached the house. It crouched before her like a bad-tempered animal, its brows the shaggy ivy overhanging the dirty window panes. Uncle Ronnie had clearly been unable to do much with the great barracks of a place, but perhaps now the war was over . . .

He had sounded nice on the telephone. He had explained very civilly that he was the scion of an extremely large and scattered family, the younger members of which were not as well known to him as he would like them to be. However, as Miss Ripley-Trewin had a photograph, if she could possibly get out to Bolton . . .

Madeleine stood before the door. The paint was cracked and peeling, the knocker's brass dulled. She had mounted three mossy steps to reach it, steps flanked on either side by a stone balustrade. An imposing entrance, even in its present state.

Madeleine raised the brass dolphin and let it fall. Its knock sounded firm and self-confident, very different from the way she felt. Was she really nearing the end of her search at last? Was it possible that after all this time she and Tarot . . . she and Tarot . . .

The door swung open and a very small, very old man stood smiling at her. He was bald, bespectacled, Pick-wickian.

'Miss Ripley-Trewin? Come in, come in! I've asked my niece, who takes care of me and the house, to make us a nice cup of coffee, but first of course you must show me your photograph.'

He ushered his guest into a lofty room overcrowded with Victorian furniture, the walls invisible beneath the heavily framed pictures which jostled, shoulder to shoulder, for space. Every table had an elaborately embroidered cloth on it, every cloth was almost hidden by knick-knacks. There were vast chiffoniers, huge sideboards, dark carved corner cupboards, stools, spindly legged chairs with velvet seats and silver braid, overstuffed armchairs, their arms and backs protected from life by more embroidered squares and oblongs of cream-coloured linen. It was like walking into a museum, Madeleine thought uncomfortably, taking a seat. But her host was talking, so she straightened her back and paid attention.

'. . . you mentioned a David Carding. As I told you, we are a very large family . . . if I might see the photograph?'

Madeleine tugged the cutting out of her pocket. She held it out.

'Does this help?'

The rosy face crumpled into a frown as he took the paper and focused on the face Madeleine indicated.

'So that's your friend, eh? Nice-looking chap, but no, my dear, I'm sorry . . . as I said, the younger generation is practically a closed book to me. No doubt the last time I saw the lad he was in short trousers. The years make a big difference.' He sighed, shaking his head sadly. 'Now I wonder whether I might put you in touch with someone who is more *au fait* with the young ones than I?'

Madeleine was starting to say how grateful she would be when she heard an approaching clatter, closely followed by a crash of fairly large proportions. It sounded as though someone had dropped a tray of china just outside the door. She started to get to her feet but Mr Carding waved her back, smiling indulgently.

'Here's my niece now with our coffee. She's never quite got the hang of the trolley – it nearly always hits the door before she can get it open.'

As he spoke the door swung inwards and a spare, elderly lady with grey hair and a rather forbidding expression entered the room, pushing before her a very large walnut-wood trolley bedecked with a lace cloth, a great deal of good Georgian silver and some delicate china. There were also cakes, sausage rolls and a silver salver covered with fancy biscuits.

'That looks awfully nice, Olivia,' Mr Carding chirruped. 'Meet our guest, Miss Ripley-Trewin. Miss Ripley-Trewin, my niece, Olivia Carding.'

Miss Carding gave Madeleine a penetrating glance swiftly followed by a very sweet smile. Then she poured tea – not coffee – from the Georgian teapot into three cups.

'I understand you're trying to trace a friend, Miss Ripley-Trewin,' the older woman said, handing cups. 'Was my uncle able to help you?'

''Fraid not, m'dear,' Mr Carding admitted. 'Gal even brought a photograph, but you know how it is . . . the younger generation . . .'

'They all look alike to us,' Miss Carding said, giving

256

Madeleine a broad smile. 'May I have a look, Miss Ripley-Trewin?'

Madeleine took the proffered cup and handed over the cutting. Miss Carding looked at it, and then went very still. She put it down on the trolley before her, still without speaking, and handed Madeleine a plate and a selection of sausage rolls and small cakes.

'Ah yes. David. It's years since Uncle saw him, of course, and in fact his name is David Terence, so the family called him Terry until he was old enough to choose to use the nickname they gave him at school – Tarot. Which may be why Uncle didn't realize . . . his sight isn't what it was, and the name.' She leaned towards the old man. 'It's Tarot, Uncle,' she said, her voice low but very clear, the voice of one used to addressing the partially deaf. 'It's Tarot in the picture.'

The old man looked up, his expression suddenly unhappy.

'Tarot! I never thought . . . my dear, I'm so sorry . . .'

Madeleine found herself on her feet, her fingers curled into fists, the tension so great that she would not have been surprised to find she had actually levitated several feet from the floor. Indeed, she felt that flying was not beyond her at that moment.

'Tarot – that's right! That was the only name I had for him until I found the newspaper cutting. So you *do* know him!'

'Yes, we knew him.' She glanced at her uncle, who was consuming a very large piece of chocolate cake with every appearance of total absorption. She lowered her voice. 'Tarot was . . . he was my son.'

'Your *son*? But I thought . . .'

Madeleine stopped short, feeling the blood rush to her face. She pressed her hands to her cheeks, realizing she had nearly said something unforgivable. 'I'm sorry . . . is he here? Where can I find him?'

'Oh, my dear! Tarot was shot down during the Normandy landings. I thought you knew . . . I thought you'd read the report in the paper . . . Oh, my dear child!'

Madeleine frowned. She was seeing the room from a long way off. Small, small, was the great room and the laden trolley, small the woman who stood before her, kind eyes brimming with tears, mouth twisted with grief.

She knew she must get out, find some air. She stumbled to her feet, lurched towards the door . . . and crashed down in a dead faint.

Later, she and Olivia Carding talked far into the night. Tarot was Olivia's illegitimate son and had been brought up by her old nanny, not knowing who his mother was until he was twenty.

'I wasn't young when Tarot was born,' Olivia explained. 'And before he was ten my mother died and I found myself looking after my father, who was past seventy and . . . well, really very difficult.

'There was never any question of my keeping my child with me, but Nanny had a cottage down on Ladybridge Lane and she agreed to take him in. She was a dear old lady . . . too old, really, to take on another child. The boy was often unhappy. He never quite knew who he was, you see, because Father had forbidden me to admit I'd had a baby and after all he paid for my keep and for Terry's as well, so . . . I'm afraid Terry always thought he came second with me, even when he only knew me as his guardian. And in a way he did, because my father was so demanding, and anyway I owed him so much that I couldn't . . . I didn't feel I could make waves.

'Father died when Tarot was twenty and then I felt I was entitled to admit I was his mother, but he never said much about it. He was still affectionate – he was always marvellously affectionate towards me – but his hurt showed through. I'd . . . well, I'd denied him, you see. And though he was a wonderful son and the kindest boy you could hope to meet, he was wild . . . very wild.'

'Ladybridge Lane! The times I rode my pony down there! Oh, God, and he was so close . . . so close!'

Olivia Carding touched Madeleine's hand timidly.

'He left when he was twenty, and only came back to see me from time to time. But when Nanny died she left him her cottage and he moved back in. That would have been . . . let me think . . . about thirty-seven or eight.'

'I was living on Victoria Road,' Madeleine said through stiff lips. 'But I probably hardly ever crossed Chorley New Road, and I had my car so I didn't use the buses much.'

'Don't blame yourself,' Olivia said. 'You must be thankful for what you had, my dear. I'm just glad that Terry never knew how nearly you must have missed one another. Although perhaps I shouldn't say it of my own son, he was a sensitive young man. A first-rate painter, too, and I think creative people have more than their fair share of sensitivity . . . I still have some of his paintings in my room, but they aren't Uncle's sort of thing so I keep them to myself.'

'I loved his work,' Madeleine said. She was still wrestling with the cruel fact that she had searched far and wide but never near, never near! 'I tried to find him around the London art galleries. I went to heaps of shows, but I never saw him.'

'No. He didn't think much of big cities.' She paused, looking straight into Madeleine's eyes. 'Forgive me . . . but what is your first name, my dear?'

'Madeleine. Why?'

'Ah! Then I have a letter for you. He left two letters,

to be opened in the event of his death. One was to me, the other is simply addressed to Madeleine. I take it he never knew your surname, as you never knew his?'

'No. We didn't think names were important,' Madeleine whispered. 'Do you have the letter here?'

'I do. He always thought you'd find each other, you know. He searched for you . . . I don't believe he ever stopped searching.'

Madeleine had cried all her tears but now her eyes ached with a dry, dull ache. She nodded, her fingers clutching her notebook as though it was the only way she could hang on to her sanity.

'I searched too. But I only once came near . . . and then although I ran and ran I never caught up.'

Miss Carding reached for her handbag, a solid affair in dull black leather. She opened it, dredged around, and produced the letter. A large white envelope, grubby now from its incarceration in the bag, with 'Madeleine' written on it in a flowing hand. Tarot's hand. Madeleine would have known it anywhere.

'There. Open it. And don't worry. I've never known a kinder man than my boy.'

Madeleine opened it and spread out the single sheet. She began to read.

Maddie, I've tried to find you, I've searched everywhere, in all the places we went together and all the places we talked about. No luck. I've worried a lot, too. About the kid. What happened to her? I always thought it was a girl and I couldn't bear the thought of you trying to bring her up alone. You were just a kid yourself – how have you managed?

But this is stupid, because if you read this it's because I'm dead, killed in action, maybe, but definitely dead. Awful thought. I hope you're all right, but you're so

pretty that I guess you'll be fine. What about the kid,
though? My daughter. If you read this, you'll know that
I didn't have it easy. Never knew quite who I was or
what was expected of me. Made my own way, in the
end, but it's a whole lot easier for a bloke.

So I want to help her, my daughter. Can she draw or
paint or anything? Money isn't everything, but I can tell
you it helps. I've made money, Maddie, quite a lot of
it. I would have left it to you, but I reckon the kid may
need it more, so I'm leaving it to you in trust for her.
Give it to her if she needs it. With my love. Not all of
it, because you've got most, Maddie. Most of my love.
But there's a bit left for her . . . oh, God, Maddie, I've
bloody missed you!

Remember me.
Tarot

Madeleine thought she had cried herself dry; she hadn't.
The tears ran down her cold cheeks and she held the
letter out wordlessly for Olivia Carding to take. Olivia
read it and cried too. It comforted Madeleine that they
wept for Tarot together, two women who had done him
harm, two women who had loved him more than anything
else in their lives.

Later, when they were calm again, Madeleine told
Olivia about the twins.

'If it takes me the rest of my life, I'll find them and see
they get their inheritance,' she said at last, dry-eyed now
and determined. 'There could never have been anyone
for me but Tarot . . . but I would have loved a baby of
my own. If that's to be denied me, then at least I'll have
done what I could for the children I did bear.'

'Ye-es . . . but don't forget how my boy loved you,'
Olivia Carding reminded her. 'He wanted your happiness

very badly, my dear. I'm sure he never guessed that you, too, could only be happy with him. If he had . . . but there, it's no use wishing. Find your daughters if you can, but don't forget that life owes you something, too.'

What did life really owe her, though, Madeleine wondered? She had abandoned the twins, left Tarot. It was almost as though she only prized what she no longer had . . . but she had been half-mad when she left the twins to their fate, only concerned with finding Tarot.

Life, she concluded drearily now, had certainly seen that she suffered for her multitudinous sins. Looking back, it was just a long catalogue of loss, starting with Tarot and the twins, going through her parents, Dickie, Neil and his baby, even Lizzie. Yet, long ago, the Stones had made her a promise. She felt that They had been responsible for most of the bad things which had happened to her, but she still had a vague feeling that they would be true to that promise.

Happiness will be yours, little Stone maiden, willing sacrifice.

The words no longer sang in her head, because she had believed, in her heart, that happiness meant Tarot. But now she must accept that he was never going to cross her path, never saunter back into her life.

And she must reach for what happiness could still be hers, because she was only thirty-five. There was a lot of life left to be lived.

But first she must be true to Tarot. He wanted the twins found and kept safe and if it took the rest of her life she would do it.

She told Olivia, and found in the older woman that strength and understanding which she had felt in Tarot. She said she would give up her job with the newspaper and start trying to trace her girls at once, and she would find them even if it took years.

Olivia said she was right to do so, but asked her to keep in touch, let her know how the search went on.

'Imagine, an old spinster like me suddenly discovering she's got twin granddaughters,' she said, her eyes shining. 'If you find them, Madeleine dear . . .'

'I will find them,' Madeleine assured her. 'And I'll tell them about you – bring them to you, if I can.'

Olivia sighed tremulously.

'When I first had my boy I was racked with guilt – so much that I could scarcely enjoy holding him in my arms. I let him down; I've always known it. He died so young, with all his life still to live, and I'm old. Finished, really, except that I help Uncle to keep going. Yet I get rewarded. A lovely girl like you, and twin granddaughters!'

It was late at night when Madeleine tore herself away at last. In the balmy darkness she climbed into her small car, started the engine and drove off down the road.

She looked around her as she left; she had come here earlier with such high hopes, such bright, optimistic feelings, and they had all come to nought. There was an aching hollow in her breast and, lurking in the back of her mind, a pit of black despair.

Yet she had a purpose, now. To find her daughters and to see that they received Tarot's inheritance. And in doing so, she might indeed find the happiness that the Stones had promised her.

Little Stone maiden. Willing sacrifice.

CHAPTER SIXTEEN

The trawler was ready for sea at last and the men had gone down to the waterfront pubs for a celebration drink. Megan knew women went into pubs these days though she had never done so herself, but Da disapproved and even Danny had said that the Five Sisters were not the sort of pubs to welcome change, particularly a change which might mean a curbing of tongues as well as a cutting down of spirituous liquor.

So Megan, Mam, Dewi's Louisa and Siân, who was going with English Phil, all sat themselves down on the seats further along Landsend where they could watch the traffic, and drank genteelly from the large jug of ale and the smaller one of sweet sherry which Danny, with a wink, had brought out to them.

English Phil had worked on a trawler before the war, so he had more experience than the rest of the crew, though Da and Danny, of course, had been small boat fishermen for years. But Phil helped them a lot with the fitting out of the *Claudia*. He recommended a dry-ice supplier, advised on the shape and depth of the trawl, and warned of various malpractices which they might encounter from men wanting to sell and none too fussy about how they did it.

He was a tall man with a bunchy, humorous face, reddish curls and a free way of talking which had immediately attracted the notorious Siân. Megan, who had always rather liked Siân, welcomed the company of both English Phil and the girl, but Mam, she knew, had reservations. As though Siân's easiness was infectious and might be picked up by Megan, she watched the two girls to see they didn't get too close – though how she thought she could possibly prevent the friendship from growing Megan could not imagine.

It had been a fine summer, Megan reflected. The weather was still lovely, but there was a frailty in the sunshine, a slight nip in the air, which meant that autumn was near. Soon the first leaves would colour, the duck and the geese would fly in to Penrhos Bay and the land would begin to hunch its shoulders against winter.

'Well, Meg! Pleased with yourself, are you? They tell me you've changed your job!'

That was quiet Louisa, who had married Dewi last spring and lived with him out at Pont-rhyd-y-bont and so was not always aware of the changes which happened in Holyhead, the big city.

'That's right. Got experience working for a chemist, see, so they've taken me on at Boots. Nice it is and no Saturdays, so I can give Mam a hand.'

'And how's Danny settling?'

It was a facer, that. He was happy again, he took her out when he could, but he seemed afraid of permanence. Megan frowned, trying to understand Danny's attitude, but before she could speak Mam butted in.

'Danny's settling fine. Give him a season with the trawler and he'll be thinking of settling further.'

'There's no doubt he's keen on our Megan,' Siân said, shooting a quick, almost furtive glance at the other girl. 'I can't get more than a smile out of him, meself.'

'Nor you should,' Mam said, her tone frosty. 'English Phil's quite enough for you, young lady.'

Her tone implied that English Phil was more than Siân deserved and Megan rushed in, wanting to pour oil even if as yet the waters were scarcely troubled at all. Siân was smiling placidly enough but Megan did not have to see

Mam's face to imagine the expression on it – the tight lips, the flared nostrils, the disapproval implicit.

'Danny's fine, but he isn't thinking about marriage or settling down just yet – why should he? He's only twenty-two!'

'Dai proposed when he was twenty-two,' Mam said smugly, obviously forgetting whose side she was on. 'I was only seventeen on my wedding day!'

'Things were different then, though,' Louisa observed, sipping sweet sherry from the tumblers Danny had brought. 'You hadn't got the war . . . Dai wasn't in the first one, was he?'

'No. And you're right, war does change things.' Mam took a drink of her beer and pulled a face. 'Horrid old stuff this is . . . let's try the little jug.'

'You'll get drunk, Mam,' Megan observed, as Louisa poured sherry into her mother's glass. 'I don't think you should have beer one minute and sherry the next.'

'I only had a mouthful of the beer,' Mam admitted, smiling conspiratorially round at them. 'Well, girls . . . a toast! To the *Claudia* and all who sail in her!'

'The *Claudia*,' the others echoed.

Megan drank the toast with the rest. She was happy, she told herself. Danny was her feller; what more could she ask? But happiness was tinged with uneasiness still. They went off on the motor bike bird-watching, seal-spotting, sometimes on simple expeditions over to the mainland to see what was happening in Caernarvon, Bangor, Llandudno. He hugged, kissed her, cuddled her. But never, not once, had he sought to extend their intimacy. Megan knew herself to be innocent in many ways, but she was no longer a child. She knew that all the talk about 'respect' and 'old-fashioned morals' was just words to a young man like Danny. He had once got amorous with her, she remembered it well. He had drawn back because she was so young, because she had shown her fright. But he had promised that later . . .

'Let's go and see if the fellers have finished their boozing,' Siân said prosaically. She shivered, rubbing her rounded arms with the palms of her hands. 'Cold I'm getting, now the sun's gone down.'

Megan came back with a start from that occasion in Porth Trecastell to see that Siân was right; dusk was falling and it was distinctly chilly. She got up, feeling the wooden slats of the seat cling lovingly to her rear.

'I've got myself a striped bum,' she said ruefully, holding out her hands to heave Mam to her feet. 'Those men and their pubs we can't go inside . . . I bet they have real chairs, not an old wooden bench that marks you for life.'

'Well, I don't envy 'em,' Mam said as she, too, stood up and smoothed down her skirt. 'Straight home, us, and a big pot of tea with homemade scones. How's that?'

'Lovely,' the younger girls chorused. Even Siân, not a home-lover, looked pleased at the proposal.

'Well, there you are,' Mam observed to Megan as, arm in arm, they crossed the road and headed once more for Newry Street. 'All that cold old drink is what men make such a fuss about, and why I'll never know. What's more, I do want to wee desperate bad.'

They all laughed and Megan squeezed Mam's arm against her side and thought how lucky they were. She was sure everything would be all right. She and Danny would marry and have babies and a little house of their own further up Newry Street, perhaps on Newry Fawr . . . there's posh! Then she could pop in and see Mam every day. The business of Danny's not wanting . . . well, what she was beginning to want . . . in the way of kissing and cuddling would resolve itself as soon as he realized that the trawler was going to succeed. And if it did not, the remedy was in her own hands. She would persuade Danny to take her back to the underground chamber at Porth Trecastell. And she would not fight or fear; next time she and Danny would make love together.

They reached the house and trooped into the kitchen. The air was pleasantly warm after the September chill and the sight of Uncle Reggie watching the kettle hiss on the hob was a sure sign that tea would not be long in coming.

In a few weeks, Megan told herself, we'll have sorted ourselves out, Danny and me. As Mam says, just give it time.

Marsha enjoyed university. Her grasp of languages ensured an easy ride and she was beginning to see that she could find an interesting job if she got a good degree.

What was more, Mummy and Daddy had lent her their super flat, the one they had used before the war. Mummy had stored things there all through the war too, once the house was requisitioned. She had given her daughter carte blanche over whom she invited to share it, but Marsha lived there alone, to date.

But they had let her down this Christmas. It was a hard winter, that was the trouble, and Daddy was still not quite himself, so the invitation from friends to go to the Caribbean for the month of December had been grasped, by Mummy, as an ideal opportunity to 'take Daddy's mind off things'.

They had invited her to go with them, but that would have meant abandoning her class before the end of term, and somehow the long and lonely journey to join them later did not appeal.

Anyway, Marsha was not sorry. London at Christmas, even with austerity still the watchword, would surely be fun? A tree was being erected in Trafalgar Square, there would be lights, parties . . . it will be quite like New

York, Marsha found herself thinking wistfully. She still missed it, though she admitted, now, that Britain was doing its best to drag itself back from the depths to which it had sunk because of the war.

Besides, she was making new friends, meeting lots of people, and some of them were fun, some of the men not bad, though not perhaps quite as hunky as American males.

Men, she admitted to herself now, were a problem. She was not supposed to invite them to the flat, and the devil of it was she dared not do so because Daddy had been so firm about it. If you break the rules you'll have to leave, he had warned. What was worse, he had a spy actually on the premises. The caretaker and his wife lived in the basement and by a piece of really foul luck Mr Higgins had been one of Daddy's mob during the war. He and nosy Mrs Higgins had promised to keep an eye on Marsha, and they jolly well did, too. She could scarcely sneeze but Mrs Higgins was up offering hot lemon and aspirin. If I brought a fellow home it would probably be a chastity belt she trotted upstairs with, Marsha told herself bitterly.

But there were compensations. Mrs Higgins kept the flat tidy for a small weekly sum (Marsha hoped it was a small sum; she did not like to think of Daddy lashing out yet more money on her). And since Marsha did not have the slightest intention of cleaning or cooking each evening, it was a bonus that Mrs Higgins was prepared to help out. Marsha handed over her ration book quite complacently, knowing that Mrs Higgins got out of it at least twice what she herself would have managed.

But at the moment Marsha was at a loose end. She had finished term and looked around for her crowd and what did she find? That everyone, or at least everyone who was anyone, had gone home for the holiday!

Unbelievably, the only people left in London were the dim girl who worked in Harrods' food hall and a spotty youth who was so brilliant that he had come up a year early and so was still only seventeen.

These were not the people Marsha had in mind as her companions, no indeed! She wanted people like Peggy Horsham-Wynn, or Dulcie Carruthers, or luscious young men like Rupert Reid-Jones or Laurence Elgar.

She contemplated taking a train back to Bolton, because the town would be full of friends back for the holiday. But that would mean coping for herself in the huge, battered house. No, she had much better stay here, with Mrs Higgins to take care of her.

But now, with Christmas only three days away, Marsha found herself at a loss. She had done as much shopping as it was possible to do with the shops so empty and rationing so strict. She had gone round Harrods and tried on countless garments, probably infuriating the sales staff, but she had enjoyed it and had bought a pretty pink cardigan, splurging her coupons rather than come away with nothing. Money didn't matter – Mummy had a charge account – but coupons were a difficulty.

So on this extremely cold morning Marsha got up late, had a cup of instant coffee and some toast for breakfast and was now sitting on the windowseat, watching the passers-by and wondering what on earth she should do with herself. It was Mrs Higgins's day to clean so she would be up later, but there really wasn't an awful lot for her to do – Marsha had been out most of the previous day – which meant she wouldn't stay long.

What shall I do, Marsha fretted. If only she had a friend still in London! She could think of several people who would have been keen to have her as a houseguest over the holiday, though people were not quite so free with their invitations now because of rationing.

Still. She had put out no feelers, made no suggestions; told no one, in fact, that she looked like enduring a solitary Christmas, so in a way she had only herself to blame.

Down in the road, people went about their business, bending double against the gale which blew a beastly mixture of snow and sleet into their faces. The streets had been cleared of snow by traffic, Marsha supposed, but it lingered on pavement and precinct, not clean and white tand exciting, as in the country, but grey and hopeless-looking, thickened with grit and gravel, half-melted with salt and then refrozen.

If the sun comes out later I'll go out and see what's happening, Marsha decided. But what did people do in London? You could see a show, but that was for evening, not for daytime; shopping was now impossible for lack of coupons; and galleries and museums had never appealed to her.

Marsha wandered through into the kitchen and put the kettle on. She would have another cup of coffee. She made it, tasted it, pulled a face. Oh hell, there must be more to life than this!

Why don't you go to the zoo, a voice in her head suggested. I've always wanted to go to London zoo.

For a moment Marsha was baffled; the zoo? What in heaven's name had made her think of that? And then she remembered. It was the Other, doing a trick she had not pulled for years, not since they were both small. Entering Marsha's mind with a suggestion, as she had done long ago over learning to ride, so that Marsha had suddenly had to have a pony.

Why the zoo, though? Marsha put the thought into words and got the unanswerable answer: why not? And it wasn't such a bad idea at that. Zoos were fun, neither instructive like museums, nor boring like art galleries.

They had big animal houses, centrally heated, where you could wander at will, and smaller houses, too, where at least you could spend time out of the elements.

Mrs Higgins arrived at that point, slamming her mop down on the hall floor.

'Morning, miss. 'Ave you 'ad your breakfast?'

Mrs Higgins's small head, with its tightly curlered hair hidden beneath a scarf, appeared round the living room door. She always looked anxious, like a mouse who isn't too sure where the cat is, Marsha decided in a rare flight of fancy.

'Yes, I've eaten, thanks. I say, Mrs Higgins, have you been to the zoo lately?'

Mrs Higgins came right into the room and rested her weight on the mop handle. She scowled down at her truly dreadful carpet slippers, at the thick lisle stockings already wrinkling down towards her bantamlike ankles.

'Well, not lately . . . but I used to go a lot. It's a nice warm place on a winter's day. You goin', then, miss?'

'I might,' Marsha said guardedly. 'Can I get a meal there?'

'Well, I dunno, not 'avin' been lately. But there's a British Restaurant quite close – ever such good value, miss, and the food ain't bad, either.' Mrs Higgins's small face took on a crafty look. 'Nice day out it makes, a trip to the zoo – goin' with friends, are you?'

Marsha knew that Mrs Higgins had been bitterly disappointed to discover that Marsha would be in London on Christmas Day, and a suggestion that Marsha might like to join the Higgins family gathering had been speedily refused. Marsha might have a lonely sort of Christmas Day, but she would not be reduced to eating in the caretaker's basement flat.

'No, I'll be going alone,' she said cruelly, seeing Mrs Higgins's face fall. If I have a miserable Christmas Day, she found herself thinking, then at least I won't be the only one!

'Oh. I see. Want me to ring for a taxi, then, miss?'

'No, I'll do it,' Marsha said. 'I'll have to get changed first. These clothes aren't right for the zoo.'

She was wearing a pale green skirt with tiny pleats, a crisp white blouse and a dark green cardigan. Far too good for walking round the zoo – and she would need something sturdier than her low-fronted court shoes, as well. If she went, of course.

But she knew she would go. Suggestions from the Other were usually complied with because past experience had taught Marsha that in some ways their tastes were very similar.

Going to her room, she flung open the big wardrobe doors and examined the contents. She had brought a great many clothes back from the States, and had managed to have a good few of Mummy's things altered to fit, but even so she longed for more choice. She had recently lightened her hair and had a perm, and really wanted clothes which showed off her new, angelic fairness, but the sophisticated black for which her soul longed was not approved of by Mummy, who kept telling her to be young whilst she could, whatever that might mean. Anyway, for the zoo all she needed was a warm coat and stout shoes.

But her wardrobe failed to come up with anything, so she got out a pair of Mummy's brogues which fitted her quite well, and then went into the master bedroom.

She could have slept here herself, of course, when Mummy and Daddy weren't in London, but she preferred her own smaller room. Now she prowled over to the wardrobe, opened it, and took out Mummy's cinnamon coat with the dark brown fur collar. It was warm and soft, and she felt inclined to act like the child she no longer was and cradle it in her arms, breathing in the soft scent

273

of the fur which was Mummy's perfume, pretending for a moment that Mummy had only gone out for a shopping trip and would soon be back.

But that was silly. She draped the coat round her shoulders and then remembered that Mummy had a delicious silk scarf which she wore with it. The scarf was gold-coloured, decorated with tiny horses.

Where would Mummy keep such a scarf? In her dressing table, first or second drawer.

Marsha pulled out the first drawer. Gloves. All different, all smart. She helped herself to a pair in the same brown as the coat-collar before closing that drawer and opening the next.

Scarves. Lots and lots. But the one she wanted was not immediately obvious.

Marsha searched. No gold-coloured scarf rewarded her. Sighing, she shut the second drawer with a bit of a snap and went on to the third, which she knew very well was really an underwear drawer, but still . . .

She burrowed beneath the undies, tossing them to one side. And right at the bottom of the drawer she found several bundles of letters, some personal, some official-looking.

Marsha started to shut the drawer and then paused. Nice girls didn't read other people's letters, not even when it was snowing outside and they were bored to tears. But these weren't private letters; they were all in Daddy's fine, sloping hand. Probably her parents would be amused and delighted if Marsha read what Daddy had written. As for the official missives, she wouldn't bother with them.

Marsha picked up a pile at random and saw her own name. This might well be interesting! She began to read.

* * *

An hour later she sat back, eyes wide, still finding it difficult to believe what she had read.

She was not Mummy's little girl and Daddy's darling at all. She was adopted! She came from a very good family, Daddy had said so, but he gave no details. Instead, he had waxed quite lyrical over her as a baby; how sweetly pretty she was, how quick and intelligent. And he had felt that Marsha should be told she was adopted in case something happened to him or Mummy during the war.

Infuriatingly, for Marsha, there was no mention of her mother's name. Daddy constantly reiterated what a good family she had come from – this was as important to Marsha as it seemed to have been to Daddy – but the only clue to her real identity was that she had been born in Wales. Until, that was, Marsha put two and two together.

It had worried Daddy, apparently, that someone called Dickie Steadman had bought a house quite near to their own home in Bolton. *I wonder whose idea it was? Daddy had written. Not hers, surely? She can't have any idea we live so close.*

So I was a Steadman baby, Marsha reasoned. She remembered talk of a Dickie Steadman but could not recall whether she had heard good or ill of him. Which was a pity, if he was her father.

Presently she heard Mrs Higgins call out that she was off, and was Marsha sure she didn't want a taxi, and Marsha called back that she would telephone for her own cab presently. She continued to sit on her parents' bed until she heard Mrs Higgins's footsteps fade into silence and then, with an abruptness which startled even herself, she flung herself face down on the rose-satin bedspread, and cried as if her heart would break.

Later, when the inexplicable fit of weeping had finished,

leaving Marsha feeling like a wrung-out dishcloth, the sun came out, it stopped snowing and the wind gentled to a breeze. It was not the best of days still, but it was better than it had been.

Marsha sat up, then went into the bathroom and washed her face. She peered at herself in the mirror; a bit pale round the mouth, a bit red round the eyes . . . so what? She had made a pretty earth-shattering discovery. Several times, as a small child, she had indulged in the dream that she was adopted; the child of royalty, perhaps. What was different now?

But she knew, sadly, that the reality was very different no matter how she might try to disguise it. She had her father's repeated assurance that she had come from a good background, but what sort of woman gives up her baby to someone else?

A young woman, something said inside Marsha's aching head. A very young woman, who isn't married and can't cope with a child.

It was odd, the words almost popping into her mind, but it made her think, for the second time that day, about the Other. Was she a real sister, then, someone with whom she had shared her early childhood? And had they both been adopted, both sent away from their natural mother? She could not possibly know for sure, yet suddenly she was certain it had happened. And that, of course, was why she and the Other had remained close, on the same wave-length.

Marsha picked up a brush and attacked her long hair, then marched through into her bedroom, the coat still round her shoulders. It was not late, not even midday, for all she felt as though she had lived through a dozen years since finding those letters. She would go to the zoo as she had planned; would not let the day be ruined. In fact, she decided, going to the telephone to ring for a taxi, it would be a good day. She would make sure of that!

CHAPTER SEVENTEEN

When the taxi driver rang the bell Marsha ran at once to the door. She brushed past the man, who turned and followed her back to the cab, barely getting the door open in time for her to swan in, very regal.

'In a hurry, are you?' the cabby said, but he spoke with good humour and the words were accompanied by a grin. 'Thought you was going to leap in and drive off yourself.'

'I can't drive,' Marsha said. 'The zoo, please.'

'Right you are.' He started his engine and pulled out into the traffic, then slowed. 'It's raining again – want to go back indoors and change that classy coat for somethink a bit more practical, like?'

'No,' Marsha said flatly. 'This will do.'

'Rain won't do much for the fur collar,' he pointed out reasonably. 'No trouble; wouldn't take a mo.'

'Drive on,' Marsha said. 'And hurry. I want to reach the zoo before it closes.'

'Sorry, I'm sure.' The cabby did not actually go much faster, but he revved his engine and started off at lights as though he fancied winning the grand prix. 'Which entrance?'

That stymied Marsha, who had no idea that the zoo had more than one. But naturally she did not intend to let the driver see the extent of her ignorance.

'The main one.'

'Why not go in the south gate? There's a nice little caff where you could have a cuppa till the rain eases up.'

'If you're so set on it,' Marsha said, letting her impatience show, 'the south entrance it is.'

'Good for you. Not meeting anyone there, then?'

'No.'

'No? Can't say I'm surprised; gal of few words, aren't you? Cat got your tongue? That's what my old mother used to say to us kids when we was quiet.'

It surprised a muffled snort of amusement out of Marsha, and for the first time she looked at the cabby. Really looked, noticing his thick and curly black hair, the clean pale skin on the back of his neck, even his hands on the wheel – rather square, practical-looking hands, but with short, neatly trimmed nails and a few stray black hairs on the backs of his fingers. She moved a bit and could see his forehead and eyes in the mirror. Very black eyes and an unlined forehead. She guessed he was no more than twenty-four or five; young, she thought, to be driving a taxi in this confusing city.

'Well? Know me again?'

'Probably not,' Marsha said dryly. 'It's not obligatory, is it?'

This time, he laughed. And, since they were stuck in a long queue at traffic lights, turned round to speak to her directly. To her surprise, Marsha saw that he was very good-looking, his face lean and his long chin deeply cleft, his whole cast of countenance dramatic, exciting. Probably used to getting his own way with his type of girl and fancied trying his luck with the other type, Marsha decided prosaically. Well, he had picked the wrong one in her!

'Not obligatory, no. But it would be nice, wouldn't it? Nothing like a tame taxi driver to take madam here and there, to the zoo, the park, Harrods . . .'

'Oh, I expect I'd soon get bored with you. I do get bored,' Marsha said truthfully. 'I'd rather have a different driver every time and not remember any of them.'

He raised a brow; just one. It gave his face a dangerous, rakish look.

'Poor little rich girl, eh? My girls don't ever complain of boredom.'

Marsha wished she could raise one eyebrow like that; he probably practises each morning, she told herself. But it was time to depress his pretensions.

'Yes, I'm rich. Is that why you're trying so hard to pick me up?'

It would have silenced most men, but not this one.

'Don't flatter yourself,' he said promptly, though over his shoulder now, because the taxi was moving once more. 'I don't need to pick up rich girls. Just you ask yourself what difference it makes to a feller whether a girl's rich as Midas or poor as a street rat. Women are all the same when the lights go out.'

'So are men, I suppose,' Marsha said doubtfully. He had cheated, taken the wind out of her sails; besides, money did matter, she was sure it did. Looks were tremendously important too but she had those, and men liked her enormously. Why, she had had lots of boyfriends since she started college!

'Nah! Men's more exciting than women. Ask anyone.'

'The only person likely to confirm that is a hermaphrodite,' Marsha said crossly. 'Do stop talking and concentrate on your driving; I realize you think you're God's gift to women but frankly I'd rather chat with the parrots at the zoo. I dare say they'd make more sense.'

She could no longer see his face but she could tell even from the back of his head that he was grinning.

'Temper, temper,' he said softly. 'Here we are, madam.' He drew the taxi into the kerb. 'That will be three shillings, please.'

Marsha got out, fiddled in her handbag and found her cream leather purse. She extracted a ten shilling note and held it out. She was always short of money – Daddy's allowance seemed to go nowhere – but on the other hand she didn't need to spend much, with Mummy's charge accounts all over London.

'Ta,' he said laconically. He fished out three florins and a shilling and held them out to her. 'Want me to call back for you when you're done?'

She took the florins but waved the shilling away, about to refuse his offer when she heard her voice say, albeit grudgingly, 'Oh, all right, then. It'll save the trouble of hailing a cab. I'll meet you here . . .' she stamped one small foot on the ground to emphasize the point '. . . at four o'clock.'

'Four on the dot. Fine. I'll be here.'

She turned away and was across the road and contemplating the wicked but pleasant thought of letting the man come back just in time to see her leaping into someone else's cab when she heard a shrill whistle behind her. She looked back. Her driver was leaning out of his window, grinning.

'You wouldn't do it,' he shouted. 'You're a little lady you are – and rich! You told me so yourself!'

And before she could gather her wits or slay him with a filthy look he had gone, driving off into the traffic, black eyes on the road ahead, hands gripping the wheel.

Promptly at four o'clock, the taxi drew up beside her at the kerb. The cabby was smiling, his dark eyes sparkling.

'Hop in,' he said briefly. 'Enjoy yourself?'

As it happened, Marsha had had a wonderful time and was dying to tell someone about it. The zoo was quiet, and an elderly keeper had let her hold a baby monkey and had given her some fish to throw to the seals. She had spent ages in the elephant house and Rajah, a magnificent bull, had taken a great liking to her, actually stroking her hair with his trunk whilst people stared and took snaps.

And then there had been tea, an unexpectedly good one, and her accidental meeting with Annabel Fines, a fellow student who was taking a niece round the zoo and had fallen in quite happily with Marsha's suggestion that they should go and see the lions together.

All this was bubbling away inside Marsha and the cab driver, it turned out, was a good listener. He asked intelligent questions, too, and seemed to know a lot about the zoo and the animals, talking knowledgeably about feeding and habitat, characteristics and peculiarities.

Because he was so friendly Marsha felt almost guilty over her earlier behaviour, but it was clear the man did not bear a grudge. So, to show him she was the same, Marsha told him about her parents going off to the Caribbean and leaving her alone over Christmas.

'That's rotten,' the cabby said seriously. 'What'll you do? Go to friends just for the day?'

'Well, I can't. All my friends went home to the country, you see,' Marsha explained. 'What do you do for Christmas? You must have a day off, surely?'

'Oh, sure. Three days. And I'm going home, too, though it's a teejus long way for such a short time.'

Through the mirror, their eyes met. Marsha smiled. 'Are you Irish?' she hazarded.

'Sure I am. Tony Bondellini's my name, which makes me Irish-Italian. But it's to Ireland we go when Christmas comes – too far to get to Florence, though I've been back most summers since I was small.'

'I'm Marsha Loxley,' Marsha said.

'Nice to meet you, Marsha. Well, here we are, right to your front door.'

The cab drew in at the kerb. It was late getting dark and the snow was falling again. Marsha thought of the lonely flat and immediately remembered the letters, which she had managed to put right out of her head all afternoon. Tears formed in her eyes but she ignored them, scrambling out of the cab, feeling the sudden chill of wind on her face as she turned to scrabble in her purse.

'How much do I owe you?' she said, and heard with horror the tremble in her voice. What on earth was the matter with her, for God's sake? An empty flat, the snow falling, Christmas coming – what did it matter?

'Oh, I'm on my way home; have it as a Christmas present,' Tony said easily. 'See you again some time, Marsha.'

He revved the engine and Marsha grabbed at the door, grabbed it as a drowning man clutches a plank.

'Tony . . . don't go! If you're on your way home, can you come in for a drink? Just . . . just coffee, if you don't drink alcohol?'

He had not expected the invitation, she could see. He frowned, looked at her, glanced up at the big block of flats, then down at the pavement, lightly dusted with new snow.

'Well, I suppose . . . yes, all right, thanks very much.' He was out of the cab in one movement, turning to lock it up. 'Are you sure your housekeeper won't think it odd? I mean . . . as you said, you're a very rich girl.'

'I lied,' Marsha said in a small, flat voice. 'I'm not who I thought I was. I'm a penniless pauper. Now you can go away.'

Tears were thick in her throat, tension was making her grip her hands into fists, hold herself ramrod stiff. She looked at him, daring him to laugh or call her a cheat, but his eyes were gentle.

'I knew there was something wrong when you got into my cab in such a terrible, cold rage,' he said. He took hold of her icy hand in his own large, warm one. 'Look, sometimes it's good to talk. Want to come out with me for a meal?'

It would have been more sensible; Mrs Higgins might not realize Tony was only a cab driver, might think he was a young man, might report to Daddy. But what the hell? It no longer mattered; Daddy and Mummy had deceived her cruelly and, now that she knew, it shouldn't matter if she hurt them. They were not her rightful parents; they were just two strangers who had wanted a child.

'No. Come in and have a drink and something to eat,' Marsha urged. How Daddy would cringe, how Mummy would bleat, if they could see her now! 'It's the first-floor flat. It's rather nice, really. Oh, God, I wish . . .'

In the lift, he put his arm round her and turned her to face him.

'Are you the housekeeper, then? Only you're too young. You aren't a skivvy – you're far too snooty for that.'

'I'm adopted,' Marsha said flatly. 'They never told me. I found out earlier today . . . there were letters in Mummy's undies drawer. I was . . . bored. I read them.'

She was furious to find that she was crying again, tears pelting down her face, soaking into the fur collar of Mummy's coat, hot tears from the cold depths of her new despair.

'So what? You're their child, their little girl.'

She snuffled, burying her face in his navy donkey jacket. No one could possibly understand! How could Mummy and Daddy have deceived her all these years? Had Eff and Teddy known in New York? Who else knew? Were they laughing at her, all the neighbours, the teachers in college, her fellow students? She said something of this and he stopped the lift, putting a hand under her chin, tilting her face to his.

'You are their well-loved child,' he said again. 'And

anyway, what does it matter? You're a beautiful woman. Your future happiness lies not in your parents' wealth or otherwise but in your own two pretty, capable hands.'

It was the best thing he could have said. Marsha straightened her shoulders and smiled and presently they stepped out on to the landing and Marsha produced her key. She unlocked the door and led him in, shedding the cinnamon coat, letting it fall to the floor. Another little sign of defiance, because Mummy loved that coat, always hung it up with care. Only she was not her mummy . . . tears were sternly repressed this time. She took Tony's hand and led him across to the kitchen.

'What would you like, tea or coffee? Or there's some whisky in the living room.'

'Tea will be grand.' He sniffed the air. 'There's a good smell coming from that oven!'

'Take a look,' Marsha invited. She plugged the kettle in and went through the familiar routine of making the tea. 'What is it? There'll be enough for two; there always is.'

'It's a fat brown dish with . . .' He yelped, backing away from the oven, sucking his fingers. 'God above, it's red hot!'

'It's casseroled beef in the brown one, and creamed potatoes and leeks in the white one,' Marsha announced, having tilted the lids of both dishes, hand protected by a quilted oven-glove. 'Want to get a couple of plates out? They're on the dresser.'

Tony laid out the plates and fetched a long-handled spoon. Marsha dished up, her mouth watering as the delicious steam teased her nostrils. Presently she went and fetched a bottle of wine and poured them each a glass, and then she and Tony sat down on opposite sides of the kitchen table and smiled at each other. Tony looked very much at home, his donkey jacket slung over a chair, his blue cotton shirt-sleeves rolled up.

'Here's to your bright eyes, Marsha. Beginning to feel a bit better, are you?'

'Much better,' Marsha said with conviction. She drank her wine like lemonade and blinked when it caught at the back of her throat. 'Much, much better. Tony . . . ?'

Tony was tasting his stew; reverently. He looked up when she spoke.

'Yes?'

'Do you really think it's all right – to be adopted, I mean?'

'Why, of course it's all right. An adopted child is chosen specially by the adoptive parents, whereas a child belongs to its natural parents whether they like it or not.'

'That's true. And they must have wanted a baby very badly, I do see that, to adopt one. But it sticks in my craw that they didn't tell me as soon as I was old enough to understand.'

'It mustn't. You have to let people explain; you can't punish them without knowing what made them take a certain action. More wine?'

Marsha nodded and drank down the second glass; it was a heavy red wine, fruity and strong, but she was thirsty despite the tea.

'Right. I'll be undersh . . . undershshtsh . . . I'll be sensible. Oh dear, how very silly I feel, as if my legs would just fold up if I tried to stand.'

Tony, eating steadily, glanced casually across at her, and his eyes widened a little.

'For heaven's sake, girl, eat something. Don't just sit there tipping wine down your throat or you'll be drunk as a lord!'

'Awright,' Marsha said owlishly. She took a forkful of

food and refilled her glass. She drank it and saw that Tony was smiling, shaking his head at her.

'Drowning your sorrows only makes sense if you've got sorrows to drown, kiddo,' he said. 'At the rate you're going I'll be putting you to bed instead of having a chat.'

'Shounds good to me,' Marsha said thickly. 'Shounds ver-ver-vereee good to me.'

Tony sighed and stood up. He had grown a great deal taller, Marsha saw. He looked down at her and his face was patient, almost resigned. She felt quite insulted by his expression.

'All right. You'll be fine after a night's sleep. Where's your room?'

'I can't tell you that!' Marsha said, astonished that he should expect her to show him her bedroom, and him a stranger as well as a cabby. 'Lesh have a little talk.'

He patted her shoulder absently, then turned and went out of the room. Whilst he was gone, Marsha passed the time by pouring herself another tumbler full of wine. It was a very old and dusty bottle, but it tasted nice. She wondered why Daddy and Mummy kept such things to themselves, never encouraging her to have a drink, and then remembered: they were not her daddy and mummy; she was a charity child.

She was in tears once more when Tony came back into the room. He said cheerfully, 'Up with you, now,' and helped her to her feet. Or rather he heaved her to her feet and then stood with an arm supporting her whilst she swayed giddily. 'Now don't go crying again; you're a chosen child, remember? And now you're going to bed.'

He led her to her room and sat her down on the covers. Kneeling, he took off her shoes and stockings, undoing the suspenders with fumbling fingers which, she tried to tell him, showed that he was a nice boy. Only she could not quite get her tongue round the words and all that came out was 'nice boy', repeated rather too often.

He unbuttoned her cardigan and blouse, undid her pleated skirt and slid it off. She tried to co-operate but she kept falling sideways in the most annoying fashion. And giggling through her tears.

He got the cardigan off but hesitated over the blouse. Beneath it her breasts were encased in the pink satin brassiere which matched her pants. Sitting on the bed, swaying, Marsha waited patiently for Tony to take her clothes off, and then began to try to wriggle out of them herself.

'Why not sleep as you are?' Tony suggested. 'It's a cold night, so you won't be too warm.'

'Mushn' sleep in clo'es,' Marsha mumbled, truly shocked that he should even consider such a thing. 'Mummy an' Daddy wou'n't like it. Gotta get 'em off.'

She tugged again, futilely, since her fingers had mysteriously ceased to have bones or joints and had become small cottonwool sausages. Tony sighed. He slid off her blouse and then picked up her nightie.

'Arms up, and I'll slip this over your head,' he said briskly. 'My word, you're well away, gel!'

'Take off my knicks firs', an' my bra,' Marsha said. She watched Tony's face and wondered why it was going so red. Had he had a little too much to drink? If so, perhaps she ought to send him on his way . . . but he was awfully useful, helping her with these stupid fastenings.

Apparently he found a compromise, though, for his grin suddenly came back. Ignoring Marsha's incoherent protests he put her nightie over her head, and then she felt his fingers fumbling with the fastening of her brassiere. He undid it, helping her arms to free themselves from the straps before removing the pink satin garment under cover of the nightie's soft blue fullness.

'Knickers now!' Marsha shouted, lurching to her feet. 'Off with knickers, Tony!'

His face had gone red again, she was interested to note. You could never understand men, she informed herself, if you lived to be a thousand. Why won't he pull these damned drawers down, so I can get into bed?

'Come on now, Marsha, you can sleep in your – your knickers, can't you? They'll keep you nice and warm.'

Marsha scowled at him, sitting on the bed whilst she swayed uncertainly before him. What on earth was the matter with the chap? Did he not know that nice girls absolutely *never* slept in their knickers?

'Don' wanna be warm; want air,' she informed him. She tugged fruitlessly at her waist, but the nightie impeded her. She sighed, heaving it higher, higher . . .

'Marsha, just stop it, will you? All right, I give in. Stand still.'

She stood still. He knelt on the floor and his hands ran up her sides beneath the nightie, fingers delicate on her bare skin. He hooked his thumbs in the elastic at her waist and pulled. She teetered, then overbalanced. Trapped by the knickers, now at knee-level, she fell back on to the bed. She started to laugh, rolling on to her side so that she could see his face.

He was not laughing. He looked cross, yet . . .

'There you are!' He tossed the pink satin knickers down. 'Goodnight, Marsha.'

She began to protest but he picked up her feet and swung them into the bed, then pulled up the covers until only her face was free of them. He still looked a little annoyed, she was sorry to see. But not with her, surely? She had done nothing wrong!

'Tony? Don' go, stay with me! Oh, Tony, do stay! Put your arms round me . . . oh Tony, don't leave me all alone!'

But he was not to be cajoled into remaining. He walked to the door, then turned.

'Go to sleep now, Marsha. If you feel sick, there's a basin beside the bed. Goodnight.'

Marsha tried to follow him, but he had tucked her in too firmly. And presently, despite her tears, for she cried long and hard over his abandonment, she found that she was tired; very, very tired. Not long after, she slept.

By rights Marsha should have woken next morning with a thumping head, but instead she woke with a nasty taste in her mouth which she remedied by climbing out of bed and cleaning her teeth.

I was drunk last night, she reminded herself; me, Marsha Loxley, nineteen next March, drunk as a tinker for the first time in my life. Why don't I have a hangover, like Daddy's had once or twice, and people at college talk about?

But it seemed a hangover was to be denied her, so she swilled her mouth round with cold water, still tasting the pleasant minty flavour of the toothpaste, and tried to decide whether to go into the kitchen and make herself some breakfast, or whether just to go back to bed.

A glance through the window showed it was early. But people were hurrying along the pavements, traffic was humming past, and she could tell even through the frosted glass that more snow had fallen in the night. She thought about going back to bed but she was too wide awake. I'll get myself some coffee, she decided, padding across the hallway, kitchen-bound.

It was a surprise, not to say a shock, when she opened the kitchen door to find a man clad in her father's dressing gown and slippers standing in front of the stove, turning two rounds of toast white-side-up under the grill.

'What . . .'

The man turned. For a moment she could not think who the hell he was, then remembered. He was her taxi driver of the day before! What on earth was he doing here, in Daddy's dressing gown, making toast? Honestly, some people . . .

'Good morning, Marsha. I was just about to wake you up with tea and toast, but you're obviously still alive . . . come to that, you were alive earlier, and snoring fit to bust, what's more.'

Snoring? Earlier? Marsha felt the colour drain out of her face. She had been drunk . . . he had been here, in the flat, all night! Had he been not only in the flat but also in her bed? Heavens, had he . . . had they . . . ?

'What? What did . . . what . . . ?'

'Oh, I popped in to see if you were okay and you didn't stir, so I came out again to make the tea. I spent the night in the big room next door to yours; your parents', I imagine. I knew they weren't around because you told me so. If you remember.' He looked hard at her, then grinned suddenly, showing his very white, slightly crooked teeth. 'Do you remember *anything*, old lady?'

Marsha frowned. She remembered going to the zoo, and before that finding letters proving she was adopted, but after that, after arriving home . . . had she asked this young man in? She must have, though it was not the sort of thing she usually did. She remembered Daddy's threat and then reminded herself that the threat was pretty empty, now. She was not Daddy's little girl, so she could please herself. Couldn't she?

'I don't remember much,' she admitted. 'Oh . . . your name's Tony!'

She sounded so pleased that he laughed, turning from the job of pouring tea to give her a shrewd glance.

'You picked me up, luv, in the most blatant way and invited me to stay with you all night, though I doubt you

knew by then just what you were saying. In fact you . . .'
He broke off, glancing at her in her cloudy blue nightie
and looking quickly away, back at the tea he was pouring.
His face had reddened slightly but he was still smiling, an
oddly reminiscent smile, Marsha thought hollowly. Oh
God, what had she done?

'Umm . . . I was upset, wasn't I?' she ventured. 'That
was why I drank so much wine. Oh!'

She had been looking at his hands as he stirred sugar
into one of the cups and immediately a picture popped
into her head. Those same hands trying to untangle her
knickers from her knees!

'Yes, you were upset and yes, you drank too much
wine. Which was why I helped you into bed and left you
to sleep it off.' He held out a cup. 'Go on, drink up and
you'll feel better.' Having seen her take a firm grip of the
teacup his eyes returned to her face, quizzical, alarmingly
intimate. 'Mind you, you look absolutely grand,' he added
in a slightly puzzled voice. 'No headache? Did you chuck
up in the night?'

'No,' Marsha said repressively. 'I'd better go and put
my dressing gown on. I hadn't realized you intended to
stay the night.'

She half turned away and was firmly grabbed. Tea
lurched over the rim and met the tiles with a slap as he
took the cup from her and dumped it on the dresser.

'Me, intend to stay the night? You really don't remember a thing, do you? You begged me to stay with you . . .
you insisted that I undress you . . . you were all too willing to let me do anything, provided I stayed.'

'I wasn't! Besides, I was drunk!' Marsha shouted, furious that he should dare to insinuate she had been willing
to do it with a cabby. 'Anyway, you can bloody well go
home. I don't want you here!'

She had sworn twice in her life, now. It was really quite

exhilarating! But she had little time to enjoy the sensation. One minute she was furiously facing him, the next she was crushed unceremoniously against his broad chest and his mouth was clamped on to hers as though he intended to push her lips through the back of her head.

Marsha struggled and kicked and tried to push herself away and then, all of a sudden, found that she was enjoying it. She let her body relax in his arms, let his mouth overcome hers, exploring, tantalizing, until she moaned beneath her breath. He swung her up in his arms and carried her out of the kitchen, across the hall and into her room, all without moving his lips from hers. And Marsha flung her arms round him and moved her body in a thoroughly provocative way and thought to herself that now she knew what working class men were like as lovers – and it was grand!

There, on that nice soft bed, he kissed and cuddled and Marsha remembered the hot hands and eager, inexpert shovings and pullings of previous boyfriends and decided that this was definitely better.

'Tony, oh, oh, Tony!'

'Marsha, you little darling, you soft, sweet, honey-child . . . oh, oh, oh!'

And then, just as she was getting really excited, the thrill seasoned by a dash of fear at what was to come . . . would it hurt? should she stop him now? . . . he drew back from her. His face was reddened, his mouth trembled, but he still drew back.

'Marsha . . . we shouldn't . . .'

'I don't want you to stop,' Marsha moaned, trying to get back into his arms, aware that her nightie was a frail barrier and glad of it. 'Tony, Tony, make love to me!'

But he would not. He put his arms round her but above her head his voice went on talking and his body was still.

'No! Tomorrow you'd scream rape.'

'I wouldn't! Oh, Tony, you shouldn't have gone so far if you didn't mean . . .'

'It's not like that. Marsha, you don't want to have a baby, do you?'

It stopped her. She drew back, looking at him doubtfully, her eyes large, her bee-stung lips swollen with his kisses.

'A baby? But can't you . . . isn't there a way . . . ?'

He laughed and kissed her lightly on the nose.

'Yes, there is. But not right here and now. Believe it or not, when I set off in my cab yesterday morning I didn't know I was going to end up in bed with a beautiful woman! Marsha . . . come to Ireland with me.'

'To Ireland? To your family? Oh, I couldn't. They'd think it was most peculiar!'

'We'll go to my family just for the day – Christmas Day – and after that we'll book into a quiet little hotel somewhere and make love, the safe way, like you want.'

Marsha looked hard at him. It was what she wanted. Just now her heart – or some other, less romantic part of her – was most definitely ruling her head. But would she still want it in two or three days, to the extent of making excuses – well, telling lies – and going off with him across the sea, to another country?

'You'd love it, Marsha, you know you would.' He was being sweet to her now, the hand that was not round her shoulders taking delightful liberties under the flimsy material of the nightie. She could feel her breathing begin to speed up and her heartbeats quicken. 'Say yes, because it's what you want, you know it is. Or would you really rather I went now, and left you to your lonely Christmas?'

'Umm . . . yes,' Marsha said breathlessly. 'I'll come to Ireland.'

And as she said it, the oddest thing happened. Instead

of seeing Tony's dark face, the bedroom behind him, she saw a picture she had thought long forgotten.

A boy and a girl scrambling over the rocks on a far shore. The girl was wearing a faded cotton dress tucked into navy bloomers, and she had long, pale gold hair.

She looked most awfully like Marsha.

CHAPTER EIGHTEEN

'I'm glad the weather's bad if it means the boys won't go out, but what sort of Christmas will it be, all this snow and cold everywhere? Ah, the poor little birds, and the gulls desperate for a bite!'

Megan was helping Mam in the kitchen, stopping every now and then to peer disgustedly through the window. Only another day to Christmas and in the early hours of the morning a storm had blown up, the sort of storm which made it impossible for the *Claudia* to sail. Outside, the lilac tree which leaned comfortably over the gate into the back lane was lashing tormentedly and the washing line, empty now of even the thin line of frosted snow which had topped it, was held out in a permanent curve by the force of the wind.

Mam, part-cooking the turkey, turned, red-faced, from her contemplation of its charms, shutting the oven door gently.

'Phew, there's hot! In half an hour, Meggie, that old bird will be cooked just right . . . well, nearly cooked, I should say, since tomorrow it'll need a couple of hours to finish it off. Done the sprouts, have you?'

'Nearly.' Megan peered with distaste at the tight green buds. 'Horrible little things – but at least it's been so cold that they aren't full of greenfly or baby caterpillars.'

'It's been so cold we're lucky to have any sprouts,' Mam reminded her. 'Williams-Bread told me a couple of days ago that his carrots had got frosted even tucked up warm in the clamp, with a good six inches of hay round them before the clay was put on top.'

'Ours are all right,' Da volunteered. He had come into the kitchen from outside and was rosy with the cold, his curls blown all over his head instead of being watered flat, as usual. 'I come from the allotment not an hour since and I munched on a carrot, coming up the hill.' He grinned at Megan, making a ring with his thumb and forefinger. 'There's sweet that carrot was, and sound . . . sweet and sound as our girl, eh, Mam?'

'Oh, get along with you,' Mam said. When he kissed the side of her neck she squealed and gave him a push, but Megan knew she loved it by the way her eyes shone. 'Now what do you want, Dai, in my nice neat kitchen?'

'A nice neat cuppa,' Da said at once. 'Toast, too, a bit burnt on the outside and all warm and soft and white inside. Butter, of course, and a scrape of marmalade. And the paper, if anyone's seen it?'

'Uncle Reggie took it to his room,' Megan said. 'No fishing today then, Da. Not even out in the bay.'

'Oh, well,' Da said tolerantly. 'Not much sale for fish, Christmas Day. And we'll be out before the New Year, never fear.' He sniffed the air, nose up, eyes closed, like one of the Bisto kids. 'Something smells good!'

'Tomorrow's dinner,' his wife said. 'That was a good bird Aunt Ennys found up for us. And the pudding's one of my best, eh, Meg?'

'Full of Irish raisins,' Megan said, smiling. 'Not to mention Irish whiskey . . .'

'. . . and butter, and sugar . . .'

'. . . and black treacle and suet . . .'

'Less of that, you wicked women,' Da protested, but he was smiling still. 'What about our good Welsh apples, then? And our flour?'

'A fine apple dumpling that would make, but not much of a Christmas pudding,' Megan pointed out. 'Won't we miss Dewi, Mam, when he comes off the mailboats and goes full-time fishing?'

Dewi helped with the engine and went out with the *Claudia* when he was not aboard the cross-channel ships, but it had not been deemed sensible for a man with a young wife to throw up a good job and go adventuring. However, as Da said, they had a ready market for their fish, and provided they continued to bring in first-rate supplies could be sure of selling them at good prices to the hotels and boarding houses on the island and along the Lleyn peninsula.

'Miss him? We'll see even more of him.'

'Yes, but you know what I mean – we'll miss the raisins and the butter and . . .'

'Oh, that. Well, when Dewi leaves, why don't you get a job aboard, Meggie?'

'I get seasick,' Megan said promptly. She was happy in Boots, reading the library books to her heart's content on quiet days, chatting with the customers and helping them to choose books when it was busier. 'But I could always make friends with a sailor, I suppose.'

Da raised his brows, and Mam smiled placidly. Everyone knew, Megan thought crossly, that she would do no such thing, but at times she was tempted – seriously tempted. Why did Danny not suggest that they get engaged, even if he did not yet want to marry? He takes me for granted, Megan told herself, and he shouldn't, it isn't fair. But on the other hand he's a great deal better than he was; he laughs more, mucks about sometimes, isn't so serious. And he doesn't ever sit in a chair and stare in front of him as though he was seeing dreadful things, nor tap his fingers on the table when I speak as if he can't wait for me to stop and then, when I do, just stare at me.

But winter was no weather for motor biking and she

missed it, was sure Danny felt the same. They had gone on one expedition in November, inland to the big reservoir to see migrating duck and geese, and coming home it had simply poured down with rain. The rain had driven horizontally, she had been really frightened, and in the end Danny had suggested they should take shelter. He had turned the bike off the main coast road into a side lane which wound down towards the shore.

'There's no shelter round here,' Megan had shouted, turning her back into the worst of the gale and shrugging her shoulders up to her ears like an old tortoise. 'Only the beach and the rocks . . . and that damned old hump of a hill . . .'

Her voice had died away. They were at Porth Trecastell, and that damned old hump was the burial chamber she and Danny had visited years ago.

'I know it. Want to come down under the mound?'

She looked at him. He was blue with cold, his face running with water, but his eyes were bright – wicked. She could not help smiling at him, though her teeth were chattering like a flock of starlings.

'Oh, Danny, and both of us near dead of cold! We'd freeze if we . . . I mean, it just isn't . . . oh, Danny, take me home!'

He had. But she knew, and she was sure Danny knew, that it had been the tentative start of a change in their relationship. He had been saying, *It's going to be all right; if not today, some other day*. And since then she had been aware that Danny no longer tensed up each time someone asked him when he was going to make an honest woman of Megan Prydderch.

'Give us a chance,' he had said to Arthur, who was cross-questioning him. 'Let's get this trawling business straightened out and then we'll talk about weddings until even your Mam is satisfied.'

'What's for dinner today, then? Old bread and a kick, I dare say.'

Megan, dragged back to the present, turned from the window in time to see Mam swing at Da, and Da catch her in one arm and pretend to pinch her nose with the other hand. Mam squealed again and beat on Da's forearm with one small, clenched fist. Da growled under his breath and lunged at her, pretend-biting the white of her neck just below her ear.

'Teach you some respect I will, girl! Better feed me or I'll take a bite out of you, big though you are!'

'It's cold lamb, tinned beans, fresh-baked bread and Mam's rice pud for after,' Megan said, gathering up the sprout-leaves and the stalks and wrapping them in newspaper to throw away. 'Cooked the pud under the turk, see – save fuel that way.'

'Save fuel – anyone would think there was a war on,' Da grumbled. He released Mam, though, and went over to the sink, rolling up the sleeves of his tattered blue sweater. 'Better wash up, even if you aren't feeding me a good hot meal,' he announced, pumping water into the white enamel bowl. 'Can't come to the table with fish scales all over my fists.'

'Fish scales? I thought you hadn't been out today,' Mam remarked, opening the bread crock and bringing out one of the big, oddly shaped loaves which she baked Mondays, Wednesdays and Fridays. 'Where would you get fish from today, Dai?'

'Where but the sea, woman? A man like me doesn't need a boat to get fish. Danny and I went down to the breakwater and cast a line out. Pulled half a dozen each aboard in as many minutes. My, they were biting despite the weather!'

'What did you get, Da?' Megan asked, looking round. There was no sign of fish that she could see.

'Bass. Danny's got 'em. He's hawking them round the neighbourhood . . . quick Christmas Eve meal, see – grill 'em in two minutes, serve 'em hot and fresh . . . give him a few shillin' for over the holiday.'

'Wonder what he wants extra money for?' Megan spoke without thinking, just idly voicing the obvious.

Mam and Da exchanged glances; Megan saw them, but could not read their expressions.

'Who doesn't want extra money?' Mam said lightly, since Da said nothing. 'Keep him going till the weather clears, likely enough.'

'Sure. Shall I get the lamb out, then, cut a few slices? Who's in for dinner?'

Mam was replying when there came a thunderous knock on the front door, followed by a crash as the door was flung open. Before anyone could move, the kitchen door was also bounced back and Peris stood in the doorway, kitbag over one shoulder, shock of dark hair falling across his eyes, big grin bisecting his face.

'Mam! Da! And the brat herself!' Peris dropped his kitbag on the floor and grabbed first Mam, then Da, then Megan. Hearty hugs all round, exclamations, questions asked too rapidly for answers. How was he, how was the Air Force, how had he come, by train, by bus, why hadn't he let them know . . .

'Let me get a word in,' Peris said. 'My pal brought me in his car – Roger Pendennis from Beaumaris. Right posh he is, but we're still good friends. Can he come in for a moment? Like to meet you he would.'

Da promptly surged out into the hall, to return almost at once with a tall, fair-haired young man who smiled pleasantly round at them all. Megan had half-expected him to be shy, but he was very self-confident, with an air of quiet authority which made him seem a good deal older than the ebullient Peris. He was introduced and it

301

transpired that both young men were learning to fly with the same squadron of Tiger Moths.

'No speaking Welsh now,' Da shouted in that language as they ushered Roger into the kitchen. 'Have to talk barbarian now, since our guest has no *Cymraeg*.' He turned to Roger, switching to English. 'Just reminding them you don't have a word of God's own language, so we can say what we like and you none the wiser.'

Roger grinned.

'I'm learning,' he protested. 'But we've only been in Beaumaris a couple of years. Before that I was in the States.'

'I thought you sounded American,' said Megan wisely. She had heard a lot of transatlantic accents in the canteen down at Quiet Corner. 'Why are you in Britain though, Roger?'

He turned to her and started to speak, and then a big grin spread over his face.

'Marsha, don't you recognize me? You know, Roger and Billy, from the ship? You danced with Billy most, but you did condescend to . . .'

His voice faltered into silence as Megan blushed scarlet, embarrassed for him, and Peris nudged him.

'What you on about, Roger? That's my kid sister Meg. Never been off Ynys Mon in her life, poor little rabbit.'

'Never? No, I see now . . . I'm sorry, Megan, but you're most awfully like a girl I used to know. I could have sworn . . . but it's just one of those things. Everyone has a double, they say.'

The matter passed off and then Mam, with a cry, was diving at the oven, turning it off, scolding them all, in Welsh and English alternately, for letting her forget her bird. How would they like it, eh, if they had to share a shrivelled little bit of meat tomorrow?

'All right if Rog stays for dinner?' Peris asked easily as Megan began to lay the table. 'A long old drive he's had.'

So the food was brought out – the cold lamb, the beans, the bread – and set on the table in the kitchen for family and their guest, with Uncle Reggie joining them as he usually did for the midday meal. Under cover of laying the table and Da carving the joint and chatting, Megan had the chance of a word with Peris.

'Peri, why's your pal staring so?' she muttered, as she sliced the loaf and buttered the slices. 'Rude it is, unless I've a smut on my nose the size of a house, mun!'

'Struck by your stunning beauty,' Peris said. 'And by the smut the size of a house, of course. Does it matter? He'll stop presently, when he gets used to you.'

'He'd better,' muttered Megan. 'A punch on the snout he'll get, else. Tell him that, when you get him alone!'

But despite Peris taking Roger off to wash his hands the staring continued, albeit covertly, throughout the meal. By the end of it Megan was not only embarrassed, she was also cross. When Peris suggested that the three younger ones might walk down to the harbour after the washing up had been done, to clear the cobwebs and settle their food, she was eager to go. Roger might not be told home-truths in the house, since he was a guest, but walking by the harbour, howling gale or no, he would learn a thing or two!

'Wrap up well, my dears,' Mam said, holding Megan's thick duffel coat whilst Megan squiggled into the arms. 'Cold it is . . . I don't want no wheezes and sneezes on Christmas Day!'

'We'll walk fast to keep the cold out,' Megan promised. 'If Danny comes round, tell him we're down by the break-water, will you?'

Once outside the house, she linked arms with Peris

303

against the gale, and found her other arm taken by Roger Pendennis.

'We'll all hang together and if one gets blown down we'll go over like ninepins,' Roger shouted, above the howl of the wind. 'Now that I don't have your father watching me, Megan, may I tell you what a pretty girl you are?'

'May I tell you that it's rude to stare?' countered Megan crossly. 'Keep your sweet talk for those who want it, you!'

'Did I stare? If I did, it was because I've always been crazy about blondes and you're not only blonde, you're very beautiful.'

'Don't talk so silly,' Megan said shortly, not at all softened by what she termed 'his old flannel' to herself. 'Just don't stare at me again, or I'll land you one.'

He laughed, then glanced down at her, the puzzled look in evidence once more.

'I'm sorry . . . I know Peris says you've never been off the island, but the girl I knew on the ship . . . she really was most awfully like you. When I first saw you I was quite sure you were Marsha.'

Megan felt a tiny, cold frisson of shock race up her spine and into her neck, where it brought the hairs on the nape tingling erect. Marsha? How very odd!

'I thought you said Marsha before. I had a friend once . . .' she began, then stopped short. Stupid to tell him that the child she had invented, to give herself a companion in her loneliest years, had also been called Marsha. He would think her a half-wit – or, if he didn't, Peris most certainly would.

Hanging on to her other arm, Peris jerked it to get her attention.

'Don't listen to old Roger,' he shouted above the wind. 'Biggest liar in four continents, always soft-soaping some

304

woman. Just you stick to dull old Danny and leave the dangerous ones alone.'

They emerged from the end of Newry Fawr and, as they turned down towards the harbour, met the wild wind head on. It robbed them of breath so that they had to turn their heads to one side to breathe comfortably. But Megan was so incensed by Peris's words that she opened her mouth to speak and felt the wind roar down her throat, trying to make her breathe in when she wanted to breathe out, forcing itself into her lungs until she turned her head.

'Danny isn't dull! He's the best bloke on the island,' she shrieked. 'Don't you dare call him dull, Peris Prydderch!'

'Who's this Danny?'

'Oh, come on, Meggie. If Danny had any fire in his belly he'd not be stuck here, fishing in a dirty little trawler with Da and the lads! Why do you think I didn't come back, eh? Because I want adventure, life! I don't want to vegetate in a little backwater, I want to get somewhere, be someone. I can't imagine why you've not gone as well.'

'No, but who is Danny?'

'So we're not good enough for you, Peris, is that it? You worshipped Danny once, you thought he was absolutely wizard! And if he'd not had ambition he could have stayed a farmhand, but he went trawling instead so don't you dare sneer at him . . .'

'Chaps, chaps, chaps . . . do just let me ask once more: *who is Danny?*'

It made them laugh, albeit reluctantly, and turn to him.

'Sorry, Roger,' Megan said. 'Danny's my boyfriend. He was in the Navy during the war and saw enough of the world and the adventure Peris is on about to know that the things which really matter are here, on the island. He's a remarkable person, is Danny.'

'He's all right, really,' Peris contributed. 'I was just

trying to get Meg mad – and didn't I succeed? You could have torn my head off and thrown it to the gulls, couldn't you, my little one?'

'I still could, so watch it,' Megan growled. 'Oh, look at that, will you?'

They had reached the harbour. They stood at the top of the green, looking down on it. Within the encircling arm of the great breakwater the boats and ships were moored, and they bounded upon the bosom of the deep as though there were fathoms of water under them instead of feet. One was already loosed from her moorings, drifting sideways across the harbour, tossed like a cork on the waves. She would do damage when she came in contact with other shipping but there was little anyone could do with a sea like that running. And outside the breakwater . . .

'Will you look at that!' Peris was staring at the sea, his eyes shining. 'Ah God, what a sight!'

Great, white-crested waves were rearing up and breaking over the wall, sending a crossways surge to tangle still further the small boats at anchor. It looked as though a giant hand was stirring a small bucket, getting the water to lash this way and that, its fury never allowed full rein in the restricted space.

'God help sailors in a storm like this,' Megan murmured. Mam's cry, heard many times during the war years. 'Thank God the *Claudia* didn't try to sail. She'd never have lasted.' She turned to Roger. 'The *Claudia* is Da's trawler,' she explained. 'She's an old boat – she was a minesweeper during the war – and though she's had no end of work done on her she's creaky in the joints – a bit slow to come head to wind, Da says. He and Danny and English Phil want a bigger boat one day. But not yet. Not until the *Claudia* has paid for herself.'

'Where's she moored?' Peris shouted. 'We could take Roger down and show him.'

'She's in the inner harbour . . . the docks, really,' Megan told him. 'It's a good old way, but if you want . . .'

'I wouldn't mind,' Roger said. 'I like a walk.'

'So do I,' Megan said at once. 'We could call for Danny. Then you can judge for yourself.'

Roger grinned.

'Sure. Fine. All right by you, Peris?'

'Certainly,' Peris said. 'Lead on, Mac-Megan!'

Danny lived with his mam and Uncle Ned in a flat above a small general store and bakery on London Road. The shop was run by his mam and Uncle Ned baked the bread. People talked about Danny's mam, but Megan thought it was all past now and no one really cared any more.

They talked because Danny's uncle was no relative but Ceinwen Williams's lie-beside, and they said it wasn't right. Not that they knew for certain what went on . . . but Megan knew there were only two bedrooms and Danny slept in the smaller one, alone.

Now Danny's Uncle Ned was pushing seventy and his mam was in her mid-forties, though, it did not seem quite as shocking as it once had. But even so there was some disapproval and Megan's mam, who was good and kind, would not speak to Danny's mam save for a cool 'good morning' when they met in the street, and the minister never called at the flat on London Road.

Megan had visited once or twice, but had not been encouraged either by her own people or by Danny's. No one held his mam's behaviour against Danny, so far as Megan could tell, but no one approved, either.

'They could not marry, see,' Megan's mam had once told her daughter. 'Small chance of that, with Ned's wife off with a black man from Liverpool these thirty years

307

since, and never a word save to tell Ned she was a good Catholic and would never divorce him.' Mam had snorted. 'A good Catholic, and her living in sin from the day she met that black feller.'

'Then why is everyone horrid to Danny's mam?' Megan had asked, not understanding this at all. 'It isn't her fault, Mam, is it?'

'Well, in a way, no. When Danny's da was killed aboard his ship she had no money and a small child, and when Ned offered her a home . . . well, I suppose she was desperate. But a stronger woman would have managed somehow, without falling into sin.'

So now Megan went into the bakery alone whilst Peris and Roger waited outside. Mrs Williams and Danny's Uncle Ned knew Megan well, though Danny's mam, who was small and shrill with a sharp pair of eyes and a tongue like a whetted razor, had never made Megan feel welcome.

'Umm . . . is Danny in, Mrs Williams?'

Danny's mam was weighing sweets into small brown bags. She looked up, let her eyes wander slowly and disapprovingly over Megan's navy duffel coat and sensible brown shoes, then sniffed and jerked her head at the stairs which led up to the flat.

'Up there.'

'Oh. Thanks. Can I go up?'

'Best give 'im a shout.'

Megan went to the foot of the stairs and called softly.

'Danny? It's Meg. Peris is home . . . can you come down for a minute?'

After rather more than a minute, Danny came quickly down the creaking wooden stairs. He had a guernsey on, still a bit fishy – Megan could smell it from where she stood – and faded denims. He looked as though he had just woken up from sleep, but he smiled at her.

'Hey, Meggie! Who's the feller with Peris? I was watching them from the window.'

Megan shrugged. She could feel the slow waves of pleasure and comfort breaking over her, now that she was with Danny. All the fury she had felt over Peris's unkind words, all the annoyance over Roger's staring, faded into insignificance beside the warming joy of Danny's presence.

'Him? Oh, he's an Englishman from Beaumaris, Roger Pendennis. He's in Peris's squadron and he gave Peris a lift home, so Mam asked him for dinner. We're taking him down to see the *Claudia*. Can you come down to the harbour with us?'

'Why not?' Danny turned to his mother, who had resumed her sweet-weighing. 'Shan't be long, Mam.'

'Tea's at six,' she said sharply. 'Don't be late.'

'He can come to us for tea if he likes,' Megan said eagerly. 'Danny's always welcome, Mam says.'

Mrs Williams grunted ungraciously.

'It's up to Danny. His tea will be on the table at six sharp and in the bin at quarter past. He knows it.'

Poor Danny, Megan thought as the two of them made their way out of the small shop. Poor Danny, tied to that cross-grained creature with her bitter mouth and sharp, suspicious eyes. It was a miracle her son had turned out as well as he had . . . and when we're married, Megan vowed to herself, I'll see that he gets the sort of spoiling he needs, not cruel rules about meals on time or meals in bins!

For now, however, all she could do was take his hand and squeeze it, and to her delight he looked down at her, his blue eyes showing that he knew what she meant and was glad of it, and squeezed back. Not too hard, but lovingly, lingeringly.

'Roger, this is Danny Williams. Danny, this is Roger Pendennis.'

Rather to Megan's surprise Danny's smile and handshake were both rather stiff and formal, Roger's glance wary. But at least a foursome was easier than a threesome. Roger and Peris went ahead, she and Danny followed. Across London Road, down Turkey Shore, to the spot where the *Claudia* was berthed.

It was more sheltered here, with the docks and the big ships breaking up the wind's force, and of course this inner harbour was always calmer, though the roofs of some of the warehousing clattered in the gale, the sheets of corrugated iron lifting and booming as the wind caught them.

'There she is!' Danny said. 'What do you think, Peris?'

It was the first time Peris had seen the *Claudia* since the early days, and he should have been impressed. But perhaps he did not want to show it in front of his friend. At any rate he took only the most cursory glance before turning away.

'Oh, she's all right, I suppose. But I wouldn't want to risk myself in any boat when it's blowing a gale like this. Give me an aircraft every time.'

'You couldn't get a kite up in this weather either, Peris,' Roger remarked. He sounded surprised.

'It's been done,' Peris said shortly. 'It was done time and again during the war.'

'I went out in worse weather too during the war,' Danny said quietly. 'Sometimes in vessels no bigger than the old *Claudia*. But we weren't hunting fish. We were the hunted.'

'But it's over now, thank goodness,' Megan said fervently. 'These days no one goes out to find fish when the sea could have you before you got more than a few yards outside the harbour. What'll we do now, then?'

'Walk home, I guess,' Roger said when no one else answered. 'To your home, I mean. Say, it was awful good of your mother to invite me for lunch.'

'Any friend of Peris's would be welcome, the same as any friend of mine,' Megan told him. She pulled at Danny's arm. 'Come on, let's go back. The wind's strong enough to get in through the buttonholes of this coat! Besides, I haven't finished wrapping all my presents.'

'What about Peris? Hadn't you posted him a parcel?'

Megan groaned.

'Of course. So he'll have nothing to open, unless . . .' She turned and shouted back to the two young men following them. 'Peri, where's the parcel we sent?'

'We brought it with us,' Peris shouted back. 'Got a bit of old nonsense for you, I have, so I thought I'd better bring my parcel for opening tomorrow.'

'Thank God,' Megan said devoutly. 'No good at inventing nice things, I am.' She looked up at Danny, his face set and serious, his wind-blown yellow hair streaming out behind him making him look like a figurehead. 'Will you come to tea, Danny?'

Danny looked down at her thoughtfully, then shook his head.

'Not today, Meggie. But I'll be round tomorrow morning, early as you like.'

CHAPTER NINETEEN

Marsha was in two minds about what to tell the Higginses. If she told them the truth – that she was off to Ireland with a man she'd only known two days – a telegram would be despatched to the Caribbean at once, closely followed by hysterical telephone calls. It would all be far too late, of course; she would have gone, and serve Mummy and Daddy right for having deceived her, but . . . it would be much easier to make up a convincing story about a cousin in Manchester, telephoning to invite Marsha to join the family Christmas celebration.

Besides, you never knew with the elderly. Mr and Mrs Higgins might be so distraught that they called in adult assistance of some kind . . . the police? . . . and this might easily queer her pitch.

So, in the end, discretion proved the better part of valour. Or, to be more precise, Marsha opted for large lies convincingly told.

She did the job well, too. Mrs Higgins drank it all in: the cousin in Manchester; the telephone call very early this morning – she was *so* sorry if the bell had woken them – and of course the money for the train fare which would come out of her allowance.

Perhaps it was partly because the Higginses had no desire to wait on her over Christmas, but whatever the reason, they believed her. Mrs Higgins said she was glad to think Marsha would be with other young people, Mr Higgins offered to get her a taxi for the station. They were wreathed in smiles, poor old dears – Marsha could almost hear the cries of delight which would ring out as soon as she was safely gone.

Still. Better that way than the other. She had to tell a few more lies before she got away, though. Oh, that's most awfully kind of you, Mr Higgins, but actually I caught a cab home last night, from the zoo, you know, and booked the driver for this morning, too. I told him I'd be going to the National Gallery and then on to Harrods, but I'm sure he'll be equally glad of any fare. Goodness, Cousin May's telephone number . . . yes, of course she's on the phone . . . look, tell you what, I'll ring you as soon as I set foot in Manchester – that bit was certainly true – so you'll know I've arrived safely. Don't worry about a thing; just enjoy your Christmas!

When Tony drove up ten minutes later she was already beginning to wonder whether she had made a mistake, to feel the knot of apprehension tightening in her stomach. He rang the bell, all very correct. He fetched her suitcase and gave her a kiss before leading the way downstairs. In his arms she felt secure once more, sure she was doing the right thing. Why shouldn't she have a life of her own – it appeared to be all she did have!

He slung her case in the back of the taxi and let her follow it, but once they were well away from the flats he stopped the cab and came and opened the rear door.

'Come and join me,' he invited. He held out both hands and pulled Marsha out of her seat and on to the pavement, where he put his arms round her very lovingly. He was wearing a big cream-coloured wool sweater; she put her face against it and liked the smell and the feel. And then he kissed her, not demandingly, quite gently, and she liked that too.

'We'd best get a move on,' he said after a moment. 'No trouble, I take it?'

'No trouble,' Marsha said, snuggling back in her seat.

313

It was nice and warm in the cab and a delicious sense of her own wickedness warmed her even more. That she should have dared! And if she played her cards right she could have her cake and eat it too, go back to the flat after having had all the excitement of being a fallen woman over the holiday, and become, to all intents and purposes, a good girl again. Daddy's pet, Mummy's little helper.

'Got all your stuff?' Tony said presently. 'Clothes for the country and that?'

'Yes. You?'

'Sure, in a hold-all. I've bought our tickets, too – third-class, I'm afraid.'

'Oh. I thought we were going all the way by taxi,' Marsha said. 'Why can't we?'

Tony pointed out the petrol restrictions and the amount of fuel a cab used, and her slight disappointment was tempered by the reminder that they would get a meal on the train.

'Right. Which station do we leave from?'

'Euston, in half an hour. We catch the boat train to Holyhead, then the cross-channel ship to Dun Laoghaire, and after that it's another train and a bit of a walk and we're there.'

'I never asked you whereabouts in Ireland,' Marsha said presently, as the taxi dodged in and out of the heavy traffic surrounding the station. 'And what will happen to your taxi whilst we're gone?'

'A friend's waiting at Euston. I'll give him the keys and he'll drive her back to the garage. And we're going to Connemara.' They swung off the main road and into a side street. 'Almost finished the first part of the journey, Marsha; excited?'

Marsha was about to deny, loftily, that a trip to Ireland could possibly thrill such a seasoned traveller as herself when she realized that she was absolutely simmering with excitement.

'A bit,' she said. 'I never asked . . . do you have sisters over there? Parents?'

He laughed, giving her an indulgent sideways glance.

'You don't think much about other people, do you? I've a couple of sisters in England and three brothers in the United States . . . we're a big family . . . but no one in the Old Country. Just grandparents, aunts and uncles, and a gross of cousins.'

'And . . . and are they all very fond of you?' Marsha asked rather timidly. An only child, she was uneasily aware that large families did not always welcome an outsider into their midst. 'I wouldn't want anyone to think . . .'

'They're a friendly lot; they'll love you,' Tony assured her. 'But I thought we'd stop off in Dublin and buy a few presents. There's no rationing there, so we'll have no trouble.' He slowed to let an old man shuffle across the road in front of him, glancing sideways at Marsha before pulling off once more. 'They're not rich . . . in fact you could call them peasants, I suppose.'

'Oh,' Marsha said rather feebly. 'Well, it's you I'm with, Tony.'

This seemed to please him; he flashed her a grin and drew in to the kerb.

'True. See that tall fellow in the old flying jacket with the collar turned up? That's my mate.'

'I see,' Marsha murmured. 'Oh, Tony . . . I wonder if this is a good idea?'

But she spoke too quietly, too late. Tony pipped the horn and the man turned and came towards them, showing long, yellowy teeth in a wide grin. Tony was getting out, heaving their luggage from the back, talking,

315

gesticulating. He handed the keys over, then came round to Marsha's side of the cab and opened the door.

'Hop out,' he said briskly. 'I'll carry your case and the hold-all. You just hang on to me . . . there's bound to be crowds all trying to get to Ireland for the holiday.'

'Did you book seats?' Marsha asked anxiously, panting in his wake as they traversed the station. She had not yet had the doubtful pleasure of standing in a corridor for hours and did not want to make today a first.

'Sure I did. Hey, there's the train . . . we're in Coach F.'

'I see it. Tony, I was wondering whether I'm going to regret . . .'

But they were scrambling into the carriage, Tony pushing her ahead of him, apologizing as the suitcase and the hold-all rammed into people. He was cheerful about it, and his victims, caught by his engaging grin, took it all in good part.

'There we are . . . two seats, side by side, so you can go to sleep on my shoulder if you want.'

Tony slung the luggage up on to the overhead rack and struggled out of his donkey jacket before helping her out of her coat. Then he sat down and pulled her down beside him.

'How's that? Comfy?'

The carriage was filling up; it was a non-smoker but already someone was trying unobtrusively to light up. Tony advised him, kindly, to use the corridor and the man did so, standing outside puffing his miserable weed whilst people pushed and scuffed past him, calling out, laughing, advising others that this one was full, try further along.

'Yes . . . I'm all right,' Marsha said feebly.

In fact, she felt very out of place indeed . . . except for the part of her which was cuddled close to Tony. She

316

looked round the carriage, half-expecting to find an accusing, Higginish eye fixed on her. Did she look like a woman running away from home with a man – no, with a taxi driver? But no one seemed to care, and they were a cheerful lot.

'There's no buffet car,' someone was saying. 'What a sell, eh? Time after time I catch this train and it always says a buffet car is available and it hardly ever is. I wonder if that sandwich seller has gone, or if he's still somewhere on the platform. We don't leave for another seven minutes, which means seventeen . . . I'll go and forage, I think.'

Tony gave her shoulders a squeeze and stood up as well.

'I'll get us some sandwiches and crisps, and a bottle of beer,' he said. 'Stay put, you.'

He grinned at her, then swung out of the compartment and down on to the platform. Marsha sat, frozen, in her seat. Suppose he missed the train? Suppose she was stuck here alone amongst strangers, with her escort – and her ticket – left behind on Euston station? How would she explain? What would she do in . . . in wherever it was they were bound? She had very little money and her suitcase contained only a few warm jumpers and skirts, a couple of frocks, and her undies.

You could telephone the Higginses, tell them you'd got on the wrong train by mistake and woke to find yourself in a strange town, she thought, made inventive by terror. Or you could go to the police . . . you've done nothing wrong, not yet.

When Tony came back into the compartment six minutes later she was so relieved and delighted to see him that she could have kissed him. All her doubts and fears simply melted away in the pleasure of his company. Together, they read the papers he had bought, together they ate the sandwiches, drank the beer, crunched the potato crisps. Together, after their impromptu lunch, they slept.

'Well, Meg, and what are you thinking, staring out of the window like that? I doubt you can see much out there.'

The family had gathered in the front room, Dewi and Louisa, Mam and Da, Henry, Peris and Megan. But Megan sat in the window, with the heavy curtains still drawn back, and gazed out into the gathering dusk. The men had been playing cards whilst Mam sewed and Louisa knitted socks but now, at Mam's words, Da flung down his last hand and heaved a sigh.

'Good thing there was no money on it, eh, lads? A pauper I would have been, for not a decent card have I had all afternoon. Meg? How about a nice cup of tea, now, and one of them little cakes Mam made this morning?'

Megan wrenched her eyes away from the darkening street and turned into the warm and lamplit room. Flames danced on the hearth, licking at the coal, making Mam's lovely brass scuttle glitter and gleam like gold, and in the soft light faces were gentled, expressions lost their sharpness.

'Tea, Da? Is it time? There's sorry I am to be dreaming when you're all thirsty.'

'Well, we could all do with a cup, I dare say,' Mam admitted. She stood up, laying her sewing down in her chair. A new shirt for Da made from old, the material cut so that it would look its best. 'Come on then, Meg, love, you can slice some bread and the men can toast it against the fire.'

'All right,' Megan said. She followed Mam into the kitchen and began to cut the loaf, then put the knife down. She frowned down at the table, at her two hands,

318

one still gripping the crust. 'Mam? There's odd I do feel! Stuffy it is in here . . . can I go out for a while?'

'After tea, you mean, Meg? Surely, if Peris will go with you, or Louisa. But just now take some butter through to stand and warm in the hearth, and some bread and a couple of toasting forks. The men can make themselves useful for once.'

'I'd like to go now,' Megan said. It was odd how she felt drawn, today, to the outdoors. It was still bitterly cold, though; as she had watched through the front window she had seen snowflakes gusting past. 'Just for a minute or two, Mam.'

She looked up, to see Mam's eyes fixed doubtfully on hers.

'What's the matter, chick? Is it Danny?'

Mam had been disappointed that Danny had not come back to tea, though she had accepted Megan's explanation that Danny would come round in the morning instead.

'Not really . . . or perhaps it is,' Megan said. She was unsure herself why she so desperately wanted to go out. 'I'll take the bread though, and the butter . . .'

Back in the warmth of the front room her urge to venture into the cold and wind seemed silly. She lingered whilst Peris and Dewi speared the first slices of bread, then returned to the kitchen. Here, where she could not even see the street, the longing to go out came back more strongly, insistent. Was it Danny? Was she worried by his apparent desire to see no more of her today? But she knew very well it was not that. Danny was probably wrapping her present and did not want to be disturbed. She had to go out because someone, somewhere, was urging her to do so.

The realization that there really was something, or someone, pressing her to leave the house was weird, even worrying. And once she realized it, a picture kept coming into her head. Of an autumn day, long ago, when she and Peris had been mucking about on Rocky Shore, fishing with homemade lines. It had been fun, but why should she suddenly start to think about it now? And why, for heaven's sake, should she keep seeing the scene from the outside, so to speak? Not through her own young eyes but as an observer must have seen it – Megan, with her long fair plaits dangling forward as she bent over her string, Peris beside her, baiting his hook with the worms he had acquired from somewhere.

'Megan? You carry the tray, love, and I'll manage the pot. We'll send Louisa back for the cakes.'

'Sorry, Mam. Dreaming, I was,' Megan said apologetically, seizing the tray. 'Get this all set out in a minute, I will, and then I'm off.'

Mam gave her a quizzical look.

'Off, are you, madam? Well, don't be long and be sure to wrap up well. It's fierce out there.'

Wonderful, understanding Mam, who never forbade just because she didn't fully comprehend! Megan smiled and reached her old coat down off the back of the kitchen door.

'Oh, Mam, I do love you! Shan't be long.'

The wind was stronger, now, than it had been earlier. It hustled Megan along the road, pushing her hard in the back, so that the scarf, which she had slung casually around her neck, was almost blown away. Megan took it off in a doorway, wrapped it firmly round first her head and then her neck and tucked the ends into her coat. Damned thing, it should not get the better of her and go sailing off inland. Mam had knitted her that scarf twelve months ago, and it was still warm and new, a welcome addition on a night like this.

She had reached Stanley Street, the snow whipping her face quite painfully, before she began to wonder where

320

she was going. Not down to the harbour, that was next to impossible with the wind blowing a gale. She turned right on to Landsend, a little more sheltered by the high wall, then crossed over the railway bridge. She paused here, looking down on the tracks, seeing the whirling snow now thicker now thinner as it was dashed to one side or the other by the fickle, bitter wind.

Near her, a signal clunked; was there a train coming? Should she wait here as it thundered to a halt in the station and watch the people pouring out, heading for the cross-channel ship?

But it was too cold, and besides, what could she see from up here? Very little, in weather conditions such as these. Megan walked over the bridge and glanced at the barracks, on her right, where the railwaymen lived. If she walked past it and continued along London Road she could go and see Danny. But instead she turned left, towards the station.

Halfway down, she stopped, frowning. Was she not going to visit Danny, then? But it seemed as though she was not, since after the briefest of pauses her feet continued to carry her down the road.

She reached the square of the station yard and found a little more shelter, though not much. There was no one on duty in the tiny office, no one selling tickets or collecting them. What would happen when the boat train arrived? The cross-channel ship would probably not sail tonight – would they let the passengers aboard or would they send them into the town to find lodgings until the weather cleared? It would be terribly hard on people going home for the holiday to find themselves stuck here on Christmas Day itself . . . but better that than to end up struggling in that bitter sea.

She went past the ticket office and on to the platform and immediately knew that the train was about to arrive.

She could hear the rails vibrating and despite the storm, the shrieking wind, thought she could just catch the noise of it as it sped towards the station.

She was right. The engine drew in, and the long line of carriages. People poured out, the knowing ones who had done the crossing a hundred times hurrying along the platform, quick to try to get aboard the ship so that they could bag a warm spot in one of the lounges.

There were chalked notices which Megan hadn't read before, but now she saw them because the passengers did. They gathered round them, shouting to friends, blaming the railway authorities, steam pouring from their open mouths.

'No passage . . . no passage until the weather improves . . .' The words were read out, discussed, exclaimed over. People began to drift over to the ticket office, a couple of men in uniform appeared, a woman wept, tears running down her thin, lined face. Oh, poor things, who had relied on the ship to get them home tonight! What would they do, where would they go?

There was a girl approaching. She was with a young man, who had his arm round her and was explaining what had happened, what they must do. The girl was wearing the smartest coat Megan had ever seen, in a beautiful shade of reddish brown, with a fur collar so dark it was almost black turned up to hide most of her face. She had a little fur hat pulled well down over her forehead and not a strand of hair could you see, but Megan felt sure she was fair.

The couple came towards her. Megan, muffled in hand-knitted wool, guessed they could scarcely see her smile through the snow and the scarf. But it didn't matter, because the young man was speaking.

'My fiancée and I are stranded until the ferry sails,' he

322

was saying. 'I wonder if you might know a guest house which would put us up for a night or two?'

'There's several,' Megan said. 'But I do know one house, not too far . . . they take guests in the summer, and I'm sure they could fit you in.'

'It's very good of you,' the girl said. She smiled inside her rich, fur-collared coat.

Megan frowned.

'Do I know you?' she said slowly. 'I met you, I think, long ago . . .'

The girl stared back at her. She had very dark blue eyes, Megan saw. Like her own. And then two slim hands came out and gripped Megan's and there was a shake in them, and a fierceness in her grip.

'You? Can it really be you? Oh, I've dreamed of meeting you again . . . you know me, don't you? I'm Marsha.'

'Marsha,' Megan said in a low, breathless whisper. 'Oh, Marsha . . . I'm Megan.'

'Of course! I think I knew your name when we were small, but somehow I'd forgotten.'

The man had been looking from one to the other; now he frowned and leaned forward, gently tugging at Megan's enveloping scarf.

'What is it with you two? Are you old friends? Relatives? Only you do look rather alike, both muffled up in coats and hats and things, and your voices . . . well, they do sound similar.'

'Oh! I'm sorry.'

Megan unwrapped her scarf and Marsha took her hat off. The two girls smiled at one another, not seeing the likeness so much as the differences, but Tony took a step back, looking as though he would have liked to cross himself.

'Dear God . . . you're identical! You could be twins!'

Megan glanced at him, then back at Marsha.

'Perhaps we are,' she said dreamily. Her hand stole out and the girls clasped fingers again. 'Perhaps we really are.'

Megan would have taken them home, she told herself, but for the family being there. Mam was wonderful, but it would scarcely have been fair on her.

But there were plenty who would take them in and be glad to help out. Megan accompanied Marsha and Tony out of the station and down London Road to Wian Street. At the third house she ushered them up to the door and knocked on it. Old Ella Bedsocks, as the kids called her, kept a clean and tidy place, a good table. Her eyesight was failing and she didn't have many visitors now, but those who came once came again.

'I'll put your friends up gladly, Megan my little one,' Ella said when Megan had explained how she came to be at the door. 'Did you explain that the cross-channel ship will hoot three times when she's ready to leave, and sail exactly an hour later? Well, listen out for the hoots I will, and wake these young people in good time to go. Remember me to your mam, and Dai Prydderch, won't you?' She turned to Tony and Marsha, laden with their cases, cold and bewildered by this sudden change in their fortunes. 'Come you up to my best spare,' she said formally. 'And a good meal I'll make you this night, for I've plenty of food in for the holiday. What does your wife like to drink, young man? Would she rather have tea or coffee?'

Megan had opened her mouth to explain that they were not married when Tony put his arm round Marsha's shoulders and turned towards Megan with a flutter of his right eyelid.

'My wife would love a hot cup of tea, and so would I,

324

but we'd like to clean up a bit first. If we could go to our room . . .'

Megan, feeling very uncomfortable, called her thanks up the stairs to Mrs Ella's plump back, and her farewells to Marsha's slim one. She was shocked when the Other turned round for a moment to give her a bright, twinkling smile. Did she know what would happen if she did not disabuse Mrs Ella smartly? They would end up in the same room all night, she and the young man – in the same bed, very likely, for Mrs Ella wasn't a modern woman with twin beds, but an old-fashioned one with goosefeather mattresses and pillows of down in which a person could sink to depths of sin previously undreamed of.

I'm glad now I didn't take them to Mam's, Megan told herself as she fought the storm, heading home. She was cold, and whatever it was that had brought her down to the station had simply fizzled out once its job was done. She trailed home, noticing for the first time that evening her freezing feet, the stinging snow against her skin.

She felt let down, cheated in some way. She should have been on top of the world, for had she not always known that the Other was real, related to her, a sister or even a twin? And now they had met and she had been proved right. But somehow she hadn't expected the Other to have a man with her, nor that man to have claimed – falsely, she knew it in her bones – that he and the Other were married.

She's going smiling into sin, Megan told herself miserably. She'll burn in hell, if Mam's right, and I don't want her to do that. I can't bear it if that happens.

Only . . . why should it? Even Mam admitted that things were not always what they seemed. Look at Mrs Williams, now, whom no one spoke to or thought a lot of. She had done wrong, but no one ever said she'd burn in hell, just that she should have managed things differently.

Times change and people with them, Da had said the last time Mam had been talking fire and brimstone about a young girl who'd been foolish. Besides, Da had gone on, you can't deny it's a beautiful baby, my love.

And of course Mam couldn't deny it, hadn't wanted to deny it. She had scolded Da and kissed him and squeaked when he kissed her back, and that had been that; no more fire and brimstoning for a bit.

I wonder what Danny would say, though? Megan thought, slogging wearily back up Landsend, Stanley Street and Newry Street and collapsing through their own front door. What would he think if I told him about a girl I've always known, who is probably my twin sister, who goes to bed with a young man she isn't married to? In one of Mrs Ella's goosefeather beds, with a hot meal inside her and the young man's kisses to make her reckless. Oh, I wonder what Danny would say?

In her heart, though, she could not believe that Danny would condemn. He might envy, but he would never condemn. So it followed that neither should she.

CHAPTER TWENTY

Megan woke. She felt excited, yet for a moment she could not remember why, nor what had happened to bring this feeling of anticipation so much to the fore.

Then, of course, she knew. It was Christmas Day and all the people she loved, even the girl she had loved without ever really knowing her, were gathered on the island.

She would have liked to lie quiet and dream a little while longer, but something got her out of bed and over to the window. She pulled the curtains back with a triumphant swish and pale sunlight flooded the room.

For a moment she felt exalted but then her heart sank, just a little. The cross-channel ship would have sailed, carrying Marsha and her young man over to Ireland. Would they ever come back? Last night had been so unexpected, so totally strange, that it had simply never occurred to her to ask what their plans were.

She went over to her clothes with a dragging step, then perked up and began to dress. Of course Marsha would come back, because they had unfinished business, the two of them. The young man might come or go as he pleased, but she and Marsha must meet again. She must know our real mother, Megan thought, starting to dress. I've never thought about my real mother, never let myself, because Mam is the best mam in the world and I never want anyone to take her place. But I would like to know a bit about the woman who gave birth to me . . . perhaps a bit about my real father, too.

Dressed, she stole out on to the landing. Mam would

be in the kitchen, preparing a real Christmas breakfast. Bacon, sausages, kidneys, fried eggs, bread . . . the list was endless and the wonder of it was that they could eat any dinner at all after it, let alone the huge one they would all put away presently.

But Megan would not go to the kitchen, because she had an errand of her own. She would go down to Salt Island, running all the way, and see if she could watch the cross-channel ship as she sailed towards the horizon, carrying the mystery that was Marsha, the Other, off to Ireland.

Megan stole out of the house, down the path and into the street. It was cold and still. Icicles hung from the guttering, and the tree by the front gate was furred with frost, iced like the loveliest confectionery imaginable.

The sunshine caught everything, turning the frost to silver, the ice to diamond. The very flagstones twinkled with a thousand tiny bright eyes of frost and a solitary spider's web, slung precariously between Evans-Newspaper and Williams-Corsets, was transformed into the finest, crispest crocheted lace.

And of course, the town was quiet, like the Sleeping Beauty's palace at the start of the hundred years. Not a curtain twitched as Megan stole along the pavement, not a voice was raised. It was as though day had not dawned, the sun had not risen; as though night still reigned in the pale blue sky.

Yesterday's storm might never have been. Megan speeded up a bit, hurrying downhill at the point where Water Street sloped sharply to join Landsend, and slid a yard along the icy paving. Jolted, she slowed down. No point in rushing so much that she broke a leg, and besides she would only run out of breath if she went too fast.

It was a good walk to the end of Salt Island. She hastened along, past the shipping offices, closed of course, past the custom house, under the Admiralty Arch which except for size was identical, so they said, to the bigger one in London. Here she skirted the sailors' hospital and went towards the sea, which surrounded her on three sides.

The storm had left its mark on the sea, of course, hard though the frost had tried to subdue it. The waves, blue and silver in the morning sun, were still choppy, fringed with foam. The gulls cried and swooped above them, no longer blown sideways, riding the wind at their will.

And out to sea, a faint plume of smoke coming from its blackened funnel, was the cross-channel ship. Stout and stubby-looking at this angle, but breasting the waves with determination, becoming smaller with every blink of Megan's suddenly sun-dazzled eyes.

Marsha had gone, then. And her companion, with his dark, kind eyes and his crooked grin. Megan stood on tiptoe and waved until the toy-boat which looked no bigger than a ladybird slid over the horizon and vanished from view, leaving not even the palest stain from its smoke stack to tarnish the incredible silver-blue of the sky.

Breakfast with the family brought her back to earth, helped to take the sour taste of anticlimax from her mouth. Megan was ravenously hungry, her run having awoken in her a desperate need for hot food and drink. She was at the toast stage when Danny's head poked round the door. He looked excited.

'Meg? Got your present here, I have.'

'Ooh, what is it? Mam, can I go with Danny for a moment?'

Mam shook her head at them both, but indulgently. 'No, my love, that you can't. We open our parcels when breakfast's finished – I can't change the habits of a lifetime just because . . .' She looked from Danny to Megan, then back again, and sighed. 'Oh, what a pair you are! Very well, but don't be long. There's others have managed to scrape up a bit of a gift for you too, you know.'

'Oh, Mam! It doesn't matter. It can wait, can't it, Danny? We'll have the presents like we always do.'

But Da, with a paper hat saved for God knew how long perched on his whitening curls, shook his head, speaking thickly through his mouthful.

'Off with you, my little one! Mam was only teasing you – plenty of time there'll be to unwrap before we have dinner. Uncle's not even up yet and we couldn't start without him, could we?'

'And that bad Peris still abed and saying he'll be down for dinner and not a moment earlier. The idea – as if I'd let him miss a good cooked breakfast, to say nothing of chapel,' Mam said. 'Though if Uncle isn't down soon we'll leave the parcels until after service.'

'Groans all round,' Danny whispered as she joined him in the hall. 'Hello, Meg. You look very beautiful today!'

'There's nice to hear you say so! And what do *you* want, Danny Williams? Oh, hold on here whilst I get your parcel . . . where shall we open them?'

She scuttled for the stairs, hearing his voice floating after her.

'Outside. What a morning, eh, Meg? After yesterday it's like heaven out there.'

Danny and his love of the outdoors! He would never settle to a quiet shore job. Probably his idea of married bliss was a tent on the headland and her cooking his supper over a fire of dried seaweed!

Smiling to herself, Megan pulled a face at Screech and ran a finger across his bars. Screech tried to grab her finger as it flashed by and used sailorly language when she escaped unscathed. Well, if he shrieked like that at least the godless Peris would wake up, even if he immediately buried his head beneath the bedclothes once more, cursing all parrots.

In her room, she heaved the great, untidy parcel from its place in the bottom of her wardrobe. 'A labour of love', Mam had called the shaggy jersey which Megan had toiled on for months and months. But it was finished at last. She had darned the slipped stitches in as neatly as she could, and grudgingly allowed Mam to sew it up after her first effort had somehow managed to create the impression that the garment had one sleeve at least a foot longer than the other. Da had laughed until the tears came and the boys had tutted over it, but Danny would know how hard she had worked – surely he would?

His parcel must be tiny. They walked out of the front door with Megan bowed down under the weight of hers, but Danny was carrying nothing visible at all. Megan knew that the brown paper was splitting in several places, that the string with which the parcel was cocooned was fraying and old. She just hoped the entire shebang wouldn't suddenly give way and deposit her toil on the frosty pavement.

It held up. Danny had come over on his motor bike, a foolhardy thing to do on such a frosty day, but he took one look at the parcel in her arms and, to her relief, did not suggest they rode anywhere.

'Sit on the Green we will, and get our bums numb on the grass,' he said, steering her up the street and through St David's Road on to Walthew Avenue. 'All downhill now, Meggie, so keep going!'

He did not offer to take the parcel and Megan was glad; it would have been too humiliating if it had burst asunder in his grasp, spoiling the surprise, the unwrapping ceremony.

They gained the Green at last and sat down. As Danny

had foretold, the grass was very cold and stiff, but it didn't matter. They stared at one another for a moment, curiously shy, and then Danny fished in his pocket and brought out a tiny box wrapped in pale pink tissue paper and tied with silver ribbon. It must have taken Danny's big, fisherman's hands a long time to wrap such a small parcel so neatly. Megan felt deeply guilty over the state of her own offering.

'Oh, Danny . . . will you open mine first?'

She knew he was longing for her to open his, but her arms did ache so . . . and anyway he could put her present on and avoid having to carry it altogether!

'Right. Give it here, mun.'

She handed it over. Danny tackled the string briskly with his pocket knife, as though eager to see what was inside. Except that only an idiot would not have guessed it was clothing. Still. What mattered was that he should like it.

The jersey was unfurled at last, and shaken out, held up admiringly against the blue sunny sky. Danny seemed speechless, then he crushed the woolly between them and hugged her hard, kissed her chin, her cheek, the side of her mouth.

'Oh, Meg, you must have worked so hard, my little one! What a wonderful jersey . . . I shall wear it always when the weather's bad. I'll be proud to wear something that's taken you such a lot of time. You are good to me!'

'Oh, it isn't much,' Megan said gruffly. 'Blue is your colour, Danny; that's why I chose it. Do you like the little bits of red and yellow? It's called tweed wool . . . and I bought all the blue, so you won't see anyone else in a jumper like yours.'

'No, you bet I won't,' Danny said. He pulled the jersey over his head although he was already wearing a woolly: a dull old navy thing, Megan thought quite viciously. She would have liked to see him throw the old one in the sea, but perhaps that was asking a bit much. After all, her jumper would need washing from time to time, and he would need another one then. From within the wool came his muffled voice, 'Lovely and warm, Meg . . . a treat on a day like this!'

He pulled the body of the jersey down. And down. And down. It was almost at knee-level, looked as if it was heading fast for his ankles.

'Is it a bit large, maybe?' Megan asked anxiously, seeing Danny's strong hands disappear into the sleeves like a couple of rabbits into a burrow. 'I dare say I could shorten it a wee bit, if you think . . .'

She had made a roll collar. Danny was industriously rolling it down, somewhat hampered by his hidden hands but working at it. His face appeared, blue eyes, the tip of his nose, his white and beautiful smile.

'Too big? Nonsense! What could be better, indeed, on a cold day, than a jumper I can roll up around my neck to keep my head warm, with arms that mean I shan't need any old gloves. I want it just as it is, Meggie, because it's just right – it's perfect.'

'Oh, Danny!' Megan sighed. She put her arms round him, which was difficult with all the additional bulk, and kissed his bearded chin. 'Oh, I'm so glad you like it! The boys were a bit rude and Da laughed, but Mam said you'd like it just fine, and Mam always knows best.'

'So she does,' Danny agreed. 'Will you open my present now?'

Immediately the little box became the most important thing in the universe. Megan held it in her hands, laid it on her pointy knees, gently untied the silver ribbon, began to pick industriously at the coloured paper. She looked at Danny and his face was as excited as though he, too, had no idea what was inside.

'Go on, mun, open it!'

She lifted the lid.

A tiny, dainty ring! The circlet was of gold and very fine; at its apex tiny green stones glittered, surrounded by chiplets of diamond. She was breathless, too astonished, too touched, to say a word. A ring! He was giving her a ring!

'O-oh, Danny! Oh, it's so beautiful! Can I try it on?'

'You can. Want me to put it on for you?'

She held out her left hand, as unself-conscious as a child, and saw him hesitate. It was enough to make her drop the hand, hold out the right one.

Danny took her right hand and held it to his mouth. He turned it over and kissed the palm. She could feel the softness of his lips and the rough bristles of his moustache, the softer hair of his beard. She felt her heart begin to beat more quickly as he kissed across her palm, then up each finger, then into the soft hollow of her inner wrist where the pulse jumped and the blood sang faster. Oh Danny, oh God, why don't you . . . why can't we . . .

'No, not that hand. The other.'

Wordlessly, she gave him her left hand. He played with her fingers for a moment, then selected one of them, smiled at her with meaning and mystery and put the little ring delicately on the very tip of the third finger.

'With this ring . . . Megan, you know how I feel about you, you know what I want, even if I can't put it into words. If I push the ring right down on to your finger, and you don't pull it off, that will mean I've asked and you've said yes. Okay?'

She could not have dreamed of a more romantic moment than this. She breathed 'Okay' beneath her breath and felt the ring sliding down the third finger of her left hand. Then she held the hand up, against the blue sky, and flung herself backwards on the grass. She wanted to sing and shout, to hug and kiss, but somehow it would not have been right. She turned and looked up at Danny, silhouetted against the sun, eyes serious though his mouth smiled down at her.

'So we're engaged. Is that right?'

He nodded, not even smiling any more.

'That's right. Are you going to give me a bit of a kiss, like, to show you're pleased with my present?'

'Oh, Danny, you fool, it's the best, most beautiful present in the whole world.' She bounced up, grabbed him in a throttling embrace, dragged him down with her on to the wet grass, both of them laughing, breathless. 'I do love you so much!'

He planted an elbow on each side of her, looking down into her face. She could not read the expression in his eyes, but he was suddenly all serious, and somehow dark, taking away the lightness and the brightness and the excitement from her mind, making her think that this was a solemn moment, in truth, and one which they must treasure.

'I love you, Meg.' He spoke slowly, as if the words were being torn out of him. 'God help me, I do love you!'

'Oh, Danny!'

'Megan, I'm just going to . . .'

'Well, would you look at that! Kissing on the Green for all the world to see – disgusting, I'd call it. Megan Prydderch, come you home at once, you bad girl. Have you forgotten about chapel?'

Megan and Danny had both shot up, conscience-stricken, at Peris's first words, and now they scrambled to their feet.

'God, Peris, you damn near gave me a heart-attack,' Danny grumbled. 'Let's go, then.'

'Not in that . . .' Peris's eye had fallen on the blue tweed jumper but he looked up and caught Danny's steely

335

glance just in time. 'I mean . . . we're wearing suits, so I thought . . .'

'I'll walk down with you and then I'm off home for some breakfast. Think your mam will let me have some toast, Meg, if I make it myself?'

'Of course,' Megan said at once. She smiled at Peris as the three of them made their way back across the Green and up Walthew Avenue. 'Look, Peris!'

She held out her left hand. Peris glanced, stared, and then turned to Danny, shooting out a thin brown hand.

'Congratulations, old feller. I hope you'll both be very happy. When's the wedding to be? I need to know in plenty of time so's I can get leave.'

'Oh, not for a while. Probably not for years,' Danny said, suddenly gloomy. 'When the trawler makes me a man of means, then we'll get spliced.'

'Next summer!' Megan shouted, capering ahead of them, feeling lightheaded with happiness, and with relief, too, for she had begun to believe Danny would never ask her. 'Don't you worry, we'll all be rich next summer!'

Despite the storm's having blown itself out, it was still a bit bouncy aboard the cross-channel ship. Thanks to their activities in that big feather bed, what was more, Tony and Marsha had had to be wakened when Mrs Ella had realized they had not heard the ship's siren hooting. And that had meant hasty dressing, a scrambled breakfast and then a breathless run, hand in hand, through the brightening dawn down to the inner harbour.

There they had reclaimed their luggage and lined up to get aboard the ship, Marsha craning her neck to see up to the deck high above and feeling very excited, considering she was a much-travelled young lady who had crossed the Atlantic at the age of eleven.

But this was different, everything was different, because Tony was with her. And because of Megan.

It was wonderful to know that the Other really did exist, was more than a figment of one's imagination! Equally wonderful to know, with absolute certainty, that they would meet again. Holyhead, in the glow of sunrise, did not look a big town, though as the ship emerged from the harbour and sailed towards the open sea Marsha realized that it was not as small as she had thought.

Still. If we really are alike – and Tony thought we were – then probably I shan't have a hard time running her to earth, Marsha told herself. I wonder if she really is my twin, or if we're just sisters? In the bright light of morning she found the previous night taking on some of the aspects of a dream – the storm howling, the snow blowing into her face, the girl walking out of the storm and offering to find them somewhere to spend the night. She knew it had happened because Tony had seen the girl too; otherwise she might easily have thought she had imagined the whole thing.

As the ship left the harbour, however, Marsha had other things to think about. The movement was jerky, and she felt best out on deck, with Tony's arm round her, his face close to hers, pointing out landmarks on the shore.

'See up there? There's been quarrying work done up there. Still doing it, I dare say. And there's a lighthouse, inland against the swell of that hill . . . see that great bird? Bigger than a gull, isn't it? I wonder what it is? Oh, look, sweetheart, see the little island with the swing bridge? And another lighthouse on it. I wonder what that one's called. Look at the height of those cliffs . . . the gulls look like dots . . . can you see the cave, down low? There are others, further along the cliffs. Bet you can only get into them by boat . . . it's an exciting coastline, isn't it? I wouldn't mind spending a week or so on that island, exploring.'

Marsha agreed to everything he said, but she was seeing pictures again. A girl, golden-brown hair floating free, facing into the breeze from the sea, standing on a dull, greyish-looking bit of beach, with chunks of concrete in the background. Standing on tiptoe and waving, waving. She looked a lot like Marsha.

After Christmas, the weather was unreliable. Like a woman, said Danny, and then looked guilty. But he wore his terrible Christmas jumper most of the time, which Megan saw as another sign that he was trying to come round to the idea of having a wife some day.

There was no talk of weddings, despite the ring. Not from Danny, that was. Mam talked about weddings all the time and Da was almost as bad. Saving up for a new suit, he told people – Megan would have blushed for him save that she was too busy blushing for herself.

She loved her ring. It was always catching her eye, but she grew shy of showing it off because of the inevitable question – *When's the wedding, then?* People must know that a fellow like Danny, who had been in the war, didn't have a lot of spare cash. He had his demob suit, of course, but he had spent a lot on the ring; more than he could afford. More than I'm worth, Megan thought miserably. Why, with this lovely ring, and Danny, should I hanker after a stupid old wedding – or a home of my own when I've got Mam's good cooking to come back to at the end of a day's work?

'An engagement is short for "engaged to be married",' Mam said repressively, when Megan voiced her thoughts. 'Every right you have, girl, to expect to set a date, even if it's ten years in the future.'

'Ten years!' Megan's horrified shudder spoke volumes.

She felt like shouting at Danny, *I'm only flesh and blood – I want you even if I'm too well brought up to say so!* but in truth she would never dream of voicing such thoughts – she really was too well brought up.

She had seriously considered seducing him. His love-making stirred her up and made her hungry for more, and he always stopped – oh, much, *much* too soon. Sometimes she thought he stopped as if he was afraid to go on, but surely it could not be so? Everyone knew that all men wanted to have their way with girls, so why should Danny be any different? What did Mam think?

'It's the war,' Mam said, looking wise and sorry at the same time. 'Awful things it does to a sensitive man, my little one, and Danny is a sensitive feller. Remember what I told you? Patience and understanding. Danny wants you to be his wife; let him choose the pace for a bit.'

Megan was quite relieved that seduction seemed to be out. She would not have known where to start – or possibly where to stop. Awful things might have happened to sensitive Danny if he thought she was trying to force not only his hand but other, more intimate parts as well. Though he did not seem particularly sensitive when he was stripped to the waist cleaning fish or lying flat along the petrol tank of the bike, sizzling along the straight main road which ran down the middle of the island like a backbone and giving her heart-attacks.

And strangest of all, she missed Marsha. She had told Mam about the girl in her dreams who had suddenly materialized on Holyhead station, with a young man and two suitcases. Mam had said, in her sensible, practical way, that Marsha might very well be Megan's twin sister, for hadn't stranger things happened, after all? And how would Megan like to try to trace her again, through the Deiniol Evans Home?

'I don't think she was ever there,' Megan said hesitantly. 'She went before I got to the Deiniol Evans.'

She didn't tell Danny, though, for two reasons. She thought he might not believe her, which would have hurt very badly, and she had only just discovered her own uniqueness, her particular charm for Danny. She had no desire to go to him and say, 'There's someone just like me only with curls – you two must meet, you'll love her.' So he might; and that would never do!

It was a help telling Mam, though. And when she thought about it, though she was sad Marsha hadn't tried to find her when she came back from Ireland she didn't let it hurt her, because the other girl probably had a job and a home to go to and no time to waste. But later, Megan told herself, later she'll come back. I know she will.

Marsha and Tony arrived in Ireland on a fine winter's afternoon, intending to leave after a few days.

They stayed for several reasons, the main one being that they suddenly found themselves in love, in Marsha's case certainly for the first time. The second reason was that Tony got a job.

They had Christmas Day with the family, as Tony had planned, and spent a long time talking to Tony's long-lost Cousin Patric. Cousin Patric thought Tony was a fine-looking chap, now, and wasn't it strange that he drove a taxi, for didn't Patric know a man with a big estate no more than thirty miles off who was desperate for a driver? A nice little cottage went with the job and old Mr Quinn, who had recently suffered a heart-attack, was the best of good fellers and would be eternally grateful so he would for someone to live in the cottage and drive him to Dublin each weekday.

'But it would be irresponsible of me to leave my cab

for any longer,' Tony said. 'I don't know that we can stay, even for your bright eyes, Marsha.'

But he went and saw the old man and they got along splendidly. And then they went to look round the cottage, and it was a treat, so it was, clean and sparsely furnished, with big fireplaces, an old-fashioned feather bed upstairs, and views of the mountains from the back windows which would have melted a harder heart than Tony's.

Mr Quinn was wealthy, eccentric and, to those he liked, generous. He liked the young Bondellinis – for it was only sensible, in a strange country, to say they were married. Tony, in anticipation of questions, had bought a cheap Woolworth's ring, and Marsha wore it all the time.

And of course they were only playing at housekeeping, which doubled the fun of it. Marsha bought a couple of wrap-around aprons and cooked dreadful meals for Tony. He was not a fussy eater, fortunately, but sometimes he grew tired of undercooked spuds and scorched chops and donned an apron himself, making Marsha watch step by step as he worked. He was a good cook, and as a result by the end of their time in the cottage Marsha could make spaghetti bolognese, produce excellent omelettes, and soufflés light enough to fly away . . . but she still singed the chops and served up half-raw potatoes.

And they made love. Lying in the big feather bed whilst the soft and soaking Irish rain misted the view and obscured the window panes, Marsha learned much about her own body and more about the giving and receiving of pleasure, because Tony revelled in her enjoyment as much as his own, and saw to it that Marsha was always as satisfied as he.

'Will we ever go home?' Marsha wondered aloud one night as they lay in each other's arms, sated and snug. 'Will we ever go back to London, and all the noise and smells and fuss?'

'Not unless you want to,' Tony said drowsily. They were both naked, Marsha's head with its soft burden of darkening gold hair resting on the hollow of his shoulder. 'I'm very happy working for old Quinn, with you to come home to each evening.'

'I'll never want to,' Marsha assured him. She turned her face sideways and licked the side of his neck, then kissed it. 'Isn't it funny, Tony? I thought being at college was marvellous. I loved being a student and meeting other students and I loved being good at languages. And then you came along and nothing else seemed to matter, nothing at all.'

She should have said, 'Nothing but Megan, that girl in Holyhead,' but she didn't because she had not yet acknowledged, even to herself, that for some strange reason Megan did matter, that there was still unfinished business between them. When she saw pictures now they no longer seemed so mysterious, but they were still food for thought. Megan, whistling down the long hill towards the sea with a basket on her arm and her hair pulled back from her head by the wind. Megan again, crouching down on a sled, careering over the snow, laughing . . . but soundlessly, of course, because Marsha's pictures weren't the talking sort. Megan down at the dockside, cleaning fish with a big gutting knife, nearly blue with cold but smiling.

And the young man. Marsha could never see the other people in her pictures clearly, only her sister, but she saw a lot of the young man. He had yellow hair and was tanned and muscular. He interested her but he was never in the forefront, always just glimpsed before the scene faded.

So to say that Tony was the only thing that mattered in her life was not quite true. Not quite, but almost. Daily she got up when he did, made him breakfast, cleaned the cottage, took the long walk into the village to do the marketing and went up to the farm for fresh eggs and milk. In the evenings she boiled kettles to fill the old tin bath in front of the kitchen fire, and sometimes she scrubbed Tony's back for him and other times she climbed into the tub on top of him, splash splat, and they played love-games in the water, on the rug, until one was as wet as the other and they were both exhilarated and ready for a meal and then bed.

And all the time the weather was dreadful, with snow and gales and draughts which whistled under the doorsill and came hissing in around the small windows set deep within the thick old walls. March came in like a lion and departed like one too, gales shaking the cottage and loosening slates and bringing a branch crashing down on the end wall, so that Tony had to chop it up for firewood . . . and they needed fires still although it was April. The persistent rain saw to that.

'Does the sun never shine here?' Marsha asked as she bought soapflakes and tea and flour at the village shop.

The neat, middle-aged woman behind the counter looked at her disapprovingly over the top of her spectacles and primmed her mouth.

'Sure, and doesn't it shine all summer long?' she said in her soft brogue. 'But here in the country we're used to the winter being cold and the spring desperate wet.' She weighed broken biscuits into a brown paper bag on her big, old-fashioned scales. 'Isn't it like that in England, then? I dare say you have bright sunlight all t'rough the winter and you brown as a berry by March!'

Marsha, recognizing sarcasm, or thinking she did, counted out her money and left the shopkeeper to her weighing up, but she did look forward to summer, even if she had a sneaking suspicion that it would prove no better at producing constant sunshine than March and April.

And then the telegram came.

'I'll have to go back, just to settle things,' Tony said when he had read the printed message. 'It's Jack, the feller who's been driving my taxi – he's had an accident. My cab's a write-off and he's broken both his legs.'

'I don't see why you have to go back, though,' Marsha complained. 'What's the point? If the cab can't be mended, then what would you do for a living? And you can't help with Jack's legs – you aren't a doctor! And spring is almost here – you said we'd plant the garden, and you'd show me wild flowers and tell me the names of all the birds and the fishes in the river . . .'

'No, I'm not a doctor,' Tony admitted, ignoring the rest of her remarks. 'But my cab was insured and Jack should have been insured too. Look, sweetheart, I won't be gone long . . . a week at the most . . . and then I'll be back here with you and we'll do the garden together.'

Was the gilt already wearing off the gingerbread? Was the spring weather too wet, summer too long in coming, the living too spartan? Marsha did not know; she only knew that if he left it would be over.

She said as much.

'Darling, don't be so silly! Why don't you come with me? You owe your parents some sort of an explanation, after all. You could see them and tell them how happy we are.'

But Marsha had no desire whatsoever to see her parents. Tony was all she wanted.

'If I come back to the mainland you won't see me again. I mean it, Tony.'

'Then stay here! Don't you see, I must go? I owe it to Jack and even to myself. That cab and my flat were all I'd got in the world . . . you never saw my flat. Come back with me and see what you're missing.'

344

Marsha glared and said nothing more, but her mind was becoming fixed. For the past week she had been miserably aware that something was not quite right. She felt as though there was a bubble of air in her chest all the time, and she found fault with Tony over the smallest things, brooding to herself, planning smart retorts which she never actually made. Why must he go? She knew very well she would not want to live in a cabby's miserable London flat, nor follow Tony like an Arabian woman, three paces to the rear, when he returned to his old haunts. She did not want him to drive pretty girls about the city. She wanted him to stay here, in Ireland, with her, the cottage and old Mr Quinn's undemanding and occasional companionship. She was in the mood to chuck the whole thing yet, at the same time, miserably aware of her own foolishness in not valuing what they had.

So she played her last card, sure of success.

'Mr Quinn won't want you to go. He likes you a lot, but he'll give the job and the cottage to someone else . . .'

'Sweetheart, he understands. He's happy for me to have a week or so away to settle my affairs. Come on, Marsha, you know I've no real choice.'

She stuck out her lip and sulked and he made a fuss of her, trying to make her see his point of view. When she refused to discuss it, he sighed and said nothing more.

Marsha congratulated herself on making him see reason and decided to roast a chicken as a treat next weekend.

Two days later, he woke her in the early hours, getting out of bed. She stirred, snuggled down, then opened an eye and saw, through the uncurtained windows, that it was raining again. That fine, persistent rain which, the natives say, gives the emerald isle its astonishing variety of greens.

It looked cold outside. Marsha peeped at the alarm clock by the bed and guessed Tony had nipped out for a piddle, because it was still quite dark and must be very early indeed. So far as she could recall he had not mentioned having to get Mr Quinn anywhere by nine.

Presently, it occurred to her that he must have had to use the outside privy, since the chamber pot on the landing was not sufficient for his purposes. He could be a while, then. She let herself drift back into comfortable slumber.

When she woke two hours later, he had gone. He had left her a note, some money, a firm promise to be back with her in no more than three days, and a present. He had bought it in Dublin, he wrote, knowing that he would have to leave her for a short while.

It was a ring. An inexpensive ring, with a little green stone in it, because she loved emeralds. Well, if that's an emerald it must be the smallest one in the entire universe, Marsha decided cruelly. She tried the ring on, though, and it looked quite nice against the whiteness of her fingers. It had little chips of glass, or possibly even of diamond, around the central gem. A cheap way of persuading me to stay, Marsha told herself crossly. He's hateful and I meant it: I shan't be here when he gets back because I'm going to spend a few days with Megan in Anglesey! And he'll come back here and find me gone and get the most terrible scare . . . and it will serve him jolly well right!

She got up, dressed and packed. The fire had gone out, but she did not intend to light it. That had always been Tony's job, and if he chose not to do it just because he had left so early in the morning that was one more nail in the coffin of their relationship.

As she drank tea and ate toast she wondered whether to leave him a note letting him know where she was. But she decided against it. He could just sweat! She caught a

346

bus to Dublin, found her way to the shipping office and booked on the cross-channel ferry bound for Holyhead.

She did feel a pang when she climbed aboard, but she stiffened her resolution by reminding herself that this was the ideal way to find out whether her affair with Tony meant anything or whether she was half out of love with him and should move on.

She stayed in the saloon throughout the crossing because it was cold and windy on deck and because she still felt unaccountably low and depressed. And as soon as the ship docked she took her little suitcase and headed for the taxi-rank. She examined three drivers closely before choosing one who, apparently, matched up with her requirements.

'I'm looking for a girl who lives in this town,' she announced, climbing into the back seat. 'She looks a lot like me. Where am I likeliest to find her?'

'You don't know her name, then?' the driver said, peering at her over his shoulder. 'A help it is, a person's name.'

'Of course I know her name . . . it's Megan,' Marsha said stiffly, wishing she could remember the surname as well. And then, whilst the taxi driver was saying that Megan was a popular name and he knew half a dozen himself, Marsha suddenly had a brainwave. At some time or other, someone had mentioned a Dai Prydderch . . .

'Megan Prydderch! I know the lass well; lives on Newry Street,' the man said. 'Know her mam and da, and all . . . I'll drive you there now.'

And suddenly, for Marsha, the cold, grey day became sunny. She was going to meet her sister again, and this time she would give the other girl her full attention, not having Tony to distract her.

It was not far. The taxi climbed the hill, turned right over a bridge, continued along a road with shops and public houses on the left-hand side and a high wall on the right, and then swung left into a steep road which wound gradually higher and higher into the town.

'Here we are; Newry Street,' the cab driver remarked conversationally. 'See that tall, thin house, whitewashed new and clean last spring? That's the one – her mam do take boarders.'

And Marsha was stepping out of the taxi, the driver behind with her case, eyeing the deep blue paint of the door and the bright brass of the letterbox with apprehension . . . lifting the knocker . . .

Within the house she could hear voices, then footsteps. The taxi driver had left her and gone back to his cab. She found her eyes getting wider and wider as the footsteps drew closer and the door swung open.

CHAPTER TWENTY-ONE

Boots the Chemist was very busy before Christmas, but afterwards trade slumped, so much so that the manager had to lay Megan off. He would re-employ her, he said, as soon as business allowed.

'Even Arthur won't be needing me,' Megan said sadly, coming in the night she got her cards. 'Oh, Mam, and Danny and I are trying so hard to save up!'

Da was mending a net, a job often undertaken of an evening, after the delicate mesh had been caught and snagged on underwater rocks. He was wearing his glasses the better to see what he was at, but looked at her over the top of them as she spoke.

'It's always been the same in the town; likely everywhere's the same,' he said placidly. 'You do help Mam and gut for us when we've a good catch . . . and Meggie, love, why don't you learn to drive?'

'To drive?' Only the rich did that. Megan could scarcely think of a single girl she knew who could drive a car, though farmers' daughters drove the farm machinery capably enough, and during the war girls had driven as a matter of course.

'That's right. It would cost, but it might be worth it in the long run. Danny passed his motor bike test easily enough, didn't he? Reckon he'd pass his driving test the same way, but right now he's no need. You have. With a driving licence you could go to the mainland for work, or we could get hold of an old van and you could take our fish round now that Arthur's got a thriving business.'

Arthur had opened a fishmonger's in town as well as keeping on the mobile fish and chip shop.

'But Da, Arthur sells your fish!'

'Yes, but he can't take our whole catch, and the price isn't as good as it would be if we sold direct. How about it?'

'It's a wizard idea . . . but could I do it? I've never even had a go on Danny's bike – I mean, I did try, but it was too heavy for me.'

Mam, seated opposite Da in her old armchair, tutted. She was knitting, fast and beautifully, and now she, too, looked over at Megan.

'No reason why not; you're a bright girl, and driving a car is something many a stupid man learns. You have a go, girl!'

'But the money . . .' Megan began, to be cheerfully interrupted.

'I'll pay for your lessons,' Da said, pointing at her with his netting needle. 'A good little creature you are, and well we're doing with the fish but better when you're selling it direct. Go you to the office in Market Street and book yourself a course. Do it first thing Monday.'

'Well, I will,' Megan said, going over and bestowing a kiss on the top of her father's head. 'You're good to me, Da! And I'll see Mrs Iestyn at the same time.'

Mrs Iestyn was the farmer's wife Megan had worked for occasionally during the war. She had a stall in the indoor market, selling her own produce, and Mam had remarked recently that Mrs Iestyn could do with a hand on Saturdays.

'A good idea but no need,' Da said. 'Now the finer weather's coming we'll be off on longer trips. We're going to sell at the nearest port, like the big trawlers do, if we find a fish shop and start pulling them in.'

Megan was growing used to what she thought of as

'trawler talk', and she knew that a fish shop was just the trawlermen's way of saying a big shoal. But . . . 'Longer trips, Da? How do you mean?'

'I mean, lass, that we lose out by having to be home each night, or every other night. What we'll do is fish with the fleet, land at the nearest port – whether it's Fleetwood, or Cork, or even Marseilles – sell our catch and then fish on. That way we won't lose so much time having to come in and out of Holyhead. And in the big ports, like Fleetwood or Grimsby, the fish go up for auction . . . you can make a big profit. We've been talking to the lads in the fleet, Danny and I.'

'Oh, I see. Then you might be away for two or three days?'

'For two or three weeks, if the weather's right and prices are high,' Da said, with a sort of grim satisfaction. 'Danny will be making enough money for both of you once we start in earnest. We took time to learn our trade, but now we're in business, and our first longish trip starts Monday, if conditions stay fair.'

'Then what's the point of me learning to drive?' Megan asked. 'You'll only need me once in three weeks or so!'

Da shook his head at her, laying down his net and the big, curved needle.

'That's where you're wrong. We'll need you in winter when we can't go out so far, not with the poor old *Claudia*, anyway. And to drive is a skill, Megan my little one . . . never lose the chance to acquire a new skill.'

'Right. But all the more reason to have a word with Mrs Iestyn,' Megan said. She glanced at the kitchen clock, tick-tocking the day away. 'Look at that old clock, now . . . shall I get tea, Mam?'

When the knock came on the door they were all busy. Da got up because he was only sitting when all was said

351

and done, whilst Megan continued to cut and butter bread.

She thought nothing of the knock; they always had early tea on a Saturday, and people often popped in. She did not think it was Danny, who had told her he would spend most of the day getting his gear ready to sail on Monday. On Sunday, if all the preparatory work on the *Claudia* was finished, they would go out somewhere, or if it was wet they would stay in, talking. But steering clear of the subject of weddings, for they were still a sore point, to be avoided so far as Danny was concerned.

'More bread, Mam, or will this be enough?'

From the front door she heard the quiet murmur of a female voice, then Da's deeper one. And then, even as she reached up for the big plate which would hold the bread and butter, she heard Da's voice again, raised this time.

'Megan? Come here, girl!'

She might have called back that she must just rinse her hands, for she was all over butter, but there was something in his tone which made her drop her knife and turn towards the hall.

'Coming,' she called. 'Shan't be a tick, Mam. It must be someone wanting to see me.'

She reached the narrow, dark little hall. Da was ushering someone inside, his hand hovering as though not certain whether to take a coat or to shake hands . . . not certain, in fact, what to do next.

'Megan love, here's a strange thing . . . a young lady come to see you.'

As soon as he said the words, Megan knew. She hurried forward and then stopped, smitten into immobility and shyness by the sight of her twin.

'Hello, Megan. Sorry to butt in like this, but I thought

352

as I was in the area . . . and someone said you had a boarding house and I don't have anywhere to stay . . .'

'Says she's your sister,' Da said hoarsely. 'And like as two peas in a pod, what's more! Can it be true? You never knew you had a sister, now, did you, my little one?'

Megan was saved from having to reply by Mam, bustling out, all smiles.

'So we've a visitor! Well, you're very welcome, my dear . . . come in, come in. About to have our tea, we were, and I dare say you're hungry. Come from Ireland on the cross-channel ship, have you? Meg did mention some while ago that she'd met you by chance . . . there's strange, how life do treat us. Come along in, and off with that beautiful coat . . . hang it up, Meg, on the rack in the hall, there's my good girl . . . Da, take the young lady's suitcase up to Meg's room. Nothing much it is, Marsha . . . you don't mind if I call you Marsha? . . . but good enough for Meg, and her brothers before her.'

Megan was astonished by her mother's sudden burst of speech, but guessed that Mam was really dumbfounded, perhaps even a little ill at ease. For her own part, she looked very hard at Marsha, for it is not given to all of us to see a living, breathing double of ourself, and it half-intrigued, half-frightened her.

And Marsha was so very pretty – I don't look like that, Megan told herself ruefully. Marsha's hair was the colour of cream, rich and pale, and it was set into lovely curls, framing her face with its abundance. Her eyes were a very dark blue, like Megan's own, but instead of having light brown lashes hers were black – though Megan, who was no fool, saw that she was using stuff on them – and her skin was pale as milk.

'Do you know, seeing you like this makes me wish I'd not lightened my hair,' Marsha said after a moment, having given Megan every bit as hard a scrutiny as Megan had given her. 'But the colour's growing out . . . my hair's just like yours where the parting comes.'

'Oh . . . yes, I see. But yours is curly.'

'I've had a perm,' Marsha said. 'Are we really so alike?'

'As peas in a pod,' Da said, still staring from one to the other. 'Only there is something in your expressions which is different. No offence, miss, but I'd not mistake you for our Megan for long, I'm thinking.'

'She's Marsha, not miss,' Megan said. 'What's your last name, Marsha?'

'Loxley. I'm Marsha Loxley.'

'And you're adopted, like me?'

'Yes. Only my parents didn't see fit to tell me, and I only found out about four months ago.'

'There's hard on you,' Mam said quietly. 'But I dare say your parents had their reasons.'

Marsha, who was still staring at Megan, flashed her a cursory glance.

'Oh . . . yes, sure. But I've come to terms with it now. It doesn't upset me as it did at first.'

'It never upset me,' Megan said rather absently. 'Shall we go up?' She turned to Mam, still standing in the hall though Da had begun to mount the stairs, carrying Marsha's case as though it weighed nothing. 'We'll just have a wash and brush up, Mam, and be right down for our tea!'

In the room that had once belonged to Peris, Dewi and Henry, the two girls faced one another again. They smiled, tentatively, then Megan put a hand on Marsha's case.

'Shall I help you to unpack? You'll stay a day or two, won't you? You don't have to rush off?'

'I'll stay for a bit,' Marsha said. 'I don't really know just what I'm going to do when I leave here, as a matter of fact. Things are a bit more complicated than you'd think.'

'Ah.' Megan nodded wisely. 'Your young man isn't with you, of course. Why not? Have you fallen out with him? You seemed to be sweethearts, but perhaps that was just the impression I got.' She did not add, as she might have done, that the two of them had pretended to Mrs Ella that they were man and wife.

'Oh, Tony. No, we didn't fall out, exactly, but it really is rather a long story, and your mother was right: I'm terribly hungry. I didn't have enough money to buy myself any food on the crossing.'

'And it's too bad of me keeping you here talking,' Megan said remorsefully. She went across the room and tipped some water into the basin on the washstand. 'Can you manage with a cold wash now? A fine bathroom we have, on the first floor, but nothing up here bar what I carry . . . and if you're really hungry perhaps you won't want to waste time while I go down for the kettle.'

'Cold will be grand,' Marsha said. She dabbled her hands, wiped them on Megan's clean towel, dabbled at her face and did the same with that. Megan tried not to look concerned about the dirt and face-powder now streaking her towel, but she could not help thinking that Mam would presently have something to say about such behaviour. 'I say, what an odd little room. It's an attic really, isn't it?'

'That's right. Mam takes boarders, you see, and they sleep in the real bedrooms. It's just us kids sleep up here, though now I'm the only one still living at home I've moved from my little room into this nice big one.' Megan looked contentedly round, seeing not the sparseness of the furnishings nor the sloping ceiling and uncarpeted floor but the wonderful space after so many years in the tiny slip of a room next door.

355

'I'm an only child,' Marsha said. She produced a pink frilled bag from the depths of her suitcase and began to puff powder on to her nose. 'How many brothers and sisters do you have?'

'No sisters, but five brothers. Arthur's the oldest, and then Samuel, but they'd left home before I came. Then there's Dewi, Henry, and Peris. Peris is nearest to me in age, and we were at the children's home together, so I think I love him a bit more than the others, but you aren't supposed to have favourites, any more than your mam and da can. Why are you putting powder on your face? The boarders have their tea separately.'

Marsha put her powder puff away and produced a little box with a cake of black stuff inside and a tiny object which looked like a doll's toothbrush. She spat on to the cake and rubbed the brush into the resultant mixture, then applied the mascara to her eyelashes.

'It's nothing to do with who's going to see me,' Marsha explained as she diligently brushed away. 'It's what you do to make yourself look nice.'

'But you look very nice anyway,' Megan protested as her sister put the little box away and got out a lipstick, very red and shiny and wicked-looking. Megan had never used a lipstick in her life, though she knew a good many girls who did. 'Isn't it a nuisance, putting all that old stuff on your face?'

'Not at all. I enjoy it,' Marsha said with some difficulty, since her upper lip was drawn down over her teeth in a stiff and unnatural bow to facilitate the putting on of the lipstick. 'I didn't make up in Ireland very much, but I always do in London.'

'I think Holyhead is more like Ireland than London,' Megan said timidly. 'Danny says we're awful backward, here. But I'm used to it.'

'Danny?'

'He's . . .' Megan held out her left hand. 'That's his ring,' she said, pointing.

Marsha finished outlining her lips, pressed them together a couple of times, smiled at her reflection in Megan's glass, then turned away from the mirror. She looked at Megan's hand, then held out her own.

'Well, that is weird! Aren't they like?'

Megan looked, and the two rings really were rather similar. Though mine is much nicer, she thought loyally, twisting it round so that the stones caught the light and sparkled with fire.

'A bit, I suppose. Who gave you yours? Was it Tony?'

'Of course.'

'Then you're getting married, too! Isn't that the oddest thing, now? Will Tony be picking you up here to take you back to Ireland?'

'He doesn't know I'm here, and nor do my parents, but not a word to yours or they'll probably tell on me,' Marsha said. 'Where do you keep your clothes?'

'In the cupboard there. I don't have a lot, but . . .'

'We'll have a look later, when we hang my things up,' Marsha said authoritatively. 'Let's go down for tea now. We can talk properly afterwards.'

Descending the stairs, she turned to speak to Megan just as Screech, spotting a stranger, came out with a terrible scream followed by a splatter of rich curses.

'Christ!' Marsha exclaimed. 'What the devil is that?'

Oh, she'll be in trouble if Mam hears, Megan thought, explaining aloud that the noise had been made by the parrot, and that Screech belonged to Uncle Reggie, a long-term boarder and a dear friend.

'I'd ring its bloody neck if it were mine,' Marsha said, but quite lightly. Megan, trying to sound as if she agreed without actually agreeing, thought that only child or no, rich or no, Marsha used some very odd language for a

357

gently reared girl. Megan, brought up amongst boys, knew a lot of words she would never have dreamed of using, particularly in front of a stranger. And, fascinated though she was by her sister, she knew that they were strangers still.

But we'll remedy that, she told herself as they skipped downstairs, Marsha going lightly before, herself tripping behind. I've always longed for a sister, so I must make the most of this one!

'Everything ready, Danny?'

It was early morning, the dawn barely lightening the eastern sky, but down in the dock the *Claudia* was preparing to sail. The tide was right, the boat provisioned, the men were coming aboard. Any moment now, Dai Prydderch thought, we'll go nosing out into the grey morning to start our first long haul.

There were seven men aboard now, the original four having proved woefully inadequate when they got into a decent-sized shoal. Himself, Dewi, Danny and English Phil had been joined by Owen Maddoc, Meirion-Papershop, whose father owned and ran the small general store just outside Rhosneigr on the Valley Road, and Billy O'Connor, who was Irish and wanted to learn about trawling so that one day he could buy his own boat and fish out of his home village, a tiny place called Gowlaun with the sea on three sides and the rest of Connemara at its back.

'All set, Dai.'

Danny was an ideal first mate, except that they had no titles aboard the *Claudia*, simply putting their hands to any task which needed doing. Dai was pleased with all the crew; even Billy, who was not yet twenty, had his head screwed on. But he knew he'd picked a good 'un in Danny. Quiet, immensely strong, with a sort of sturdy common sense which stood them all in good stead whether they were hauling, casting out the trawl, or bargaining for the best price available.

'Right. Cast off!'

Someone had to give the orders and Dai was master, but one day Danny would have his own trawler . . . possibly a fleet of them, Dai thought, grinning to himself. There was a strength of character in Danny, a resolve, which he could only envy. It wasn't burning ambition or anything like that, just a determination to do whatever he did as well as he possibly could. Danny watched like a hawk whenever they were in a strange port to see how other trawlers were run, and if he liked something, he brought it aboard. He read, too. In his bunk, at meals, whenever he had a moment's leisure, Danny would get out books on navigation or study coastal maps. Dai recognized his desire to learn more about his chosen career as real dedication, and respected it. He was glad to have Danny aboard, even more glad that Danny and Megan were engaged. Only to Danny could he have borne giving his precious child in marriage; only to Danny.

'We're away, then.'

That was Billy, coming up from below where he had been setting up the galley. As the youngest aboard, working as what would have been called the deckie-learner on a larger boat, Billy would do the cooking – apart from making bread, which Dai trusted to no one but himself. Rhiannon had taught him and he knew himself to be as much master of the art, now, as she. But bread aside, Billy had already proved himself a competent if not an inspired cook.

'That's right.' Dai's eyes were fixed ahead, watching the familiar harbour lights blinking palely as day crept inexorably across the sky. Soon they would be clear of the dock, seeing the quayside slide away from them; then they would pass alongside the other boats and finally they would emerge into the open sea, Ireland getting bigger on the horizon as they chugged out to the fishing grounds.

Presently, having brought them out of the harbour mouth, Dai signalled to Danny to take over and went below to see how Billy was managing. The lad was boiling a pan full of eggs and cutting bread and butter. The kettle was hissing on the stove and the pot stood ready for warming.

'All set? Good. I'll have mine now. You can feed the others on the mess deck.'

Billy nodded his thanks and Dai went up on deck, seeing Danny standing behind the glass of the tiny bridge. He leaned over the rail, staring down at the waves surging past, then looking up at the sky, clear enough, though still the colourless grey of dawn.

That girl! It was a strange affair, a girl who looked just like his Megan – only not so pretty – just walking into the house and getting her legs under the table without so much as a word of warning!

Danny hadn't said what he thought. He'd come round for his dinner the previous day, Sunday, and frowned when he saw her . . . he was taken in all right, Dai told himself now, grinning with retrospective amusement. Now I never thought it was my Meg at the door . . . but then I'd only just been talking to her in the kitchen, and the girl Marsha was so muffled up there was small chance of a likeness being noticeable, even.

'What you done to your hair, girl?' Danny had demanded quite truculently. 'Not been dipping it in that old bleach, have you, when your Mam told you to do no such thing!'

He had been half laughing, but when Marsha had turned round and smiled at him he had gone pale, had put up a hand as though to ward off . . .

And of course Megan, soft-hearted thing, couldn't bear his puzzlement and jumped out from behind the door shouting Boo! like a kid of four and introducing him to her 'sister'. That was what the two of them called themselves, though it seemed to Dai they had little enough cause, apart from the likeness, which was uncanny at times.

Danny had been very quiet after that. The two girls had chattered like starlings, so perhaps he had only been quiet because he knew he would never get a word in edgeways, but Dai thought it was more than that. Dismay, at finding his Megan was not unique? But she was, of course, and Danny knew it. Did Danny not like this strange young woman with her cultured voice and her quick tongue? Dai did not know; Danny was not a man to show his feelings.

And then there was Rhiannon, the darling of his heart. What had she thought? She was not a woman to make hasty decisions or snap judgements – none knew that better than Dai – but he had a feeling she had not altogether taken to Marsha Loxley. Worried, she had been, when the two girls had gone off together, heads close, full of laughter. But since it had been his last day at home for a while she had tried to throw it off, make light of any anxieties she might have had.

But Dai was not fooled. She feared for her Megan. Causelessly, surely?

I shan't be sorry to get home after this trip, see what's been happening, Dai decided. Yet am I not better away from whatever female machinations are going on in that house? Out here, the wind and the waves are the only things we have to worry about, apart from the fish. Oh aye, we're better off out of it whilst the women come to terms with what's happened.

Yet he would still be glad to know just why his Rhiannon was uneasy about the girl Marsha.

Rhiannon always hated the day they sailed. She inevitably felt left behind, as though Dai and the others had gone lightly off on an expedition of pleasure, though she knew perfectly well that fishing was scarcely that. Even with fine weather they would work harder and more dangerously than nine out of ten of their fellow men.

Rhiannon had got up early to see her menfolk off, which meant that she was in the kitchen and wide awake before six o'clock had struck. It would have been nice to go back to bed, except that she would never drop off for fear of oversleeping. And anyway, there were always jobs to be done. She would start the bread-making off, and then she could bake a cake or two – anything to stop herself thinking about the dangers ahead for any man who went to sea in search of fish.

Of all the men who work on trawlers, a quarter will die at sea, drowned, wrecked, or cast on to rocks by the element which is both their livelihood and their enemy. Rhiannon had no idea who had first put it into words, but she knew it was true. More men died fishing than ever perished down the mines.

But each to his own, and Dai had craved for his trawler. He could not be happy on land, she knew; he would swop the safest, most lucrative shore-job for his perpetual battle with the elements.

Odd, really, except that he had known no other life. The cross-channel ships, the fishing vessels from other ports, his own little boat . . . and now this. A trawler with the power to bring him, if not riches, at least a good living. Or death.

Oh, shut up, you foolish creature, Rhiannon scolded herself. What's the use of thoughts like those? What good will it do if you make yourself miserable worrying over what may never happen? Oh, think about happy things . . . our Megan learning to drive like a lady, and going to marry Danny one of these fine days.

But thinking about Megan simply reminded her of Marsha's presence. Why the girl should worry her so she had no idea, yet from the very first moment of seeing her she had felt as though a cloud loomed over them, shutting out the sun. It was a strange thing, no question, to see the face you loved on another human being.

Not that you could mistake them, once you knew there were a couple of them knocking around. Marsha's hair was bleached fairer than Megan's, and curled from the perm she had had some months ago. But in a few weeks the bleach will have grown out, and the curls too, Rhiannon reminded herself. And I'll still know them apart, because my baby has the sweetest, most gentle expression, and that other, oh, she's got a hard look on her and a scornful glance when it rests on you! And the way she walked in – not a penny piece on her, not a word of Welsh either, yet she simply expects us to put her up, feed her, listen to her stories . . . lies, more like . . . and accept her as Megan's twin sister.

And why should we not? Rhiannon's kind and motherly side asked as she got out the flour and tipped it into her big mixing bowl. The fact that they really are related is in their faces, so why not welcome the child? And she had welcomed her, of course, for Megan's sake. But she was still uneasy. There was something about Marsha which worried her.

Rhiannon ran water into a pan, put it on the top of the stove to warm, went through to the cold cupboard – which was not really a cupboard at all but a neat hole dug in the ground at the back of the pantry and then lined with slabs of marble from old washstands – and got out her lump of yeast. Why should she keep fretting round the problem of Marsha, when the girl was no problem at all?

If she makes Meg unhappy then I shall tell her to leave, twin or no twin, Rhiannon decided, and felt better for it.

Outside, the sky was beginning to show colour: faint azure blue, with the gulls wheeling high above the town already in sunshine.

Rhiannon finished the second kneading of her dough and pushed it into her loaf tins to prove. The fire had been damped down for the night but she had riddled it through when she first got up and now the oven was beautifully hot. In an hour or so she would put the loaves in and by the time everyone was up and about the good smell of baking bread would have permeated the house.

But now? Rhiannon looked round her; at the cosy kitchen, the remains of her baking, the hundred and one jobs she could easily turn her hand to before anyone else was around. Now I'm going out, she decided suddenly. Why not? A woman was tied to her home for long enough each day without staying in it when she had a perfect right to please herself.

Although April was well advanced, it was probably quite chilly outside, so Rhiannon put on her old grey coat and beige woollen gloves. Then she gave the kitchen a last glance, just to make sure that if anyone came in whilst she was away they wouldn't see anything awful, like unwashed pots or a dirty floor. All was as it should be, so she opened the back door and stepped out.

Balmy and fresh, the morning air caressed her face. Somewhere a blackbird shouted its shrill warning . . . people about, people about! Rhiannon looked up, to where the bird perched in next door's apple tree. The blossom was showing, tight ruby and coral buds against the gently unfolding green. We should have a good summer after such a winter, Rhiannon decided, and crossed the yard to the tall green-painted door in the old grey stone wall.

Outside in the back lane, which was so narrow that if she walked down it with her arms stretched out her hands touched the walls on either side, she saw the dew heavy on the tussocks of rough grass at the wall's foot, and a slow snail, questing horns out, timidly progressing from the safety of its dark home between two stones out into the newness of the morning. How long is it, Rhiannon asked herself, since you last came out here just to walk along and look? How long since you saw a snail gliding along and actually thought about it, instead of just picking it guiltily off the lettuce or cabbage and, when no one was looking, throwing it next door?

Years, it must have been. But she could still remember distinctly the games she and Seiriol, her brother, had played. The snail-racing in wet weather, when you would capture a whole stable of the beasts and race them along the wet flagstones in the yard, up and down, one well in the lead, galloping towards the home straight and a rewarding cabbage leaf . . . until it turned off, stupidly dense, to make with dogged determination for a totally unappetizing stretch of bare earth, or for someone's dangerously hopping foot.

That's snails for you, Rhiannon thought, moving on, leaving today's snail to its slow journey. We had other games, too, Seiriol and I. Hopscotch, played out in Newry Street on marked flagstones. Fivestones, which always seemed a waste of time to me. Whipping a top . . . that was quite fun . . . and then of course there was the sea, the fishing, the shore.

It had never crossed her mind before to wonder whether she had done right by Megan and the others, but now, confronted with the vision of Marsha in her expensive clothes, her face delicately coloured with make-up, talking to them about her life, her student days, her time in the United States, she did wonder. She had thought she was saving them from the Deiniol Evans Home, but would they have done better for themselves from there? And why had Megan, the best of girls, not been chosen by some rich family to be brought up as their own? Why had she not been given Marsha's luck?

Because it wasn't luck, not really, Rhiannon said stoutly to herself, crossing Newry Fields and plunging into the lane behind Newry Fawr, heading for the harbour partly because it was downhill but also because she so rarely went there these days. To a child there are many things more important than material wealth. Would I, as a littl'un, have swopped my snail stable and my old flour-bag on a cane for a posh house, a pony to ride, and a fishing line to dangle over an inland pond?

She thought of Megan at six, squatting on the pavement in Newry Street, watching the boys playing marbles, then joining in, winning, coming back into the kitchen bright-eyed, boastful, with a big marble held in one grubby fist . . . a marble she had 'won, Mam, all on myself!'

Maybe I've done all right by her, Rhiannon thought, trying to stop herself running downhill into the sunlight, because a woman her age couldn't be seen acting like a child of ten. And then she looked around her, at the sleeping town, at the sunshine casting long blue shadows from all the houses as she passed, and she thought to hell with them all – sorry, God – and broke into a happy trot.

No one would see, and if they did, what matter? She was Rhiannon Prydderch, a sober matron from eight o'clock each morning until midnight or past. But today she had escaped for a while. Today she would be a child again, in the brief time left to her before she must go home and start breakfast.

Megan woke when she heard the back door open and close, though she was not aware of the particular sound which had disturbed her slumber. She looked across the room and was almost surprised to see the hump of a body in the other bed . . . then remembered Marsha, and felt again the welling spring of warmth which had come over her when she first realized she had a sister.

They were two! Those long-ago days had come again, when there was someone so close to her, so much a part of herself, that she had felt always safe, always wanted. But then she remembered that she had felt safe and wanted ever since coming to the island, and thought, rather sadly, that she and Marsha had met too late. Now they were two separate people, no longer almost one, and there was little they could do to change it.

Not that I want to, she realized, with a stab of something akin to dismay at her own disloyalty. But it was no use kidding herself. She and Marsha had grown up in two totally unconnected environments and no matter how alike they might look, might even feel in many ways, they were separated by differences so basic that she could not imagine either of them ever bridging the gap. Or wanting to do so, for that matter, for though Marsha was so breathlessly pretty, so fashionable and smart, Megan realized that she did not envy the other girl any of these attributes. Nor would she have changed one iota of her own background to make it more like Marsha's.

She's very nice and I want to know her better, Megan's thoughts ran as she put a toe out of bed, wincing as it touched cold linoleum before hastily transferring itself to the rag rug and then creeping back under the blankets. She's had a wonderful life, and how odd that all the things I've most wanted in the past she has actually got! The pony I was desperate for, the riding lessons, the bicycle, a proper girl's model . . . to say nothing of the clothes.

Hanging Marsha's clothes in the wardrobe the previous day had been a revelation. She was the possessor of dresses which Megan had only seen previously in her mind's eye . . . but how distinctly she had seen them, how much she had longed for them! She felt she could have recited a description of Marsha's best things long before the case was even opened – ivory-backed hairbrushes, a pink satin make-up bag, that pale green skirt with thousands of tiny pleats; each and every item had been, once, coveted by Megan.

'Why did you choose the pleated skirt and the dark green cardigan?' Megan asked as she placed them tenderly over a hanger. 'Is green a favourite colour of yours?'

Marsha stopped shaking out her light blue linen dress and frowned.

'Hmm . . . no idea. I had this sudden urge . . . I buy a lot of blue, and I just thought . . .'

'So did I. Only I never had enough spare cash to buy them,' Megan said frankly. 'Isn't it *odd*, Marsha? I think it's far odder than looking like someone to find out that you think like them, want the same sort of things.'

'Yes, I suppose . . . but where did you see the pleated skirt? I mean, I got it in the States,' Marsha pointed out.

'In the window of Victoria House, in Stanley Street,' Megan said. 'It's that really good shop opposite the Reform Café. And I saw the cardigan in the Paragon. Just like yours it was . . . but no affording it, see? So Mam and I went to Pollycoffs and bought my grey wool with the matching cardigan . . . good value, but not what I wanted.'

Marsha smiled at her. Sometimes she seemed to forget her superiority and they were just the two of them, equal, with a lot of catching up to do. But at other times Megan could sense her twin's impatience, the way Marsha was having to crush down sharp rejoinders when she, Megan, wanted to talk about things which didn't interest Marsha much.

368

'I believe you; thousands wouldn't. Tell me about Danny.'

Now, lying in bed, staring at the brightness where the sunlight outside illuminated the faded curtains at the window, Megan thought guiltily: I'm as bad as she is in some ways. I didn't want to talk to her about Danny.

Danny was too special, too much her own. She had agreed to the deception in the kitchen, had hidden behind the door and caught one glimpse of his sudden pallor beneath the tan when he realized that something was radically wrong – he knew no more than that – with his Megan.

She had rushed out, shouting, because she could not bear his hurt, his obvious bewilderment. And Marsha had been cross, because – and Megan knew this for a fact even though Marsha had never breathed a word of it – because Marsha had wanted Danny to take her in his arms, to believe her to be Megan for one moment at least.

In those few seconds in the kitchen, Megan had seen into Marsha's mind as clearly as she could see into her mirror, and she had not liked it one bit. Oh, not that there was anything *wrong*, precisely, in Marsha's wanting to be kissed by Danny, to be mistaken for her sister. It was not exactly wrong . . . just not very wise.

And who are you, Megan Prydderch, to preach of wisdom like some old owl, Megan asked herself now. A fool you are, girl, if you're jealous of your own sister because she wants to have a bit of a kiss with a lovely feller like Danny. Well, then, a fool she was, because she could not have borne to see Marsha in Danny's arms. She's got her own feller, even though she says she doesn't want him, Megan told herself now. She'd better not try to interfere between me and Danny!

But it was absurd of her even to let the thought cross

369

her mind, and Megan was properly ashamed. And besides, her irrepressible inner self reminded her, Danny's at sea now for at least two weeks. Likely she'll be gone before he returns.

It was a good thought in one way, yet in another it sent a pang of sharp dismay through her. My sister, that Other who once lay close to my heart, and I can think with pleasure of her leaving me? No, I'm not that hard. I'll miss her something terrible when she does go, but we're women now, with our own lives to lead. Even if we'd been brought up together, going to the same school, sleeping in the same room, sharing everything from our mother's milk to our thoughts and dreams, we would be tearing ourselves apart from each other now, preparing to meet the world with only the men we love beside us.

That's the first sensible thought I've had this morning, Megan decided. Sitting up and swinging both feet, this time, down to the floor, she wondered whether to see if she could will Marsha awake, or to bend her mind to keeping her twin asleep so that she could go down and help Mam with the breakfast before bringing a tray up to Marsha.

She decided to wake her. She closed her eyes, sitting there on the bed with her feet on the rag rug, and thought herself into her sister's dreams, getting a swift but confused impression of a huge shop with so many goods on display that there was no choosing between them. And then she willed wakefulness, willed the stretch, the yawn, the slow, sleepy stirring of the slumber-fattened eyelids. She willed the mouth to wake, water to rush in to moisten the tongue, roused a fleeting longing for a cup of tea . . .

'Good morning, Megan. Why did you wake me up? I was having a lovely dream.'

'I know. So many dresses!' Megan watched her sister's eyes open so wide that she could see the whites all round the dark blue of the iris, before Marsha laughed. 'Well, how did I wake you, then? You woke yourself.'

Marsha shook her head slowly.

'Oh, God, I'll get you out of bed at two o'clock tomorrow morning to teach you a lesson, now you've shown me how! I'm dying for . . .'

'. . . a cup of tea! No, don't throw the pillow at me, I'll go down and make you one, honest to God!'

'You'd better, then!'

Megan padded over to the door, across the landing and down two flights of stairs. The kitchen was deserted but dough was proving in front of the stove and by something in the air she knew Mam had been here not long before. Gone down to the harbour to wave Da off, I dare say, Megan told herself, pulling the kettle over the heat. And isn't it the strangest thing that just when I'm beginning to think it would have been better if Marsha had gone straight home from Ireland, things should suddenly all come right again? There's something of her in me and something of me in her, and we're too close to turn away from each other. We must learn each other whilst we've got the chance.

She had made the tea and poured it, was about to carry the tray up the stairs to Marsha, when the back door opened and Mam came in. She stopped short at the sight of Megan, then smiled. Guiltily.

'Well, Meggie . . . I feel a right old fraud! I'll just go down as far as the Green, I thought, take a look at the harbour on such a fine morning, and there's me dreaming away and forgetting my dough and your breakfasts . . . oh, what a good girl you are – you've put the tins into the oven! And where might you be taking that tray?'

'Upstairs to Marsha. I woke her up by . . . well, by dinning around and making a noise, so I said I'd fetch her a cup of tea.'

371

Mam shook her head, but she was smiling.

'I wonder if that one has ever made anyone a cup of tea first thing in the morning in her life? I doubt it very much.'

But Megan, carrying the tray carefully up the stairs, was sure that Mam, for once, was wrong. On one occasion she had had a mind-picture of her sister carrying a cup of tea carefully across a small bedroom to a dark-haired man lying in bed. Marsha had made tea for Tony, once at least.

Mam isn't too keen on Marsha, Megan thought now, negotiating the half-landing without brushing against Screech's bamboos. A pity, but she'll grow to love her, I'm sure. After all, she's very like me, and Mam loves me nearly as much as she loves Da!

CHAPTER TWENTY-TWO

'Soon it'll be summer.'

'Uhuh.'

'When summer comes, Mrs Iestyn wants me for the market stall twice a week, Fridays and Saturdays. But the shop will need me then, too, and though I wouldn't like to let Mrs Iestyn down I can't be in two places at once.'

'Mm hmm.'

Megan, lying with her head on Danny's hard stomach and shielding her eyes with both hands from the strong noonday sun, rolled over and punched him hard. He didn't even wince, so he must have been expecting it. She sat up, glaring down at him.

'Daniel Williams, will you listen to me? And answer this time, instead of just grunting. What will I do about Mrs Iestyn and Arthur's shop? And then there's my driving lessons. I need Mrs Iestyn's work so's I can pay for extra lessons, only I've got my test in a couple of weeks so if I was to go back to Boots . . . Danny, don't you dare close your eyes!'

Danny's blue eyes opened. He smiled at her; the lazy, wicked smile she loved.

'Why should I be asleep, just because I close my eyes?' he demanded. 'And why should I answer your questions when you won't answer mine? When's that girl going home?'

He had come back after two weeks' trawling to find Marsha still in Megan's room.

'Making herself right at home,' Mam had muttered, when he and she were alone in the kitchen. 'Doesn't want anyone but our Meg – out of it I am, and in my own house!'

But now, at his innocent question, Megan's clear gaze clouded over and a faint line appeared between her brows.

'She's not *that girl*, she's my twin sister,' she explained. 'Mam makes me feel guilty, but I can't just ask her to go. Besides, she's running away.'

'From who, answer me that! Her feller's likely glad to be rid, from what I've heard. She may be your sister, Meggie, but she's difficult to live with, isn't that so?'

'Used to having her own way, that's the trouble,' Megan said. 'Not her fault; she's been spoiled rotten. And she's nice really, Danny. Wait till you know her better.'

They were lying on the smooth, downward sloping clifftop above the South Stack lighthouse, with the grass around them starred with the clear pink shout of thrift, the gold of stonecrop. It was a sunny day, the breeze scarcely lifting the heavy weight of Megan's silky curtain of hair, the sea below blue as the sky, the wave movement so slight it looked like watered taffeta.

They had come on the motor bike, ostensibly to see the puffins which nested on the cliffs, but really to get away. The *Claudia* had berthed three days before, but it was the first time they had been alone, and although Megan was philosophical about it Danny was not. He wanted his girl to himself, he told her, his mouth very close to her ear, as though he suspected Marsha of having hearing like a lynx.

'Mean I do feel,' Megan had said remorsefully, as she met him – by secret appointment – on the Green, having managed to leave the house early under cover of shopping for Mam. 'Poor girl – she wants to be with me, that's all.'

'She is with you morning, noon and night,' Danny said

374

frankly. 'Look, girl, I'm only home for another couple of days, then we're sailing again. Don't I count for anything?'

'Oh, Danny, you're the most important person in my whole life, but Marsha . . . it's hard to explain, especially to you, because you've never had a brother, let alone a sister. But I do owe her something. When I was *very* unhappy, before I came to live on the island, she . . . Marsha . . . was the only one, the only person who could understand, who I could tell about things.'

'But you never saw each other after you were babies, your Mam said. What do you mean, you could tell her things?'

Megan sighed. It was too much for anyone to understand, that was the trouble. How could she expect Danny to take her seriously if she told him about the imagined friend, the little girl who could comfort when life was full of difficulties? Even Mam had been unable to believe in such closeness between two people who had scarcely ever met in real life. Dreams, Megan knew, were just dreams. However, there were the clothes, the pony . . . things like that.

'Oh, I can't explain, Danny. It's just that when you are a twin – which we think we must be, because Marsha's birthday and the one they sent with me from the Deiniol Evans Home are the same – when you're a twin you have such very similar feelings, wishes, all sorts, that you . . . oh, it's no use. When you stare at me like that I feel like hitting you, not explaining!'

'Hit away,' Danny said, jutting his bearded chin at her in a very provocative fashion. 'Don't get cross, my little one. I dare say you're right and people who aren't twins can't understand. But . . . don't let her spoil you, Meggie! She's clinging like a second skin at the moment, but I've a feeling that she'll slough you off like a snake does when it's got a new shiny one to wear beneath the old.'

'Oh, no! It's not like that! We'll be friends always! We're so close, so alike . . .'

'Don't bank on it,' Danny advised. 'Want to take another look at the puffins before we go?'

She sighed and climbed reluctantly to her feet. Danny put his arm about her shoulders and squeezed her to him.

'You've caught the sun – your cheeks are quite pink,' he observed. 'Look, do you know what Marsha's running away from?'

'Yes, I think I do. But don't tell, will you, Danny?'

'Not if you don't want me to. Fire ahead.'

'She's running away from her mam and da, because they didn't tell her she was adopted.'

'Oh, rubbish! If you believe that, then all I can say is you aren't as bright as I thought you were. No girl with a grain of sense runs away from loving care for one small miscalculation, because that's all it amounts to. But if that's what she's told you with her mouth, what has she told her with her heart?'

Megan turned in the circle of his arm and stared at him, pulling him to a halt. They were at the top of the steps which led down to the lighthouse and the window in the rock from whence one could see the puffins, but she stopped him short.

'Hold on! Danny, if you understand that Marsha and I can talk without words, then you should see why I can't just ask her to leave.'

'I never said I didn't understand,' Danny pointed out. 'I just think you're mistaken to encourage her to stay when one of these days she'll do you some sort of wrong, either by simply getting out and leaving you flat, or . . . oh, I don't know, just something.'

'She won't do me any sort of wrong, because it would

be like hurting herself,' Megan said. But uncertainly. Again she thought of the little likenesses and the huge differences between her and her twin. 'As for what she says to me without words, she says she wants . . . she wants . . .'

'What?' Danny said when Megan hesitated. 'Go on, girl, spit it out. Better for it you'll feel.'

'Well, I think she wants revenge, like,' Megan said slowly. 'She says she doesn't love Tony, and in a way she doesn't, because she thinks she's too good for him – and she probably is – but in another way she knows she does love him and is cross with him because he let her down.'

'And that's the sort of girl you claim is so close to you, so like you, that you'll never really be parted?' Danny's voice was incredulous. 'And what about her mam and da, then? Has she let them know where she is?'

'If she tells them she's here they'll send for her and make her go home,' Megan tried to explain, but her heart was heavy for the Loxleys and she did not, even to her own ears, sound very convinced. 'I suggested just a letter, in case they're worried whether she's all right, but she said she wouldn't risk it. They kept her awful close, Danny.'

'They loved her an awful lot, Megan,' Danny said, parodying her words. 'Don't get mad with me, my little one, but she's not . . . not . . .'

'She's not thoughtful,' Megan said eagerly. 'That was what you meant, wasn't it? And she doesn't have imagination, Danny. She just can't imagine what her parents are going through.'

'Then you know as well as I do that she's not . . .'

'. . . not thoughtful. Look, Danny, I can't really explain why Marsha's so important to me, but you must try to understand. It isn't as if you and I were married, or – or anything, so you can't say she's coming between us, especially when you're at sea. But next time you come home . . .'

'But we're engaged . . .'

'Yes, I know. But Marsha lived with that Tony, mun, for several months! She must think . . . well, to her way of seeing it . . .'

They had started to walk down the rough stone steps and this time it was Danny who pulled Megan to a halt. Roughly, swinging her round to face him.

'You told her we weren't lovers!'

'I did not! Besides, it's wrong to be lovers. Unless you're getting married soon, I suppose.'

Danny's eyes were very bright, very wicked. He smiled, then drew her against him, putting his face close so that his eyes burned, brilliant blue, into hers. He kissed her mouth gently, then harder, then stepped back. He was breathing fast, his broad chest heaving as though he had just climbed up the three hundred and sixty-five steps from the lighthouse to the clifftop instead of merely descending half of them.

'Oh, so it's wrong except when you're getting married soon? But we're engaged! And wouldn't it be fun, my little one! Wouldn't it be just great, now, to hold you in my arms . . . like this, and to squeeze you closer and closer . . . like this, and then to . . .'

'Not in full view of the lighthouse keeper and his kids and a million auks,' Megan protested, pulling away. Her knees were trembling . . . God, how she did love Danny!

'No, there is a time and a place,' Danny agreed. He let her go as calmly as though they had been discussing the weather and began to lead her down the steps once more. 'Tell you what, I'll leave you a note where to meet and what excuse to give, how would that be? And I'll be there, on my old bike, and we'll go for a spin.'

'Yes, but . . .'

'No buts, Meg. We're engaged to be married, aren't we? Besides, I might change my mind and leave it until I can make an honest woman of you . . . only I've a feeling that your sister won't go until she's more or less forced to do so.'

'Nonsense,' Megan said at once. 'She'll go when she's ready to take on the world again.'

'Perhaps. Here we are; the window. Up with you.'

The window was a natural square-shaped hole in the rock face, through which you could see into the three-sided chimney in which the auks nested. In fact a great many seabirds nested there – fulmars, guillemots, razor-bills and Megan's favourites, the beautiful little puffins with their rainbow bills and their bright orange feet.

For an hour they watched the puffins as they arrowed down into the smooth green depths, accompanied by air-bubbles which drifted to the surface, but neither of them really took in what was happening. They were both far too involved with their own thoughts.

The following day, Friday, the heavens decided to open and pour the rain which had not fallen for three weeks down on Holyhead. Danny came round for tea and pulled a face at Megan as they ate. Outside, the rain pounded on the pavements and drummed on the slates. It made provisioning the *Claudia* a miserable business in which the whole family had to join, Mam and Megan climbing up and down the companionway with tins and packets and baskets of food which Marsha put away.

They hoped for better weather on the Saturday, but when it decides to rain on Anglesey it always makes a proper job of it. Saturday dawned grey and overcast and the rain pelted and the wind howled and Megan, bringing in Mrs Iestyn's goods from her old lorry to the market stall, got soaked to the skin so many times that she began

379

to feel like a mermaid, her long hair darkened with rain to the colour of clear honey.

Sunday was, if anything, worse. It thundered in the afternoon and the two girls, glumly watching the harbour under the shelter of Da's church umbrella, saw the lightning spearing down into the sea and forking up to slash the heavens open and thought their own thoughts.

'Will they sail tomorrow, now the weather's so bad?' Marsha asked at last.

She was shivering, hugging her borrowed coat round her. Mam had drawn the line at lending Marsha money to buy yet more clothes, even if she did need something more practical than the things she had brought with her from Ireland.

'Yes, of course they will. It isn't as if there were huge seas running, or terrible gales,' Megan explained. 'When it's so bad they can't get out of the harbour they postpone the sailing, but not otherwise. After all, once they're away from here no one can tell what the weather will throw at them.'

'No. But English Phil said they can ride out storms in other ports.'

Marsha was taking quite an interest in English Phil, which was all right, as it happened, since Siân had turned her attention to Billy O'Connor. She had decided to make a man of him, it appeared. Megan rather pitied Billy, though the lad seemed happy enough.

'That's true, thank God. Well, it's Sunday evening; I doubt we'll see much more of the lads until next time they dock. Da always spends his last evening checking his clothes and going over lists of provisions, though he knows very well we put everything aboard.'

'Oh, does he? What does Danny do?'

Megan shot a suspicious look at her, but Marsha turned innocent eyes in return and Megan immediately felt ashamed. How silly she was, to feel even the slightest tug of jealousy over Danny, when he and she were so much in love, and soon to marry.

'Danny? Oh, the same, I expect. He'll come round and say goodbye, though.'

'So will Phil,' Marsha said, sounding smug.

Megan wondered why Marsha was talking as though she and Phil were more than just acquaintances. Oh, she had flirted with him, but she suddenly seemed really interested in what the men did and when they would see them again.

'Will he? That's nice. I say, the rain's driving in on me in spite of the umbrella. Shall we go back?'

They went back and Mam was making crumpets for tea. All this must be terribly boring for Marsha, coming from a house where they probably have bought crumpets and eat them whenever they feel like it, Megan thought. But Marsha seemed to be enjoying herself. She was flushed and happy, teasing Da, being charming. Mam was a bit abrupt with her, but she hated it when the trawler left, did Mam.

Danny didn't come to tea. He came over later, when they had finished. Megan was upstairs shampooing her hair, but came to the head of the stairs and called down to him.

He shouted back that he'd pop round again if he had a moment, but he'd just called to remind Dai that they had no ice and the delivery man should be reminded, sharply if necessary, that they were off on the tide in the morning.

He did not come up the stairs nor make the assignation for which Megan had been waiting, but it was the weather, of course. Where would they go? There was nowhere a couple could be alone and under cover, not that she could think of, and anyway it was best to wait.

Later, she noticed that Marsha had a little smile on her face.

'Phil call?' she asked. And Marsha said he had, and that he and she would be going for a little walk later on.

'In this weather?' Megan said jokingly, for it was still pouring with rain. 'You're mad, girl . . . only fit for ducks out there it is.'

'Da's gone down to the *Claudia*; he and Danny want to see the ice in tonight, late though it is,' Mam said. 'Did English Phil go with them?'

'He might have,' Megan said cautiously. She stayed downstairs until midnight, hoping that Danny might pop back, but he never came.

She was in bed before Marsha returned, and fell asleep with the other bed empty for the first time for a month.

Marsha had been looking out for Danny, because she knew he would come. She just hoped it would not be at teatime, but something told her it would be later, and it was. She had suggested that Megan should wash her hair and Megan had trotted upstairs obediently as though she was all in favour of what Marsha had in mind.

Now, Marsha thanked her stars for the speed with which she had picked up the Welsh language. She had worked at it for Megan's sake, but now it would really come in useful. Danny never spoke English to her sister.

Danny arrived at last. And there was Megan, at the head of the stairs, with her hair wrapped in a towel, calling down to him . . . but of course he knew it was Marsha, because Megan had already rushed out in the pouring rain, with her old anorak on, the hood pulled well up to save her from the wet. And she had run to Danny, whispering, quick.

'Where, Danny? When?'

He had reached for her hands, in a hurry, without the

slightest hesitation. He knew who she was, in Megan's coat with the words he most wanted to hear on her lips.

'Eight o'clock, down the end of the road.'

Then he had gone to the door and delivered his message about the ice, and seen Marsha with a towel around her head. He was wearing waterproofs; if she had not known it was Danny, Marsha mused, turning to go inside, he could have been anyone, so anonymous are oilskins.

And at eight o'clock, Megan was on her knees before the fire in the parlour, drying her heavy tresses and reading a book. She had waved, absently, as Marsha took her anorak and left. No thought of where her sister was going, no suspicion that Danny might have made that assignation. What a *nice* girl she is, Marsha thought, as she sloshed along the wet pavement in Megan's wellington boots, Megan's anorak, even Megan's faded blue cotton, for she had formed the habit of wearing anything she fancied which belonged to her sister and, to be fair, she had thrown open her wardrobe too.

But the rain was getting worse, if anything. Still, in a moment she would meet Danny and he would take her somewhere warm and dry and they would make wonderful, passionate love and the little niggle of wanting Tony, the bigger niggle of hungering after anything Megan had, would be sated.

All her life she and Megan had passed needs, thoughts, desires, from one to the other. All her life, Marsha had satisfied Megan's desires, even if Megan had never known it. She had got riding lessons not because she wanted to learn to ride – it had never entered her head – but because what Megan wanted she wanted too. Likewise owning a pony, having heaps of books, buying a particular garment . . . and it was Megan who made me have my hair permed and bleached, Marsha thought quite crossly now. I was an idiot, but when she wanted it so badly I knew – or thought I knew – that it was what I wanted too. But her mam doesn't give way easily, and mine does. So I had my hair done and then Megan stopped wanting it so badly. So in a way she owes me Danny. After all, if she hadn't wanted him so desperately it wouldn't have entered my head that he was worth a bit of scheming over. And I'm risking Tony by having Danny. So it's all her fault, really.

Mind, he's a gorgeous hunk, is Danny. Her stomach clenched with delighted anticipation at the thought of the gorgeous hunk possessing her. Tony had been good, but Danny, she was sure, would be better. Oh, damn the rain . . . how glad she would be to find herself under a roof, with Danny.

Only he must not realize, not until it was too late – better if he never realized. She had never seen him angry but found she dreaded it. His rage would be terrible.

For a moment her confident footsteps faltered and the dark seemed threatening, a force for evil and not one which would, so conveniently, hide her from the eyes of anyone watching. But then she thought again of Danny's hands on her, his body against hers, and she walked on – or battled on, rather, head down, fighting the wind and rain.

It would be worth it! It would be worth anything she had to have Danny too.

He was there, waiting. He climbed aboard his bike and she got up behind, wet hands clinging to his slippery oilskins. He spoke to her in Welsh and she answered in the same language, once again glad of the ease with which she had picked it up from the family.

'You all right, love? You aren't frightened?'

'I'm fine.'

Then they were off, the wind tearing at them, the rain

almost unendurable as it was forced against them. She lay flat along his back, her head turned sideways, and prayed for the journey to end.

It ended with an incredibly bumpy ride over what felt like pasture, and then they began to climb, the bike slipping and sliding all over the place, and thick mud – she just knew it was mud – splashing all up her legs and over Megan's anorak.

Danny brought the bike to a halt. They were on a plateau with the hump of the hill rising above them. In the darkness she could see very little and the rain still pelted down. She would have liked to ask him why in God's name they had come to this wild and lonely spot – she could hear the sea thundering on rocks near at hand – but she did not have the Welsh for so much conversation. Better to keep quiet.

'Did you guess it would be here?' Marsha nodded bleakly. He laughed and gave her a squeeze through the thick anorak. 'Come on, then . . . keep close.'

She understood that all right; everyone seemed to tell her to follow them, as though she were an idiot with no sense of direction whatsoever. Which, as it happened, was pretty accurate around here.

He led her straight at the hillside, through thick, wet bushes which lashed at her, clung, showered her already soaked clothing with heavy drops. There was a lovely smell, though . . . gorse blossom! Now that her eyes were used to the dark she could pick out the paler patches and recognize the sweet, nutty scent mingling with the smell of the sea, the richness of wet earth, more powerful even than the aroma of wet anorak and rubber boots which was pretty pervasive.

They reached the side of the hill and Danny ducked down. Marsha ducked too; she had little option with Danny gripping her wrist. They were in a cave – a tunnel?

385

– which seemed to lead right into the heart of the mound. Trust Danny to have found somewhere which was still really out of doors, though they were at least sheltered from the rain.

Danny stopped. His hand left hers for a moment and light sprang up, warm and golden, filling the space around them. They were in a smallish, circular chamber and for a moment she nearly screamed at the sight of the great, silent figures spread out around them. She gasped, unable to help herself, before suddenly realizing that they were only Stones.

But what Stones! Each one richly carved, and one, at the end, laid flat, like a great granite altar. And it was towards this that Danny was leading her, pulling her along. She allowed herself to be tugged over to the Stone, and then Danny turned and faced her. His beautiful, tanned face looked down at her and suddenly it seemed as though this was not Danny at all but someone else, someone remote and stern and terrifying, who had brought her here for some purpose which he would carry out now, regardless of her wishes.

She backed a step and he smiled; the tilted, cruel smile of a Greek god. A conqueror's smile. Then he held out his hand.

'Megan, my little one!'

And then, before she could say anything or run or even move, he switched out the light.

She was frozen with terror for a moment, sure that the Stones were closing in on her, about to crush her. And then Danny's arms were round her, strong and warm, and he was muttering what she took to be endearments in her ear as he lifted her, laid her on the slab of stone. It was slightly hollowed, she found, and almost comfortable, almost like a bed.

He loomed over her. She could see nothing whatever

in the total darkness, but she knew he was near and now she wanted him worse than she had ever wanted anyone or anything, with a heat and a fever she had never known before.

The darkness no longer terrified her, but comforted with its complete anonymity. She almost believed herself to be Megan now, because it should have been Megan lying here, waiting for Danny to take her.

She heard little sounds, knew he was taking his clothes off. She sat up and began to tear her own things off so that when he finished and came down on her she was already naked and lying on a thick, soft pile of damp clothing.

He groaned, his hands touching, finding, then settling her comfortably beneath him. He must have been as desperate as Marsha for their joining but he was clearly determined that this should be no hasty, greedy coupling. He caressed, stroked, aroused, until Marsha had to bite her lips until they bled to stop herself from crying out to him to hurry, hurry, to take her now! She dared not speak because he would know, she knew he would know, and the moment she had hungered for would never happen if he knew who lay beneath him, writhing and whimpering to his touch.

But presently they were both too hot for each other to hold back. Marsha cried out, encouraged, but without a word, only with little sounds, and felt him heavy on her, clutched and clung as the slow, strong rhythm of his movements changed, quickened to climax.

And throughout their loving she was aware of the Stones, standing a-tiptoe, staring at them, greedy for their cries, drawing some sort of deep, primeval satisfaction from what was happening on the altar slab, relishing the heat of passion after so long in the lonely dark.

When it was over, when the shuddering died away,

they lay together, bodies close, and Danny soothed and whispered and told her – she thought – that she might sleep now.

Sleep? On a stone altar beneath a hill, with those weird Stones looking down? And into her head popped another thought, alien, strange, yet, she believed, the truth.

Fear nothing, for the Stones are the Guardians; whilst you are here nothing can harm you. They are supreme in this place.

And after that, though it seemed incredible, she slept as soundly as though she were in her own bed.

Danny saw her right to the door, watched her go in and close it gently behind her. In his imagination he saw her climb the stairs, creak open the attic door, slither out of her wet things and slide into bed.

He sat there in the rain and the windy darkness, astride his bike, and was glad that he had dared, glad he had taken the bull by the horns and made Megan his own, using his body and the things his body could do to tie her to him with bonds as strong as steel yet as gentle as the dawn breeze.

God, but she was wonderful, his Megan! She had laid her virginity in his hands, trusting him, and she had not been disappointed. Indeed, her response had kindled in him a kind of divine madness, so that he had possessed her three times during the course of their loving, each taking and giving equal pleasure, perhaps heightened by the strangeness of the setting, the power which seemed to stream out of the Stones and into the couple on the granite altar.

He had not thought of it as an altar at first. Just as the nearest thing to a bed in the chamber. He had known its true purpose, and that Megan was, in a sense, the sacrifice, when it was too late to draw back, even if he could have done. Images, confusing yet titillating, had spun crazily round in his head . . . a white-robed priest with long yellow hair just like Danny's own and a wreath of some dark-leaved plant on his head, a curved stone knife upraised . . . the plunge, which was, at the last minute, not the plunge of the cold knife into hot flesh but the sex act suddenly beautiful in its intensity, its power to drive out darkness.

And Megan's quivering, clutching, wholehearted response had shown him more than words that she was as involved as he, as deeply satisfied. He had known that if he could take her back there everything would be all right. He had killed the fears that if he had Megan, then fate would see that he did not have her long. He had followed his instincts at long last, ignoring the foolish, war-born terrors, and his entire body, its mad ardour gradually cooling, was whole again.

But he could not spend the rest of the night astride the motor bike, watching her house and thinking tenderly of her body relaxing into sleep. He must be up at dawn to catch the tide. He pushed the bike with his feet down the hill to the main road before starting the engine, and then as he roared off towards London Road his mind was singing his love as loud and clear as though he had actually raised his voice in song.

Megan, Megan, Megan! You are the most beautiful and desirable woman in the whole of Ynys Mon, and you belong to me, Danny Williams, fisherman, who adores you from the top of your golden head to the tip of your toes. Ah, God, but he was the luckiest devil in the whole old world, and the child within her would be beautiful and bright and . . .

He nearly came off his bike with the shock. Child? For God's sake, why should he have thought that? Could a woman have a baby the first time? All the lads he knew swore it was impossible . . . but what did it matter, anyway? If she was to bear his child they would marry as soon as his next voyage was over, make all tidy.

He reached the bridge, revved to climb the slight slope, then roared down the other side, swung right, and cut the engine. Experience told him that the bike could coast home from here.

A baby. Was it what he wanted, to tie her to him with a child? It would shame Rhiannon and Dai, except that he would marry her so quickly that the old 'uns would never be able to tell for sure. And a life, surely, was cause for happiness, not shame? Oh, damn them all, it was he and Meg who mattered, not a lot of tight-lipped chapel-goers who denied the sweetness, the rightness, of a man and a woman together, when they loved.

He parked the bike up beside the house, slid round the side and opened the back door. All was dark and quiet; his mam and uncle slept. Once he had been ashamed that they shared a bed and them not married, but no more. Let them do what they wanted, so long as they hurt no one else, made no man or woman weep.

The stairs were old friends; old friends tell no tales, he reminded them, avoiding the third, which creaked, stepping lightly on the ninth, which had a loose board he had long meant to hammer flat, gaining the upper landing without a sound made.

He had greased the hinges of his door with butter; he opened it and no squeak could be heard. He took off his boots, his oilskins, his thick working jersey and his faded old trousers. Naked, he slid between the rough, scratchy sheets.

Sleep now, until the dawn, he commanded himself. Not long you've got before we sail, so make the most of it, Danny Williams, lover of Megan!

He snuggled down, and braced his naked arms around

his pillow and trembled at his memories and wished she was with him still, soft and yielding, yet supple and firm-bodied.

He had barely been asleep an hour when the shrilling of the alarm woke him and he saw, through his uncurtained window, the heralded day begin.

CHAPTER TWENTY-THREE

Megan slept deep and heavy, as though she were exhausted, yet all she had done, dammit, was wash her hair! She woke to find the room full of light, and saw the hump of Marsha's hip in the bed opposite and the alarm clock, traitorously silent, its bell not primed to ring.

Oh, drat! She shot out of bed, reached the door, slithered across the landing and down the first flight. It was still quite early, so she would use the bathroom, and just a smidgin of the boarders' hot water, not enough to notice. But Mam would be down in the kitchen, waiting for her jug . . .

She was back in her room getting the jug from her washstand before she remembered that it was Monday. No market today, and the fish shop not wanting her yet either. No driving lesson . . . oh, damn and damn again, there was no need to be up at all. She could have had another half-hour, and she so tired and heavy and somehow stale-feeling that she could have slept for a week!

But she was awake now, so she might as well give Mam a hand. Mam always suffered on sailing day; she was always quiet, a bit abrupt. And I usually hate it when I know they've left, Megan reminded herself. And poor Danny . . . he had gone without what he wanted, but perhaps he had thought better of it, thought how much it would mean to Mam if her daughter married because that was what she wanted, not because she had no choice.

Marsha slept still, her breathing so heavy she was almost snoring. Megan nearly gave her a shove when she saw the anorak and wellington boots Marsha had borrowed clagged with mud. Oh, damn the girl, so mad for English Phil that she'd not given a thought to whose clothes she rolled in, carrying on in the long grass. And in the rain, too. Everything soaked and filthy . . . and the blue dress was old, I grant, but did she have to rip it? And there were gorse needles everywhere.

Megan picked up the dress; it lay, limp and innocent, in her grasp. Where have you been and what did she do, in you or out of you? she demanded of it, but the dress, of course, simply hung in her hands. Megan turned it over. Sodden, dirty, torn . . . she cheated. She closed both eyes and put the dress up to her face.

Pictures. A deep darkness, a smell of old earth, incense, a faint, transitory sweetness. Something hard beneath, like bones felt through a thick, damp pelt. A man, shoulders jerking, pulling you, settling into a position in which . . .

'Oh, I'm sorry! You can have one of mine – my best one – honestly you can. But you know what a bitch of a night it was, and the only spot he could find for us was pretty bloody uncomfortable, I'm telling you.'

Marsha was sitting up in bed, her face strained and anxious.

'It doesn't matter. It'll wash, and I'll mend the rip,' Megan said slowly. 'Where did you go, you and Phil?'

Marsha shrugged.

'I've no idea.'

'A hut? An old shed?'

Marsha shrugged again. She looked defensive, almost sly, as though she knew perfectly well where she had been but did not choose to tell.

'I haven't a clue. It was dark and wet and windy and he took me into the dry.'

'And what did you do there?'

Marsha's eyes fell on the dress, still held between

Megan's hands. Did Marsha know the power that handling an object could sometimes bring? Megan had scarcely
known it herself, but now she acknowledged that it had
helped her to see the pictures.

'What do you think? A bit of kissing, a bit of cuddling.
I gave him what they all want.'

Megan should have left it there, but she found she
could not. She had to know! After all, it was her dress,
her anorak, even her wellington boots!

'Did you go all the way?'

Marsha was sitting up in bed. Now she swung her feet
out and stared at her toes. She did not seem embarrassed
by the question, merely unsure how best to answer.

'Why do you want to know? Why does it matter?'

Unsaid were the words, *I wasn't a virgin when I came
here, you know, so what difference does it make whether
I did it or not last night?* They hung between them, Megan
felt, in letters of fire, and why did it matter, what difference would it make? But she still felt that she had to
know.

'I didn't say it mattered. I suppose I'm just curious.'

'Oh.' Marsha looked at her again, this time with something of triumph in her glance. Megan could not understand it at all. 'All right, I'll satisfy your vulgar curiosity
just this once. We did it.'

With the words, uttered with such indifference, a sharp
pang went through Megan, so strong that it was almost a
physical thing. Like a spear it skewered her so that she
gasped and clutched her stomach, the colour flying from
her cheeks, leaving her sick and pale. Oh, the pain of it!

'Meg? Are you all right? What is it?'

But already it had passed. Megan straightened and
smiled at her sister, sitting in her bare skin on the bed,
twiddling her toes amongst the knotted rags of the rug.

'Indigestion, I expect,' she said cheerfully. 'Are you

going to sit there in your birthday suit all morning or shall I get you some washing water when I fetch mine?'

'Happy, eh, Dan? Never see you without a broad grin this trip. Still an' all, we've had the weather, and the catches. I suppose you've a right to that great big self-satisfied smirk.'

Danny and Phil were leaning on the rail, watching as the small port settled into evening. They had brought their catch in here, the fishroom full to bursting, and had auctioned it off at the best price for cod this season. The money had been banked and Dai and Dewi were off getting more ice, whilst the other lads were having a drink. Danny was on watch, if you could call it that, because he could not imagine anyone wanting to come aboard in this quiet, well-run little West Country port. But still, you never knew. They weren't local men and in some places the locals resented fishermen from other parts of the country joining the press of trawlers trying to sell their catch.

'Smirking, am I? Well, at the rate we're going, Phil, old son, Megan and I will be setting up home together come the autumn. Enough to make any man smirk, eh?'

'She's a lovely girl,' Phil agreed. 'That sister of hers, Marsha, she's not a bad kid either. Came out with me a few times; game for anything, I thought. Strange, isn't it, how two girls can be like as two peas in a pod and yet so different? Your Megan's a quiet, shy one. Marsha expects to be taken at her own valuation, which is pretty dam' high, I can tell you.'

'Oh? Prices herself above rubies, does she? Well, she'll get respect that way, if nothing else.'

'Respect?' Phil guffawed. 'I don't know about that. Hot-arsed little piece, she is.'

Danny frowned. He did not care for Marsha, but she was Megan's sister.

'No way to talk about the girl, Phil,' he said reprovingly. 'Don't try to tell me you got your leg over that one – when did you have the opportunity?'

'Thursday before we sailed,' Phil said promptly. 'Took her over to Moelfre, had a drink in the pub, stopped for a snog on the way back in a farmer's field – he'd left the gate open most conveniently – and she was all over me, Danny, honest! I hardly had a chance to make an indecent suggestion, let alone start touching her up, before she was on top of me. I swear to God if I'd been a virgin she'd have raped me!'

'Poor old Phil,' Danny said, grinning. 'Well, who'd have thought it!'

Inside his head, the little pictures danced: the white face on her as he had drawn her into the tunnel; the wildness of her body as they began to make love; the priest with his long yellow hair down to his shoulders and his stern face, the upraised stone knife . . .

'I know what you mean. And I couldn't help wondering who else had had a slice,' Phil said ungallantly. 'I mean, when a girl makes a feller . . . you have to wonder.'

'Yeah. Well, in case you think it runs in the family . . .'

'I wouldn't dream of thinking such a thing,' Phil assured him. 'Megan's quite different.'

Danny nodded, turning back again to gaze at the little town, the lights pricking on, the blue dusk settling, stealing the red from the rooftiles, the green from the trees. Coming across the quay he saw three small figures. He touched Phil's arm.

'The lads are back. Want to go for a quick pint before we sail?'

The storm caught them out at sea, far from land. It was

a terrible one, the tail of a hurricane, Dai shouted when he and Danny met, both streaming salt water, on the open deck.

It was evening, and not a star in sight. No sign of land, either, though they knew they were somewhere off the west coast of Ireland. A dangerous shoal-shore, similar in many ways to the coast of Anglesey where a ship could founder, and her crew with it, so close to land that those on the beach could see the very whites of the eyes of men dying in the surf.

Hour after hour they fought to keep her head-on to the waves, but the *Claudia* was old. As she wallowed into each trough she groaned like a living thing, and was more reluctant to shake off the weight of the sea and brace herself to climb the great hill of the next breaker.

They knew when she decided she could struggle no longer by her sluggishness. Like an old bitch who had fought well in her time but could fight no longer, she wanted to lie down and let the sea take her. Her seams were parting, and the weight of water had smashed the Kent clear-vu screen of the bridge. Dai was at the wheel, knowing there was no hope, and Billy no longer fiddled with the RT set. He had been getting static and nothing else ever since the storm had started.

'Up on deck,' Dai bawled above the scream of the wind, the howl and crash of the waves. 'She'll not rise again . . . save yourselves.'

Vain command! The *Claudia* had one tiny boat; Danny had seen it washed away an hour since. But nevertheless, the instinct for survival being what it is, when the poor trawler met her last wave, keeled on to her side and nosed into the deep, everyone grabbed hold of something, did his best to keep afloat.

Danny had been too busy, until now, to think, but as the following wave picked him up like a bit of straw, sucked him crest-high, and then tossed him down into its trough, he thought of pretty Megan, left behind, and wished he'd not taken her, in that deep underground chamber, with the great Stones watching.

He fought his way to the surface – or was he forced there like a cork, for the waves to play cat and mouse with once more? Again he was thrown into the trough, but this time the great comber towering house-high above him broke in a flurry of foam and came crashing down on top of him, heavy as bricks and as destructive to life and limb.

Danny was turned over and over, tumbled and broken, in the wake of the great wave, now below the surface, now on it. And he thought of Megan and he remembered the fear that he had thought so foolish: that the price of her was to be his death. A slow and painful death, battered and torn and finally choked out of his good life by the bitter salt water.

Once he came to himself to find he was on a great crest, riding it like a surfer, but powerless, when the comber curled over, to resist again, to rise once more to the surface. He was too weak, numbed with a deep, bone-chilling cold. He felt the suck of the currents below and knew that he was being dragged down, lungs bursting, into that deeper darkness. And for a moment he saw the chamber, the girl writhing on the altar, and himself, bending over her.

It was Marsha! Just for that one last fleeting second of consciousness he knew, thought he had always known – it was Marsha who had coupled with him so willingly that night, Marsha who had lain in his arms. He was dying for Marsha, who meant less than nothing to him.

And even as the bitterness of his loss swept over him, so did a deeper, colder darkness. And he knew no more.

* * *

It was a week before the first detritus of the wreck came ashore, a fortnight before bodies were found. The household at Newry Street went about its business like automatons, with never a word said unless it needed saying.

All their men, gone in a single afternoon. Mam and Louisa widowed, Megan bereft, Billy O'Connor's mother childless now. Marsha seemed uneasy, started sentences and then broke them off. She was fonder of English Phil than any of us realized, Megan thought, when she could think at all. Most of the time she just sat.

She and Mam tried to comfort each other, for Mam knew that Da had meant almost as much to Megan as he had done to her. And they found his body, almost untouched by the cruel teeth of the rocks which had battered the other bodies into anonymity. Very pale and strange Dai Prydderch looked, lying in the coffin, with his blue eyes closed and his firm mouth slack. Megan took one look and rushed from the chapel to vomit grief and pain into the green May grasses already racing to reach knee-height.

The police came when they sent the bodies home, and were kind. Chief Inspector Johnny Evans who had sat next to Mam in school and knew Dai well, had served in the Navy with him, cried at the funeral.

Mam didn't cry. Nor Megan. Marsha stayed at home to mind the boarders, except that the boarders all came to the burial.

Uncle Reggie cried. And he cried again when they buried Dewi and held a memorial service for the others, whose bodies would probably never be recovered, because they were young and full of hope and laughter and should have outlived an old man like him.

Mam didn't cry. Nor Megan. They hurt too much to cry.

Sergeant Corkie Williams came round to tell them,

gently, that it would be better if they didn't come down to identify Dewi. Corkie knew the lad and frankly, Rhi, save for the hand with the wedding ring . . .

He couldn't forget what was left of Dewi, though he was used enough to the bodies that were hurled ashore along the rocky coast from winter tragedies at sea. Best remember him as he was, Rhi, Sgt Corkie said; don't go down until the coffin's closed.

In the end, no one did. Only Da was neat and nice, and oh, how those quiet, closed eyes pained Megan to the heart, the wispy, flattened curls of him, the hands, softened and whitened by two weeks in the water until there was nothing left of Da's square, strong hands with the cracked and broken nails, the seamed palms.

'How will we live?' Mam burst out one evening, when she and Megan were sitting in the kitchen, waiting for the boarders to finish their tea. 'Oh, Megan, my little one, how ever will we live?'

Megan was sitting on the floor beside Mam's chair; now she moved to lean against her legs, taking her hand, patting it as though she were the parent and Mam the child.

'I don't know. But we must,' she said slowly. She knew that Mam was not talking about money; they would manage somehow. She was asking, quite simply, how one went on existing after such a devastating tragedy. 'It happens, Mam.'

They both knew the bitter truth of this. To the woman of a fisherman or a sailor, death by drowning is a spectre always lurking in the wings. Megan remembered the death throes of the submarine *Thetis*, which went down just off the island, within a stone's throw of rescue. She remembered the young men drowned whilst trying to save the crew of a ditched plane just off Rhosneigr beach. And there were thousands more deaths, stretching back in time, men dying because the weather turned bad on them and their boats weren't strong enough to resist.

Somewhere in the house, someone turned on the wireless. Dance music was playing. The listener twiddled the knob, trying to get another station, then gave up and turned the set off. Megan heaved herself to her feet. It was odd how heavy she felt all of a sudden, as though sorrow was actually a physical weight, bowing her down.

'They'll be waiting for me to clear,' she said. 'I shan't be long.'

She left the room. Mam stared at the flames in the stove. What was she waiting for, now?

Marsha left the house and immediately felt lighter, almost a new person again. She was so lonely – and nobody cared! Megan had withdrawn from her as completely as though they were once more separated by hundreds of miles. She lay in bed no more than six feet away from her sister, she ate at the same table, and yet her mind was closed to her completely.

She knows, Marsha thought sometimes, but she knew it wasn't true. If Megan had known she would have told her; she wouldn't simply have switched off their channel of communication without a word or a look. Worse, when they did speak, Megan kept apologizing, which made Marsha feel wretched, though as God was her witness she had nothing to feel wretched about. The bloke was dead – he could no longer come between them either because Megan wanted no one but him or because Marsha had to have him too.

She woke some mornings determined to go home, imagining her parents' faces when she walked into the big hall, how they would light up, how they would hug, kiss, make much of her! But whenever she made, even in her own mind, the first tentative plans for the trip, something

401

in her stopped her short. Unfinished business, it said severely; you can't leave here until . . .

Until what? But it seemed she was stuck for the time being at least, caught and sucked down in a whirlpool of grief not her own, grief she was not even allowed to share, for although they were absently kind to her neither Mam nor Megan could let her in.

Megan started work again a week after the funerals. She appeared behind the market stall, her heavy hair falling forward, half obscuring her face, wearing her grey skirt and cardigan and a navy blouse. It was the nearest she could get to mourning, Marsha supposed.

A week after that, Megan tied her long hair up in a knot on top of her head and changed the navy blouse for a white one.

A fortnight later still, because the holidaymakers were beginning to come back, and the caravans on the headlands were filling up, she started work at Boots again. She smiled at customers, joked with them even . . . but Marsha knew that Megan was hollow with grief, that she was simply putting on an act because it was all she could do now.

Then, one morning, whilst Megan was fetching their washing water – they took it in turns – Marsha was sick. She made it to the bathroom, fortunately, but she felt exceedingly ill all the rest of the day.

Marsha was a bright girl; everyone said so. Certainly she was no fool. She walked up and down the Green, counting dates, and came to the conclusion that she had missed two periods and was very likely pregnant.

For a moment she panicked. Pregnant! But Tony had always been so careful, so considerate for her . . .

Danny. That night. It was Danny who had taken no care, Danny who had simply wanted to gratify his own desires without a thought of the consequences.

For a moment she hated him, hated him with all her strength and all her might. She was glad he had drowned . . . she hoped he had suffered. He had thought he was stuffing his precious Megan, that oh-so-nice girl, and how would he have liked to lie in his cold grave and think of Megan facing shame and childbirth alone? But because it was Marsha he was probably laughing his head off, wherever he was.

Her heart jumped and bounded in her chest and she pressed her hands against it; stop it, stop leaping about like that, heart, don't be such a fool, we can work it out. We'll go home to Mummy and Daddy and demand an abortion, tell them Danny raped me one night . . . oh, heart, don't let me down now, don't start aching!

She did not want a baby. She did not even want Danny any more. If he had walked up to her now, smiling and sweet, and told her he would marry her, make her respectable, she would have laughed in his face. Let him have his old Megan, pure and unsullied – albeit largely by accident – he was not half the man Tony was!

Tony! She could see his face as clearly as if it was only yesterday they had lain together, in the big soft bed in the little cottage, the rain tickling gently at the window and Tony giving her everything he had to offer, loving her for herself, not for what she was, or had, or might become.

Why in heaven's name had she ever left him? Just because he had not immediately jumped to do her bidding she had flown out in a temper, lost him. He would have searched; she was sure of that now, though she had told herself at the time that she was testing him. When he had failed to turn up on the doorstep she decided he had lost interest in her, was as indifferent to her as she was to him.

She had meant to go back sooner than this, to assure

him that she was just teaching him a bit of a lesson so that he didn't go against her wishes another time. And then bloody Danny had seemed such a challenge, and after she'd had him she'd waited to see what would happen between him and Megan, and one thing had led to another . . .

And now? How could she possibly go back, bearing another man's child? Tony would know that the baby could not be his because he had taken precautions. But if she explained that the father was dead, drowned in a shipping accident . . .

It would make no difference. Tony was too intelligent to believe that she had been raped, so she must get rid of the baby or she would never be able to search for him. And that, she now realized, was what she desperately wanted to do. To be held in his arms, comforted by his body, have him all to herself.

She had been fooled into chasing Danny by the old will o' the wisp of wanting whatever Megan had. She had always known it was not love which had prompted her to take Megan's place, but it was not even genuine lust for Danny's beautiful body. It had been a sort of competitiveness, the feeling that if Megan wanted something, then she must have it too.

That night she went to bed in a strange frame of mind – which was probably why she dreamed.

Darkness, first. And then the darkness grew light as a fire began to burn in the centre of the Stone circle. She knew the chamber at once; by the light of the flames she could even pick out the flat slab of the altar . . . with something or someone on it, stretched out, submissive.

There was a man, taller than all the Stones, so tall that he had to bend his neck or his head would have touched the roof overhead. He was very dark, very beautiful. He was moving about the circle and he was naked, but so proud, so slow-pacing, that he looked finer and more in command than anyone in flowing robes or full uniform.

Megan was there. Crouched at the foot of the altar, her long hair streaming across her shoulders, across her naked breast, falling like a heavy silk curtain right down to the earthen floor. Her eyes met Marsha's for a moment, and they were dark with sadness, enlarged by the tears which trembled inside the lids.

Marsha moved forward until she stood in front of the dark man. He put a hand on her arm; she could feel it, the fingers strong as steel as they sank into her soft flesh. He turned her round, to face the altar, and the body lying on it.

It was Danny. Beautiful, grave-faced. Dead, of course. And then, to her horror, he moved! Slowly, inexorably, he began to sit up. She saw Megan lift her head, saw the curtain of her hair fall back, saw the wondering, adoring face . . .

And then Marsha was shrieking at him, screaming like a seagull in a gale, shaking herself free from the tall man's grasp, going over to Danny, trying to press him back down again, on to the altar which had become his bier.

'You're dead!' she screamed, shaking all over with fury and fear. 'Lie down, damn you, Danny – the dead tell no tales!'

She felt the smooth, cold flesh of him against her palms as she fought to press him flat, and then the fire flared up and up, and she felt its heat on her body, saw Megan's face turn from a kind of simple wonder to full and terrible despair.

And woke.

It was full daylight. She lay rigid for a moment, bathed in her own sweat, listening to the pounding of her heart gradually ease. Then she opened her eyes.

Megan stood above her, bending down, with a look of

such pain, such horrified comprehension on her face that Marsha winced back from it as from a naked blade.

'You went with Danny,' Megan said in a small, cold voice. 'That last night, you pretended to be me. You packed me off to wash my hair and you took my place . . . you let him . . . you let him . . .'

'No! Meggie, it was a *dream*, that's all. No, a nightmare! Oh, Meg, I was so scared . . . Danny's dead, but in my dream he was alive . . .'

'I know. I heard. You made him do it to you, and he did it because he thought you were me . . . me! Oh, God, if it had been me, then at least I'd have something of his, some little part of him to remember him by. Someone to look after, bring up the way he would have wanted a child brought up.' She narrowed her eyes and Marsha saw, fearfully, that all the kindness, all the gentleness, had fled. 'You stole my child, Marsha Loxley. You're pregnant, aren't you? Pregnant by my man, with the child who should have been mine!'

'No . . . it wasn't like that. I don't want it, Meg, honestly I don't! I haven't had any fun yet. I don't want a baby holding me down. Look, I'll go away, back to Bolton, to my people . . . I'm sorry, I'm so sorry!'

'Yes, you will go. But not until the child is born safe,' Megan said, quiet all of a sudden but with dreadful emphasis. 'That is my baby, and I will have it born whole and well. Then you may go wailing back to Mummy and Daddy, to tell them some fine old tale about how put-upon you've been, how you were kept a prisoner by wicked people on a little island off the coast, and how sorry you are and will they buy you a new pony, please, and some nice pretty new clothes, and will they find you a nice healthy man who will do it to you once a night, all comfy in your soft bed, and never, never give you babies!'

'Megan, please . . . we're twins – we're almost one

person. You wouldn't keep me here against my will – make me give birth to a baby I don't want?'

'Well, I would, then. Because that baby is all I have left of my Danny, my heart's love, and I won't see you throw it away! What harm will it do you to wait a few more months, give birth to my child?'

'How can I stay here, with you knowing?' demanded Marsha, using, had she but known it, the only argument which had any force to Megan's pain-racked mind. 'What would your mam say if she knew?'

'We won't tell her. But you'll stay.'

'But, Meg, I can't stay, not now. Would you tell your mam whose baby it was . . . would you? People will guess – or I might even tell them.' She paused, cunning showing her a way – if way it was. 'Meg, come with me! We'll go away, just the two of us, and when it's born I'll give it to you, I swear before God, and you can come back here to your mam and they'll think it's yours by birth as well as by right. Wouldn't that do?'

For a moment they stared at one another, those two so nearly identical faces, Megan pale and marked with suffering, Marsha pink, anxious only that she might not reap the reward she deserved: her sister's lifelong hatred. Then Megan sat heavily down on the bed and Marsha, who had been leaning on her elbow, sat up properly and put a tentative hand on the other's shoulder.

'Ye-es,' Megan said slowly. 'It might work – it probably would work! But where would we go?'

'To Ireland,' Marsha said at once. 'If you offered to drive Mr Quinn, he'd let us have the cottage Tony and I had.'

'Hmm. How do you know Tony's not there?'

'I don't know for sure. But I bet he isn't. Shall we do that, then? Go to Ireland to have the baby?'

Megan began to agree, and then something occurred to her which brought her brows together once more.

'I can't. Only a person with a heart of stone would leave mam now. I can't do it. Not even for Danny's baby. You'll have to stay here, Marsha.'

'All right; but I'll think of something,' Marsha said. 'And Meg . . . ?'

Megan had stood up to go and fetch their washing water. Halfway to the door, jug in hand, she turned.

'What?'

'You're all I've got, so don't hate me. Don't lock me out. I've always wanted what you want, right from when we were just kids, when you wanted to learn to ride, remember? And the pale green skirt? It wasn't my sort of thing, but . . .'

'Danny was different, and you know it. As for hating . . .' the dark blue eyes met Marsha's, steady, unflinching. '. . . hating's your speciality, Marsha, not mine. I've had so little practice, you see – but I'm a quick learner.'

'You've got to get out, Mam. You can't stay cooped up in the house any longer, so just you come with me and Peris. We aren't saying you'll have a wonderful time; none of us will for . . . for a while. But we're saying you can't simply shut yourself away. It's not fair to the rest of us.'

It was a brilliant day, hot and sunny. There was a yacht racing round the harbour, a bonfire on the beach, spuds to bake in the embers, sausages part charred, part raw to eat in your hand, and lots of soft drinks.

Carnival! Celebrations with fireworks, because the scion of a noble house had borne a son! And Megan and Peris were determined that, with the funerals now more than two months behind them, Mam should begin to return to the world once more.

And the job of persuading her was easier with Peris here, because yesterday Peris had talked about Da and the good times until at last, at long long last, tears had welled up in Mam's eyes and rained down her cheeks, until the frozen core of her had melted with the tears so that she had cried and cried and had begun, for the first time, to accept her loss.

'Oh, well . . . as you say, Peris, Dai would have grieved sore to see me sitting indoors on such a day. Very well, you pushy people, I'll come down to the beach and eat baked potatoes, and woe betide you if you let me down and this fine carnival isn't so fine after all!'

She spoke like her old self, fire sparkling in her dark eyes, her generous mouth curved into a smile. But it wrung Megan's heart to see that thick, curly hair, which had once been so black, white now as any snow. Mam, who had looked like a girl, was an elderly woman today, and no hiding it.

'Good, Mam,' Peris said approvingly. 'Go you and get ready, whilst Meg and I put up some food for us, just in case those old sausages really are nothing but sawdust and seasoning.'

She went, laughing at them, rumpling Peris's spiky brown hair.

As soon as she had gone the two heads bent close, the brown and the gold.

'Where's that girl you wrote and told me about . . . said she was your sister or some such nonsense? Mam said she looked like never budging. I wanted to see her for myself, see how like you she really was – not that there could be two like you!'

They were in the kitchen, Megan bustling about fetching food, Peris sitting on the big old table swinging his legs. Megan turned from her work for a moment to shake a reproving head at him.

'Can't there, indeed? Well, she was my twin. Like as two peas in a pod, Da said, the first time . . .' she choked on the words and stopped short, then resumed '. . . the first time he saw her. As for where she is, she went. I tried to keep her . . .' She looked up at Peris, dark and self-confident, Peris who was so dear to her. 'I fell asleep . . . I couldn't stay awake for ever, not even for Danny's sake.'

'Why on earth should you? Meggie, my little one, you are in a bad state, and bearing up so well in front of Mam. Tell me what's been happening.'

'I can't. It's not my secret . . . but why not? Why the hell not? Peris, my twin sister is expecting a baby. It's Danny's baby.'

'Danny's? Oh, love, and Danny gone . . . but Danny was engaged to you!'

'Yes. That's how alike we are. He came for me, and she tricked him, got him to lie with her. Now there is to be a baby. Or there was.'

Peris shook his head, clearly bewildered by this tale half told.

'Is? Or was? I don't understand.'

Megan explained. Slowly and carefully, she made Peris see what had happened, and how she had longed for the child that her sister would bear.

'But she's spoilt and doesn't want a baby, doesn't even want to have to give birth to it,' she said bitterly, in conclusion. 'I said she must have the baby, and I tried to keep her here. But I had to go and fall asleep one night . . . she was pretending to be asleep herself, but she was so cunning . . . and when I woke she'd gone. Even her dresses had gone. Peris, she packed whilst I lay there and snored like a pig. And by now the baby may have been . . . taken away. Flushed down the lav. Oh, Peris, I did try, really I did!'

'And Mam knows nothing?'

'Would you tell her, and break her heart? She loved Danny like a son. Enough sorrow she has to bear without knowing he did wrong with that . . . that she-wolf.'

'I don't think Mam would see it like that,' Peris said. His voice had a tiny laugh in it. Megan looked at him and saw, suddenly, that her excuse did have its funny side. As if Mam would grudge Danny, now . . .

'You think I should tell her? But what possible good could it do?'

Peris walked across the kitchen and put a brotherly hand round Megan's neck, drawing her nearer to him. He looked seriously into her face.

'You look like death warmed up, my little one! Pale face, shadowed eyes . . . and gaunt, you are! How much weight have you lost these past couple of months, eh?'

Megan shrugged, impatient with what seemed to her to have no importance.

'Don't know or care. And I'll mend.'

'Oh yes, you'll mend. But quicker, see, if Mam knows what hurts. And two sides there are to that coin, as well. Mam will mend quicker if she can see you need her strength, her understanding. Tell her, Meggie; let her in. Don't lock her out!'

'How odd! That was what Marsha said. And it was true – I had locked her out because my head was so tight with grieving there was no room for anything else. And then, of course, I wanted to lock her out . . . I wanted worse things, too.'

She looked at Peris with apprehension, fearing to see dismay in his eyes, but there was only pity and understanding.

'Of course you did – who wouldn't? It was a dirty trick.

411

But Meggie, you mustn't let it sour you. When you come right down to it, the baby is hers, now that Danny . . .'

'It should have been mine. And she doesn't want it, Peris; truly she doesn't.'

'And you've no idea where she's gone, this sister of yours . . . this twin?'

'Oh yes, to Ireland. But I don't know where. And I can't find out, not any more. We've closed our minds to each other and now they won't open even if we try.'

Peris nodded.

'Maybe it's for the best, Meggie. Maybe ordinary people like us aren't meant to lift the curtain. You do it for good, but maybe a little evil can creep in . . . better not to look into another's mind.'

Megan nodded. It was no use trying to explain to Peris about being a twin. He had done well, she considered, to have accepted as much as he had. And he had helped her enormously with his commonsense approach, his kindliness. And she would tell Mam. Not today, because today was the carnival, but some day, some day soon.

CHAPTER TWENTY-FOUR

Back in time. Back across the months to the night of that wild storm which wrecked the good ship *Claudia* and drowned the crew.

On the shore, quite early next morning, Jim Flaherty comes, quietly, quietly, in his soft rubber-soled shoes. He comes to see what the storm has driven ashore, what largesse the waves have brought him.

Jim Flaherty lives in a little sod hut, crouched down at the foot of the nearest hill. He burns peat from the bog on his fire and he cooks fish, and vegetables which he grows himself. People say Jim is stupid, a poor old mad paddy, but Jim doesn't mind because what if he is? Who has a better life than Jim, and his old dog Bunty, and his little cat Fudge?

He buys proper, store-bought food twice, sometimes three times a year, which is why he's scavenging on this chilly morning, with the wind still blowing a gale and rain on its breath. He can sell the wood from a wrecked ship or use the stores which come ashore. Sometimes he has a good catch of fish and he can sell them for a few shillings to the townies who never come down to this remote, watery part of the coast.

As he roots along the cast-up piles of seaweed he suddenly sees, far up the beach on the tideline, something that is neither rock nor weed nor yet a fish. A seal? It looks a little like a seal: the humped back, the body gradually tapering to where the waves still tug and fret at it.

Jim hardly ever runs; life is as good lived at a slow pace

413

as at a trot, never mind a canter. But he runs now, because he has seen a movement from the seal . . . or whatever it may be. Was it a shrug of the shoulders, or a shudder wrinkling the pelt? Or a breath, raggedly drawn? Or was it just the waves, pushing it further up the beach, dragging it further down?

He reaches the hump on the sand and does not even stop to let his breathing slow but bends urgently and seizes the man – because it is clear, now, that it is a man – beneath the shoulders, towing him further up the beach, making a furrow in the hard, wet sand. A man! A sailor or a fisherman, cast up on his beach and still breathing – just.

Jim doesn't know much about resuscitation, but he has an instinct for some things, and this is one of them. He hauls desperately at the man's shoulders, then rolls him over on to his back and begins, rhythmically, to push his ribcage up and down, up and down, as though the man were doing it himself, as though he were actually breathing. And then the man gives a cough, and he turns his head and sea water comes out from him like a jet, like a fountain, he's spouting like a whale, so that Jim gives a snort of laughter because he looks dam' funny, pretty dam' funny!

But laughing doesn't help him, so Jim heaves at him again and turns him on to his face and the man brings up more water, only not so much, not so dramatically. And then he begins to make a very odd sort of snoring noise, and his eyes roll all over the place and Bunty, who is standing close, gives a little wuff of excitement and comes right up to them, and licks the man's hollow, bristly cheek.

There is a cut on the back of the man's head, sluggishly bleeding. When Jim cuts himself, he puts a handful of cobwebs on the cut and binds it in place with dock leaves and string. It always works; the cut always heals. But there are no dock leaves on the beach, nor cobwebs, either. It takes Jim a moment or two, but he realizes that he must get the man back to his hut, somehow.

He carries him, in the end, over one shoulder like a big sack of grain. Jim has to hump grain for his hens: big, half-wild birds who come running when he makes his chicken call and scatters the feed. And the man isn't much heavier than a sack of grain, either, though Jim can feel strong bones beneath the flesh.

They reach the hut and Jim dumps the sack of grain man as lightly as he can on his own bed, which is just a couch of heather covered with other soft things – sheep's wool, old jerseys, newspapers that have come his way . . . for Jim would not dream of buying one, never having learned to read. Then, because he is a practical sort of man and has often felt cold himself after a close encounter with the ocean, he puts the kettle on.

Marsha didn't go home after she escaped from the tall house in Newry Street. She knew now that there was no escape from the baby; she owed it to Megan, even perhaps in a way to Danny, to give birth, though she had no intention whatsoever of keeping the child. Let them put it in a home or adopt it themselves or do what they would. Marsha would not be held back by a wretched, puling brat!

Instead, she went to Ireland.

From the moment she decided she would leave, she began to make plans. She took money whenever she saw a unguarded shilling – which did not happen often – and she sold some of her nicer pieces of jewellery to the jeweller in Holyhead town centre. Then came the night when Megan fell asleep before her. She packed all her belongings into her case, added two thick jerseys of

Megan's and an odd little painting on the wall of the boarders' dining room which she had always coveted, and slipped into the night.

Cross-channel ships leave at strange hours. Before the sky was more than grey with approaching dawn she was aboard the *Hibernia* and heading out to sea. By teatime she had made her way half across the country, heading for Mr Quinn's cottage.

She told herself she did not want Tony to be there, though in her heart she would have welcomed even a glimpse of him. But she was safe; the cottage was empty, cold even in the warmth of summer. Marsha didn't intend to tell Tony's family anything – thirty miles is a great distance to insular people, so they would hear nothing from any other source – but she had to tell Mr Quinn.

He was a deeply religious man. He told her that he was sorry she had been deserted, that she might keep the cottage and welcome, and that he would pay her enough to keep body and soul together if she would clean for him up at the big house.

Marsha would have liked to tell him where he could put his job but she was in no position to quibble. Instead, she thanked him prettily and went daily up to the house, where her idea of cleaning did not coincide with that of the housekeeper, Mrs Mahon. But at least the house was big enough for them to keep out of each other's way, and Mrs Mahon, who was actually unmarried and used the title because she felt housekeepers should always have the edge over their staff, had no idea that her unsatisfactory cleaner was also only pretending to be married, though for a very different reason.

As the weeks and then the months passed, Marsha was off sick more than she worked, for she found that without rent to pay and with only herself to please she was spending very little money. With an expanding waistline, an aching back and thickening ankles she had no urge to buy clothes, and she didn't go anywhere, either, for fear of being seen in her hideously pregnant state.

There was a nursing order of nuns just ten miles away from Mr Quinn's estate, and they agreed to take Marsha for the birth. They were sweet, quiet women, dedicated to their task of improving the human condition, and Marsha sometimes thought that, if one had to be expecting a baby, one could not have chosen a better spot.

So she waited out her time, never letting herself think of Megan, or the tall house in Newry Street, or the little island just across the water. But Tony haunted her dreams and she knew that, when this was all over, she would find him if it took the rest of her life.

Madeleine was getting closer . . . getting warm, getting warm, the children shouted when they played hide and seek, and Madeleine knew exactly what they meant.

Every time she followed up a clue, now, which led in the right direction, she felt as though Tarot smiled at her, his approval implicit. He had wanted so badly to know his daughter – daughters – and he had died before he could do so. But he wanted Madeleine to make sure they were all right, she was certain of that.

And the clues were there for her, now that she chose to search. She went through hospital records, found the name of Nanny Evans's daughter, found her marriage . . . followed up the divorce, her flight . . . everything was grist, now, to her mill.

They had registered the baby under their own name, because at first they must have told people she was their own, until the man left and the woman wanted no more responsibility for this small child.

She was Megan Crispe, not a common name, when she was taken in by the Deiniol Evans Children's Home.

Fortunately, the superintendent remembered her well – remembered the name of her foster-parents, too.

'They took her and a number of boys,' he said, reading names randomly out of a huge ledger. 'Dewi was one, and Henry, and Peris. The Prydderchs are good people. Regular chapel-goers. You can always tell when the children want to take on the foster-name, and all Mrs Prydderch's have done that. There isn't a lot of money there, mind – he was a fisherman before the war, and she took in boarders – but perhaps money isn't that important. At any rate, her boys have done well – and the girl too, for all I know. Megan's only twenty, of course.'

'Nineteen,' Madeleine corrected automatically, her heart thumping so hard that she could feel her ribs banging against her thin silk blouse. 'Nineteen last March.'

'That's right.' The superintendent cleared his throat and closed the ledger in a rather final sort of way. 'And you'll be wanting Mrs Prydderch's address, I dare say?'

'If you please.'

Madeleine was wearing a suit of such respectability and dullness that she felt stifled by it, and her long hair was pulled severely back from her face into a French pleat. She had chosen low-heeled shoes and dark stockings – what a relief it would be to go back to her lodgings and change into something light and summery, because despite the year's being well advanced they were still having wonderfully warm weather. And I must find something suitable, Madeleine thought exultantly, something to celebrate the end of my search.

'Well, I'll have to get in touch with her first, of course. I can't just hand out someone's address when I feel like it. But if you'll come back in a few days . . . !'

'Of course,' Madeleine said numbly. So near and yet so far! Suppose the woman realized who she was, and didn't want to see her? She had told the superintendent

418

she was trying to trace her old nanny's granddaughter . . . something about a small legacy. But had he believed her? Or had he guessed?

'Right. Now, it may take me a while to get in touch with the family, since they aren't on the telephone, but if you come back, say, in a week . . .'

'Of course,' Madeleine said again, getting to her feet. Useless to think she would find them herself before then. This was Wales, and even if the name Prydderch was an unusual one there must be hundreds of them scattered over the Principality.

'Mind, I might be able to get a message to them,' Mr Glasse mused. 'One of my colleagues visits the island quite often . . . on his way to and from Ireland . . . which means he must almost pass the door. I could see if he can get a message to Mrs Prydderch asking her to telephone me, either here or at my home.'

'That would be very kind,' Madeleine murmured. An island! And an island, furthermore, from which it was possible to catch a ferry to Eire! She need not kick her heels here for a week, then. She could at least employ her time gainfully, having a long, hard look at that island.

'Not at all, not at all. I do remember the child, and I'm always glad of any good fortune that may befall a former inmate of the Deiniol Evans Home.' Mr Glasse came round the desk, holding out his hand. 'Thank you for calling, Miss Ripley-Trewin. It's been a pleasure. And of course we shall meet again – in a week, unless I hear sooner. Where may I contact you in that event?'

'I'm staying just up the road; I'll write the address down for you,' Madeleine said, walking back to the desk and reaching for a piece of paper. She scribbled the name of the boarding house, added her own, then handed the paper to the superintendent. 'There you are, Mr Glasse – and thank you.'

'What you want, Mam, is another lad to keep you on your toes.'

Peris had come home on leave because Megan was so worried about Mam. They had taken her out for a meal, then to the cinema and now the three of them were sitting, as the family had always sat, in the kitchen. They were drinking cocoa, eating shortbread and talking.

'Another lad? No, indeed, she needs a girl,' Megan protested, aiming a pretend-kick at Peris from where she perched on the tall kitchen stool. 'A lad makes work; a girl helps with doing it.'

'Oh, yeah? I was a help, wasn't I, Mam? Anyway, Mam's got you to skivvy for her, young Meg, if she needs a hand.'

Mam, sitting in the fireside chair with both hands cuddling her mug, looked from one face to the other and shook her head at them.

'Always squabbling – why should I want more kids who'll squabble worse, eh? And our Meg won't be here for always, Peris. There's many a feller sets his cap at her.'

'She'll be here for a bit yet,' Peris said shrewdly, 'and there's nothing like work for taking your mind off things. I won't mince words, Mam. Da's been gone six months, Uncle Reggie died happily in his good bed eight weeks since, Mr Jones got married . . . and you've got this big old house with only you and little Meg here rattling around in it. And you can't deny you sit and think a lot, Mam. That's why I think you need another kid.'

Mam sighed and for a moment her expression sagged from determined good cheer to melancholy. Megan's heart ached for her, because it was hard enough for Megan herself, who was young, to learn to live without Da and Danny, and Mam was older, more tired, and sometimes you could see she didn't think it was worth the effort.

'You're right about one thing, Peris. I think a lot, and bitterly, too. Because you see, Da and I had planned for the day when there would be just the two of us – no kids, no boarders. And it was going to be a good time. Now, without him, my mind is thin and stretched and empty, and the days do go on and on, marching into months and years, and no hope any more, see? Nothing to look forward to, nothing to dream about.'

'I know,' Megan murmured, whilst Peris leaned across and took Mam's hand. 'But I've got my job. You're alone too much, Mam.'

Upstairs, Screech screeched. Mam got slowly to her feet. It occurred to Megan that six months earlier Mam would have been halfway up the stairs in the time that it now took her to reach the kitchen door.

'That old bird – the times I said I'd wring its neck but for Uncle Reggie, and here I am waiting on it beak and claw!' Mam said over her shoulder, a hand pressed to the small of her back. Grief makes your bones ache, Megan knew, and pitied Mam more. Her own young bones ached enough some days to give her a reason for the tears.

'Foster a little lad,' Peris advised Mam's disappearing back. 'Come with you to the old Deiniol Evans Home I will, Mam . . . take you in a hired car, all posh, and bring back a real high-class kid!'

'I could come as well – an outing we could make of it,' Megan declared. 'Wouldn't that be a bit of a break, Mam? Time off's easier with the summer gone. And you aren't the only one who could do with someone young about the house,' she added. 'Do you know, I even miss Marsha!'

Mam continued to plod up the stairs, but on the half-landing she turned to call down to them.

'Can't say I miss that little trouble-maker . . . but

you're good children. I'll come out with you to the home, see what we can see.'

'But it can't possibly be yet. It's too early! I reckoned it up – another two months at least, perhaps even three! It's indigestion, I tell you, and pains from eating all that new bread and cheese.'

Mrs Mahon regarded Marsha with melancholy satisfaction.

'Sure and you can say that until you're blue in the face, but it won't make it any different! You're in labour, and unless you want the child to be born in this house you'd better be off to the hospital now, and no arguing!'

'I'll go home and lie down,' Marsha said with dignity. 'First babies hardly ever come early, Dr Patten says so.'

'What a good idea; you give birth alone. Why not? Do you good to do some work for once.'

Marsha sniffed and set off, but halfway down the drive she was hit by a pain so fierce and prolonged that she swallowed her pride and returned to the house.

'You're right – I suppose it might be the baby,' she muttered when Mrs Mahon came to the door in answer to her frantic knock. 'Can you phone for the doctor, please?'

'I will that,' Mrs Mahon said heartily. She did not add that she had made the call as soon as Marsha had left the house. 'Go into the front room, now, and lie on the couch. They'll send an ambulance for you directly.'

The baby was born at six o'clock the following morning, by which time Marsha was, as she put it, 'almost dead'. It was a grand little boy, they told her, and scolded her for not wanting to hold it, longing only to put the whole affair behind her and sleep.

But later in the morning they woke her, and she saw

the child. A scrap of a thing with dark hair and slitted eyes, still puffy from its birth struggles. She looked at its long fingers, each one tipped with a tiny, frail nail. At the fine and mossy down on the small, elongated skull. At the reddened skin which was so soft and smooth and velvety. In her arm, it pushed its hot face against her breast and drew up its tiny, matchstick legs under the long cotton nightgown. It opened its bare and gummy mouth in a big yawn and the nun who had brought it to her said dotingly, 'Who's a lovely feller, then? Who's his mammy's precious, eh?' She turned to Marsha, sitting up in bed trying to smile politely and wanting sleep almost more than she wanted life just now. 'What'll you call him, the darlin'?' she asked. A good Irish name, perhaps?'

'Umm . . . How about if you choose the name? What would you suggest, Sister?'

'Before I joined the Order I was Maggie O'Connor . . .' she looked round the small room as though walls had ears, her face pink with the importance of it '. . . now wouldn't Connor be a fine name for the wee feller?'

'There we are then; Connor. Can you take him now, sister, before I let him go from tiredness?'

The baby was taken out of her arms and the sleep which Marsha had craved was hers at last. But it was not the deep and delightful sleep of total forgetfulness, not the abnegation of all responsibility which she needed. Instead, she dreamed.

She was running away from something, carrying the baby wrapped in a long shawl. The child was terribly heavy and she longed to put it down somewhere, to run on without it, but there was nowhere suitable in all the wild country about. She kept seeing haystacks in the distance, but when she reached them they had turned into ponds, or bridges, or tiny roofless cottages with gaping, empty windows.

She might have been all right nevertheless, might have escaped, had the baby not suddenly begun to cry. It cried and cried, its screams echoing and re-echoing around the countryside, and she knew the noise would bring her pursuers down on them both and that would be the end of them.

She ached from running, too, and a stitch was hovering, so she stopped for a moment, ignoring the threatening sky overhead with its burden of rain-heavy clouds and the rumbles, faint and far off, of distant thunder. She looked hard into the baby's face, and suddenly it wasn't small and red and screwed up any more, but was smoothing out, the skin pale as milk, framed in long, dark gold hair, and the eyes were pansy blue and they held her gaze steadily.

It was Megan and she was smiling slightly, but there was a warning in her face.

'Don't forget what you promised,' she said. 'Don't forget whose baby it is . . . bring him to me!'

'But I can't – they're chasing me, and I'm so tired! They're bound to catch me!'

Megan's warm eyes cooled a fraction.

'No one will hurt you if you do as you promised. Bring me my baby!'

'Do you mean carry it all the way back to the island? Over the water and all? To your door?'

'To my door. Don't forget, you pr—ooo—m—ised!'

The last word was a wail which became a gull's plaintive mew as Marsha struggled out of sleep, heart pounding, body soaked in sweat. She opened her eyes. She was in bed in a small hospital room, and in a cradle at the foot of the bed the dark-haired, alien baby to which she had so recently given birth was starting to cry again.

CHAPTER TWENTY-FIVE

The Deiniol Evans Children's Home was not everyone's idea of an attractive building, but Megan, seeing it for the first time in a dozen years, was intrigued by it. For a start, it was a lot smaller than she remembered. Where were the lofty rooms, the mighty hall, the enormous lavatories so large that she had a job to gain the seat and had always balanced precariously there, half afraid of toppling backwards and being dragged down by the rush of the emptying cistern?

All she saw now was a large, shabby house with perfectly ordinary rooms, ugly utility furniture which had seen better days and a great many plainly dressed and depressed-looking children.

Mr Glasse, the superintendent, greeted them all like long-lost friends, however, which was nice if a trifle puzzling. From what Megan could remember, she had not been exactly a favourite in her time here. Quite the opposite, in fact. But he shook hands with them all, claimed old acquaintance with herself and Peris, told Mam that she was one of his most successful foster-mothers, and begged them to have a drink of tea with him.

Mam, clearly made uneasy by this reception, showed the whites of her eyes and tried to get out of it, but in vain. Mr Glasse was not letting them go before he had got them, so to speak.

'Sit down . . . make yourselves comfortable,' he said, fussing round them. 'How very strange that you should come to see us today, Mrs Prydderch . . . very strange indeed, for only yesterday I posted a letter to you . . . at least, I gave it to one of the children to post in the box at the end of the road, which may mean, of course, that it never got posted at all!'

He laughed squeakily; Megan, recognizing a joke, laughed too, then wished she hadn't when he shot round in his chair, stared at her and beamed, displaying huge false teeth of an incredible whiteness flanked by bright pink artificial gums.

'Well, well, well! That was unfair, since not a child in this place would ever betray a trust. Well, not many children would . . . the letter, my dear Mrs Prydderch, will undoubtedly reach you tomorrow or the day after, yet here you all are . . . well, well, well! *Most* fortunate!'

Peris, who appeared to have been struck dumb on arrival, cleared his throat and spoke at long last, shooting an appealing sideways look at Megan as he did so.

'Umm, Mr Glasse, we brought Mam to see you in the hope that you might spare her another foster-child. As you can see, Megan and I are quite old, and . . .' His voice, creaking with embarrassment, trailed off into silence as Mr Glasse's gimlet gaze swung in his direction. 'Er . . . so we brought Mam over,' Peris concluded tamely.

'I *see*,' Mr Glasse said, with undue emphasis. 'Oh, so *that*'s why you're here . . . you couldn't have guessed . . .'

Mam, who had been staring at him like a bird at a snake, suddenly seemed to pull herself together. She sat up straight in her uncomfortable chair and actually leaned forward and tapped commandingly on the superintendent's desk.

'Mr Glasse . . . will you tell us what your letter said, please, before I go raving mad?'

'Oh! Of course, of course! It seems, Mrs Prydderch, that your foster-daughter here may have come into a bit of money. Not much – probably not what you or I would call an inheritance – but a small sum . . .'

'I thought I was a foundling,' Megan said rather too loudly. 'Foundlings don't inherit, except in stories.'

'Apparently it's a bit more complicated than that. Anyway, I'm not sure I should have said anything,' Mr Glasse said belatedly, putting a bony hand to his round, balding forehead. 'The long and the short of it, Mrs Prydderch, is that a young woman came here a few days ago, from a firm of solicitors, I believe. She asked me for your address, but naturally I couldn't give it to her just like that, so I wrote to you, asking permission to send her to see you, and . . .'

'Where is she now?' Mam said bluntly. 'What's her name?'

Mr Glasse consulted a letter which he drew from a file on his desk.

'Miss Madeleine Ripley-Trewin,' he said. 'It seems that Megan's grandmother was nanny to a well-to-do family in Manchester, and her employer left money to old Mrs Evans when she died. Unfortunately Mrs Evans had predeceased her, but in that case the will stated that the money was to go to Mrs Evans's next of kin. Which, Miss Ripley-Trewin says, is Megan.'

'I didn't know I had a granny,' Megan said dazedly.

Peris snorted and gave her a nudge.

'Everyone does,' he muttered. 'But she must have died ages ago, or you wouldn't have come here.'

'That's true,' Mr Glasse owned. 'But we don't look too closely into past histories here at the Deiniol Evans. No point, and it could do harm.'

'And where is this Miss Ripley-whatsit now?' Peris asked. 'Do you have an address or a telephone number? Megan might want to get the business over whilst we're on the mainland.'

'I do indeed. The lady's staying just up the road, at the Moorscroft Guest House. It seems she has other business in the vicinity. Mind you, whether she'll be home now . . . but I could ring for you, if you like.'

He reached out for the tall telephone and took the receiver off its hook, looking from Mam to Megan, eyebrows raised.

'Oh, no harm to give her a call,' Mam said, seeing that Megan was still puzzling over the whole business and had probably not heard a word that had been said. 'Tell her we're here . . . see what she says.'

Mr Glasse spoke into the instrument, asking if Miss Ripley-Trewin was available. He waited, nodding to Mam, and then he spoke into the mouthpiece again.

'Miss Ripley-Trewin? As you know, I wrote to Mrs Prydderch and posted the letter yesterday, so it is still, as it were, on its travels, but by a strange coincidence Mrs Prydderch is with me now; would you care to come over?'

They all heard the receiver at the other end clatter down after a tiny, indistinguishable reply. Mr Glasse replaced his own instrument.

'There we are . . . Miss Ripley-Trewin will be here in five minutes. Now, I think I'll order a tray of tea.'

He went across the hall, opened a baize door and called through it to someone on the other side.

The front doorbell rang as he was retracing his steps. Megan saw him hesitate and knew he was thinking that it was scarcely the place of an important man like himself to answer the door. Then she saw him decide that, just this once . . .

He opened the door, smiled, stepped back. A woman came into the hall.

Madeleine had no idea what to expect; Mrs Prydderch had haunted her dreams for three days now, but facelessly. Her own age? Older? Scarcely younger, if she'd had Megan for almost fourteen years. Would her husband be with her? Was there any chance that she had brought Megan? But of course she had known nothing about Madeleine's message until she got here, so she would probably be alone.

Mr Glasse opened the front door himself and ushered her in. Madeleine glanced towards the study and saw that the door was open wide, and that there were several people in the room. A white-haired woman, seated. A young man, dark and handsome, leaning against the mantelpiece. And someone else, who had moved out of sight as Madeleine entered the hall.

'Well, this is fortunate,' Mr Glasse was saying, buzzing round her like a fly as she paused in the doorway. 'Peris, could you bring another chair, please? Now, Miss Ripley-Trewin, let me introduce you.'

Madeleine was staring at the girl. About her own height, slim, with shiny hair, a rich shade between chestnut and blonde. She had dark eyes, half veiled now by her lashes, and very pale, very clear skin.

Mr Glasse was still talking. The older woman was on her feet, holding out a small, square hand. She was striking, her hair thick and curly and white as snow, with very shrewd black eyes in a lively and intelligent face.

'Good afternoon, Miss Ripley-Trewin. This is my daughter, Megan, though as you know I never gave birth to her.'

'No, that's true,' said Megan, speaking for the first time. It was very odd, Madeleine decided, to hear her daughter speaking with a musical Welsh lilt to every word she uttered. 'But I always say I was born at the age of six, in Mam's kitchen in Newry Street.'

There was a short silence. Madeleine looked into the dark blue eyes of the child she had not seen for over

429

nineteen years and longed for a friendly softening of their straight look, for some intimation that Megan recognized her . . . for surely there must be something, some tie of blood, between a mother and her child?

'Umm . . . did you know you had a twin sister, called Marsha?' Madeleine ventured at last. 'She was adopted before you were, privately.'

'Yes, we knew,' Megan said. Despite the lovely accent her voice was indifferent, grazing rudeness. 'Came to see us, she did, about nine months ago. Ran off one night without a word of thanks to Mam, who'd kept her free for weeks and weeks. In Ireland now, I wouldn't be surprised.'

'Oh, I see,' Madeleine said feebly. Had there been a stronger tie between her babies than between either one of them and their mother? Ah, but she had behaved disgracefully, and from what Mr Glasse had told her this one, Megan, had suffered six years of hell, being pushed from pillar to post, never knowing where she would next lay her head. She longed to apologize, to explain . . . but she could scarcely do so in front of Mr Glasse, who had no idea that she was Megan's mother. 'How did Marsha find you?'

'Walked into each other on Holyhead railway station, when I was watching the trains and she was travelling to Ireland with her feller. When he ran out on her she came to me for help. And to Mam, of course.'

'Yes . . . but how did you know each other? I mean, you hadn't met since you were babies, had you?'

Megan slanted her another of those cool, level looks. Madeleine squirmed but kept her own gaze steady, not without difficulty.

'Identical, they say we are. Not inside, mind, but to look at. When you find yourself staring into your own face you're bound to ask questions, aren't you?'

'Yes, I suppose so. Well, Megan, I wonder if it would be possible . . . there are things I have to ask you . . . could we, perhaps, have a cup of tea and a chat? I'm sure Mrs Prydderch and the young man . . .'.

'Peris is my brother,' Megan said baldly. 'I don't think we've got much to talk about, have we? And I'd sooner stay with Mam. She's come here to see if she can foster another little lad . . . that's more important really.'

'You go off, love,' Mam said soothingly. She glanced at Peris. 'You stay with me, lad, and we'll all meet up later.'

Peris looked from one to the other. It was clear he was baffled by the sudden change in his sister.

'No harm in going, Meg,' he said diffidently. 'Stay with Mam, I will. Go you on, just for an hour.'

'If it's business you want to discuss,' Megan said, staring straight at Madeleine with those beautiful eyes still chilled and somehow accusing, 'then discuss it with Mam. I know nothing of business – I don't even know who I am, it seems. I thought I was Megan Prydderch, no messing, with a nain and a taid dead in the churchyard in Holyhead and another nain and taid tucked up cosy in the graveyard in Moelfre. I've several brothers . . . and no sister. Not any more. And my mam is Rhiannon Prydderch, widow of Dai Prydderch, and . . . and . . .'

Her voice broke. Her eyes were suddenly softer, but only because of the tears that brimmed in them. Madeleine took a step towards her, longing to hold her, to let her weep whilst she poured out her love, her distress. But Mam was first. She would always be first. And she gathered Megan into a warm embrace, soothing, gentling, talking. In Welsh, of course.

Madeleine turned away.

Shut out.

* * *

'What did you expect, my dear? Of course I knew who you were the moment I set eyes on you – in profile, you and Megan are mother and daughter, no question! But you lost your right to my girl when you left her, lass. And she's had a bad time these past months. We all have.'

Madeleine and Rhiannon were sitting opposite one another in a teashop, lace-tableclothed, dark-oak-beamed, with a pot of tea and a plate of scones between them. Their cups were full but the scones had not been touched.

'I didn't think properly at all,' Madeleine explained. She sighed and put a hand to her throbbing head. 'It's taken me years to get this far – and to have her look at me like that, deny me in her heart – it was hard.'

'Life's hard.' Rhiannon helped herself to a scone, drew the butter dish nearer. 'I won't ask why you left her, because I dare say you thought she was safe enough. But you do owe us an explanation for coming back after nearly twenty years.'

'Tarot . . . Megan's father . . . was killed during the Normandy landings,' Madeleine said. 'I lost him before then, though. Before the twins were even born I lost him. After I had them I tried to find him again . . . he was all that mattered to me. Only I never did, until I saw his picture in the paper. He was already dead by then, but I didn't know. And when I found out, his mother told me that David – that was his real name, David – had often talked about his child, and the girl who'd run off and left him all those years ago. The child mattered a lot to him, his mother said, though he'd never set eyes on her. And I'd lost Tarot . . . David, I mean . . . and I'd gone and lost his daughters, too. He'd left money to me, in trust for them, so I decided to try to find the twins and hand over their inheritance. Only it looked as though one of them, Marsha, was going to be all right financially anyway. My mother arranged her adoption by a very

432

well-to-do couple, and she's probably never wanted for anything in her life. Which left Megan – your Megan.'

'And my Megan's rich in a way poor little Marsha will never know,' Rhiannon said. She bit into her scone, then spoke rather thickly through it. 'Megan creates love. Wherever she goes, whatever she does, people love her because she's generous, affectionate and kind. She lost her man when I lost mine – they were both killed at sea, along with my third boy, Dewi, and all the crew of the *Claudia*. It was a mortal blow, but she's brave, and stronger than she knows. Then she lost her sister. One minute sweet as honey, in each other's pockets, always with their heads together. Then the *Claudia* went down and grief came between them. And then . . . ah, who can say what happened then? Save that Megan watched Marsha like a hawk, no love in her eyes any more, and Marsha was afraid, unhappy . . . but somehow in Megan's power. So she ran. Oh, Megan cried a river, but the girl had gone and what was the sense in weeping? When I tried to talk to her about it she wouldn't say a word, just shut her beautiful mouth very tight and veiled her eyes from me. But she came round; I knew she would. Good all through is our Meggie; wholesome and loving. And then you walk in, and though it's no fault of yours you woke the demons that had slumbered, reminded her of Marsha, and losing Danny, made her remember those first six years when she was nobody's child. And – just for a minute, mind – she hated you.'

There was a long silence. Rhiannon sipped tea, Madeleine stared into space. Then she gave a little jump and picked up her own cup.

'Yes. I see what I must do. I'll go, of course. She doesn't want to know me and she's absolutely right. I can't explain what made me decide I didn't want my own children – it was some madness which struck me as soon as

I knew I was pregnant. I would have . . .' She hesitated, looking at Rhiannon doubtfully, then squared her shoulders and continued. 'I would have had an abortion had I been able to arrange it. That shows you how desperate I was. And I blamed Tarot and left him, though I was deeply in love with him and have never loved another man since.'

'No need to rush off,' Rhiannon protested. 'She's got a kind heart, am I not telling you? Hurt for me, she was, when you first showed your face. Afraid that I, who have loved her and done my best by her, might think myself supplanted. She'll come round . . . and she'll have a thousand questions she'll want to ask you. Stay. For your feller's sake if not for your own. He wanted to help her.'

'You're right, of course. Tarot wished her nothing but good – it was my behaviour that was despicable. I'll make sure she gets the money her father wanted her to have, and then she can forget me. I realize now, having met you, that she truly doesn't need me – but if she ever finds it in her heart to forgive me . . . you'll let me know?'

'Of course I will,' Rhiannon said heartily. 'But don't do nothing hasty; don't give her more grief. I know my girl – she'll be regretting every word she uttered today by the time a week's gone. She must have wondered about her father, though she's never said, and my Dai, God rest him, worshipped the ground she trod on. She's very like you about the face, though the eyes are different and her hair's darker. But she's a country girl, with a gift for drawing wild things . . .'

'That's Tarot,' Madeleine said eagerly. 'He was David Carding, you know, the artist.'

'Oh,' Rhiannon said. 'Not a name I'm familiar with, but I take it he's well known?'

'Famous, amongst people who know about art.'

'She'll be proud,' Rhiannon said simply. 'Stay a while, my dear. Come over to the island; I won't offer you a room in Newry Street, but I've a friend who does bed and breakfast . . . she'll make you welcome.'

'I'd like to,' Madeleine said, still hesitant. 'But I don't want to hurt Megan more than she's been hurt already.'

Rhiannon shook her head.

'You won't. To be blunt with you, you can't. The only pain that lasts is inflicted by those we love.'

The folk of the little town on the west coast of Ireland where Jim Flaherty does his shopping are not a curious bunch. Life jogs by, and though they would break a leg to find out what a neighbour was up to, the scandals, the carryings-on in the big old world beyond their little town, which is more like a large village if the truth were told, leave them pretty well cold.

When Jim comes for his shopping and asks for bacon for two instead of one, they grin at each other. Sure, and isn't he a feller for his fry-ups? Eggs he has in plenty, though with winter fast approaching even Jim's marvellous fat, wild hens will lay sparingly, but he loves his bacon so he does, and a pot of dripping from the joint to go with it.

Bacon isn't all the extra he buys, though. He wants a comb. When old Mrs Dunmore at the chemist's reminds him that he had a nice new comb two Christmases ago, he says sure and hasn't she the memory now, still got it he has, and uses it, too. But this comb is for the other feller, and hasn't he got a fine crop of hair on him, calling out for a comb which won't snap in two at the job it'll have to get through that thick thatch?

Old Mrs Dunmore knows Jim is slow, but she knows he isn't daft, whatever some folk may think. So she asks him about the other feller: where did Jim meet him; is he a decent sort of man; where did he come from?

'He came from the sea, so he did,' Jim says. 'He's been a poor t'ing, Mrs Dunmore, but he's gettin' better with the eggs and the cow's milk and the warmth of me fire, lit night and day now.'

So he has a visitor, quiet old Jim! Someone convalescing after an illness, no doubt, thinks Mrs Dunmore, who has never seen Jim's sod hut and wouldn't believe a human being lived in it if she had.

'That's nice for you, Jim; company,' she nods, finding him a bright red comb and knocking a penny off the price because she's had it a while. 'I bet you and he have many a good crack when you sit by your fire of an evening, eh?'

Jim looks puzzled, as though he expects old Mrs Dunmore to know as much about his guest as he does himself.

'Oh no, he doesn't *talk*,' Jim says with an earnestness which, for some reason, sends cold shivers down Mrs Dunmore's spine. 'Not a talkin' sort of man he is. More the silent type. Just sits there, you know, lookin' ahead and thinkin'.'

'Well, maybe when he eats that fine food you've bought, Jim, and gets to comb his hair, he'll begin to talk,' Mrs Dunmore says. She is uneasy because Jim is a child of innocence, sometimes difficult to fathom. It worries her that the man came from the sea and sits by Jim's fire with never a word said. An awful thought shuffles into her neat, tidy head . . . she tries to shuffle it out again, desperate-quick, but it lingers, grinning horribly. Suppose, just suppose, that Jim is feeding and taking care of . . . well, a corpse?

'He won't use the comb; I don't think he can use a comb,' Jim is saying seriously, however. 'He's a rare 'un . . . quiet iddun the word, Mrs Dunmore!'

* * *

436

Jim gets home late, despite doing his best to hurry, to get back before dark. He goes straight into his hut, ignoring the plaintive gurgles of the hens, who haven't been fed all day and do like their handful of grain.

He left the fire smouldering this morning, but knew it would go out, so he is very surprised indeed to see it burning brightly. He looks around. Bunty comes in after him. Bunty had run to greet him the moment he came within earshot of the sod hut, but the little cat, Fudge, so named because her coat is just the creamy, browny colour of full cream Irish fudge, is sitting near the fire purring like a maniac, big yellow lamps raised to his face, white whiskers quivering at the scent of the food in his basket.

The man from the sea isn't sitting in his usual place. He hasn't fallen over, either. Jim looks all round to see. And then he hears something outside, and goes back into the darkness, taking a moment to get his night-eyes. In that moment he crests the headland so that he can look down on the beach. Surely his friend – if a silent unmoving person can be classed as a friend – has not gone back to the sea from whence he came? Surely he must enjoy life in the sod hut more than being tossed in the cold sea, crushed against the spiked rocks?

Against the pale sand he can see the man now. He is bending, lifting something in his arms, coming back up the sandy little path. Near the top he stops to catch his breath. He isn't used to moving, so it has taken it out of him, that walk. His breath is making terrible tearing noises in his throat; Jim can almost feel, inside his own quiet breast, the thundering of the other feller's heart.

Presently, the man moves again. He is almost at the top of the rise, ready to start the descent which will end outside the door of Jim's sod hut. Jim moves, just a little, to touch his hand to the smooth top of Bunty's head,

close against his knee, and the man turns. His eyes have
never focused on Jim's face in all the long time Jim has
tended him, nor has his mouth smiled or uttered.

Now, suddenly, like a miracle, all three things happen
at once. The blue eyes light up with recognition. The
mouth curves in a smile, then opens.

'Getting stuff for the fire, I am,' the man says. His
voice is flat and creaky from disuse. 'Mustn't let it go
out.'

Jim considers this proposal. He thinks about it seriously
for a moment, his hand still resting on Bunty's black and
white head. The man has a funny sort of voice, not like
the voices Jim hears around him in the small town. But
it is a nice voice, perhaps the sort of voice owned by all
men who come from the sea.

And whilst he is thinking, the man seems to be thinking
too. He doesn't rush or hurry or look as if he wants to
move. He just stands there, as Jim would stand, with his
arms full of dried seaweed and bits of driftwood and waits
for Jim to speak.

'That's right; mustn't let it go out,' Jim says at last,
having thought it over. He agrees with the man from the
sea; the fire is needed now that the evenings are getting
shorter. 'I bought you a comb.'

'A comb?'

'That's right. A pretty one. Mrs Dunmore said you
could comb your own hair but I told her you couldn't do
that yet. Do you think you'll be able to now?'

The man has fallen into step beside him. Companion-
ably, side by side, they make their way down the track
and into the sod hut. The man from the sea piles up his
fuel in a corner, then throws some on to the fire. It
crackles up, bright and golden, shedding its light on both
of them. How nice to have pretty yellow hair, Jim thinks

438

without envy, staring at the man's long, blond locks. I wish I had pretty yellow hair!

'Yes, I can comb my own hair,' the man from the sea says at last. 'I'll do it later.'

He sits down, linking his arms about his knees. He looks at home, a part of the hut. Jim sits down too, in the same pose. They both stare into the flickering flames, blue, saffron, tangerine, sparking along the hissing driftwood.

Presently, without changing their attitudes, they sleep.

The nuns would have liked to keep Marsha and baby Connor for a few days longer, but Marsha had very soon had enough. She felt well, not just better but really well. Now she would be able to face Tony and get everything sorted out between them – once she had taken the baby back to Anglesey, of course.

She did feel slightly guilty about Mr Quinn and his dear little cottage – suppose she eventually found Tony and he wanted to go back and she had made that impossible by ditching Mr Quinn without a word? – but she seldom allowed guilt to trouble her for long.

And she wanted to see Megan very badly indeed. She kept telling herself that when she went back, kept her side of the bargain, Megan would forgive her, let her in again. They would open the doors in their minds, slammed ungratefully shut by Megan on that dreadful morning, which seemed so long ago, when she had found out about Danny.

All my life I never worried that I had no friends, that people didn't seem to like me much, because I had Megan, Marsha told herself as she trudged from the maternity home to the nearest bus stop. All my life Megan was enough for me, so it must have been the same for her. How can she bear to lose all that, give it up, just because I was stupid once? Just because of this wretched, miserable, whining little scrap of nothing?

It would be wrong to say she hated the baby, but she was certainly indifferent to it. She never used its name, preferring to say 'baby' if she had to address it. She thought of it, always, as belonging to someone else. That was best because she acknowledged, now, that she herself had no right to the child. Even if she had wanted it, which by great good fortune she did not, it would not have been hers.

The baby was not breast-fed, because Marsha had absolutely refused to nurse it. She held the bottle, that was all, and the nuns had taught her how to mix the formula and bring up the child's wind. They had forced her, gagging, to change its nappies as well . . . what horrors a parent had to face . . . and to wipe oily stuff on its nasty pink, pointed bottom and between its legs where its enormous willy lived. Well, enormous when you considered the size of the rest of it, anyway.

But Megan would love it; Marsha had no doubt of that. Because it was Danny's, Megan would take it to her heart. And much though she missed Megan, much though she wanted the door opened once more, Marsha still, in a way, hated her smug sister with her common little happy-families existence and her working class outlook, working class hands, working class parent.

So far from grudging her possession of the baby, she thought having it would jolly well serve Megan right. All those slimy, disgusting nappies, that beastly, raw-looking bottom, the mucus which ran out of its hard, snouty little button nose, the screams it screamed, the farts it farted, the belches it belched . . . they would all be Megan's, and so far as bargains went Megan would, Marsha thought, most definitely be the loser.

But she'll have lots of love; even more love when she's

440

got the baby than before, a little inner voice reminded Marsha. *In their hearts, people will admire Megan for taking on someone else's baby, because no one will ever believe it's hers, now, in the way she'd planned.*

It was a pity that two entirely different reactions to Megan lived within Marsha's head. Even when she went with Danny, she had done it not to spite Megan exactly but to be quits with her, to have what she had. And later, when Megan had outlined her plans for Marsha to give her the baby, the ignoble but irresistible thought that Megan would end up not only with the child but also with the blame had very nearly kept Marsha to her promise not to leave.

Only . . . she had been so miserable and frightened, and she had simply had to escape from those cool and accusing eyes, that shuttered mind.

And now she was going back. Because of a promise? Well, partly, but also because she couldn't search for Tony if she was lugging a baby round everywhere with her. And Tony was the one thing she had which Megan had never got near. Oh, there were Mummy and Daddy of course, if you wanted to be literal, but Marsha had a sneaking suspicion that Mummy and Daddy would take to Megan.

But Tony wasn't the sort of person to love someone just because she was pretty, sweet, good, and all that dull stuff. He loved Marsha because she was fascinating, wicked, fun to be with . . . and most of all he loved her because she was Marsha and not Megan, not Susie, not Tom, Dick or Harry come to that. He loved her, she loved him, and their place was together.

And because of this, because of the promise, and because, in the back of her mind, she hated the shuttered nature of her present relationship with her twin, Marsha walked through the rain, waited at the bus stop, rode to the ferry terminal, boarded the ship, found herself a seat in one of the lounges for three and a half hours – and finally disembarked in Holyhead, to find the rain slithering down the window panes as she came through customs and driving into her face so that she was forced to bend forward, almost as though she was shielding the baby.

She wondered about a taxi, then decided it simply wasn't far enough to bother and anyway the walk would do her good. She had got very stiff sitting in the lounge with the baby, quiet for once, lying solid and soggy across her knees.

Marsha, carrying her burden, walked along Landsend, turned up Market Street, putting her back into the steepness of the hill, into Stanley Street, and so to the tall house in Newry Street squeezed in between its smaller neighbours. She was soaked to the skin by now, her hair in rat-tails, and she hoped it would make Megan sorry for her, regret what she had put her through.

She reached the gate, putting out a hand to the familiar latch, went through it, and took the three steps to the front door.

She knocked. And waited.

CHAPTER TWENTY-SIX

There was a long pause, giving Marsha time to wonder, with some dismay, what she should do if they were all out. Then she heard footsteps, hurrying.

The door opened. Megan stood in the doorway, still wearing her anorak, a wet umbrella in her hand. Clearly she had only just got in herself.

'Marsha!' Her eyes lit up as though they were still best friends, dearest sisters, and then she stopped looking at Marsha and gazed, instead, at the shawl-wrapped bundle. 'Oh . . . you've had your baby!'

'Yes. I've brought it back, like we said.'

Megan made a curious little gesture with her hands; it said: Oh, how glad I am that you've kept your word! Then it said: But I can't do what I had planned to do. And then she simply stood aside, gesturing for Marsha to go past her.

'You're soaked, and your baby too, I expect. Go into the kitchen – there's a nice fire in there.'

Mam was in the kitchen. Didn't she stare when she saw Marsha with the baby in her arms! Shocked her rigid, the narrow-minded creature, Marsha thought gladly. Knew she wasn't a saint, for all Megan thinks the sun shines out of her.

'Marsha, my little one! With a baby! Oh, my love, why ever did you run away? Nothing wrong, there is, in having a baby, though of course it's easier if you marry first . . . but the way I see it now, better a baby and no marriage than a marriage and no baby.'

Mam jumped up from her fireside chair, quick and

young despite the white hair, and caught Marsha's arm. She sat her down gently, solicitously, as though Marsha mattered to her more than anyone in the world. Warmth, and not only from the fire, flooded Marsha and the baby sighed and stirred, opening its eyes, making sucking movements with its bud of a mouth.

'There's pretty she is,' Mam sighed worshipfully. 'Oh, who's a lovely little lass, then?'

'It's a boy – he's wearing blue bootees,' Megan said. She was not laughing, but her voice was. 'Shame on you, Mam, and you such a lover of littl'uns!'

'They all look alike when they're small,' Marsha said. 'Can you take it now? I'm going up to Bolton to see Mummy and Daddy. Only I promised Megan I'd bring the baby here first.'

Mam didn't understand. You could tell by her smile that she was preparing to say goodbye, sadly giving up the idea of a long cuddle, of giving it a feed, possibly of changing its stinking nappy for all Marsha knew. In fact all she did know was that its nappy was stinking, for she could smell nothing else.

'Well, I'll hold him for a minute . . . oh, look, Meggie, is that a little smile? Is that a little smile, my precious?'

Megan moved over and looked down at the baby. Marsha watched her. There was an odd expression on her sister's face, as though she longed to look yet dreaded it, too. I hope she doesn't expect it to be the image of Danny, because as far as I can remember he was fair and it's dark, Marsha thought to herself as Megan bent over the child.

Megan frowned. She glanced at Mam, then at the baby, then over at Marsha. And then she blushed. Wave after wave of scarlet colour washed over her face and neck and her eyes slid uncomfortably away from the baby, over to Mam, back to Marsha, down to the floor. What on earth is the matter with her, Marsha thought crossly. Don't say the mere sight of Danny's horrible offspring has aroused in Megan unclean thoughts!

'Mam . . . can Marsha and . . . and her baby stay over? She'll not get a train tonight, and the baby does look . . . sort of tired. He can sleep in one of the drawers out of my dressing table.'

'That would be lovely,' Mam said eagerly. She held the little thing in a natural, comfortable way in one arm. She looked like the Madonna, her head tilted, that doting look on her face. And then she sniffed suspiciously and looked rather accusingly at Marsha.

'He's dirty,' she announced. 'Go you upstairs, the pair of you. I'll give him a bit of a wash, find something soothing for his little bottom . . . do you have a clean nappy, Marsha?'

'In the bag, I expect,' Marsha said wearily. 'And there's powder and stuff. The nuns gave me things. Oh, and there's dried milk and glucose and that. I suppose you wouldn't like to get his feed ready, would you? He's probably hungry.'

Mam's face was lit from within, glowing. She tucked the baby back into her arm and stood up.

'I'll do it all,' she said. 'Off with you now and get yourselves tidy. Where's Peris?'

'Oh . . . upstairs, changing,' Megan said. 'He was soaked to the skin, not having a brolly.'

'Send him down; he can make our tea,' Mam said. 'It'll be ready in forty minutes.'

'Forty minutes,' Marsha mused as the two girls went up the stairs. 'Not long, but long enough. It's good of your mam to let me stay the night, but I'll catch the early train, I think. I don't want to waste time. Oh, I called it Connor since it was born in Ireland, but I dare say you can change it if you want to.'

445

Megan stopped short. The rich colour had faded from her face in the kitchen but now it returned with a rush. She put her hand on Marsha's arm. Timidly.

'Marsha, I'm awfully sorry about the baby. Of course he's yours, not mine – I see that now. Even if he had been Danny's, I wouldn't have tried to take him away from you, but as it is . . . well, you'll take him when you go. That's understood.'

Marsha stared, then scowled.

'It is not understood, Megan Prydderch,' she said sharply. 'I can't take it back to Mummy and Daddy. They'd make me keep it, and the last thing I want is to be burdened with Danny's wretched baby. Don't you understand? I've got to find Tony.'

They had paused on the half-landing in front of Screech's elegant bamboo home. Now, Megan turned to fiddle with the head of sunflower seeds tied to the bars. She was pink still, but no longer scarlet.

'I don't think you understand, do you, Marsha?' she said quietly. 'Your baby isn't Danny's, it's Tony's. It even looks like him – its face is the same shape and it's got his long chin. Besides, it wasn't a premature birth, was it?'

'No, they said I'd gone full term,' Marsha said, not seeing what her sister was driving at. 'But what does it matter? You can't tell who fathered a baby by its face!'

'Sometimes you can. And you can tell by dates. Marsha, Danny's only been gone seven months! Oh, my dear girl, haven't you looked at your baby at all?'

'Once or twice,' Marsha admitted cautiously. 'But not to see a likeness . . . why should I? I can't remember what Danny looked like anyway, and I was so sure . . .'

'Danny was all golden hair and blue eyes,' Megan said. There was pain in her voice, but love, too. 'And his face was broad across the cheekbones, with a square chin. Your Tony was the one with black eyes, black hair and

446

a long chin. I couldn't take that baby even if I wanted tò, Marsha, because one day you'd want him back.'

'I wouldn't. I don't,' Marsha said wildly. 'It'll hold me up, slow me down. I must find Tony before it's too late. Before he marries someone else, or stops loving me!'

'Well, I can't take him,' Megan said firmly. 'Nor Mam, before you say. Oh yes, she'd love the baby, but I know you through and through, Marsha. The day you change your mind you'll turn up on this doorstep and take the kid away and break Mam's heart without a qualm. We want no part in that baby, Mam and I.'

'All right. I suppose if it's not Danny's . . . but I can stay here tonight, can't I? And Meggie . . . can we still be friends, sort of?'

'Sort of,' Megan said. 'Oh, and in case you're interested, our real mother turned up today – she's staying on the island. That's where Peris and I had been, to see her for a talk. She wants to meet us both, after all these years!'

And she smiled. A real smile, sweet and gentle, with so much understanding, so much real affection, that suddenly Marsha could have howled and hugged her – but knew better than to try. I'm breaking ties, not making them, she reminded herself as she began to wash.

'Our real mother? What on earth does *she* want?' she said, soaping her hands. 'I've got quite enough on my plate with Mummy and Daddy, without some other woman expecting me to do what she says. I'm nobody's child any more, I'm Tony's woman.'

'It doesn't matter; she knows your Bolton address,' Megan said soothingly. 'She'll probably contact you there. And now, if you've finished, let's go down for tea and you can meet Peris . . . he's longing to meet you!'

'I can't help it – I shall miss that baby something cruel,'

Mam sighed next morning, cooking bacon and egg and chatting to Megan whilst waiting for Peris to put in an appearance. 'There's sweet he was. That girl didn't care for him at all, and I – oh, I would have been so good to him, the dear little feller!'

'I know, Mam. But it would have ended badly; I know Marsha. She'd have come and snatched the baby back and broken your heart, see? You've been hurt enough, Mam.'

'Oh, hurt!' Mam flicked a disdainful hand. 'Mams are made to be hurt, old Megan, didn't you know that? Still and all, I've been luckier than most. Good kids I do have . . .' She slanted a smile at her daughter. 'And another lad coming in two weeks, when they've got the paperwork sorted out. Dear God above, in the old days I'd just go to the Deiniol Evans, choose a child, and out we'd walk hand in hand!'

Peris came into the kitchen, smiled at them, then looked askance.

'Where's Marsha? And the kid? Not still in bed . . . I thought she wanted to catch the early train?'

'She did catch it – the six o'clock one. At least she left at a gallop at ten to the hour, cramming bread and cheese into her mouth, so I hope she caught it.'

Marsha had missed the train. She sat on the platform sulking, and the baby, who had been good all night and all the previous day, began to cry, balling its tiny hands into fists, screwing up its small red face, turning first purple and then, alarmingly, blue.

Oh, damn the thing, Marsha thought. Any minute now it'll have a seizure or something . . . I'd better walk up and down or whatever you're supposed to do.

She started walking along the platform, thinking about the previous evening – the previous night, come to that.

Megan had spent most of it telling her all about their real mother, or at any rate as much as she herself had learned. What the woman had said about their father had fascinated them both, but as to this Madeleine Ripley-Trewin, even Megan hadn't been able to raise much enthusiasm. It was her precious Mam who mattered.

Not that Marsha altogether blamed her. What had their mother done for them, after all? She had abandoned them, one to an institution and the other to adoptive parents who had cared so little for her that they had not even revealed her adopted status. Still, she had come, it appeared, with the best of intentions, to try to give Megan some money which had been left to her.

And there's money for me, too, if I want it, Marsha reminded herself. But she didn't want it because the moment she was back with Mummy and Daddy she would have all the money she needed – and all the support, too. It did say a lot for them, she grudgingly admitted, that despite going off for a year – more – and not getting in touch once, she never doubted her welcome.

Well, if she didn't do all that badly by us, it wasn't because she tried to see us comfortably settled, Marsha told herself now. It never occurred to her, being Marsha, that Madeleine had done precisely what she herself intended to do with her own small son: hand him over to someone else. But, even if it had, being Marsha she would simply have told herself the cases were different.

Presently, walking up and down the platform palled. She glanced at her wristwatch. It was another whole hour before the train she needed would even come in, let alone go out again. She would walk up on to London Road and get a cup of coffee somewhere, and perhaps someone might be persuaded to warm up the baby's bottle for her.

She remembered Mrs Ella as soon as she got outside the station yard. Nice old trout, the sort of person to coo over the most stinking of babies, offer to hold it, perhaps even to change it – how often did one have to change babies, for God's sake? – for its exhausted parent.

And who knows, perhaps I might meet a fairy god-mother as I go, Marsha thought as she walked. Now that really would be convenient. She would wave her wand and the baby would disappear and Tony would be there instead! How wonderful!

As though half believing her own story she glanced down at the small bundle in the crook of her inexpert arm, and got quite a shock. Just for a moment, Tony's face looked back at her, red and crumpled perhaps, getting ready to bawl again, but identifiable.

And then, coming towards her along the pavement, just emerging from Mrs Ella's front garden, came a slender blonde woman in a smart navy blue suit with a navy blue macintosh over one arm.

For one startled second Marsha thought it was Megan, and then she saw that the woman was nearer forty than twenty and that she was quite clearly a visitor to the island because she was looking about her as though she did not quite know which way to go.

She saw Marsha watching her and smiled. It was a pretty smile, her mouth tilting into a happy curve, but she only glanced at the younger woman before fixing her eyes on the child.

'Oh, excuse me. I've come out to buy a paper to read over my breakfast, and the lady I'm staying with told me there was a shop just by the bridge, but I'm afraid . . .' The woman was close enough, now, to look directly into Connor's face. 'Oh, my dear, I think your baby is going to give a most almighty yell at any moment.'

Marsha opened her mouth, shut it again, then opened it once more.

'Do I know you?'

The woman had been concentrating almost entirely on the child; she looked up at Marsha and a hand flew to her mouth.

'Oh, Megan, I'm most awfully sorry. I didn't . . . Megan? It *is* you, isn't it?'

Marsha smiled too, but shook her head.

'No. I'm Marsha. And you're . . . ?'

'Oh . . . I'm Madeleine Ripley-Trewin. I came to see both of you, actually . . .'

'You're our mother,' Marsha said. 'The one who dumped us, years ago.'

'Oh . . . but how do you . . .'

'Megan told me.' Suddenly an idea as brilliant as it was simple entered Marsha's mind. She heaved the baby up in her arms and thrust it at the older woman. 'You left us . . . now you can have him! I thought Meg or Mam would take him but they wouldn't, and I don't want him.'

Madeleine Ripley-Trewin's arms accepted the tiny burden as naturally and eagerly as Mam's had. She looked at Marsha, her face eager, her eyes misty.

'For me? The baby's for me? But I came to tell you about a legacy . . .'

'You can have the legacy and the nappies and things too,' Marsha said recklessly. 'Go on, take it back to Mrs Ella's – she'll let you feed it and everything, I dare say. And now I really must go – I've got a train to catch.' She turned away, seeing her mother standing stunned in the first faint rays of the October sun. 'His name's Connor,' she shouted across the gradually increasing distance which separated them. 'Take better care of him than you did of us!'

Standing there on Wian Road, with the baby in her arms, Madeleine looked down once more into her grandson's beautiful little face. And as though he was suddenly

451

conscious that he was being watched, Connor opened his eyes and stared straight up at Madeleine.

They were very dark eyes, set beneath a very definite line of brow for such a young child. Madeleine took a deep, shaky breath.

'She wants me to have you,' she breathed, turning away from the town, her original errand forgotten. 'She's given you to me – oh, and isn't it the strangest thing that you look just like my Tarot?'

'Goin'? Why? Today an' all? Us'll miss you.'

Jim stands in the doorway of the sod hut, watching as the man from the sea gathers his things together. He doesn't have much, just a patched pair of trousers, a thin old shirt and a pair of short rubber boots. But everything he has, Jim has given him. They are friends.

'I'm a long way from home, Jim,' the man says.

He has grown much stronger over the weeks and months, not just in his body but in his voice, his mind. Jim loves him, hates to see him go, but understands that a man needs his home. Jim needs his sod hut, his dog, his cat, his hens. He needs the sea growling and grumbling at the rocks, sucking and nibbling at the sand; he needs the sweet grass and the black earth from whence his vegetables spring. He even needs the wind, to howl in winter, showing him how snug is the sod hut, to blow gentle on him in summer, cooling his toil-warmed body.

'Long way? But you'll come back one day?'

The man from the sea smiles at him. It is the nicest smile in the world, apart from Bunty's. He reaches out and gently ruffles Jim's rusty brown hair.

'Course I'll come back. Me and my woman, we'll come and see you when we're settled. It may not be for a bit, mind . . .' He thinks; Jim can still see him thinking, the

452

slow thoughts gathering like stormclouds, when he worries. 'When the leaves fall. We'll come then.'

Jim understands this and is sad, because it is spring now, and autumn seems a long way off. But summer is a good time, the best; he can live through a summer without the man from the sea, for hasn't he lived through countless summers – and springs, autumns, winters – before, with only his animals for company?

'It's far, where you live. Does it take long?'

'Tramping, a few weeks, maybe. But I'm fit now, I can work. I'll earn money for a ride, perhaps.'

Jim prefers to tramp; vehicles other than horse-drawn ones frighten him. He nods slowly, trying to show that this is a natural thing to do.

'Wish I had a donkey,' he murmurs. 'One day . . .'

'That's right. You'll have a donkey soon, Jim. I promise. When the leaves fall.'

Jim watches silently as his friend says goodbye to Fudge and Bunty, then claps him on the shoulder and says things which don't have any meaning, not to Jim. Things about saving life and debts and gratitude. But Jim smiles anyway, and wishes his friend well and waves and waves until the man from the sea is just a little dot, climbing the high ridge.

When he's out of sight behind the ridge, Jim settles down once more. To loneliness.

It was a Tuesday and the weather was dreadful. Dark clouds scudded fast across the sky before a spiteful wind, gusting rain blew into Megan's face and the cloud was right down over Holyhead mountain. As for the sea – well, it was all you could do to make it out until you were down on the shore, and then you could see it all right. There were white horses as far as the horizon and the waves were coming in crosswise, slanted, any old how, as the wind harried them from their natural course.

Megan had woken cross. Her day off and look at it! Didn't it know it was supposed to be May? But she had made her arrangements for today and go out she would, come hell or high water. She had vowed she would find somewhere wild and quiet today and just sit down on a rock somewhere and scream from sheer frustration and that was exactly what she would do, rain or no rain.

She was annoyed and upset because she hadn't got the job. Oh, the interviewing board had been very nice about it. Mr Pringle, who seemed to be the boss, had explained that they really needed a man because some of the work was quite heavy, but such a man would need an assistant and if Megan was really serious about helping to start a nature reserve on the island he would certainly advise she put in for the assistant's job.

'And if you know of a suitable young man for the warden's post we'd gladly interview him,' Mr Pringle said hopefully. 'We've not had many applicants. And you're ideal, Miss Prydderch; what a shame you're a woman!'

Danny would have loved the job – would have been very good at it – but failing him she could think of no one. She began to say so, and then the stupid lump had risen up in her stupid throat and her stupid voice had gone and put its foot in it, saying the very thing to put the three men who had conducted the interview against her.

'I'm only half a woman,' she had heard her voice remarking sadly.

There had been an embarrassed silence, and then Mr Pringle had cleared his throat and repeated that they would certainly consider her for the job of assistant, should they find a suitable applicant for warden.

But they wouldn't consider her. Not after that. Only

half a woman, indeed! And what had she meant? That she had a twin sister who completed her as a person? Or that, without Danny, she could never be a whole woman? Not that it mattered – she had ruined her chance and now she was going out to scream and shout and kick rocks somewhere quiet, where she could let go completely without anyone's being any the wiser.

She had thought about Rocky Shore, but she and Danny had spent such happy times there! So she had decided to go further afield, to Penrhyn Bay, where she had worked on the farm during the war. During her time there the beach had been mined so she and Danny had never visited it together, but a short while ago the mines had been removed and the beach was safe once more. She decided she would catch a bus, walk up past the farm, take to the shore and tramp along it until she got to the wide and sandy beach. There, on a day like this, she could walk until her knees gave way, shriek until her throat was sore, and no one would think the less of her because of it.

She queued for the bus; it was full of soggy people returning from market. But they were cheerful despite the weather, chatting, laughing, asking her where she was off to on such a fine day now, and wasn't she a duck in all but feathers to be going visiting in such rain?

Despite her resolve, the talk and laughter began to melt the core of fury and self-disgust which Megan had nursed since the failed interview four days earlier. She found herself laughing as well, giving as good as she got, and when the bus stopped in Llanfwrog, which was the nearest it went to the farm, she got off into the rain quite happily, hunching into her duffel coat, striding out with her wellies splashing through puddles, ignoring the touch of the long, soaked grasses of the verge.

It was a fair walk, though. And although the rain stopped within moments of her getting off the bus she was still pretty wet by the time she rounded the corner and saw the farm buildings ahead of her.

Should she go in? They would make her welcome, give her a cup of tea, probably feed her as well. She was almost tempted . . . but then the recollection of her own stupidity and her desperate need to scream overcame her once again.

Fool, fool, *fool*! The only job she had ever desperately wanted and she had mucked it up! To be able to draw and paint birds from life whenever she had the time, to spend her working day with the gentle creatures who had lived on the island long before Man ever came . . . and she had not only failed to get the warden's job for which she had applied, she had made certain, by her sheer unadulterated stupidity, that she would not be considered for the assistant's job either. Half a woman! Oh, God, Megan Prydderch, how could you be such a *fool*?

She sheered away from the grey stone farmhouse with its ivy-clad walls and dropped down on to the shore. The tide was half out, and it would be a simple enough matter to walk round the coast, trying to reassure herself that this was only a temporary set-back. Now she knew what she really wanted to do, there would surely be other jobs coming up? Nature reserves were a new idea but the island was the perfect place for them. Miles and miles of unspoilt country, more miles of unspoilt coastline, and already the birds, the seals, the porpoises were regular visitors, coming in their hundreds if not their thousands.

The shore was grey with shells and shingle here, the black volcanic rocks patched with yellow lichen. Megan climbed over them and down on to pebbles, then over more rocks, these crowned with crackly brown seaweed which would turn lush and glossy only when the tide returned. She continued to move down the shore until she was below the tideline, where the rocks were thick with wet seaweed: dark brown bladderwort, golden mermaid's hair, brilliant green sea-lettuce. She tried to avoid treading on the millions and millions of inhabited shells – bright orange ones, yellow ones, brown and pink and chestnut ones – but it was impossible so she took to the water, wading through pools and inlets, seeing a shoal of shrimps dart away from her alien boot, stopping for a moment to watch two hermit crabs wrestling over the same large empty shell.

She reached Sandy Beach at last, just as she heard the cross-channel ship sounding its siren to warn a fishing boat out of its path. It had been docking when she climbed aboard the bus, so it had had a fast turn-round. She shaded her eyes with her hand to watch it, and, with the action, realized the sun had come out. It was pale and watery and had not yet reached Sandy Beach – she was still poised on the wet, fawn-coloured reaches of sand beneath the scudding clouds – but over towards Ireland the sky showed blue, and the sunlight caught the ship – was it the *Hibernia*, or the *Cambria*? – and painted it brilliant white, the funnels flame-red.

We nearly always get our weather from Ireland, Megan reflected, moving out of the water and up the beach to where the sand had dried to a tropical whiteness. Well, I've been a fool and I've lost a lovely job, but I will *not* despair! Look at today, for instance. When I set out it was grey and rainy, but any moment now the sun will shine and I'll be far too hot in this old duffel.

Still, she had come here to rage at fate, and rage she would. Further up the beach was a large, smooth-looking white stone, just the sort to travel a mile when kicked with sufficient force. Megan fixed her eyes on the stone and began to run her hardest. She had played a lot of football as a child and prided herself on having a very strong kick for a girl.

She reached the stone and curved round it, whanging it with the side of her wellie as hard as she could.

It should have skimmed towards the sea. It would have skimmed towards the sea had it not been the tip of Everest, Megan concluded bitterly from a position of pre-natal agony, curled up on the sand and holding her toe. The bloody, bloody stone hadn't been a stone at all, but the topmost peak of . . . well, of some bloody, bloody mountain . . . and her toe was broken into a million damned splinters and whose fault was it? Oh, damn and damn and damn, it was bloody Megan Prydderch's own stupid fault, and that was the unkindest cut of all!

Presently, when the pain in her toe had subsided to a bearable level, Megan sat up. She sniggered to herself, holding her foot with both hands and rocking slowly to and fro. What an idiot she was being! She couldn't even kick a rock without doing herself an injury, and as for screaming . . .

She tried to scream. It sounded pathetically small and thin against the boisterous bellowing of the wind. She screamed again, louder, putting more force into it, and a seagull, hovering overhead, came closer. It only had one leg and for some reason one-legged gulls don't seem able to get their under-carriage to work properly, so that the leg always dangles a bit instead of tucking neatly into the tummy feathers the way two legs will.

I'm a bit like that gull, Megan thought. It's learned to cope awfully well with its affliction, but it can't quite merge in with the other birds. She watched as it swung lazily above her, then came in head to wind with lovely nonchalance, managing to make a perfect landing on its one little grey pin.

Megan found an old, sandy wine gum in her pocket

and threw it towards the gull. It hopped forward, seized the wine gum without overbalancing, and tipped its head up. Seconds later it eyed Megan once more, clearly wondering whether she was good for anything else.

'It's not that I grudge them to you, I just don't have any more,' Megan told it. 'You'd better get fishing if you want any supper tonight, old bird!'

The gull waited a moment, then hopped round again and managed a good takeoff, winging its way out to sea.

Megan had kicked her mountain-top when she was halfway along the beach. Now she turned back, glancing at her wristwatch. She had plenty of time before the bus went back again, and now that she had done her screaming and rock-kicking she did not fancy just wasting the afternoon. Suppose she bathed? She had no costume, but the beach was deserted still and likely to remain so . . . and she had a perfectly good bra and pants on.

But one did not bathe just like that, and imagine the walk back to the bus with sand and salt stickiness making every movement miserable! Megan retraced her steps along the beach to where it curved into a clifflet with rocks at its foot. She chose a warm and sheltered spot, shed her duffel coat, kicked off her boots, took off her grey woolly jumper and settled down to bask in the sun.

It was a rare treat to relax so completely. She was out of the wind but she could still hear it buffeting the island, driving the sea to splash against the rocks, to hiss along the sand. Behind her lids, the sun's gold continued to shine. Now and then a cloud passed over its face and Megan's lids cooled from gold to pink, then warmed back to gold again as the cloud was driven on.

Presently she decided to forgive herself for losing the job. And later still, she slept.

* * *

He came across the sand, searching for her. He had only just missed the bus, had seen it pull away, bulging with passengers, as he came running down Landsend.

His first call had been to the house in Newry Street, and Mam had taken one look and shrieked . . . rushed at him, hugged him tight, then pushed him out the door, her voice high and trembling, her cheeks pink and tear-streaked.

'Run, Danny boy, run hard! Off to Penrhyn she is, on the bus . . . her day off, see, and her so miserable . . . oh, *run*, Danny!'

Running hadn't been enough, but he'd still had money left from his journey home. He'd got a taxi to Penrhos, then borrowed a row-boat – not that the owner knew, mind. He had pulled good and strong, the wind at his back helping him every yard of the way, and arrived just now, beached his small craft and come up the shore, quiet over the fawny-gold sand, crunching loud across the pebbles and shingle.

He looked along the stretch of the bay; no sign. Turned back, to the little cliff with the rocks at its foot. Saw her at once, heart lifting, beating suddenly loud in his ears, suddenly uneven.

She was asleep! Curled up, hair all anyhow, mouth open, sand blown by the wind on the duffel coat which pillowed her head, on her neck, in her fingers, even dusting her cheek. Oh, beautiful she was, beautiful beyond any woman Danny had ever known!

How to wake her, though? A shriek was all right, but a heart-attack would kill the pair of them! Danny stood over her, between her face and the sun, and waited.

She frowned like a baby, and ducked her chin. She half-turned on her side and popped her thumb into her mouth, cuddling down, bringing her knees up, reaching for an imaginary blanket to pull over her shoulders. She thought she was in her own bed, the darling!

'Megan! Meg, my darling . . . Meggie, my little one, wake up!'

He knelt by her, brushing the sand off her cheek with gentle fingers, seeing her lids begin to stir, watching for the dark blue eyes to open, focus, waiting for realization to dawn . . .

She shook her head crossly and opened her eyes, knuckling them into wakefulness. She sat up and looked. He put his hands on her shoulders and smiled.

'Meggie? It's me!'

She stared, the colour rushing up into her face, staining it a clear, pale pink. Then she lunged forward, into his arms, her own straining round him with a desperate strength.

'Danny! It really is you! Oh, Danny . . . oh, Danny . . . oh, God, hold me!'

He held her very tightly and felt her fluttering heart against his own, felt her soft breath panting against his cheek.

'Meg? Are you all right, now? Oh, but you feel so good . . . and I thought I'd never hold you again, I thought I was drowned-dead for sure.'

'So did we,' Megan said. Her voice was lazy and warm, a bee's hum in high summer. 'Oh, Danny, we all thought you'd gone down with Da and the *Claudia*.'

'Nearly. Not quite. Oh, Meg!'

There was a long, sun-filled pause amongst the rocks. Danny and Megan were content just to hold and be held, wanting nothing further, not even words. But at length Megan broke the silence.

'Danny . . . they all died, you know, the others on the trawler. I didn't want to believe you . . . you . . . but it seemed as though you must have gone down with the rest. Oh, God, how I prayed . . . and how happy I am now! Just to hold you, be with you . . . seen your mam, have you?'

'No, not yet. Saw yours, because I went straight to Newry Street. What a shriek she gave! But I'll see my mam in good time.'

'Yes, you'd better. I'll come with you, shall I? And what will we do tomorrow? There's lots who'll want to give you a hug, Danny.'

'Before I do anything else I've got to buy a donkey,' Danny said, his arm still cradling her. 'A nice little she-donkey, with a foal in her if possible.'

'You can have my savings,' Megan said at once. 'I haven't spent much this past year.'

'Aren't you going to ask me what I want with a donkey? Woman, you have no human curiosity!'

'What do you want with a donkey?' Megan said obediently.

'Shan't tell you!'

They rocked with laughter, holding each other still, Megan wrinkling her nose at Danny, Danny suddenly kissing the soft skin just beneath her ear.

'No, but really. I am interested, honest!'

'Oh. Right. There was this feller, see . . .'

ALSO AVAILABLE IN ARROW:

ALL ARROW BOOKS ARE AVAILABLE THROUGH MAIL ORDER OR FROM YOUR LOCAL BOOKSHOP AND NEWSAGENT.

PLEASE SEND CHEQUE, EUROCHEQUE, POSTAL ORDER (STERLING ONLY), ACCESS, VISA, MASTERCARD, DINERS CARD, SWITCH OR AMEX.

☐☐☐☐☐☐☐☐☐☐☐☐☐☐☐☐☐

EXPIRY DATE .... SIGNATURE ....

PLEASE ALLOW 75 PENCE PER BOOK FOR POST AND PACKING U.K.

OVERSEAS CUSTOMERS PLEASE ALLOW £1.00 PER COPY FOR POST AND PACKING.

ALL ORDERS TO:

ARROW BOOKS, BOOKS BY POST, TBS LIMITED, THE BOOK SERVICE, COLCHESTER ROAD, FRATING GREEN, COLCHESTER, ESSEX CO7 7DW.

TELEPHONE: (01206) 256 000
FAX: (01206) 255 914

NAME ....

ADDRESS ....

....

Please allow 28 days for delivery. Please tick box if you do not wish to receive any additional information ☐

Prices and availability subject to change without notice.